ALWAYS BEEN MINE

VICTORIA PAIGE

ALWAYS BEEN MINE

By Victoria Paige

Edited by: Hot Tree Editing

1

A CLAP of thunder jolted Beatrice awake.

Disoriented, she took in her naked body under the cool satin sheets. She smiled like a cat who'd had her fill of cream. Pure feline satisfaction. A night of wild sex with Gabriel Sullivan would do that to you.

She frowned at the empty space beside her. *Where is he?*

Her brows furrowed deeper when a streak of lightning and the ensuing rumble followed too closely behind it. Damn spring storms. They better not delay their flight to Barbados in the morning.

Beatrice swung her legs to the floor, stood and slipped into a robe. Eyeing the open suitcase laid out on the floor, she remembered the whirlwind development of their relationship in recent weeks. She'd been seeing Gabe on and off for the past four months. It was only in the last three weeks that the dark-haired former Navy SEAL finally staked some sort of claim on her. Well, really staked a claim. Beatrice had been having drinks with a male friend when he rudely butted in and asked to speak to her.

He laid it out. He wanted their relationship to be exclusive.

This four-day trip to Barbados was a way of cementing the definition of said relationship: Gabe and Beatrice were a couple.

Shaking her head at how easily he had changed her rules about dating someone who was currently serving or had served in the military, she went to look for her man.

She descended the stairs of her two-story row house and found him in the study, standing by the French windows with the phone to his ear. His voice was low and gruff. He heard her come into the room; lightning illuminated his grim face and tight mouth.

Something was horribly wrong.

"I need to go," Gabe spoke into the phone. His whiskey eyes were black in the darkened room, but she could feel them drinking her in. "I'll see you in a few."

"Is everything okay?" Beatrice asked anxiously as he ended the call.

Gabe lowered his gaze. Striding past her, he exited the study, crossed the living room, and mounted the steps leading to their bedroom.

A familiar knot of abandonment tightened her gut, freezing her where Gabe had left her. Taking deep breaths to calm down, she followed him upstairs.

The sight that met her in their room unleashed her worst fears. Gabe was pulling out his stuff from the meticulously packed suitcase and was shoving them into his black duffel.

"What are you doing?" Beatrice asked hoarsely. "Our flight leaves in six hours. Are we canceling?"

Gabe paused; the muscle tic in his jaw pulsed a few times before he finally looked at her. "I made a mistake."

Beatrice forced herself to smile; sure she had misheard him. "What do you mean? You don't like Barbados? We don't have to go if that's not your thing."

"Us, Beatrice." His tone was calm. "We're not going to work."

His statement doused her denial of what was clearly unfolding before her. He was ending it.

"Explain, Gabriel," Beatrice said coldly. "Three weeks ago, you practically bulldozed me into a committed relationship. Now you're wimping out? Uh-uh, a simple 'we're not going to work' *is not* cutting it."

Gabe flinched, but didn't respond. He pulled the zipper on his duffel and tried to get past her. She was having none of that and stood smack in front of him.

"I deserve an answer."

Gabe's eyes blazed at her. Wait, was he angry at her?

What the hell!

"You want the truth?" Gabe rasped. "I have a job to do."

"You're done with the SEALs or did you lie?"

"No. This is something else."

"You're working for Dad," Beatrice whispered. The disapproval of her father regarding their relationship dawned on her.

He looked straight into her eyes. "No. Someone else. I need to leave."

"No. That's not a freaking explanation," Beatrice fired back.

"You deserve more—"

"Don't feed me that bullshit!" Beatrice screamed. Tremors shook her body. This wasn't happening. Why was this happening?

"Okay, you want the fucking truth?" Gabe replied tersely. "I'll always care for my job more than I'll ever care about you. I realize that now."

She inhaled sharply at his blunt, if not cruel, declaration. Heat burned behind her eyes. She wasn't going to cry. Oh, no, she wasn't. She wasn't becoming her mother.

A tear slid down her cheek.

Gabe cursed. "You asked for the fucking truth. You got it."

He made to move past her again, but she couldn't let him go.

Against her better judgment, she raised a palm against his chest.

"Please, Gabe—"

"Jesus, Beatrice," Gabe growled. "You're an admiral's daughter. Have some fucking pride. Don't beg a man to stay if he doesn't want you."

The final stake was driven into her heart. She dropped her hand and swallowed hard. She stepped aside. Gabe didn't even hesitate as he walked briskly away from her.

Yet what hope was left inside her made her walk to the window. The rain had slowed to a trickle, and there were still rumblings of thunder in the distance. The scene outside was pretty much what she felt inside—pure desolation. She watched the headlights of Gabe's car flash as he bleeped the locks. Seconds later, his tall silhouette emerged from the sidewalk fronting her house.

Look up. Look up. Don't leave, Gabe.

He never looked up.

THREE YEARS later

"RISE AND SHINE, BEATRICE PORTER!"

The smell of coffee hovered around her nose, but Beatrice shoved her face further into the pillow. "Go away."

"Tsk. Tsk. Late night? Or can't sleep?" The amused masculine voice teased.

"Both," Beatrice grumbled, finally flopping on her back and sitting up. She glared at the leanly built blond man smirking at her. Douglas Keller—her personal assistant, her confidante, her everything actually. Because he did everything for her security consulting business that she had no patience to do. Besides, he took good care of her. She eyed the Styrofoam cup of morning brew held so tantalizing close to her face.

"From your favorite corner coffee shop," Doug said as Beatrice grabbed the cup from him. He sat on the edge of her bed. "Drink up. You'll need it."

She groaned, "Don't tell me there's another article."

"Front page of the DC Tattler," Doug said. "Not too shabby a picture of your altercation with Rocker Boy in front of a Georgetown restaurant."

Eric Stone, lead guitarist of Titanium Rose, was a moment of female weakness. She had succumbed to all those tattoos and bad boy image, and somehow fell into an intense fling that lasted for five weeks. That ended two weeks ago when she walked in on him snorting cocaine off a naked groupie.

It was official: Beatrice Porter had become a cliché and she hated it. Right now, she hated the disapproving look Doug was giving her. He had warned her, after all.

"He's spreading the word that he's begging for a second chance. He accepts full responsibility for the breakup."

"He said he had stopped using." Beatrice took a big gulp of her coffee and thought she should have brushed her teeth first. Setting the cup down, she padded to the bathroom, leaving the door open so Doug could talk to her.

"He said he was missing you."

"Seriously? That's his excuse? I was gone for less than four days. If I had not cut my trip short . . . I would have . . ." She shuddered before sticking the toothbrush in her mouth. It was a good thing she refused to forego using condoms with him. God knows if this hadn't been the first time. Still, it was a good thing to have herself tested.

"I'll schedule an appointment with your doctor," Doug said, reading her mind. She later shooed him out of the room so she could take a shower. While she let the spray of water wake her up, she contemplated the damage to her reputation. So far, none of her clients had canceled their appointments. Her friends Travis Blake and Nate Reece, who ran a partner security firm, Blake Security Inc. (BSI), offered to beat Eric up and make it look like an accident. All her other friends simply teased her about this whole situation. She snorted inwardly. Her clients were probably afraid of canceling on an admiral's daughter. Though she hated leaning on the clout of her father, she admitted it had its uses.

Beatrice didn't know what her father, Admiral Benjamin Porter, exactly did for the CIA. Their relationship was an ebb and flow. Sometimes tumultuous where they clashed, sometimes cordial, sometimes cold. Turning off the water, Beatrice grabbed a towel and dried off.

There were times when he let his guard down and showed her some genuine warmth. Those occasions were rare. Beatrice wondered if he just wanted her to toughen up for whatever life plan he had in store for her. She wasn't obtuse enough not to realize her father's deft manipulation of her life had landed her as a security consultant.

Doug was already pounding away on his laptop in her home office. Beatrice lived in a penthouse apartment right on Pennsylvania Avenue. She realized as a consultant, she didn't need to rent office space and just conducted her initial meetings in one of the many swanky restaurants inundating the nation's capital.

"I've already typed up a brief for your lunch appointment with Senator Mendoza and his Chief of Staff."

"And they only want security for their delegation to South America?"

"Yes. That's their immediate requirement."

"Have you done a background check? Any known threats to the senator?"

"He's a member of the Intelligence and Homeland Security committees, so there are the usual threats. However, there is concern regarding his travel to Colombia."

Beatrice sighed, trying to remember what she knew about that part of the world.

Senator Alex Mendoza was second-generation Colombian American. A success story. The son of poor immigrant parents, he impressed his teachers in school and won a scholarship to Harvard and graduated with the highest honors. He would facing a delicate challenge when the Immigration and Border Security bill hit the floor early next year.

"Cocaine jungles," Beatrice said. "Russian-supplied guns arming private armies." She inhaled her coffee. "Source of one of the best coffee beans in the world. Should be interesting. What else is on the agenda today?"

"We have that Mayflower Charity Ball tonight," Doug piped in.

"Ah, yes," Beatrice scoffed. "You're still fine as my date?"

"Of course."

"Great. Right now, I don't want to go by myself, what with that little scandal with Eric. The last thing I want to look like is some pathetic woman scorned."

"Don't worry, we'll look great as a couple." Doug waggled his eyebrows.

Beatrice pouted. "Why can't you just fall in love with me?"

Her assistant smiled wryly before leaning in and giving her a kiss on top of her head. "I do love you, sweetie."

Beatrice exited the G Street level of the Metro Center stop and walked up to La Grenouille—a ritzy French restaurant in the heart of DC. She checked the time on her phone. It was almost noon, and she was sure the place was already buzzing with lobbyists dressed in Armani suits. It was the first week of November, so everyone was pushing their agenda before

Congress adjourned for the Christmas break. Heads turned her way as she neared the restaurant. She was used to the attention that her willowy, designer-clad figure attracted. She'd been approached several times by top modeling agencies, but sashaying down a catwalk held no appeal for her. No. She relished playing hardball in a business dominated by men. She thrived on the challenge. However, Beatrice was not her confident self today; she cringed at the attention. Were they looking at her as a beautiful woman, or the woman who walked in on her cheating rock star ex-boyfriend? The details didn't even come from her. Her only response to the media was "no comment." All the information came from the groupie who she caught with Eric.

Unbidden feelings of another rejection came to mind, one that happened one stormy night, three years ago. Beatrice shuddered as bile churned in her gut. Thankfully, she didn't even love Eric. He was good in bed, although nowhere near as—

Damn it, Beatrice Porter. Snap out of it.

Irritated with herself, she heaved and pushed the brass bar of the wood-framed, glass revolving doors of the restaurant.

"Ah, Ms. Porter, your party just arrived," the maître d' greeted her. "We have you seated at your regular table."

"Excellent." Beatrice smiled, shrugged off her cream peacoat, and handed it to a member of the waitstaff while another led her further into the dining area toward one of the secluded corners. The nutty aroma of browned butter wafted through her nose, and the earlier turmoil in her stomach receded.

A distinguished gentleman, clearly of South American descent, rose from the table and smiled at her. Senator Alex Mendoza's shrewd dark eyes crinkled at the corners, and a dimple appeared. "Beatrice, it's been a while."

"Senator."

"How have you been? How's the Admiral?"

"I'm fine. Dad is doing well, too." The truth was, she had not seen or spoken to her father since the scandal broke out. Knowing him, it was his silent disapproval. Thoughts of her father didn't linger in Beatrice's mind for her eyes landed on the senator's companion. *Well, hello, handsome.*

The senator gestured to the man beside him. "Zach Jamison, my new Chief of Staff,"

Beatrice held out her hand and it was caught in a firm handshake and held a bit longer than was normal.

Her eyes locked with Zach's. The man was all-dark. Dark hair, dark eyes, and deeply bronzed skin. He looked sinful. She should be used to blatant male perusal, but she was caught off guard and felt her skin blushing.

"Pleasure to meet you," Beatrice said, wanting to congratulate herself for her steady voice.

"Pleasure's all mine." Zach's eyes penetrated deep into her.

Pulling her hand away, she addressed the senator and expressed condolences regarding the untimely death of his former Chief of Staff.

The senator nodded gravely as all three of them took their seats. Senator Mendoza's former Chief of Staff recently passed from a heart attack. She had met the man twice before. Sharp and very protective of the senator, his death was a big blow to the senator's office.

Zach Jamison had big shoes to fill.

Regaining some of her composure, Beatrice launched straight into business. "I believe my assistant has sent you the questionnaire?"

"Yes, we received the paperwork from Mr. Keller," Zach answered. "We're concerned with some of the questions. They're very intrusive."

She was prepared for the pushback. "Understand this, Mr. Jamison. Each principal is encouraged to answer the questions truthfully. People who want to harm Senator Mendoza will use every dirty trick in the book, every weakness. A food allergy, a relative who has a debt, etc. We need to prepare for every threat."

"I have nothing to hide," Senator Mendoza said. "Though my medical—"

"We're not discussing that here," Beatrice cut him off. "That's for when I determine which security company will be most suited to you. I'm merely assessing your high level needs for now."

Both men nodded.

Their server arrived to fill their glasses with water and take their drink orders. While each of them perused the menu, Beatrice led in with her questions. "I understand the Immigration and Border Security bill is high on your priorities right now."

"That is correct." The senator nodded. "My constituents are divided regarding some key aspects of the bill."

"Understandable. Florida is a melting pot of different ethnic groups, and yet, a majority of the demographic is white." Beatrice shut the menu. She knew most of the entrée items listed by heart. "You'll have to find a happy medium."

"As I've stated in our advance brief, the President wants me to meet with several heads of state from the South American continent. Our last stop is Colombia. Their government is beginning to gain control over the drug trafficking problem, but that will largely depend on talks with the left-wing guerrillas and the right-wing paramilitary groups."

The waiter arrived with their drinks. After giving her lunch order, Beatrice took a sip of her Riesling. "There was a recent flare up of violence between the government and the guerillas. You may need bigger guns."

"No. I want BSI," Senator Mendoza said.

"That's for me to determine."

"I know which firm you are considering, but we couldn't afford them."

"I'm not sending BSI into known hostile territory. Their specialty is executive and dignitary protection. You almost need a team that functions as a private army," Beatrice reiterated.

"Listen, Beatrice. May I call you Beatrice?" Zach's mouth tilted in a grin. Oh, the man was turning on the charm. "Bring the matter up with BSI and see if they'll take it. Travis Blake is a living legend—the Navy SEAL who saved a senator from an assassin. Folks on the Hill talk about him whenever extra security is needed."

Beatrice inwardly agreed that Travis's guys were very capable of handling extreme life or death situations. She was just more protective of them. She considered them her boys.

"All right," Beatrice agreed. "I'll bring it up with Nathan Reece. Travis is on his honeymoon right now and should return this Friday."

"I've met Reece." The senator nodded in approval. "I really think BSI has the team we need. They provided outstanding security for the senate contingent the U.S. sent to Ukraine. I heard you negotiated that deal."

"I did."

"So what made you go into the security business?" Zach asked. "You are not what I expected."

"Should I be offended?"

"I meant that as a compliment," the Chief of Staff replied smoothly. "Your reputation precedes you."

Beatrice winced. Zach, realizing his faux pas, turned a shade darker under his tan. The senator chuckled. "You shouldn't worry about the tabloid write-ups, Beatrice. You've worked hard for where you are now."

Fortunately, their food arrived and the elaborate way the dishes were served gave her enough time to gather her wits about her.

"It'll blow over," Beatrice quipped and shrugged her shoulders. She looked at Zach who was staring at her with remorseful eyes. She raised a brow. His eyes turned mischievous, and then he flashed her a toothpaste-commercial-worthy smile.

Suddenly, Zach's attractiveness diminished, and the devilish grin of another man came to mind.

Beatrice Porter! Get a grip!

"Now, I believe, I'm the one asking the questions?" Beatrice brought the conversation back to point.

"BITCH WHORE!"

Beatrice watched in horror as a wave of red ruined her new cashmere wool peacoat.

What the hell?

She had just returned from her successful lunch meeting with the senator and was about to ascend the steps leading to the lobby of her condominium when she heard her name. Three women, all of them wearing Titanium Rose t-shirts, attacked her with red paint. How did they find out where she lived?

The older of the women, who sported bottle-blonde hair, continued to call her all manner of derogatory female names.

Building security rushed out and was about to restrain the women when Beatrice signaled them to back away.

She also noticed a tall figure rapidly approaching from her right peripheral vision.

Doug.

She kept her eyes on her attackers.

"Can you repeat what you just called me?" Beatrice said to Eric's rabid fans.

"Ms. Porter . . ." one of the guards started to say, but she raised a finger to shush them.

"Bitch whore!" Blondie repeated, her lips curling in a snarl.

"Is that right?" Beatrice said, wiping paint from her face. "I'm the bitch? I'm the whore? Didn't you read the papers?"

Blondie's eyes widened. "Well, yeah, Eric wants you back."

"Not that part," she said irritably. "You do know he cheated on me, right?"

"That was just a groupie . . ." Blondie's voice faded. "He's Eric Stone. Everyone wants to fuck him."

"So that makes it okay?"

No answer from the three women.

"You think it's okay for your man to step out on you when you've agreed to be exclusive?"

All three shook their head.

"I've made my point. You three are lucky I'm not about to press charges, because I'm so done with this fiasco, it's not funny," Beatrice snapped. "Now get out of here before someone takes pictures and I find myself splashed all over the tabloids again. This is DC. I understand there's no place more symbolic where freedom of expression is demonstrated every day, but dousing a person with red paint is not part of your first amendment rights. Do I make myself clear?"

The women just stared at her. The guards started snig-gering but stopped when Beatrice glared at them.

"Go on before I change my mind."

All three women slowly backed away before turning and running off.

"Beatrice," Doug said. His eyes were sympathetic, but his lips were twitching.

"Don't laugh," she warned. "Damn Eric." She whipped out her phone and called him. She got his voice mail. Just as well. She didn't want to talk to him, just leave him a message. A warning.

"Eric. Beatrice. Call off your fans. You and I? Not happening again. Get that through your damn head. The next time I get attacked or harassed, you *will* not like what I'll do to you."

She ended the call. Doug sighed.

"What?"

"You threatened your ex over the phone."

Beatrice paused. *Shit.*

"That's not the way to keep yourself out of the tabloids."

"Damn it," Beatrice hissed.

"Come on, *Carrie*, let's get you cleaned up."

Beatrice grunted.

"You're lucky they didn't use pig's blood."

She grunted again.

They were making their way up the steps when Beatrice felt a shiver go up her spine. She stopped and looked around.

"What's wrong, honeybee?" Doug occasionally used that annoying endearment on her, but right now, Beatrice's attention was riveted to her surroundings.

"I feel like . . . I feel like someone's watching me."

"You're just spooked by the attack," Doug reassured her. He was probably right. He put his arm around her and she leaned into its comfort as they walked into the lobby together.

THE MAYFLOWER CHARITY Ball was a black-tie affair, but Beatrice decided to forgo the formality of a limousine. Too much fanfare to pull up at the entrance of the trendy Larkspur Manor in McLean. At the moment, she preferred to remain inconspicuous, asking Doug to pick her up in his low-profile Toyota sedan. Some part of her hated how she seemed to be hiding, but the ugly scene in front of her condo earlier only proved the prudence of her decision.

Pulling up by the valet, a doorman opened the passenger door and assisted her from the car. Beatrice was wearing a simple satin sheath gown. Its platinum color set off her creamy skin tone. She set her hair in big curls and gathered them in a sophisticated off-center ponytail. Doug offered his arm, and together, they walked the short distance to the main entrance. They veered to the side walkway, which led to a discrete door that guests who preferred anonymity used during such events.

"Your hands are clammy," Doug murmured. "Are you still shaken from this afternoon?"

"I wish I could blame the incident earlier," Beatrice replied, "but that's not it."

"Don't tell me fearless Beatrice Porter is afraid to face down this crowd?"

"Of course not." *Lie.* But that wasn't it either. The idea that she was being watched had been festering for weeks now. The mess with Eric Stone had thrown some white noise into her intuition, and she could not, for the life of her, determine what was causing her all this disquiet.

The door opened to reveal a brightly lit, opulent ballroom.

Showtime.

BEATRICE EXCUSED herself from the huddle of diplomats and lawmakers to get another drink. She had sent Doug off to eavesdrop on another conversation of a rival security consultant.

A dark-haired woman with a pageboy bob, dressed in a tacky emerald-sequined gown, waylaid Beatrice on her way to the bar.

Kelly Winters. Her nemesis and the main society reporter for the DC Tattler.

"Beatrice."

"Ms. Winters. I didn't know they allowed barracudas in these functions." Beatrice's voice was glazed with saccharine sweetness.

Unfazed, the reporter shrugged. "You're not the only one with political connections, Beatrice."

"It's Ms. Porter to you," Beatrice responded. "Well, if

you're going to be mixing in these social circles, I suggest you fire your fashion consultant."

The gloves came off. The reporter's face turned ugly and she sneered, "You'd do best not to antagonize me. Your reputation is not exactly stellar at the moment."

Beatrice gave a short burst of mirthless laughter. She shook her head. "Don't threaten me, Ms. Winters. You print one lie, and you and your tabloid just bought yourselves a lawsuit."

"Everything all right here?" a low baritone voice interjected.

Zach Jamison.

Kelly's brow arched. "You've moved on pretty fast."

"Come on, Beatrice," Zach gently grasped her arm as he glared at the reporter. "Looks like you need a drink."

When they reached the bar, Zach asked what she wanted and ordered their drinks. Giving her his full attention, he asked, "Was she a reporter?"

"Yes."

"She the one who's been printing all this garbage about you?"

Beatrice nodded.

"How did she manage to get into this exclusive event?"

"No idea," Beatrice replied tersely and winced when she saw Zach's face fall. "I'm sorry. I'm just not very good company at the moment. It's been a weird day."

He frowned and Beatrice realized how her statement came across. "Oh, no. No. Our lunch meeting was the most productive part of my day, actually."

Zach grinned at her. "Okay. You got me worried there for a moment. We're pretty set to work with you and whomever you choose for us."

"Bee!" Doug reached them. He looked worried. "I saw Winters ambush you. I couldn't get away from the French ambassador."

"No worries, man. I got her covered," Zach replied.

Both men exchanged strange looks she couldn't decipher. Beatrice suddenly felt suffocated. She needed a blast of November chill.

"Guys, do me a favor? Make sure Winters doesn't leave the ballroom," Beatrice said. "I'm stepping out for a bit."

"It's forty degrees out there," Doug said. "I'll come with you."

"Doug," Beatrice said sternly. "I'll be fine. Keep an eye on things."

"Well, at least put this on." Her assistant removed his tuxedo jacket and draped it across her shoulders.

"Thanks," Beatrice said, and then nodded to Zach. "Thanks for rescuing me from Winters."

"Not a problem, lady."

Afterward, Beatrice couldn't walk fast enough to the French doors that opened to the balcony. Because of the chilly weather, there wasn't a soul outside. She closed the embellished glass door behind her and took a couple of steps toward the marble balustrade. Invigorating air refreshed her lungs. She had the odd desire to run.

"Beatrice."

Whatever breath she took in was punched right out of her. She turned in the direction of the familiar voice and stilled.

Gabriel.

2

Gabe couldn't breathe. She was still the vision he remembered.

His Beatrice.

No. Not his. He lost that right three years ago when he left her. Now, he had to earn her forgiveness, and hope she'd take him back.

She didn't know it yet, but he wasn't giving her a choice.

In that moment where time stood in a vacuum, he studied her. Beatrice always had the face of an angel, an almost perfect oval that tapered to a delicate, yet stubborn, chin. It really depended on her mood. Cutting wit and dry humor were some of the traits Gabe loved about her. His eyes zeroed in on the jacket keeping her warm and his jaw tightened. When his gaze returned to her eyes, he realized the shock had left her only to be replaced by pure unadulterated fury.

Gabe turned rigid with anticipation. What did he expect? That she would welcome him with open arms?

"What are you doing here?" Her tone was sharp. The hatred dripping from her voice bore a hole in his gut like acid.

"I hoped to see you."

"And then what?" Beatrice snapped. "Be friends? I'm sorry, Gabe, but friends do not leave the way you did."

"We were not friends when I left, do not delude yourself. You were my woman." Giving Beatrice an inch would only make her take a mile. He couldn't waver and fuck around with what he wanted. Not with her. He'd have to make it clear. His voice turned hoarse. "I threw you away—"

"Yes, you did."

"I want you back, poppy—"

He expected it, the stinging slap. It cracked in the silence of the night.

The coat over her shoulders fell to the ground, drawing Gabe's eyes to her nipples, which were pushing against the fabric of her gown, tempting him to just rip that dress from her, suck on her tit, and fuck her senseless. The burn on his cheek was insignificant to the lust that seized him. He'd had a semi since he'd seen her. Now his cock was threatening a full-blown erection.

"You're the fucking delusional one," she hissed. "I will never, ever take you back." She cursed. "Stop looking at my boobs!"

He couldn't help grinning, but resisted the urge to make a sexual innuendo.

Eyes on the prize, Sullivan.

"I know it's going to take some time, babe."

"Oh? For what?"

"For you to trust me again."

"Trust you to make a fool of me again? You really think I'd waste my time on you? Are you really that hard up, Gabe? If all you want is a fuck, I'm sure there'll be—"

He didn't let her finish. Something broke inside him when she had dared think he would fool her again. He wanted her to feel how much he needed her. His hand snaked out and yanked her against him. His mouth came crashing down on hers. Her lips were sealed tightly. Gabe growled low in his throat as he backed her into a dark corner. His fingers dug into her ass, preparing to boost her against the wall.

That was when he felt it.

An unholy pain between his legs.

He lost the ability to breathe, to think. He imploded like a pile of bricks.

"Fuck." Was that his voice? *Fuck.*

"Boy, that felt amazing," Beatrice gushed. Triumph and exhilaration were rolling off her in waves.

Gabe was on his knees, his hands over his crotch, looking up dazedly at her. "You do realize, poppy," he pushed between gritted teeth, "you could have ruined our chances of ever having children."

Fuck, he felt like puking. Cold sweat started beading his forehead.

"Hmph, still delusional. I don't freaking care if you ever get another erection. Period."

"That'll be a shame for you, babe."

"You deserve to be castrated, you asshole!" Beatrice spun on her heels and stalked away from him.

Gabe tried to get up, but the pain was still so intense, he crawled. "Damn it, Beatrice! Wait!"

"What's going on here?"

This just keeps getting better, Gabe thought darkly. Beatrice's assistant showed up and he was down on the floor like a pathetic bastard. Not that he didn't deserve it, but he'd rather not look too diminished in front of a potential rival, even if the admiral assured him Douglas Keller wouldn't be competition.

The blond prick glared at Gabe and acted like he was going to beat him up.

Really, buddy? I just got kneed in the balls.

"What did he do, Bee?"

"I took care of it, Doug. Don't worry," Beatrice cast another wrathful stare his way. "The air out here has gone rotten. Take me home before I get sick."

Gabe watched the woman who meant everything to him walk away with another man. A searing pain burned in his chest. He deserved it, but he wasn't giving up. Not by a long shot.

"So who is Mr. Hottie?"

Beatrice collapsed against the passenger seat of Doug's car. The calm she was feeling left her, and now she was a bundle of anxiety.

"That—is Gabriel Sullivan."

"The *Gabriel*?"

"Yup. So stop perving. I don't want to talk about it either."

Doug was silent for a while and then, "He's the reason you're so messed up about relationships, honeybee. We need to talk about it, but not tonight. This day has sucked you dry."

Understatement.

They were quiet on the ride home. Doug would have normally dropped her off, but this time, he insisted on accompanying her inside. It was only when Beatrice stepped into her condo that she felt safe enough to let go. It started with tremors in her hands until her whole body started shaking. Years of suppressed emotion, of keeping a facade that she had gotten over Gabe, finally caught up with her.

She broke down and wept.

Doug reached for her and clasped her neck, bringing her head to his chest.

Pain, rooted so deeply, prevented the sounds of her cries from escaping. She opened her mouth, but it was a silent cry. It hurt. The pressure in her chest pushed against her throat.

All the inadequacies and insecurities she had held in for years threatened to unhinge her completely.

"Breathe, sweetie," Doug whispered in her ear.

After one mighty indrawn breath, a wail of anguish finally escaped her and she sobbed until she thought she couldn't stop.

"Why . . .wh . . . why did he have to . . . come back . . ." she mumbled between sobs. "I was fine. I. Was. Fine."

This went on for a while—speaking incoherently between her tears. All through this, Doug held her and didn't say a word.

Finally, Beatrice exhaled a shuddering breath. A feeling of cleansing and calm overwhelmed her. "Whoa, that was cathartic."

"Feeling better?" her friend asked her quietly. His face was grim.

Beatrice nodded and pulled away.

"You should have let me beat the shit out of him."

"I can fight my own battles."

"I've never seen you this way, Beatrice." Doug's eyes flashed angrily. "Whatever happened broke you. I don't like it."

Beatrice shook her head. "Maybe tonight was the closure I needed."

Doug looked at her dubiously. "He doesn't seem like a guy who'd give up easy."

Her heart pinched. "Wrong, Doug. He gave me up easily once before."

When he kinda promised her an eternity.

She remembered that night, three days before he had left her.

Beatrice liked clubbing; Gabe did not.

They had gone out to dinner, and then at her insistence, to a dance club afterward.

Beatrice had to drag his ass out of the chair more than once to dance with her.

Even then, he was as stiff as a board and clearly uncomfortable.

Fed up, she called it a night and decided to go home.

"You need to loosen up, Gabe," Beatrice groused on their way back to her row house.

"I told you when we got together I'm not dancing."

"I know, but I thought that was just macho-man speak."

Gabe shot her an annoyed look, but didn't say anything.

She remained quiet on the way home and heard Gabe exhale a resigned breath.

When they entered the house, he gripped her hand and led her to the study.

"What're you up to, Gabe?"

He grinned and shushed her. Letting go of her hand, he walked to the antique cabinet that held a vintage turntable and old records.

"Can't let your mom's collection go to waste," Gabe said, rummaging through the records. He picked one and loaded it on the sound player.

Strains of Etta James's "At Last" filled the study.

Beatrice started shaking her head. A silly grin formed on her lips as her frustration with Gabe melted away. He opened the French doors that led to the patio.

"Shall we?" He held out his hand.

"Gabe, you don't have to." For some strange reason, a lump formed in her throat.

Their hands linked, Gabe pulled her close and whispered, "Anything for you, poppy."

They slow-danced on the stone patio to the tune of Etta James's haunting voice, her head on Gabe's chest, his chin against her temple. When the music ended, she looked up at him and asked, "Why do you call me poppy? Is it because of my hair?"

Gabe nodded. "Yes. Also, in some cultures, the poppy is a symbol of eternal love."

His eyes were intense as they stared into hers. Unable to speak, she hid her face on his chest, contemplating what he just revealed. They swayed together in silence.

Eternal love, Beatrice fumed as she snapped back to the present.

Fool me once, Gabe. Only once.

GABE WALKED into his house and dropped the keys on the small table by the foyer. His rescue military dog, Rhino, a nine-year-old German Shepherd, was sitting right by the small table. His tail thumped eagerly, waiting for Gabe to greet him.

"Hey, buddy." Gabe crouched and gripped his dog's head in an affectionate squeeze. "Ready for your walk?"

The minute Rhino heard "walk", he started whining excitedly and shuffling his front legs. Chuckling, Gabe reached for the leash and hooked one end to Rhino's collar. He had long since removed his tuxedo bow and unbuttoned his shirt.

It had been almost four months since he had shed his Dmitry Yerzov persona. The first few weeks were a challenge to integrate back into normal society. Gabe had no close relatives. His parents were dead and he had no siblings. This made him an ideal CIA operative. The only family he knew were the SEALs, and even then he had to give up his brothers to descend into the twisted world of the Russian mafia. He had killed all his emotions to take the job. Once he had ceased to exist as his deadly alter ego, images of every person he had assassinated flooded his dreams. It was hell. He'd been to see the CIA shrink at the NEST—the agency's special rehabilitation center. Screw the stigma. The sooner he fixed his fucked-up self, the sooner he could go after her. Beatrice was his prize.

He exited his all-brick Victorian row house in Old Town Alexandria, Rhino at his heels. Beatrice had sold her old house in this area and moved into her new condominium a few months after he'd left her. Guilt clawed at him. She loved that house and this area. He had thought to buy the same house back for her, but decided maybe it was best to start fresh. The back patio needed some work, but the front of the house had a small yard with mature landscaping and wrought-iron fencing. He remembered Beatrice stopping to gaze at this house in particular whenever they went for their walks in the neighborhood.

Confident aren't you, Sullivan? She kneed you in the junk.

Gabe winced at the memory. His Beatrice was still a spitfire.

He walked a couple of blocks more, Rhino happily marking each tree, when he noticed a black sedan parked a couple of cars up. Rhino must have felt the change in Gabe's body language and started growling softly.

"Easy, boy," Gabe said tightly.

When the back door swung open, Gabe knew who was stepping out even before the figure fully emerged.

Admiral Benjamin Porter—top-level recruiter and strategist of CIA black ops and Beatrice's father. A reminder of everything Gabe told himself he shouldn't be, and yet he admired the man. However, from what little Beatrice had told him during their time together, the admiral was a shitty father and husband.

Rhino's growl grew louder as the admiral approached.

"Gonna call off your attack dog, Commander?"

"Not sure."

The admiral sighed. "We have a problem."

"Not mine."

"Gabriel—"

"I told you, sir. I'm done with the agency." Rhino started snarling. Gabe decided to calm down his dog. "Friendlies, Rhino."

The dog immediately stopped his aggression.

"My priority is Beatrice."

"I know that," the admiral said. "That's why I procured your admission into the Mayflower Charity Ball. I've given you information about her whereabouts for the last two weeks and stood back while you stalked her."

Gabe snorted but didn't contradict the admiral, because that was exactly what he did. Thankfully, he didn't catch her at a time when she was with Eric Stone. Judging from the tabloids, the relationship was a hot mess. He was so proud of how his girl handled herself with so much class against three crazed fans earlier this afternoon.

The admiral had now fallen into step by his side as the three of them continued to walk without missing a beat.

"I don't want to fuck up again with her. I want to prove to her that I'm in it for the long haul."

"Is that what the dog is all about? A show of your commitment?"

Gabe didn't answer, so the admiral continued, "Or is he helping you regain your empathy. Teaching you how to feel?"

"Don't psychoanalyze me, Ben," Gabe snapped. "Rhino was a loyal military dog who was about to be classified as equipment and left behind. He may be partially deaf and blind, but he deserves a second chance."

"Sounds familiar."

Gabe cursed. "Look, say what you gotta say. Be done with it."

"Someone might be aware that Dmitry Yerzov is still alive."

"Impossible. How?" Gabe was used to the admiral's penchant for drama and constant scheming. Gabe should know. He had let himself be a part of it.

"Philip Crowe aka Leonid Belov must have had a partner that we weren't aware of," the admiral said. Crowe/Belov had worked with Gabe in an undercover capacity in the Zorin

Bratva—a Russian arms dealer they had brought down almost four months ago.

The admiral had his full attention now. "Go on."

"The off-shore account that Crowe was going to use to siphon the thirty-five million dollars was shut down before we could get our hands on it. All indications point to the Fuego gang."

"Shit. The Colombian gang that we sent after Travis and Caitlin?"

"The same."

The wheels started spinning in Gabe's head. That would mean Crowe had an "in" with the gang. Nothing would stop Crowe from having insurance just in case something happened to him, which it did. Crowe knew most of the true identities of CIA agents involved in the Zorin Bratva takedown.

"What else?"

"Nothing as of now, but I may have to call in a marker from an old friend."

A pained look crossed the admiral's face.

"Something tells me this old friend isn't really a friend."

"A buddy from my earlier days in the Navy. We had a falling out. Or rather, his ideals didn't align with the U.S. government any longer."

"Look, I'll help if I can. I don't want a crosshair on you or Beatrice," Gabe said. As much as he despised Porter sometimes, he cared for the crazy bastard.

"All I wanted was to give you a heads up," Porter said. "I'm not sure if there's anything you can do. I'm sure if Crowe gave Fuego all the information from the Zorin takedown, you're compromised."

"I'm adept with disguises, in case you've forgotten." Shit. Did he just volunteer himself? Backtracking, and in a harsh tone, he repeated, "Beatrice is my priority. I'm not officially involved. I'm out of the agency. Don't ask me to refer someone to help either, because I'm not having another friend's death on my conscience."

"It wasn't your fault, Gabriel."

"I know, but for a long time, I felt it was. It's done. He's not coming back. He's dead, and the people responsible are dead as well," Gabe stated flatly. His skin prickled as his alter ego reared his head. "Are we done?"

The admiral nodded. Gabe hastened away with Rhino. There was an urgent need to distance himself from Porter.

~ *Dmitry, about three years ago*

The twelve-year-old boy stared up at him—bound, gagged, and crying quietly, snot mixing with all the tears. He'd been brave for the most part, defiant even. He would have made a good lieutenant for the Bratva, except his father was a traitor, and Zorin wanted the bloodline ended.

Starting with the first born son.

Angel of Death.

The poor lad peed in his pants.

For a moment, Dmitry wavered, and then he said, "You won't feel a thing. I'll be quick."

Present

"Refill?"

Gabe looked up to see the diner waitress holding a carafe of coffee.

"Sure."

"You must like our food a lot; you've been here for the past two weeks."

"Yeah."

"All you ever order are pancakes and bacon," his chatty waitress pressed on, leaning against the table suggestively. "You need to try other items on the menu."

Gabe was amused. "Are we still talking about this menu, hon?"

"I don't know, handsome, you tell me."

He looked around the diner. It was after 9:00 a.m. and the crowd had thinned considerably. He leaned back in the booth, taking in the woman's red-striped uniform, a size too small and five inches too short. Gabe smiled wryly. "I'm taken, sorry."

"Shame." She leaned closer. "Well, if you get untaken, let me know."

"I believe you were going to pour me some coffee."

The waitress's eyes flashed angrily as she poured coffee into the cup. Gabe made a mental note to change the location of his stakeout because the waitress would probably spit on his food the next time.

He stared across the street at Beatrice's condominium. She usually didn't leave her residence until noon. Doug's car frequently passed the front of the condo around 8:30 a.m., rounding the building to pull into the underground parking, but he didn't see him arrive this morning. Gabe was sure Douglas Keller was gay, but he definitely wasn't the flamboyant or even the effeminate type. Gabe knew Beatrice's assistant would have had no qualms beating him up last night, not that Gabe would have let him. Balls kicked or not, he would have flipped the guy over before he'd even gotten to throw a punch.

A flashy car stopping in front of the condominium drew his attention. With recognition came swift fury. Rock dick Eric Stone. Gabriel forced himself to remain in his seat and wait before getting himself involved. The last thing Beatrice needed was an ex-boyfriend getting into the business of another ex-boyfriend.

It didn't take long. Eric the dickhead started causing a ruckus. Shaggy brown hair, t-shirt, torn-jeans, and sporting converse sneakers, he was arguing with the guard who apparently had orders not to let him in. Twenty minutes later, his spitfire flew down the steps of the condo to confront him. Beatrice was speaking normally, but Stone was yelling at her and gesturing wildly.

The escalation of tension was inevitable.

Gabe stood and threw a couple of bills on the table as he hurried outside. He was just in time to see Stone lay his hands on Beatrice's shoulders to yell further into her face. Even from the distance, Gabe could see the fire in her green eyes, and for a second, he was feeling sorry for Eric.

"Take your hands off me, Eric."

Wait for it.

"Stop being so fucking stubborn, Bee—oomph!"

Rocker boy released his hold on her shoulders and doubled-up on his stomach.

Punched in the gut.

Gabe had taught her that move—tip of fingers to fist—not much momentum needed.

Eric was lucky he didn't get kicked in the balls.

Gabe slowed his approach as a smirk formed on his lips. Beatrice spotted him.

"I don't believe this," Beatrice yelled. "What are you doing here?"

"Watching over you," Gabe stated simply.

An undecipherable look passed over her face. Then her eyes shifted between him and Eric.

"Who's this asshole, Beatrice?" Eric wheezed through his mouth, glaring at Gabe.

"Her man," he responded levelly, ignoring Beatrice's gasp of outrage.

"You fucking replaced me with this gorilla?" Eric snapped.

Gabe paused. He'd gotten back his muscles after he'd deliberately shed some pounds to fit the mold of a lean assassin who looked good in a suit, but he was far from ape-size right now.

"I didn't know Beatrice's taste had changed to pansy-assed rock dicks," Gabe drawled in response.

Eric straightened and balled his fists at his sides. Indecision was written all over his face whether he should take a swing at Gabe or not. As for Gabe, he almost wished he had, so he could have an excuse to thrash him.

"Hit me. Come on. You know you want to," Gabe goaded softly.

"Screw this," Beatrice snapped. "I don't care if you two kill each other."

She turned and stalked back into the condo.

Eric started to follow Beatrice, but Gabe blocked him.

"Be a good boy. Get back into your overpriced car and get out of here." His hands were itching to squeeze the life out of this little shit.

"We'll have to ask both of you to leave the premises or we're calling the cops," a building security guard announced firmly.

Gabe sighed. The last thing he wanted was to get arrested. He raised both his arms in acquiescence. He looked in the direction of the condo and saw Beatrice with her arms folded over her chest, staring at them. He lifted his hand to give her a two-finger salute and walked away.

"So, HOW ABOUT SOME DINNER?" Zach Jamison asked Beatrice after they concluded their first meeting of Senator Mendoza's security detail. The senator was busy with senate committee hearings and couldn't make the appointment.

Beatrice had dreaded the question throughout the whole meeting because Zach had hinted at it earlier when he arrived at the BSI office. Doug was frowning at Zach. Nate pretended he didn't hear the question, and excused himself politely, heading into his office.

"I've got a load of paperwork to do." Beatrice hoped her smile softened the lame excuse. She'd been tense as violin string ever since Gabe had returned. Two days had passed since that confrontation in front of the condo. Eric continued to hound her with phone calls, but hadn't shown up at her building again. There was no contact from Gabe, which was adding more to her uneasiness.

Zach shrugged. "Some other time then. Great meeting. The senator will be pleased." The senator's Chief of Staff grinned brightly before heading out to the reception area.

When he was out of earshot, Beatrice said, "That smile of his gives me the creeps."

"Something is not adding up with that guy," Doug said.

"Huh? How so?"

"He's coming on to you in public—"

"And?"

"I was pretty sure he was eye-fucking me three nights ago."

Beatrice stilled, her lips were twitching. "Maybe he's bi. Look, he's all yours if you're jealous."

Doug huffed. "Don't be silly. I just don't trust a guy who does that."

"Maybe he's making you jealous?"

"Well, he's not my type."

Beatrice had to agree with her assistant there. Doug preferred blue-collar. For all his clean-cut, neatly pressed look, he favored rough-looking guys.

"I'm heading out. I need to drop a couple of contracts with our attorney for them to look over," Doug said. "You leaving?"

"Nah. I need to catch up with Nate."

"See you next week then?"

"Enjoy Florida!" Beatrice stepped toward Doug and gave him a hug.

He held her tightly. "I won't go if you need me here, sweetie. There's way too many things going on with you."

"Don't worry, Nate will take care of me."

BEATRICE FOUND Nathan Reece going over some building blueprints. He was the other partner in Blake Security Incorporated. Because he had been a clandestine agent with the CIA, he preferred not to be identified with the company name. Nate worked more as a silent partner, having Travis handle most of the face-to-face meetings with the client—or the principal—as was the term professionally used in the security business.

"So what do you think of Zach?"

Nate looked up briefly from the prints before him. "Uh . . . seems like a nice guy."

"Lame. What is up?"

"Look, Bee, I don't want to make an assessment of someone based on one meeting."

"Lie. You were formerly CIA, Nate. Rapid assessments are your forte."

"He's our client. I shouldn't let it affect me."

"What are you talking about?"

Nate squirmed uncomfortably. "I think he likes me . . . uh . . . that way."

Beatrice burst out laughing. "Oh, God, how could I be so blind in all this? Well, I don't ever get any sexual vibes from him except his cheesy smile. How come I'm the one getting a dinner invitation?"

"Search me," Nate shrugged. "He's a client. I'll deal."

Beatrice walked beside Nate and tucked her arm into his. "We need to find you a nice girl."

"Leave me alone, Bee. You're the one who needs to get her ducks in a row."

Beatrice harrumphed.

"I wasn't going to say anything, but you better not consider taking him back."

Who was Nate talking about? Gabe or Eric? Had Doug mentioned something to him?

"Uh, who?" Beatrice hedged.

Nate rolled his eyes. "Who else? Eric Stone." Ever the astute observer though, his eyes narrowed. "Why? What aren't you telling me?"

"Don't say anything to Travis yet, okay?"

Nate nodded.

"His SEAL buddy, Gabriel Sullivan, is back in town."

Nate silently cursed. "You better not consider taking him back either. Is he bothering you? Do you want me to put someone on you?"

"I can handle myself, Nate," Beatrice snapped.

"He's bothering you." Her friend's brown eyes grew cold. "That fucker. You wanna stay with me for the weekend?"

Beatrice sighed. This was so sad. Before her was the perfect male specimen: tall, a physique that belonged on the cover of a sports magazine, a smile that wouldn't creep women out, but most likely make their panties drop, and she was friends with the man.

"Why are you looking at me like that?" Nate asked warily.

"Like what?"

"Like I was a bug you crushed under your shoe."

Beatrice shook her head in amusement. "I'm just pissed that all the reliable men in my life are not relationship material. First there's Doug. Gainfully employed. I don't know what the hell I'd do without him. He cares for me, loves me, but he's gay. Then, there's you. Women drool all over you, and yet you do nothing for me."

"Wow. Thanks," Nate said sarcastically, but his eyes glinted merrily. "You're sexy as hell, too, Bee. I see men look at you and it pisses me off."

Beatrice raised a brow.

"Because it's like they're ogling my little sister," Nate chuckled and caught her head under his arm and ground his fist on the crown of her head.

Beatrice squealed and kidney punched him. Nate grunted, but continued chuckling.

"Ugh! Stop that. You're not much older than me," Beatrice yelled.

"Okay, okay." Nate let her go. "What do you want?"

"Jeez, you really sound like an older brother being pestered by his five-year-old sister."

"What do you want, Beatrice?"

"When will Travis and Cat be back?"

"You know when," Nate said, annoyed. "Tonight. What do you really want?"

Beatrice perched half her butt on his desk, eyeing him knowingly.

"I'm not giving it to you," Nate said. "I shouldn't have told you about the inner room at the Diamond Owl. Why do you want to learn about BDSM anyway? You're not made for that shit, you know."

"Are you?"

"No." Nate sat on the chair and leaned back. "It's not as simple as leather, chains, and whips, Bee. It's about trust. People think it's all the rage and think a set of handcuffs translates to BDSM. It doesn't."

"You sound knowledgeable."

"I know some folks who are into that lifestyle. Not for me."

"I'm curious to know how to control a man's orgasm. They say—"

"Christ! This conversation has gotten weird—"

"I read that there's this sub-space—"

"Stop!" Nate growled. He reached for his sticky pad and scrawled a word on it. "Here. It's Friday night. Now get out of here. I need to get some shit done."

Grinning triumphantly at a scowling Nate, and with the

password to the BDSM club safely in her clutches, she gave him a quick hug and skipped out of the room. Friday was the day after tomorrow. Caitlin should be back by then, and Emily was easy to persuade. She didn't need to tell them exactly where they were going. For the first time in days, Beatrice felt more like herself—in control and conniving.

3

"I KNOW, Mom. I wish I could visit for Thanksgiving, but it's a bad time for me right now."

She also didn't like the idea of flying to California on the most traveled holiday of the year. Lorraine Woodward divorced her father fifteen years ago when Beatrice was seventeen. It had been an amicable divorce unlike the simmering resentment that reigned throughout their marriage. Any child would be hurt when their parents' marriage ended, but Beatrice had been relieved.

"You should stop wasting your life away in that job, Beatrice," her mother scolded. "Find a nice young man to settle down. You're becoming too much like your father."

She'd heard this lecture before. Her mom had already laid into her about the Eric Stone debacle when it first happened. She was surprised the topic had not come up again. So she said what she always did, "I love you, Mom."

Her mother sighed. "I'll talk to you before Thanksgiving."

Obligatory Friday morning call to her mom over, Beatrice switched on the television and set it to the international news channel. She pulled a couple of files on her lap and started working, but her thoughts drifted back to the events leading to the divorce. Beatrice didn't remember much from her childhood, except her mother's constant drinking. Her father was rarely home. There was a point when her mother lost it and just went ballistic and attacked her dad. Beatrice had cowered under a writing desk and heard her mom screaming about her dad's ambition ruining their marriage. The fight ended with a slamming of doors.

Beatrice emerged from under the table. She took tentative steps down the stairs and found her mom on her knees, quietly sobbing into her hands.

"Mom?"

Her mother looked at her and tried to smile. "I'm okay, bumblebee."

"Where's Dad?"

A pained expression came over her mom's face. "I tried, Beatrice. He can't be here for your birthday."

She knelt beside her mother and hugged her. "It's okay. We'll be okay, Mom."

Her mom only sobbed harder into her shoulder. It was then at the age of almost ten that Beatrice started to shoulder her mother's tears.

Despite her mother's bitterness with the state of their marriage, Beatrice was thankful that during the times she was sober, she performed her parental duties well. But because she'd been drunk half the time, Beatrice had learned to be independent, so she had taken more responsibilities at a young age. She'd forged her mother's signature on payment checks and on her school release forms. She would race home from school to fix dinner. Some of her friends picked up on her mom's nickname for her and turned it to "Busy Bee" until it was later shortened to "Bee" and the name stuck.

Beatrice suspected it was during her high school graduation that her mom had given up on her father when he didn't show up until weeks later. Her mother filed for divorce not long after.

Interestingly enough, it was about this time her dad took an active interest in Beatrice's life. And like a dry sponge starved for water, she soaked up whatever attention he gave her until she was old enough to realize he was molding her into someone like him. Of course she rebelled then, but it was not long after, and with much horror, that she realized she liked the path her dad had carved for her.

The divorce and the eventual distance did help her mother overcome her alcoholism. She eventually checked herself into rehab where she met her second husband—a popular Hollywood producer. She was now living the life of a Stepford wife in a Beverly Hills mansion.

Sadly, Beatrice knew her mom was still in love with her dad. That was the reason Beatrice avoided men like Benjamin Porter. She rose from the couch and walked over to where a couple of picture frames sat on top of a mantel. Her pictures with her mom. One with her dad. No one could probably tell, but Beatrice had arranged the pictures in a way that started with her mother at her most vibrant and youngest. It ended with the pictures during her graduation. Her mom's beauty had faded into a face etched with bitterness, its vibrancy snuffed out by a force other than age—the indifference of a man who was supposed to love and cherish her.

After Gabe had left her, Beatrice made it a ritual, a therapy, to stare at the photographs first thing in the morning and, when she remembered, the last thing at night. She had since stopped doing it after a year, thinking she had gotten over Gabe. Her breakdown a couple of days ago proved otherwise. So she was getting back into her picture therapy. No way was she going to end up like her mother.

SHUTTING the lid on her laptop, Beatrice sighed in relief. She just finished following up on her doctor's medical portal regarding her STD tests. She was clean. Health scares like this one should be enough to keep her legs shut, preferably bound together, for the next five years or so. How weird was it that she was going to a sex club tonight? Maybe she should content herself with voyeurism and a dildo for the said five years.

Her phone chimed with a text message. Caitlin was running ten minutes late.

She missed those two, Travis and Cat. Caitlin Blake was an amnesiac and hacker genius. She had recently started fielding freelance assignments from the National Security Agency (NSA). Though Travis, in all his caveman glory, wasn't happy about his wife working for another secretive part of the government, he gave in grudgingly. Caitlin never did remember her past. Any pertinent clue was sealed in CIA-classified files. Caitlin told her that Project Infinity had been corrupted. The mastermind of the cover-up in the agency was still a mystery. The specter agent program had gone beyond the level of top secret and that was all Caitlin knew. A friend and fellow agent, Jase Locke/John Cooper, lied to her about their relationship and tricked her into a life on the run. The truth about her disappearance that night was only revealed through a posthumous letter from Jase. Digging deeper would put herself and Travis in the crosshairs of an unknown enemy, and with Travis and the admiral at odds, Travis was one ally down.

"I want a clean start with Travis, Bee," Caitlin said. "I hate that I deceived him when we were married. He loves me anyway. I'm sure my reasons were to protect him. So I'm leaving it alone."

If there were two people who deserved a happily-ever-after, it was those two. They had been through so much, especially Travis. To see her friend now so deliriously happy should be nauseating given her blasé opinion on relationships, but Beatrice was genuinely thrilled for them.

After exactly ten minutes, the doorbell chimed.

Beatrice opened the door to a gorgeously tanned Caitlin Blake. Her blonde hair was bleached lighter by the sun, and her unusual hazel eyes were sparkling with contentment. In short, she was positively glowing.

"Don't you look so sun-kissed and annoyingly beautiful."

"Are we doing this mutual admiration thing?" Caitlin smirked and walked in.

Beatrice snorted. "Nah, my ego is brimming right now."

The other woman eyed her outfit. Beatrice was dressed in a mid-length flounce, flirty skirt in a teal color that complimented her red hair.

"So what am I wearing?"

Beatrice smiled in feline smugness. "You will love *the* dress."

THEY HAD BEEN in the inner sanctum of Diamond Owl for a few minutes now. Beatrice wasn't feeling it. No way could she do what she was witnessing to a sex partner. What made her think she was a domme? Those damned erotica books she loved reading in her spare time would be her downfall.

Caitlin, Emily, and Beatrice managed to snag a good spot near the stage where a barrier kept the crowd at bay. On display was a woman shackled to what Beatrice knew was a St. Andrew's Cross. Said woman was being flogged and then felt up for her wetness.

"Oh, my," Caitlin whispered. "You think you can whip a guy like that, check how hard he is, and then whip him again?"

"Shut up," Beatrice retorted, feeling like slinking away and escaping. So much for her big bluster earlier.

Caitlin whispered something to Emily. Beatrice leaned in to listen to their conversation when a hand gripped her upper arm firmly.

"Come on, Bee."

Nate.

What the hell was he doing here?

Beatrice caught sight of Travis's unmistakable form

crowding Caitlin. *Uh-oh. Busted!*

She had an uncontrollable compulsion to laugh. Maybe it was the couple of drinks she'd had, or she was just finding the whole situation amusing. The minute she and Nate left the room, she burst out laughing.

"Oh, my God!" she chortled. "Poor Caitlin. She's going to get it. Wait until Travis gets a load of that dress."

"You are so much trouble, Ms. Porter," Nate declared.

"You're one to talk. You ratted us out again."

"Hey, bros before hoes and all that, you know." He smirked.

"You owe me a drink."

"Come on, then."

They both started for the bar when Beatrice stopped in her tracks. Gabe was standing before them, glowering at Nate. Her friend tensed beside her, clocking the threat immediately.

"Am I right to assume that's Gabriel Sullivan?" Nate murmured in her ear.

Beatrice nodded.

Nate immediately stepped in front of her, facing Gabe squarely. Both men were almost the same height, Gabe maybe an inch taller at six-four and definitely bulkier. However, Nate was no slouch with his lean compact muscles either.

"Turn around and walk away," Nate growled softly.

"Nathan Reece, right?" Gabe said with a tight smile. "I guess I don't need to tell you who I am. You should also know that this won't end well if you stop me from talking to Beatrice."

"So you wanna take this outside?" Nate goaded.

Yep, time to step in.

"I got this, Nate."

"Beatrice—"

"He'll only keep coming back," Beatrice whispered harshly to her friend. "My problem. My solution. Stand down."

Nate's jaw clenched. Indecision was written all over his face. He nodded jerkily then returned his gaze to the other man. Without another word to Gabe, he deliberately shouldered past him.

"Hey, poppy," Gabe greeted her quietly.

Beatrice nodded to the exit. "Let's go."

THE SECOND they cleared the club steps, Beatrice whirled on Gabe and shoved him on the shoulder.

"What is wrong with you, huh?" Beatrice screeched. "You keep following me everywhere. Do you know how creepy that is?"

"Since when have you become so violent, babe?" Gabe mock massaged his left shoulder.

He wasn't taking her seriously. Nothing had changed. He could still annoy the hell out of her and at the same time turn her on. Seeing all that hardness underneath his navy blue shirt over jeans that hugged well-muscled thighs sent a palpable twitch between her legs. *Hell. No.*

"What's your game, really? I'm so tired of you popping up everywhere I am—"

"No game, Beatrice." His face turned serious. "I wouldn't say leaving you was a mistake. Saying I had no choice is a lie. I can't tell you why."

"I don't care why. It doesn't matter—"

"Can we go somewhere to talk?" Gabe cut in gruffly. Oh, God, his whiskey eyes were boring straight into her and she could feel herself weakening. Damned alcohol.

"Nothing matters, don't you see?" Beatrice's tone was almost pleading. How could she make him leave her alone? "We were a mistake from the start. You chose your job like my father always did. You just proved to me that I was right all along."

"Let's go somewhere else. Please, babe."

Beatrice frowned and narrowed her eyes. There was something wrong with Gabe. He was still larger than life, but obviously diminished. What happened to him? Damn it, she shouldn't care. Stilling herself, she bit out, "I am done with you."

A commotion at the entrance of the club drew their attention. Beatrice felt her gut fall from under her when she spotted Travis with an unconscious Caitlin in his arms.

Beatrice hurried to them. "What happened?"

"Passed out," Travis clipped. "You and I are going to have words, Bee."

Gabe chose that moment to grab her arm. "I'm not done with you."

Travis's shocked eyes fell on Gabe.

"Hello, Lieutenant."

"Shit. Gabriel?"

"You have no right following me here!" Beatrice was feeling desperate. "This is stalking."

"Oh, please, Bee, your scream can wake the dead," Caitlin muttered.

"Cat?" Travis whispered in relief.

"You can put me down, Trav. I'm fine. I think."

"No way. I'm taking you to the hospital. You fainted once during our honeymoon, too. Ed's bringing the car around."

The Escalade pulled up in front of the club.

"Gabe, we need to catch up. Man, you just disappeared off the face of the planet," Travis said. "I have to take my wife to the hospital."

"I'll be in touch."

Nate was flying down the steps of the club just as the Escalade was pulling away. "What happened?"

"Caitlin fainted," Beatrice announced.

"Shit. That must have freaked Travis out." Nate glared at

Gabe. "You done with this guy? I can take you home. I don't think you should be driving."

"We took a cab—"

Gabe's hand shot out and manacled Nate's throat. "I told you this wouldn't end well if you got between me and Beatrice."

"Bring it on, asshole." Nate didn't even flinch, just stared at Gabe in challenge. "That all you got?"

Beatrice recognized that gleam in Nate's eye. For all his playful nature, he was such a war freak. She inserted herself between the two, and extricated Gabe's fingers from Nate's neck. Not releasing Gabe's hand, she tugged him alongside her. "Go home, Nate, or go back to the bar. I told you I got this."

GABE FOLLOWED Beatrice's lead as she dragged him toward the back of the club. He found himself getting hard as they approached the darkened alley. The possibilities of what could happen in this secluded area were playing havoc with his resolve to talk first.

"Beatrice, what are you doing?" he asked tightly.

"You said you wanted to talk," she said flippantly.

"There's a 24-hour diner across—"

"But we know it's not talking you really want." Beatrice pushed Gabe against the wall. "You want to fuck, don't you?"

Before Gabe could reply, Beatrice pressed her lips against his and slipped her tongue inside his mouth. Her taste was a heady mix of berries and wine. He groaned. He wanted to devour her, but not like this. She was drunk.

With as much strength as he could muster, he grabbed her shoulders. "Damn it, poppy. We need to talk."

"Talking is overrated," Beatrice murmured and kissed him again while stroking the bulge in his pants.

"Not here." He tried again.

"Take me against the wall, Gabe."

Fuck. He could feel her softness overwhelm him. His head was swimming.

"Beatrice. Not here."

He held her firmly from him.

"I'm not drunk, Gabe. But I want to feel your cock inside me," she purred as she cupped his heavy balls through his jeans. Gabe raised his eyes to the night, praying for self-control. She was driving him insane with lust.

Eyes on the prize, Sullivan.

She backed away coquettishly from him. "Now there's a hotel down the street. I'm just going to check-in rather than go home. Follow me there or not, I don't care."

"What is your game, Beatrice?" Gabe asked in a strangled groan. She was toying with him, but fuck if he could control his cock from responding.

"No game," Beatrice shrugged. "I'm tired of fighting this attraction. But before I commit to taking you back, I just want to make sure the merchandise is in working order."

Gabe didn't know whether to laugh or get pissed. "Not sure I like being objectified, sweetheart."

"Oh, get your head out of your ass," she snapped. "Men do it all the time. Now. Are we wasting time here?"

THEY FELL through the threshold of the hotel room in a frantic tangle of limbs. Lips ferociously locked on each other, three years of separation condensing into an explosion of lust. As soon as the door slammed shut, Gabe had Beatrice up against it, his fingers going under her skirt, snaking up her thighs and inside her panties. Wet. Fucking wet and drenching his fingers. She moaned into his mouth.

"You want this, huh? You want my mouth on that greedy pussy?"

"No mouth tonight. Just cock."

"Why not?" Gabe coaxed. He'd been dying to get his face between those beautiful thighs. "Why not?" he repeated as he got down on his knees, shoving her skirt up, and started trailing his tongue up her inner thighs. She moaned. His cock grew hard enough to pound nails as his nose inched closer to her feminine heat. He could smell her, the intoxicating arousal of Beatrice. He took a swipe at the fabric covering her pussy, eager to plunge his tongue inside her.

Her fingers dug into his hair, yanking his head viciously to look at her. Gabe winced. *What the hell?*

"I said no mouth. I want you inside me. Just cock."

Glaring at her, Gabe stood and muttered, "Why?"

"Too intimate."

Damn her. She was determined to fight him the whole way. Fine. Gabe unbuckled his belt, lowered his zipper, and freed his erection. All through this, Beatrice eyed him hungrily. There was no mistaking the want in her eyes.

"Okay, babe, you want to test drive the merchandise?" Gabe mocked, but deep down he was fuming. It was demeaning, but he took it. Because he'd hurt her, he would take anything right now. He rolled on the condom. "You wanna know if my cock can fill you the way it used to?"

Beatrice licked her lips. That did it. Gabe lost all control and boosted her against the door. Nudging her panties aside, he plunged inside her. They both yelled at the first stroke. Jesus Christ, she felt so good. So snug.

"How am I doing so far, babe?"

"Stop talking. Start fucking."

Damn her. "You got it."

Gabe pulled back and slammed back inside her. This was not how he envisioned their first time back together. Why did he allow this to happen? But rational thinking soon unraveled into an elemental need. The need to fuck. He continued pounding her into the door as she clung to him. Her wet heat squeezed his cock with such agonizing pleasure, it felt unreal. He squashed down the consequences of this reckless union. All he cared about at this moment was that Beatrice was back in his arms, and he was buried deep inside her. She clenched around him as her orgasm hit her. Gabe followed, coming the hardest he'd had in a long time, probably since her.

THE RUSTLE of fabric woke him, and for a moment Gabe didn't know where he was. Then it all came flooding back. He had fucked her two more times. Both times were a basic quenching of lust that was missing a certain connection, which was why instead of feeling sated, he felt empty. A thud further jolted him out of his sleepy haze.

"Beatrice?"

No answer.

He squinted and saw her dark form against the available light streaming from under the door. What time was it? He checked the bedside clock. It was almost five in the morning.

"Beatrice?"

"What, Gabriel?"

Her voice was flat.

An uneasiness roiled in his gut. He reached for the lamp and turned on the lights. Beatrice had her clothes on and appeared to be looking for her shoes. She found them under the coffee table.

"What are you doing?"

"Isn't it obvious? I'm leaving."

"Well hell, babe, if you weren't satisfied with the merchandise, maybe you'll give me another chance to prove you wrong," Gabe said bitterly. He got up from the bed and walked toward her. Since Beatrice was sitting on a chair slipping on her shoes, his semi-erect dick was right in front of her face.

Beatrice snorted a short laugh. "No need to be crude,

Gabe."

"No. Crude is you propositioning me and then making this all about sex," he whispered harshly. "It isn't. You know it isn't. Why are you doing this to us?"

"Seriously? I did this to us?"

"I'm talking about right now, Beatrice. I want you back. What do you need me to do?"

Her face was impassive. He wasn't getting through to her. Gabe crouched in front of her. "Three years ago—know that I had to leave, Beatrice. I had to. I hurt you because I wanted you to hate me—"

"It worked."

He flinched but pressed on. "Because I didn't know if I could make it back alive. But I came back to you, babe."

"Three years too late and the same fucking problems, Gabe," Beatrice snapped. "You said you cared for your job more than you did me."

"I had to lie."

"Your actions proved it wasn't a lie."

"It was the right choice at that time."

Beatrice sighed and stood up. "Same excuses my dad probably had in his head when he forgot he had a family. Look what that did to my mother. She's pretending to be happy with someone else when in truth she's still in love with him."

"I'm not your dad, Beatrice," Gabe said quietly. "If I'd decided to stay with you then, that choice would've torn me up for the rest of my life. Now, there's only you. You're my priority. My job? I don't have one. I quit. I'll probably go private."

She stilled for a beat. "I've changed."

"What?"

"I don't want a relationship right now after what happened with Eric."

Gabe rose from his crouch and leaned into her, his face a

hair-breadth away. "Don't bring that fucker between us. He's out of your life. Got me?"

"Ah, there you are. The old Gabe," she smiled derisively. "For a while I wondered who this sentiment-spouting fool was." Beatrice reached for the door.

"Don't do this, poppy," he growled, gripping her arm. "This is not you. You walk out now, I might not follow."

"Pride, Gabe?" Beatrice mocked. The look in her eyes fisted his heart in a vise of panic as it was looking more and more certain that they were truly over.

"This isn't about pride. It's about you walking away from what we just shared."

"It was just sex—"

"Keep telling yourself—"

"Just. Sex." Beatrice reached in her bag to pull out a card. "You're good. One of the most delicious fucks I've ever had, but the entire package is a bad investment."

At that moment, Gabe hated her. He dropped his hand from her arm and clenched his fists at his sides as he tried to control his anger.

"Stop," he bit off. Each word pounded another nail in his coffin, sealing him in a tomb with no redemption.

Still he couldn't let her go, so he reached for her again, but she stepped back. Her body language warning him not to touch her.

She flicked the card in the air; his eyes followed it to the floor.

"If you want to do this again, give me a call," Beatrice said, pulling the door open. "But if you have any pride left in you, Gabe, you won't."

He wished she had slammed the door behind her. At least that way he knew she still felt something for him, even if it was anger. The click of the lock echoing in the silence of the room made it seem more final.

He had lost her forever.

4

DMITRY ENTERED THE WHOREHOUSE.

The madam had cheated Zorin out of his cut, and his boss had lost patience.

He passed the rooms where drugged-up teenage girls were held; his mouth curled in disgust. None of his kills were innocent; today wouldn't be any different—a righteous kill.

He could have made this quick, but Dmitry wanted to exact revenge for the young women who might never recover from their horrific fate.

The madam writhed underneath him.

In the throes of her climax, his other hand circled her neck.

And squeezed.

His face came closer. She started struggling, her eyes dilating in fear.

"It may be too late to save those girls," Dmitry snarled softly, "but you will never, ever harm another innocent again." His fingers tightened. "Feel their pain, their fear."

She choked for a while.

Before he snapped her neck.

THE WHISKEY DID nothing to drown the pain. Each time Gabe remembered Beatrice's words was like being stabbed by a dagger to the chest. Repeatedly. It was a physical pain and a constant lump in his throat. He hoped hard liquor would wash it away, but it didn't.

The prospects of rekindling their relationship were bleak.

The situation had turned ugly.

If Gabe were honest with himself, he didn't think he was ready to be with her, for he had no idea who the fuck he was. The old him wouldn't have let Beatrice walk out of that room after firing those words. He would have hauled her over his shoulder, dumped her on the bed, and fucked her into submission. As Dmitry Yerzov? He'd probably shackle her to a bed and keep her on the brink of orgasm before he fucked her. In the ass.

He tipped his whiskey back and signaled the bartender for another one and took in the packed establishment on a Saturday night. He had contemplated camping out at Beatrice's condo, but the sting of rejection was still too fresh and there was only so much a man's pride could handle. Because if she rejected him so soon again, Gabe didn't know what he might do. Fuck. Was this how she felt when he had left her?

How could they come back from all this ugliness they were inflicting on each other?

His brain was telling him to let her go, but that muscle he called his heart was screaming at him to beg her to take him back. His loins were a different matter. They craved her, as well as wanted him to fuck her out of his system. He looked around at the meat market before him.

Maybe if he could bring himself to fuck someone else, he could move on from her. She obviously didn't want him back. Why the fuck was he trying so hard?

Gabe shook his head. *What the fuck, Sullivan? Tucking tail and running already?*

The alcohol not only made him a limp dick, but stupid as well.

As if the fates were taunting him further, a redhead squeezed in next to him.

"Buy me a drink, sugar?"

Gabe glanced at the woman briefly before nodding at the bartender to give her a drink on his tab.

"Thanks," the redhead gushed when her prissy concoction was served. She pressed her breasts against Gabe's arm. His cock stirred. Not a whiskey dick after all.

"I've been watching you," the redhead said. "Looked like you could use some company."

Gabe didn't say anything, just simply took a sip of his whiskey. He should just order the whole damn bottle.

"Not much of a talker?" This time her hand went on his thigh and started inching up, destination unmistakable. Gabe didn't stop her. He glanced at her, taking in her red hair. She was attractive enough, a bit too much makeup for his taste. His eyes rested on her mouth, which tipped up in a knowing smile. "I can show you a good time, sugar."

Gabe chuckled as he returned his attention to his drink. "Not here for that, hon."

The woman's giggle grated on his nerves. What the fuck was he doing? Why was he allowing this woman to fondle him?

Her breath fanned his ear. "I think I can change your mind."

She finished the last of her drink and jerked her head in the direction of the back exit, coyly walking away.

Gabe stared at the remainder of his whiskey for a beat. He slugged it back and pushed away from the bar. He left a couple of bills to cover their drinks and followed the redhead.

SUNDAY EARLY MORNING was a relatively quiet drive up the Beltway. Gabe guided his SUV toward Chevy Chase, Maryland. He felt like shit. His head was pounding, and the sunlight was too bright even while wearing his sunglasses. He deserved this hangover from hell.

He nearly wrecked what he had tried for months to accomplish—being the man who Beatrice deserved. In a pathetic attempt to erase her cruel rejection and to soothe his shredded ego, he contemplated letting another woman suck him off.

In the back alley of the bar, the redhead pushed him against the wall, reminiscent of how Beatrice came on to him the night before. When the woman tried to kiss him, Gabe buried his fingers in her hair, and that was when it hit him.

Rough, wiry hair.

Not Beatrice.

The madness stopped instantly. He was jolted out of his drunken stupor, his erection deflated, and he walked away with no small amount of self-recrimination. He was spiraling between his past and present. He couldn't find his purpose. He quit his job to be with the only person who could anchor him, who could prevent the darkness from sweeping him away, but she didn't want him. Hated him in fact.

Angel of Death.

"You won't feel a thing. I'll be quick."

Gabe shook the images away and spotted the exit for Chevy Chase. He really shouldn't be doing this, but he needed a reminder that even when he was at his vilest, he had a shred of humanity left. He pulled into a relatively affluent neighborhood and parked a couple of cars up from a Tudor-framed house. He waited, sipping from a thermos of hot coffee he had brought with him.

Two hours later, a boy of about fifteen emerged. He was bundled up in a hoodie and an overlay jacket, wearing jeans and sneakers. He was dribbling a basketball on his way to the side of the house. There was a ring fixed at the center of a two-car garage.

The boy started playing hoops.

Gabe watched.

"Here's your coffee, hon."

The barista handed Beatrice her order. It was good to leave the condo this morning because she had remained holed up in her unit all day Saturday after her disastrous encounter with Gabe. Something wasn't sitting right with her. She should be feeling the sweet triumph of revenge, not this unsettling guilt for what she had done.

She ran a couple of miles this morning to clear her head, trying to remove the unsavory taste of how she left Gabe so callously. He did the same to her, why couldn't she pay him back in kind? Damn it, why couldn't he leave well enough alone? He was forcing her to become the biggest bitch in history. The stricken look on his face right before she turned away almost made her reconsider. If he wasn't all hard-ass male perfection, that would have been a kicked-puppy look. Why did he have to remind her of how good he was with his cock? He filled her perfectly, stretching her between the point of pleasure and pain, and hammering out her orgasms effortlessly.

Nowhere near serene and still as conflicted as ever, Beatrice walked into the lobby of her condominium. An anxious concierge rushed toward her.

"Ms. Porter!"

"What's going on?" she asked, baffled.

"There are two detectives here to see you."

Detectives? That was when Beatrice noticed the two trench-coat clad guys rise from the lobby couches. Not missing a beat, she nonchalantly walked to the concierge desk to pick up a newspaper and tucked it under her arm before she faced the approaching detectives.

"Detectives Moore and Smithers of the Metropolitan Police Department." Both detectives flashed their badges.

"To what do I owe this visit?"

"Can we talk somewhere private, Ms. Porter?"

The penetrating look on Detective Moore's face indicated that the matter was grave. She tried to wrack her brain on what could be wrong?

A knot of anxiety formed in her gut.

She nodded to the elevators to take them to her condo.

BEATRICE SET her keycard and coffee on the foyer table, turned and folded her arms in front of her. "What's this all about?"

"Where were you between three and seven a.m. yesterday morning?"

Oh, my God, did something happen to Gabe?

"Did something happen to Gabriel Sullivan?" she blurted out, panic in her voice.

Both detectives frowned; one of them started writing on his notepad.

"Well?" When she heard herself shriek, Beatrice forced herself to calm down. But the silence of the two detectives was making it extremely difficult.

"Were you with this Gabriel Sullivan?"

Warning bells and self-preservation trilled in Beatrice's consciousness. "Do I need a lawyer? If you don't tell me what this is all about, I'm not saying anything else."

"Eric Stone was found dead last night. Time of death initially puts it around the early hours of Saturday morning."

Beatrice felt the room spin. Shocked at Eric's death, relieved that Gabe was okay, it was too much. She forced her unsteady legs to walk across the foyer toward her living room and sat on the couch. The detectives followed but remained standing.

"How?"

"We can't disclose the circumstances for now," Detective Smithers said. "So, were you with this Gabriel Sullivan?"

"I was drunk; I'm not sure of the time frame."

"Do you have his contact information?"

"No."

"Really? That's—"

"He was a one-night stand." She had the resources to track him down, but linking Gabe to Eric was not a good idea given the two had an altercation a few days ago. The detectives might eventually find out. She didn't even want to dwell on her reasons for wanting to protect Gabe.

"Oh." Detective Smithers smirked.

"I'm sorry, I don't have more information to help you," Beatrice said. She wasn't even going to volunteer information about Eric's drug use. "Eric and I broke up a few weeks ago."

"When was the last time you saw him?"

Beatrice clenched her jaw.

"I understand he was harassing you two days ago," Detective Moore pressed immediately after Smithers's question. "Even after you'd threatened him in a voicemail to leave you alone or else."

Shit.

"You've got connections with private security groups—"

"Gentlemen, either charge me with something or this meeting is over. I will not entertain any more questions without my lawyer. Got it?" Beatrice snapped.

"Very well, Ms. Porter," Detective Smithers said, still sporting an annoying smirk. "Don't leave town."

With that parting shot, the two detectives left.

Beatrice called her father.

It was early evening when Gabe let himself into his house.

Poor Rhino must be ready to explode. If he had been thinking straight, Gabe would have thought to bring his dog along. After his stop in Chevy Chase, Maryland, he just drove around until his gas tank was almost empty.

After walking Rhino for half an hour, he returned to the house. Admiral Porter was waiting for him. The admiral was sitting on the top steps with his head in his hands, elbows resting on his knees.

"Admiral?"

The older man looked up and rose from the steps. "Where were you, Gabriel?"

"I'm not accountable to you," Gabe answered coldly as he moved past the admiral to unlock the door. Porter followed him in without waiting for an invitation.

"Is it true you were with Beatrice Saturday morning?"

Gabe stilled, suddenly unsure where this was going. "She told you?"

"Is it true?"

"Yes," Gabe bit out. "If this is some form of belated fatherly outrage, you can turn around and walk out that door. It's between me and her, and I don't know what the fuck she was thinking telling you." His nostrils flared. "Unless you had one of us followed."

"Fatherly outrage is the least of your concerns right now," Porter shot back. "Eric Stone is dead. Beatrice is a person of interest. She left a damning voicemail on that man's phone, threatening him."

All the anger leached out of Gabe as concern for Beatrice took over. "They think she killed him?"

"Or hired someone to do the job. Woman scorned and all that," the admiral said dismissively. "I know Beatrice had nothing to do with it. Besides, autopsy and tox screen show death by natural causes."

"Which is?"

"He died in his sleep."

"Fuck!" Gabe muttered.

"Exactly."

The degree of separation from Eric Stone to the admiral and even to Gabe was too close, and death by natural causes, too suspicious in the world of covert ops and assassins. "You're thinking it's a professional hit?"

"I'm pulling some strings to have our own techs run some tests to check for lesser known toxins."

"Hybernabis," Gabe said softly. "It's untraceable, makes the victim look like he died in his sleep, or if he has an existing heart condition, a heart attack. There's a chemical you can add to flush it out so it'd show up on the report."

"Are you breaking the assassin's code, Gabriel?" Porter asked.

"No. That compound is on the CIA watch list. One of the elements is hard to procure, which is why it's a very unpopular popular drug if you know what I mean."

"Did you use it?"

"You know I did, Admiral."

"Beatrice doesn't want to use you as an alibi."

"Why ever not?" Gabe growled.

"She said you had a confrontation with Stone last week and it might shift the investigation to you."

Gabe inhaled sharply, not sure whether to feel elated that she cared for him enough to protect him, or annoyed that she would think he'd let her go through this alone.

"It's time for you to get your head out of your ass, Commander."

His eyes narrowed at the older man, pretty sure he knew what the admiral meant, but he was feeling masochistic right now. He needed a push.

The admiral snorted. "I've left you well enough alone these past few months, Gabriel. I know coming back from being Dmitry Yerzov is tough. But, son, you've gone all the way to the other end of the spectrum, a level above being a pussy. You should be ashamed to be called a Navy SEAL."

"Now wait a goddamned minute—"

"From what I've gathered from my daughter, you're nowhere near getting through to her—"

"Yeah? Well, her daddy issues ain't helping, and I'm really uncomfortable talking to you about your daughter. She's an adult. Fine time for you to be showing concern—"

"I'm more concerned about you."

"What?"

"Didn't you hear a thing I said?" Porter huffed in irritation. "You're not the man you used to be, Gabriel. The man three years ago was the man my daughter fell for. You're not even close. You treat her with kid gloves. Hell, if she takes you back the way you are right now, she'll eat you alive. Drag you around and spit you out like a chew toy. Don't make me regret helping you with my daughter."

"Back the hell up," Gabe snapped. "I do not treat her with kid gloves. What do you think I should have done to her when she kneed me in the balls?"

Porter froze; then his eyes crinkled at the corners before he burst out laughing.

"Glad you find it amusing," Gabe grumbled. "I can take it from here, Admiral. I've done some soul-searching so to speak. I'd appreciate it if you let me handle Beatrice from here on."

"Handle?" The admiral quirked a brow.

"The woman needs some wooing and a firm hand. I'm handling her with care this time, Ben."

The admiral's brows shot to his hairline. "This should be interesting. You may still be the right man for her after all."

"What the fuck, Ben? I don't care what you think, especially since you didn't give a shit for most of her life."

"Tread carefully, Gabriel," Porter warned.

"No. You need to come to terms with a few home truths," he shot back. "Your fuck-ups as a father are not helping my cause with your daughter at all. I'd prefer it if you stay away from me while I'm trying to get Beatrice to take me back." Gabe felt pain lance through his chest, thinking of the girl she used to be. "I don't get it, Admiral. She's beautiful, intelligent, and larger than life. How can you not cherish and protect someone as precious as her?"

The admiral paled, his face was a mask, but the tension rolling off him was palpable. Gabe knew he'd gone too far, but someone had to say it. Someone had to fight for Beatrice, for the girl she had been who needed the love of a father.

"You think I don't cherish her?" Porter said softly. "The second biggest mistake of my life was getting in too deep with the CIA and then realizing I've made enemies. Having personal attachments had suddenly become more complicated. Protect her? Why do you think I've hooked her up with so many security firms? Do you know how many allies she has made, willing to protect her?"

He regarded the admiral skeptically. "No matter how you emotionally detach yourself from Beatrice, the threat will always be there by association. Are you sure this is not a defense mechanism on your part, so if anything does happen to Beatrice, you would be as you are—apathetic?"

"I'm warning you, Commander." Porter's face was etched in tense lines.

"I guess I've made my point."

The admiral sighed in resignation. "It's too late for me, Gabriel, but not for you. Be the man you used to be. Protect her because I can't do it forever. One of these days, my enemies are going to catch up with me. She will get caught in the crossfire."

It chilled Gabe that nothing had happened as yet. He knew several missions the admiral had orchestrated that threatened serious blowback.

"I'm sure Beatrice knows this. She's not obtuse."

Porter nodded and walked to the door. "She's at the condo right now—"

"I don't get it, Admiral, why are you helping me so much?"

"I don't want you to make the same mistake I made."

"What?"

"The greatest mistake of my life." An expression of regret flashed across the admiral's face. "I didn't fight for the woman I love. I let her go."

"You divorced her when you had seventeen years to fix your marriage," Gabe scoffed, angry and confused at the admiral's words.

"I'm not talking about Beatrice's mother."

And with that bombshell, the admiral left. Gabe stared at the door for a while.

"Well, hell," he muttered.

5

THE INTERCOM BUZZED in her kitchen.

Beatrice hurriedly wrapped herself in a robe. It was 11:00 p.m. Travis, Caitlin, and Nate had just left. They didn't waste time showing their solidarity with her current situation. Before they had arrived, she spent almost an hour on the phone with Doug, who wanted to fly back from Florida tonight. Beatrice convinced him not to change his flight and just return the next day as he originally planned.

"Yes?"

"Hey, babe, buzz me in."

Gabe.

"It's almost midnight. I need some sleep, and I'm in no mood for a booty call."

"I won't touch you. Well . . . unless you beg me to."

In your dreams, Sullivan.

"Go home, Gabe."

"I made hot chocolate," Gabe cut in abruptly. "Old-fashioned way. Just how you like it."

Beatrice paused. "Bittersweet?"

"Seventy-percent Belgian chocolate, babe."

That sneaky bastard. She could feel her mouth drooling.

"Poppy?"

Damn Gabriel Sullivan.

FIVE MINUTES LATER, she opened the door to a tousled-hair, scruffy-jaw, hot as hell man holding a thermos of liquid ambrosia. Gabe had learned to make proper hot chocolate—thick and bittersweet—from a friend who lived in Paris. Beatrice had never tasted anything quite like it. But hot cocoa aside, she thought this was the perfect opportunity to give him a logical argument to his idea of getting back together. He needed to stop turning up at her condo, announced or unannounced.

"Hey," he whispered, tawny eyes, warm and melting like caramel, gazed down on her.

She said nothing, just stood aside and waved an arm to let him in. Closing the door behind him, she walked to the kitchen to get some mugs. Beatrice was very aware that Gabe was checking out her condo.

"Nice place, great view," Gabe murmured. "Must have cost a mint."

"It did."

Beatrice consciously tugged her robe together as she sat on the couch. Gabe took the armchair adjacent from her. This surprised Beatrice because there was plenty of room on the couch. "The hot chocolate was a sneaky move."

Gabe chuckled and unscrewed the top of the thermos. "It worked, didn't it?"

Oh, yes. The aroma of hot cocoa was intoxicating.

"I didn't even hold out for a proper dinner date."

"I can take you out to dinner tomorrow, if you'd let me," Gabe responded instantly.

"Why are you pushing this? Isn't what happened Saturday morning enough?"

"That was a mistake."

Beatrice bristled. "Excuse me, but didn't you get off three times?"

"So did you. But I should've stopped you." Gabe handed her a cup. "We weren't ready, emotionally—"

"Where is this all coming from? Have you grown a vagina or something?"

Gabe scowled. "I've been to see a shrink."

Beatrice didn't know what to say to that, so she kept her mouth shut.

"I've been back for four months now," Gabe continued. "Gone for three years, I can't tell you what I did, but know that"—he paused and inhaled sharply before pushing the air out slowly—"I did things, Beatrice. Horrific things."

"Gabe—"

"The last thing I want from you is pity," he said. "I'm dealing with it. I think I can be the man you need, but I can't prove it to you unless you give me a chance."

"You can't waltz back into my life and expect to pick up where we had left off. You're not the only one who's changed. The woman you knew three years ago was willing to bend her rules by dating a man like you. That woman now wants something else altogether," Beatrice said. "It's not about what you did, Gabe. It's what you represent. You're everything I don't want, and I have to remember that."

Gabe's eyes wavered from hers and stared at a spot on her carpet. His jaw was set in a tense line. "I'm not your father, Beatrice."

She smiled sadly. "That's where you're wrong."

His eyes returned to hers. "Can we at least be friends?"

She didn't trust him, or maybe she didn't trust herself. "Gabe, I don't know."

"I heard about Eric Stone. I'm sorry."

She nodded. Tears welled up in her eyes and she didn't dare respond. Even if she didn't love Eric, some part of her still cared for him despite how it ended between them.

"How's it going with the investigation?"

"I think they're going to declare it death by natural causes," Beatrice said. "I've gone to the station with Dad and his lawyer. Given my statement. The lawyer assured me I'm not a suspect."

"You think any of Stone's fans are going to blame you?"

"The building's security is very solid, but Travis and Nate are talking about putting someone on me. I told them they're overreacting—I'm not exactly helpless you know." *Nope, she isn't.* She had good self-defense skills and was a crack shot with a 9mm—kind of important to have on the résumé when you were a security consultant.

"I can protect you, Beatrice," Gabe declared, his voice so warm and tender, it sent a shiver up her spine.

She took a sip of her hot chocolate. It was thick and creamy with just the right amount of bitter and sweet. "Still the master of hot chocolate."

"Thank you. Don't change the subject. What time do I need to be here tomorrow?"

"All right. Stop. Right there." She could feel tendrils of smoke rise from her ears. "I'm covered."

"Sure you are. By me." Gabe stood up.

"Where are you going?"

"Home."

"You just got here."

Gabe grinned at her. "Are you asking me to spend the night?"

"Absolutely not!"

His face sobered. "I'm serious about making this work, babe. I can be patient."

He tipped back the mug and finished his beverage.

"But—"

"I have to get home. Rhino won't be happy being cooped up in the house again."

"Who the hell is Rhino?"

"My dog—"

"You have a dog?"

Gabe took the mug from her and set it on the table. He pulled her to her feet and gently pressed a kiss on her forehead. "I'll see you tomorrow morning at eight thirty."

He strode to the door, pulled it open, and said, "Lock up behind me."

What the hell just happened?

AFTER TOSSING and turning for most of the night, Beatrice gave up on sleep and decided to go for another brisk run early that morning. An hour later, she was back at the condo, all showered and dressed for the day. She sipped her coffee as she pored over the morning newspaper.

The escalating tensions in the Middle East and Ukraine topped the headlines. Below that was the death of Eric Stone. There was a statement from the lead singer of Titanium Rose asking the press to give the band some privacy as they grieved the passing of one of their own. Beatrice winced when she saw a picture of herself and Eric exiting a Georgetown bar holding hands. They had some good times. She quickly noted where and when the wake and funeral was. When she turned the page to follow the story in another section, that was when she saw it.

A small article with the title: "Gang violence escalates in Cloverleaf District." A familiar picture of a dark-haired woman stared back at her, except Beatrice knew her when she was blonde. It was Blondie who attacked her with red paint a week ago. She quickly scanned the article. The bodies of five people, three women and two men, were found in an alley in the worst area of Northern Virginia. The Cloverleaf District was home to abandoned warehouses and dilapidated buildings. Street gangs basically ruled the vicinity. It was a constant battle of dominance and alliances, cooperation and competition. Russian, German, Latino, and even Asian gangs vied for control.

Beatrice pondered whether to call the detectives with this information, but something held her back. Besides, Cloverleaf wasn't their jurisdiction.

Her intercom buzzed.

"Yes?"

"A Gabriel Sullivan is here to see you, Ms. Porter."

Her eyes drifted to the clock, 8:15 a.m. "Send him up." She could probably use Gabe for some sleuthing and muscle. Hah! She didn't even feel guilty.

There was a light knock on her door. Her heart rate skittered the same time she berated herself for feeling as though she was going on a first date. She stopped her knees from wobbling and opened the door, trying not to gape.

A leather-jacket clad Gabe stood there, holding a bag of what might be baked goods and a tray of fresh coffee. But what made her jaw almost hit the floor was how he was smiling at her. A grin that reached his eyes and transformed his face from hard planes to pure masculine hotness. Gabe was the guy who could make her panties drop with a smile.

"Uh, are you going to invite me in?" Gabe asked. Beatrice wanted to smack him on the head when his smile morphed into a semi-smirk. The asshole knew his effect on her and was turning on the charm.

"Sorry, caffeine hadn't kicked in yet. Doug has a key and I don't have to bother with opening doors in the morning." She was babbling while she inhaled his scent as he walked past her—leather and soap. Hmm . . . what if sweat was added to the mix?

Sex-induced sweat.

Oh, Lord, this man could turn her brains to mush. She finally noticed him frowning at the open periodical she had on her table.

"What were you reading?" Gabe asked.

"I was attacked a couple of days ago by random, red-paint throwing, Titanium Rose fans," Beatrice said. "I'm not sure it's so random now."

Something flashed across Gabe's face. It was a look Beatrice knew her father used when he was masking his reaction. She would play along for a while.

"I'm not following," Gabe said finally when Beatrice didn't elaborate.

She pointed to the picture of Blondie. "She's one of them."

"Okay, let me play devil's advocate here," Gabe said steadily, looking her in the eyes. "Why would someone kill Eric Stone and some fans? Are we talking about a stalker?"

Beatrice took a sip of her coffee. "I'm saying I don't think they were fans at all, but someone hired them to mess with me using my relationship with Eric as a cover. Now they're dead, so they couldn't snitch. With the news of Eric's death, those women who attacked me must have freaked out."

"You're probably reading too much into the news, babe. It's—"

Beatrice lost her temper. "Don't tell me it's a fucking coincidence because you know in our line of work there is no such thing as coincidences. Believing so will only get you killed. What are you hiding, Gabe?"

"I don't know what you're talking about."

Beatrice snorted. "Really? You get that same look my father does whenever he's trying to throw some misdirection my way. It's pathetic."

"I really don't know." Gabe repeated, and the frustration on his face told her he knew something was up, but he didn't know what, so she decided to throw him a bone.

"My father never shares any information with me," Beatrice said. "He likes keeping me in the dark because he thinks he's protecting me. But you can relay this message to him. In case he doesn't know who my recent client is, it's Senator Alex Mendoza. The biggest threat to his security right now is his trip to Colombia. I'm still trying to figure out why." Beatrice tapped a finger on the gang war article. "The news says it's a Colombian gang who may have killed these five people. No one is sure because no one is talking. I'm going to dig—"

"Leave it alone, poppy," Gabe growled.

"It's my job, Gabe," Beatrice replied coolly. "As the senator's security consultant, I'm supposed to assess high level threats."

"Why can't the security company you hire do this for you?"

"Again. It's my job and it appears to be personal. I want to know why."

Gabe raked his fingers through his hair. "What were you planning to do?"

Beatrice eyed him warily. He stepped forward and planted himself squarely in front of her.

"Try keeping it from me," he threatened softly. "You'll find yourself shackled to the bed. I'm sticking to you like white on rice, so it's best now to tell me your plans."

Beatrice glared at him, but he only stared her down. The muscle tic in his jaw told her just how dead serious he was with his words.

Shackled to the bed by Gabriel Sullivan doesn't seem so bad, a sultry voice gushed in her head.

"Shut up," Beatrice whispered.

"Excuse me?"

"Sorry, voice in my head," she muttered. "I have a meeting with Senator Mendoza at ten. I'm planning to ask him some specifics about his agenda for Colombia. Then I'm heading to the Cloverleaf District to find out more about the killings or executions or whatever the hell it was."

"Like hell, Beatrice! Are you nuts?" Gabe said incredulously. "You can be sure I'm not letting you out of my sight."

Beatrice grinned slyly. "That's what I'm counting on, sport. I trust you to have my back."

The look he cast her was a mixture of surprise, pleasure, and annoyance.

Good. Nothing had changed.

GABE DIDN'T KNOW whether he wanted to strangle Beatrice or fuck her. She was a damned handful. But taking his personal stake out of the equation, she was right. It was her job to investigate threats to a client. Well, it was his job to protect her. She'd just gotten herself a bodyguard whether she liked it or not.

He walked down the curb of the U.S. Capitol until a black sedan pulled up.

"I don't have much time," Gabe told the admiral as he got into the car. "Beatrice is in back to back meetings. One is with Alex Mendoza. How didn't you know of her business with the senator?"

"I don't keep tabs on my daughter all the time," Porter said derisively. "The world is keeping me busy."

Gabe snorted. "What do you have for me?"

"The woman in the picture is Luisa Delgado," the admiral rattled off the other names of the victims. "She's half-American, half-Colombian. She has a fresh tattoo on her back that tells me she had recently been initiated into the Fuego gang. Their attack on Beatrice must have been part of their hazing, or so they were led to believe."

The two men exchanged grim looks. There was their link.

"Anything on Eric Stone's cause of death?"

The admiral shook his head. "Not yet. I expect the results by the end of the day. I'm dealing with some red tape."

"What?"

The admiral had carte blanche on mostly everything in the agency. Red tape wasn't in his vocabulary.

"There's something bigger at play here, Gabe," the admiral said gravely. "What's happening is merely the gravel in a landslide. I'm getting closer to the traitor inside the CIA responsible for everything, and he's throwing wrenches at me in the system."

"Spy games? What do you mean *everything*?"

"I could trace anomalies back to the specter agent program. There were big ethical issues that came about with the Berserker serum that was administered to agents and turned them into killing machines. The lead scientist who created BSK had disappeared. Soon after, Project Infinity was shut down, agents cut lose. Those who weren't hunted down joined the Russian mob. Someone high up was involved. I started the op to infiltrate the Zorin Bratva, partly to draw the mastermind out, but he was too smart and stayed hidden."

Gabe couldn't believe what he was hearing. Was Admiral Porter saying there was someone wilier than he was inside the CIA?

"You better give me the CliffsNotes version, Admiral, I need to head back."

"We're playing cat and mouse with this guy. He's still one step ahead. We've shut down the Zorin Bratva, his coffers are running dry. Thanks to your undercover work, we've determined it's through the sale of cocaine into the homeland that allowed the drug traffickers to buy their guns."

"He's the guy allowing the shipment of cocaine into the U.S.?"

"The point is, Gabriel, I was expecting our guy to start shifting his attention to the conflicts in Ukraine and Iraq. That's where more arms dealers would make money. With the Colombian government in talks to lessen, if not end the armed conflicts, he should have abandoned the country a year ago. Yet he continues to have a vested interest in Colombia. The question is why."

"Where do we go from here?" Gabe looked as his watch.

"Right now, there are very few I trust inside the agency." The admiral sighed. "I'll have to depend on unconventional assets."

"Who?"

"The enemy of your enemy is your friend," the admiral said. "The Iron Skulls MC and Fuego gang are known mortal enemies. Even with the death of that Marko guy who caused all the trouble for us over five months ago, this had not eased tensions between the two organizations. They're competing for market share in drugs, cocaine versus meth, both under the control of the Russian gang, which is controlled by the Russian mafia. Skulls are under protection of the Russian gang whenever they're in the Cloverleaf District—a frequent artery for their operations."

"Lesser evil?"

The admiral nodded. "I've spoken to their president. Nicholas Crane used to be in the U.S. Navy."

"How can you be sure you can trust him? His MC is running drugs, Admiral."

"I'm helping them get clear of the drugs. The town they're protecting is booming. Once they become self-sufficient, they'll cut their meth runs. They'll have your back when you get into Cloverleaf District to do whatever Beatrice needs to get done. They'll have their eyes on you, but won't get involved unless the situation deteriorates. They don't want to jeopardize their standing with the Russian gang."

"Do you know if Beatrice is the target?" Gabe realized he was clenching his fists tight.

The admiral held out his smartphone to Gabe. "This was sent this morning to one of my email addresses."

A picture of the admiral and Beatrice.

"That was taken yesterday at the Metropolitan Police

Department. Someone is either trying to make me visible or making sure I know my daughter is not safe."

Fury and helplessness rendered Gabe speechless. Beatrice was heading straight into the belly of the enemy. Nostrils flaring, he pushed through gritted teeth. "We have to tell her what's going on."

"Not yet."

"Damn it, Admiral. Travis lost Caitlin because of Project Infinity. Are you willing to lose a daughter now, too?"

"Are you willing to tell her your part in the op that nearly got Caitlin killed? Are you willing to tell her what you've done for the Zorin Bratva, Gabe? That you've killed people in cold blood to become the most feared assassin in all the echelons of Russian organized crime? That you are the Angel of Death—Dmitry Yerzov?"

"If I have to. If that will keep her alive."

"You've really chosen my daughter above everything else, haven't you?" the admiral said softly. "Be careful what you tell her; do not compromise other ops or agents."

"Goes without saying, Admiral," Gabe said darkly. It angered him that the admiral would feel the need to tell him this. The sedan stopped a hundred feet away from the U.S. Capitol complex.

"Take care of her, Commander."

"I'M READY!" Beatrice chirped, stepping out of her bedroom. She insisted on changing her clothes before going sleuthing in Cloverleaf. Gabe agreed, because no way could she blend in the rough neighborhood wearing one of her designer suits, cashmere coat, and thousand-dollar shoes.

Right now, she was wearing jeans that hugged her slender form and black combat boots. She slipped on a ratty coat, her face scrubbed free of makeup and hair twined in a fat braid.

She looked incredibly young and beautiful.

"How do I look?"

"Like a female version of Oliver Twist," Gabe teased.

He grunted when Beatrice jabbed an elbow in his gut as she passed him to pick up her messenger bag. She transferred some items from the purse she used earlier, and then she opened the middle drawer underneath her kitchen counter and took out a gun.

Gabe arched a brow. If he was finding her hot before, more so now. She never failed to surprise him.

"You seem to have scenarios like this down pat."

"I told you, Gabe." Beatrice tucked her gun in her bag. "It's what I do. I'm not reckless. I would never go alone. Usually Nate goes with me, or one of the other BSI guys, but since you're here, I don't need to bother them."

"Damn straight," Gabe muttered.

"I'm assuming you're doing this for free." She eyed him teasingly.

Gabe stared at her lips. "I accept different forms of payment."

He watched a blush steal up her cheeks. He didn't regret the innuendo, and he wanted nothing more than to strip her naked and slide inside her instead of traipsing across town and probably getting shot.

"That better be a joke, Sullivan." She was glaring at him, which only made him want to fuck her more. Her attitude was a definite turn on for him.

"Come on. Save your attitude for later." His lips twitched in amusement. "I've a feeling you'll need it."

"This is Luisa Delgado's address," Beatrice informed Gabe. They were in front of a ten-story building. The entrance consisted of a collapsed expandable metal gate that had seen better times and dusty aluminum-framed glass doors.

She was about to step inside when Gabe pulled her back. "Wait. Let me go in first. You have a bodyguard. Use me."

Beatrice huffed in irritation. "Fine. Lead the way."

Gabe speared her an irritated look. She wondered how long before he would strangle her. She'd been sniping at him all the way from DC to Cloverleaf, and except for the tightening of his fingers on the steering wheel—probably imagining her neck—he'd been amiable.

They used the stairs since the elevator wasn't working. Walls were covered with graffiti and the rickety steps were littered with garbage and people. Most of them were junkies —stoned, filthy, and most likely homeless. Beatrice thought she did a good job of blending in with a skull cap over her head, but Gabe was a big guy, and everyone who wasn't drugged out eyed him warily. She noticed a boy of about ten run out of the building.

The little snitch.

"We don't have much time," Beatrice said. "I think we're about to have company soon."

"I know," Gabe muttered.

When they reached apartment 405, Gabe rapped on the door. They heard shuffling in the room.

"What do you want?" A voice asked from inside.

"Luisa owes me money—" Beatrice started to say.

"She's not here. Go away."

"I'm not leaving until I get my money," Beatrice fired back. She threw Gabe a dirty look, warning him to wipe the smirk off his face. Didn't he know how to do undercover work? Jeez.

The door cracked open. A woman peered through the small opening. "You will get us killed. We have nowhere else to go. Go away."

A rush of footsteps pounded up the stairs. The door was slammed shut. Gabe tensed beside her.

"Now that was productive," Beatrice grumbled, trying to make light of the situation, but her heart thudded against her chest with anxiety.

"Babe, I think things are about to get interesting," Gabe said grimly.

Sure enough, three Latino guys armed with metal pipes and guns appeared in the hallway.

Shit.

6

"Let me do the talking."

Beatrice whispered to Gabe as she stepped in front of him. He cursed softly beside her. She was certain he was ready to throw her over his shoulder and run away with her.

"Lost?" the Latino man with the nose ring sneered.

"Not at all," Beatrice said with false bravado. "I'm looking for Luisa. You know where she is? Bitch told me this was her address." She mentally begged forgiveness for speaking ill of the dead.

"Haven't you read the news? She's dead."

Beatrice feigned shock. "No! Damn it. Well, hell, how can I get back my three hundred dollars?"

The Latino guys laughed. "We can give you three hundred dollars, but you'll have to spread those long legs and let us fuck you." More laughter.

This wasn't going well at all. She could feel Gabe ready to come out of his skin. Growly noises were coming from her man. Her man? When did he become her man?

Focus, Bee!

Beatrice shifted her attention back to the problem at hand.

Walking forward with all the sass she could muster and

pretending she didn't hear Gabe call out her name in frustration, she stopped in front of Nose Ring guy.

"Hmm . . . she also promised me quality *cabello*." Beatrice hoped she pronounced the Spanish street name for cocaine correctly.

"You better not be a cop, chica." Nose Ring scowled at her.

"Do I look like a cop to you?" Beatrice swore she could hear her pulse in her ears. Her voice wavered.

Shit.

Nose Ring's eyes narrowed with suspicion, his mouth curled in a snarl as he reached for the gun tucked in the waistband of his jeans. "Yes."

Beatrice heard, "Fuck this," right before Nose Ring's head jerked back in a spatter of blood.

Gabe yanked her behind him where she landed on her ass. Ignoring the pain on her bottom, she kept her eyes on the scene while reaching for her gun. She quickly extended her arm to shoot the guy about to clobber Gabe with a metal pipe.

Gabe was finishing off the last thug, avoiding knife jabs, and blocking strikes while countering with his own punches. It seemed he had the situation under control so she crawled to Nose Ring's body and searched for identification. She barely had time to grab his wallet when Gabe pulled her to her feet and growled, "Let's go."

She was thrown over his shoulder and saw the stairs streak past her vision so fast, it made her dizzy. When they reached the street level, she was dumped on her feet. He grabbed her hand firmly, dragging her back to where they had parked. "Walk fast, but act normal. There may be more of them."

"Gabe—"

"We do not want to draw any more attention."

The demand in his voice was absolute, so she shut up until they got to their car.

She winced when she saw his face. He was blazing with fury, and it was directed at her. "We need to check for—"

"Got it," Gabe bit off, disappearing from view to check for trackers or explosives that may have been planted under their vehicle in their absence.

"Are you hurt?" she asked worriedly when he got back to his feet. His face looked okay, but bruising was usually delayed. He didn't appear to be bleeding, but he was wearing a leather jacket that could be masking an injury.

"Get in the car."

"I'm sorry that—"

"Get in the fucking car, Beatrice!"

He started for her but stopped when two men approached them. They didn't look Latino. Both of them were tall, one of them even taller and bigger than Gabe. The younger guy had blond braids. They were wearing leather cuts over their hoodies.

Bikers.

"Both of you all right?" one of them asked.

"Where the hell were you guys?" Gabe snapped.

"We were in the room across from Luisa's," the blond one said.

"Our orders were not to interfere unless things got dire," the bigger biker added. His eyes crinkled as they landed on her. "Looks like you had things under control. I'm Ashe by the way."

He extended his hand to Beatrice and nodded to his companion. "This is Duke."

"Those guys Fuego?" Gabe asked.

Ashe nodded. "Things are too hot right now. We can't stay and chat, but here's our current number. That'll be valid for at least two days." He handed Gabe a piece of paper. "The Skulls don't usually stay long around these parts. We do our drop and leave. We have the protection of the Russian gang, but things can turn on a dime."

Beatrice was feeling a sense of outrage growing inside her. She turned to Gabe. "Am I to understand I've wasted a trip here and you already know for sure it was the Fuego gang?"

Gabe's non-answer was answer enough.

"Are they the same ones who hired the victims to mess with me?"

"Not sure," Gabe answered curtly.

Beatrice turned back to the bikers. "We need names of whoever is related to the victims. Who hired them, who killed them. You have all the info to get started?"

Ashe nodded. "We have an intelligence guy. I can put him on it. Give us 24 hours and then call us on that burner."

Beatrice nodded.

When the bikers were out of earshot, she pivoted on Gabe, glaring at him. "You could have saved us the trouble of almost getting our heads blown off."

"Don't start, Beatrice," Gabe snapped. "I'm so pissed at you right now; you don't want to test me."

"You? Pissed at me? You're the one who withheld information."

"I didn't have *all* the information. Now. Get. In."

Something told her this wasn't a conversation to be had on the streets, so she did as she was told, but slammed the door hard in protest. Gabe got in beside her and cut her another angry look.

They didn't say anything for a while. Beatrice was busy checking out the contents of Nose Ring's wallet when she realized he missed her exit.

"You missed the DC exit."

Gabe glanced at her. "You're coming home with me."

SHE FROZE BESIDE HIM, but the blowup didn't come. Baffled,

he glanced over to her and saw her brows were furrowed as she was inspecting the seam of the wallet.

"No comeback?"

"I'm spattered with blood," Beatrice said matter-of-factly. "Makes sense to clean up over at your place before I walk into my condo." Her head finally turned his way. "You do intend to return me to the condo, right?"

"We'll discuss this later."

She simply shrugged. This annoyed him. It was probably still the adrenalin pumping through his veins that fed the desire to strangle her, squeeze her, hug her, and feel her. There were many things he wanted to do to her, with her, and for her, but they needed to talk first. Gabe didn't know where he stood with Beatrice. Well, he kind of knew, but he couldn't accept that they were over. They still had a story of *them,* and he wanted their story to begin now. Not later, not tomorrow, and definitely not never.He didn't know how to convince her to give him a second chance. Beatrice understood the meaning of duty and country. She understood why he had to leave her. The thing was, she was prepared not to be with a man like him. That scared him, because how could you reason with something logical?

Twenty minutes later, he was pulling up beside his house. He noticed Beatrice looking around the neighborhood, an emotion on her face that pinched his heart. She was remembering *them*.

"You live here?" she whispered, her eyes glazed.

"I do."

"Why here?"

"I missed us, poppy," he replied simply.

An anguished sound escaped her as she exited the car. She started stalking up the sidewalk away from his house.

"Beatrice!"

"Fuck you, Gabe!" she yelled, not slowing down.

He caught up with her, gripping her arm. She spun

around and her fists went flying, hitting him on the chest. She started crying and it broke his heart. He didn't know what to do, except hold her, clenching her tight against him as she sobbed into his chest.

"I'm sorry, Beatrice," Gabe whispered. "God, I'm so sorry."

"How dare you do this to me!"

"I'm sorry—"

"Why couldn't you just stay away?" she cried into his chest, trying to push at him, but he wouldn't, couldn't let her go. This was the closest he had gotten through to her, and he was not backing the fuck down from anything she wanted to throw at him. "Why, Gabe?"

"Because . . . I just can't." His mouth was by her ear. "Please, babe, give me another chance."

Her crying faded into hiccups. She tried again to push away, but he only tightened his arms. Finally, she relaxed, much to Gabe's relief. No way was he letting her go to build up that wall again. No fucking way.

Her body seemed to have lost all the fight as she leaned heavily against him.

"Let's get you inside and cleaned up."

She crumbled. She just fell apart and there was nothing she could do to stop the avalanche of hurt and rejection she had felt when he left her without looking back. The pain in her heart was excruciating, threatening to rip her chest wide open. When Gabe turned onto the street that looked so familiar, the street where they'd walked hand in hand so many times, it was simply too much. Now, with Gabe's arms around her, gripping her like he would never let her go, they walked side by side toward his house.

It felt like coming home, and yet, it didn't feel real.

Because it really wasn't. She had made up her mind never to be with a man like him, but her treacherous heart was screaming at her to take the leap again.

She was suddenly yanked out of her internal musings by the most handsome creature she had ever seen, and for a moment her spirits lifted.

"Oh, my God," Beatrice gushed as she sank to her knees in front of Gabe's dog. "Can I pet him?"

"He would love that," Gabe replied. "His name is Rhino."

"Aren't you a handsome one?" She scratched the dog behind his ears and his tail thumped enthusiastically in response.

"Looks like someone else is in love with you," Gabe said gruffly as he walked past them. What did he mean by that? Beatrice looked past Rhino's massive head to see Gabe walk into a room. She rose from the floor when he came back and handed her a shirt—a freshly laundered one judging from the smell. She resisted the urge to inhale deeply to absorb the essence of him.

"There's a full bath in the room down the hallway. Everything you need should be in there, shampoo, towel, stuff." He headed up the stairs. "I'll clean up as well and then take Rhino for a walk. Make yourself at home."

Beatrice heard the door slam and the scuffle of feet approach. Rhino's head poked through the door of the guest room. She had finished drying her hair and was now wearing Gabe's shirt, which came about mid-thigh for her. No panties.

"Hey, boy," Beatrice held out her hand. The dog came into the room and immediately nosed her palm, trying to snort it. She laughed.

"He really likes you." Gabe was standing by the doorway.

"Shame on you, Sullivan, using your dog to get to me."

"That obvious, huh?"

Silence.

This went on for a while. Beatrice playing with Rhino's muzzle, feeling Gabe's intense stare on her. She felt herself squeezing her thighs together. Maybe no undies wasn't a good idea after all. What was she thinking?

"Got a minute?" Gabe finally said, exhaling deeply. "I need to tell you something."

GABE WASN'T sure it was a good idea now to bring Beatrice home with him. Seeing her in his shirt, hiked up, exposing her bare legs, sent all the blood in his head to his dick. Was she even wearing panties?

He cleared his throat and jerked his head toward the living room. Seeing her sitting so close to the bed was wreaking havoc with his resolve to talk and not screw. "Uh, I'll wait for you in the dining room."

He sat on the chair and scooted it under the table to hide the growing bulge in his crotch. Going commando in sweatpants was not helping the situation at all. He linked his fingers together and bent his head. *Shit. Down boy.*

Beatrice took the chair right across from him. She was right to put the table between them.

"Okay, Gabe. Talk."

"Remember when we met?"

Beatrice smiled, her face wistful. "How can I forget? I bumped into you on your way out of Dad's study. It was during a cocktail party. You weren't supposed to be there."

"There was an op that was brewing. There were months of prep work to be done. I was the top choice to go on that mission. It was going to be deep cover, dicey, and a long one." Unable to help himself, Gabe reached across the table and linked their fingers. "You took my breath away."

"Gabe—"

"You really did, babe. That night, I couldn't get you out of my head, so I stalked you, bumped into you on purpose, and asked you out. I couldn't afford the distraction, really. When your dad found out, he was furious. I couldn't blame him. It was the worst possible timing."

"So you were going on a mission, and then you asked me to be exclusive anyway?"

"No. I said I was the top choice, but I wasn't the only one. Ryker, a good friend of mine, had the same skill set as I had. Had the same background as I do—no immediate family to wonder if we were gone for a long time or if we never came back. I chose to be with you, Beatrice. I bowed out of the mission."

"But you still left . . ." her voice trailed off.

Gabe closed his eyes as he remembered the memories of that night, and the harsh decisions he had to make. He was breathing hoarsely when he spoke, "Something went horribly wrong. There were so many vendettas within the organization we were going to infiltrate—Ryker got killed when the plane he was in exploded."

"Oh, my God," Beatrice whispered.

"It should've been me."

"Gabe—"

"There was only a small window of opportunity to insert myself into the op, otherwise, we would have lost the chance."

"You blamed yourself that night—"

He shook his head.

Beatrice's face contorted in anguish. "You blamed me?"

She tried to pull her hands away, but Gabe held on. "It was a fucked up night, babe. As soon as I drove off, I blamed myself and did for a while. What I regretted these past three years was every single hurtful word I said to you that night, because they were a lie. I cared for you more than the mission. I could walk away from it—all things being equal. But a friend died because I chose to be with you, and I knew if I didn't see this mission through, I could never live with myself."

"If you only told me, Gabe—" Beatrice choked.

"What?" Gabe snapped, letting go of her hands and pushing out of the chair. He paced the room. "Ask you to wait for me? I wasn't even sure I was coming out of this alive. As much as I regretted saying those words to you, in the end, I felt it was best for you to forget me. I just wish I handled it differently."

"You have no idea how damaging those words were." The expression in her eyes chilled him.

He walked back to the table, bracing his hands across, he leaned in. "They were a lie."

"The words festered inside me, you know," Beatrice said softly.

Gabe's heart rate quickened with the direction the conversation was taking.

"Babe—"

"That I will never be worth more than a job. That I was so pathetic I almost begged you to stay."

His chest was hurting with the pain his words had inflicted on her all those years ago.

He couldn't take it anymore. He walked to her side and hauled her to her feet. He needed to kiss the pain away, so he pressed his mouth against hers. He tasted the salt of her tears, so he pushed his tongue between her lips and she opened beneath him. He devoured her, wanting to absorb her hurt into him.

"I'm so sorry, Beatrice," Gabe whispered hoarsely against her lips. "So fucking sorry."

Her arms came up around his neck as he lifted her and spread her on the table. His hands sought her heat. Finding her bare almost short-circuited his brain. He bent over her and continued kissing her, rubbing his hardness against her core. She moaned into his mouth, so he quickened his thrusting until she convulsed against him as he swallowed her cries. He swept her up from the table and headed straight for his bedroom. Kicking the door shut so Rhino wouldn't follow, he carefully lowered Beatrice on the bed.

"I don't think—" she protested.

"Shh . . . let me show you just how much you mean to me." Gabe pushed her legs apart and buried his face between her thighs. He hungrily licked, stroking her from the base of her sex and hovering just around her clit. Her hands dug into his hair. "Please, Gabe."

He stimulated the bundle of nerves with his tongue, fastening his lips, and gently sucking the tender flesh. When she undulated her hips to shove her pussy closer, he knew she was close. Her taste was heaven and he wanted more. He wanted every last drop of her arousal. He released her clit and licked down to her entrance, plunging his tongue inside, seeking the source of his addiction. She shrieked, screamed, and moaned. He welcomed the warm gush of sweetness into his mouth. The starvation of the past three years for her taste came to a fore in this moment where he had her.

"You taste so fucking good," he growled as he crawled up her body, pulled the waistband of his sweats down and thrust into her. "Fuck, babe." He leaned his forehead on hers as he savored the initial sheathing of her warmth around his cock. He started to move. "So good, so good. Fucking tight. So slick . . ."

Shit, condom.

Gabe was tempted to blow his load inside her, but he didn't want to push his luck. He pulled out reluctantly. Beatrice's whimper of protest almost made him want to thrust back inside her. His fingers shook as he ripped the foil of the condom.

Fuck. Fuck.

He quickly rolled it on. Lifting her hips, he punched forward, burying himself so deep inside her; a feral sound escaped him. He wouldn't last. He would never get enough of her. Beatrice's hands came up his shoulders. He grabbed her wrists and slammed them above her head as the need to dominate surged inside him. Their eyes locked, watching each other as he moved above her. He lost himself once again in her emerald depths. When her eyes shut, the grip of her silken channel tightened around his girth. "I can't hold back . . . FUCK!"

It started from the base of his spine, the pleasure shooting up his back, his neck muscles tensing as his astounding climax took over. He continued pumping his hips furiously until he was spent, and all he could do was collapse on top of her.

He rubbed his cheek against hers, their faces slick with sweat. He was overtaken with contentment. She was back. She was once again his Beatrice.

There was a deep indrawn breath that sounded suspiciously like a sob. Frowning, Gabe levered himself on his elbows, and what he saw splintered his heart.

Beatrice was crying silently.

"I can't," she whispered brokenly.

Two words. She shattered him with two words.

THEY AVOIDED each other's eyes after having had mind-blowing sex. What did she expect? That they could simply pick up where they left off three years ago? She wasn't ready and she let lust control her actions. She could blame Gabe for taking advantage of her moment of weakness, but she knew that wasn't his intention. He wanted to comfort her the best way he could. Things got out of hand and they both gave in.

So, they were adults, right? It was just sex. Big freaking deal.

But it was a big deal.

She and Gabe hadn't discussed the present Colombian

problem. They let their personal issues come between them. They couldn't work together like this.

The doorbell chimed. Beatrice sighed in relief. She had called Doug to bring over a change of clothes and be her ride home. Gabe gave the command for Rhino to settle down and opened the door to her assistant who promptly glared at Gabe. Not bothering with any greeting, he headed straight for Beatrice and hugged her. Fortunately, she didn't cry. She'd had enough of that. It wasn't funny because she rarely cried. Doug handed her her clothes and she disappeared into the guest room.

She could hear harsh whispered words being exchanged in the other room. She quickly donned her clothes because Doug's voice was getting louder. Gabe's was still a steady baritone cadence, but that didn't mean they wouldn't come to blows.

"Doug, can you wait for me outside, please?" Beatrice gave her friend a nudge when she returned to the living room.

"No, Bee. Enough is enough; you don't need to say anything more to this asshole."

"Wait for me outside," Beatrice repeated in exasperation. When her assistant still hesitated, she added, "Please? I'll be fine, truly."

Casting one more dirty look at Gabe, Doug said, "I'll be right outside the door."

When they were alone once more, their eyes finally met.

"I don't want to see you for a while," Beatrice said.

Gabe's eyes flashed in anger. "Is that your answer? Avoiding me?"

"I need to process what you told me, Gabe. I can't just turn off three years of hurt. I understand more of your reasons now, but it doesn't mean I want us back together."

Frustrated, guttural sounds worked in his throat. "Bullshit."

"Excuse me?" This time her temper flared.

He prowled toward her. She held her ground as they both stared challengingly at each other.

"You heard me. I call bullshit," Gabe repeated. "Fireworks. You deny we just burned those sheets between us."

"A relationship is not simply about sex."

"I agree. But the most honest reaction I've ever gotten from you is when I watch you come when I'm buried deep inside you. I want you back. I'm not about to let you push me away because of some fear that I'm walking out on you again because I won't. I swear. I'm all in, babe. All yours." His hand came up to cup her face. "So tell me, what's the problem?"

"I . . . I just need some time."

"I'll give you a day."

"What the hell kind of time is that?"

"I give you a day. I need to get some shit done anyway, and you're not leaving your condo tomorrow."

"I have a meeting with BSI."

At Gabe's unbending stare, Beatrice sighed. "I can have Nate pick me up."

"What is Nate to you?"

"He's a friend."

"Have you fucked him?"

"Not that it's any of your business, but no," Beatrice retorted.

"Oh, I'm making it my business, babe." He bent low, his warm breath fanning her ear. Releasing her jaw, he trailed the back of his fingers down the length of her torso, her hips. "Everything to do with this sweet body of yours, down right to here"—he cupped her between her legs and she couldn't bring herself to stop him—"is my business. Do you know why?"

"No, but I'm sure you'll tell me."

He grinned at her defiance. "Because you've always been mine. Your brain has not caught up yet, but your body cannot fucking deny how it wants mine."

"Again, sex, no matter how good it is, does not make us together." Beatrice wanted to pull her hair out.

"We will be."

"WE ARE NOT TOGETHER!"

Gabe sighed. "Take some time tomorrow and think about us."

"There is no us!" Gah! What an annoying man!

"Beatrice," Gabe whispered, brushing her lips gently. "I love you, babe."

She melted into a puddle right there.

7

"SO YOU'RE SAYING we might expect a hit in Colombia?"

Edward Shepard was the BSI team lead assigned on Senator Alex Mendoza's security detail. He was studying the threat-analysis report Beatrice prepared for them, which included some speculations of the related violence in the Cloverleaf District. Travis and Nate were also in the room.

"That's where I see the biggest threat coming from," Beatrice said. "I met with Alex Mendoza yesterday and informed him we're close to forming a team for him. His South American trip won't begin until next year, but he agreed that it would be best to be familiar with his personal security in the next few months. Then we can expand it next year to include his entire delegation."

"What's with the Fuego connection?" Travis asked, his eyes most likely skimming to the last page of the report.

Beatrice sighed. She had not discussed this with Gabe yet, and her father had been off the grid. She would need to get with Ashe and Duke soon to see what else they dug up. "I'm not sure where they exactly fit. It just seemed coincidental that the women who attacked me last week are now dead and linked to Fuego. I'm having someone look into it."

"Who's looking into it?" Travis cut in. "Beatrice, you know better than to involve too many people in this."

"I had no choice, okay?" Beatrice's eyes flashed in annoyance. "Apparently, Gabe, and I hazard a guess, my dad, were already one step ahead of me and made the connection before I did. I dunno why they would use a motorcycle club to do their—"

"Motorcycle club? Not the Iron Skulls?" Travis didn't look happy.

"Uh, yes," Beatrice replied warily.

Nate cursed. "Who?"

"Ashe and Duke."

Travis bolted from his chair and paced the room, his hand rubbing against his jaw in a gesture of agitation.

"Am I missing something here?" Beatrice asked.

"Remember that time Travis took Caitlin out of town after the Russians ambushed them?" Nate asked.

"Yes?"

"They had a run in with the Iron Skulls and later the Fuego gang."

"Oh, my God, was that the shoot-out in the small town?"

"Yup. We couldn't account for the sniper who took out one of the Fuegos. Travis speculated that sniper was Crowe, the man who shot Caitlin and worked for your dad," Nate added.

"I remember him," Beatrice murmured. No coincidences.

Travis stopped pacing and sat in his chair. "I bet the admiral has the necessary answers to make sense out of all this, and I have a feeling we're not going to like it."

Gabe definitely had more explaining to do as well, Beatrice fumed.

"We did have a run-in yesterday at Cloverleaf," Beatrice confessed. "That two dead and one critical from gang violence yesterday—"

"I caught that in the news this morning," Travis said. "Damn it, Bee, was that you? Was Gabe with you?"

"He was."

"What's going on with you two?" Nate asked sharply.

"All right, let's stay on point in this meeting," Beatrice retorted. "We can talk about my personal life later. Anyway, I managed to filch the wallet off one of the dead guys to see if I could find a connection to any threats to Senator Mendoza, but the guy's a dead end. He is a U.S. citizen and I couldn't find any links back to Colombia."

Ed flicked through the brief. "What exactly were you hoping to find?"

"From what the senator told me, his trip to Colombia is to pressure their government to increase monitoring over some of the businesses that may be working with drug traffickers. With no drug cartels to speak of, most of the drug traffickers are using the Mexican cartels to move their stuff and it's cutting into their profits. I hear they've gotten creative."

"How so?" Nate asked.

"Remember that recent bust in Virginia Beach regarding a hundred million dollars' worth of cocaine stored in juice cans?"

The men nodded.

"Well, there's speculation that they're moving it under the guise of sacks of coffee beans or cans of ground coffee."

"Holy shit!" Ed muttered. "That would be hard to track. Colombia is one of the world's largest exporters of coffee."

"Exactly. So, instead of increasing funding for Border Security and Customs, it would be better to address the problem at the source. The senator is hoping to convince the Colombian government that it's in their best interest to do so."

"Good luck with that," Nate muttered.

"Corruption and bribery is rife in Colombia," Beatrice agreed. "The outcome of the senator's trip is not our problem. Our concern is making sure the senator will be protected against harm. We need to do background checks on the businesses that stand to lose in case the government decides to crack down on drugs. We're also going in at a time when the peace talks between the government and the left wing guerrillas and right wing paramilitary groups are at a flashpoint. Senator Mendoza and his delegation can be a target if talks break down, so we have to consider routes, convoy formations, and safe haven alternatives in case of an ambush."

"We've got this." Ed nodded in reassurance.

"I'm proud of you, Dmitry."

"Thank you, sir."

Grigori Zorin clasped his shoulder. "Almost three years you've shown your unwavering loyalty. You know you're almost like a son to me."

"I know, sir. Again, for that I'm grateful. You have been most generous."

"You should marry one of my daughters."

"Sir?"

"You'd do well to run the Zorin Bratva one day."

Dmitry nodded tightly.

Gabe sat in the outer offices of BSI, waiting for Beatrice to be done with her meeting. It was almost 7:00 p.m. The rumors were true: Travis Blake was a slave driver. He observed Emily Shephard, who worked efficiently at the reception area fielding calls, filing documents away, and doing whatever she was doing in front of the computer.

He couldn't stay away for 24 hours. He couldn't wait until tomorrow to see her again. He'd met with Ashe and Duke earlier. Gabe knew he was being underhanded filtering information before any of it reached Beatrice. She was a damned loose cannon, and with Porter not answering his phone, Gabe didn't know what he was going to do with the information. There was still that matter of Crowe having an accomplice in the Fuego gang, and if this killing had nothing to do with Beatrice's client, it was best they kept the information classified. Luisa Delgado was killed with a garrote, while the others were killed execution style—single bullet to the back of the head. The question Gabe had was why not execute everyone with a bullet?

"They should be finished soon," Emily smiled at him.

The office door opened and a blonde woman walked in. Travis's wife, Caitlin. Gabe felt a stab of guilt. He knew her when she was Sarah.

"Hey, Emily, is Travis almost done? We don't want to be late for our dinner reservation," Caitlin said.

"Why don't you head on back and shoo them out of Conference Room 2. Ed and I have to be somewhere as well."

Gabe decided to re-introduce himself and got up from the couch just as Caitlin pivoted toward him.

All color leached from her face. A mixture of terror and anger took over her entire body as she leapt behind the reception area, startling Emily. Before he knew it, a 9-mm was pointed at him.

Fuck. Gabe was not having a good feeling about this. He raised his arms instinctively.

"Cat, what's going on?" Emily screeched.

Travis's wife continued glaring at him. A stampede of footsteps rushed from the hallway. She must have pushed the panic button.

Travis burst into the room.

"Cat?" Travis's eyes widened when they landed on Gabe. "Why are you pointing a gun at Gabe?"

"Gabe?" Caitlin asked. "What are you talking about? That's a Russian hit man."

Double fuck.

"Cat, put the gun down."

Beatrice cleared the door and froze when she saw the scene before her. She had never seen Cat look so terrified. And why the hell was she pointing the gun at Gabe?

"He's Bee's Gabriel?" Caitlin asked.

"I'm sure she doesn't want to admit it right now," Gabe said, smirking. Only Gabe would smirk with a gun pointed at him. "She's in denial, but she'll come around."

Beatrice rushed to Gabe's side even before Caitlin fully lowered the gun.

"You must have me confused with someone else," Gabe added.

Lie. Beatrice knew. She just knew Caitlin was right, and with that knowledge came a whole new level of anxiety.

"I don't understand," Caitlin whispered. "I saw you meet with Jase. He didn't know I followed him. I was worried because he said he was cutting a deal with a Russian hit man. It was you." Beatrice hated how Caitlin looked troubled. "It was you," she whispered again.

Travis walked to his wife's side and put an arm around her shoulder. He jerked a chin at Ed, who understood and walked straight to the exit door, locking it.

Beatrice felt Gabe turn solid beside her. These guys were not letting him out without answers.

"Care to tell us the truth, Gabe?" Travis said icily. "I figured that's how the admiral got Jase's letter?"

Gabe didn't say anything. Fury was evident in every line of Travis's body as he left Caitlin's side and stalked toward Gabe.

"Tell me, Sullivan," Travis said coldly. "Did you know my wife was alive? Were you part of the whole fucking cover-up?"

No answer.

A fist flew. And then another and then another. Travis hammered away at Gabe until they both fell to the floor.

Travis straddled him and continued punching; Gabe blocked some blows, but didn't fight back.

Beatrice yelled for Travis to stop; Ed held her back. It was Nate who finally dragged Travis away from Gabe.

"You motherfucking son of a bitch," Travis roared. "You were my friend! My brother. How could you?"

"I wasn't a part of the accident," Gabe said quietly, getting to his feet. "I only found out about Caitlin six months before you found her."

"You're lying!" Travis growled.

"You know how it is, Lieutenant. I can't reveal specifics of a mission."

"You've been working with Porter?"

Gabe inclined his head.

"Are you Dmitry?" Caitlin asked, walking toward Gabe. "Porter called a guy named Dmitry with the coordinates for the plutonium cache."

"Wait a minute," Travis's eyes narrowed. "The Zorin Bratva. Dmitry Yerzov was his assassin." Travis's arm wrapped protectively around Caitlin. "Fuck, Gabe. That was you?"

Gabe's throat worked convulsively. He wanted to come clean, but he decided against it. "I'm not confirming or denying."

Travis growled, dropped his arms around Caitlin and started for Gabe again.

"Hit me again, Lieutenant, but this time I'm retaliating," Gabe warned.

Beatrice decided to step in. "Let's calm down for a moment, Travis." She looked at Caitlin who nodded and hugged her husband's waist to calm him down.

"This is too much to take in for everyone," Beatrice said. It certainly was for her. She was reeling, but she could feel the tension in Gabe right now, even some self-loathing. She should be pissed at him for being party to what happened to Travis and Caitlin, but now was not the time. She wanted to tend to his injuries, but this revelation made her wary. Did she really want to know what he did as this Dmitry Yerzov guy? She decided distance was best right now while she sort herself out. "Gabe, go home. I'll talk to you tomorrow."

Travis balled up his fists at his sides, and Gabe squared up. He meant it when he said he was fighting back this time.

"I agree," Nate said. "Sullivan, get out of here before we change our minds."

"I'm not leaving without you," Gabe scowled at Beatrice.

"Bee is not leaving with you," Nate snapped.

"Oh, yes, she is," Gabe muttered, his arm reached out and yanked her against him. His eyes drilled into hers.

"I'm not leaving without you," he repeated.

The air was charged with testosterone, seeing that the only levelheaded man right now was Ed, who would definitely side with Travis and Nate if the situation deteriorated.

"Okay," Beatrice looked at a furious Nate. "I got this, Nate."

"Bee—" Nate reached for her.

"Seriously? Fuck off." Gabe shoved Nate.

"Jesus! Enough!" Beatrice yelled in exasperation. She yanked on Gabe's massive arm and dragged him toward the exit. "Stand down, Reece, before you piss me off."

Men!

Gabe was relieved Beatrice left with him. He didn't want her to be out of sight. Not right now. Not when he didn't know how she really felt when he had all but admitted he was the Russian assassin, Dmitry Yerzov. He thought he was ready to tell her everything, but it was harder than he first thought.

"Come home with me, please," Gabe said quietly, casting a furtive glance at her.

"I can't, Gabe. Look, come over to my condo and I'll take care of your cuts. Travis did a number on your face. Is your nose broken?"

Now that she mentioned it, his face felt like one fucking swollen pulsating lump. He moved his jaw; it hurt, but thankfully it wasn't broken. Most of the blood was from his nose, but he didn't think it was fractured either. "I'm fine."

"Now is not the time to act all macho—"

"I'm not. We can swing by your condo and pick up some clothes."

"You said you'd give me space. I'm still trying to process yesterday's revelations and now . . . this happens."

His fingers tightened on the steering wheel, fighting to stay quiet and not blurt out his defense. Should he even be saying anything? He couldn't. Not in good conscience could he volunteer information.

He heard her sigh.

She didn't want to be here with him.

He felt deflated.

He had been so hopeful last night and today.

Right now, not so much.

Twenty minutes later, Beatrice let them into her condo. She gestured for him to head straight for her bedroom. Gabe wondered if she felt the sizzle and electricity between them, because anywhere he had Beatrice all to himself, he couldn't help but think of doing wicked things to her.

It was the first time he saw her bedroom. There was a four-poster bed with a prissy canopy. Thankfully, not pink. The whole room was feminine, but not cloyingly so. He entered the bathroom. The scent of Beatrice was all over. Something floral, something citrusy. A flash of her thighs spread out with his head between them came to mind. He had a strong desire to boost her on the sink and go down on her.

"Why don't you sit over there?" Beatrice pointed to the closed toilet seat. Gabe dutifully obeyed, staring at her ass while she moved around the bedroom. She had kicked off her heels and was in her stocking feet. Was she wearing garters underneath that skirt?

She came back with some soaked cotton balls on a towel.

"So talk."

"There's nothing really to say."

"Are you Dmitry?"

"You know the answer to that."

"I want to hear you say it." Beatrice took that moment to dab his face—none too gently—with a soaked cotton ball.

Gabe gritted his teeth. "I did what had to be done."

"Did you have anything to do with Fuego's involvement in that shoot-out that nearly got Caitlin killed?"

"She's alive, isn't she?" Gabe snapped. Beatrice made a noncommittal sound and picked up another soaked cotton ball and jabbed it on a cut near his eye.

"Fuck!" Gabe roared. That fucking stung. "What the hell was that?"

"Alcohol," Beatrice said calmly. "Are you going to give me answers at all?"

"What do you want to know?"

"You killed people for the mob."

"I told you I did horrific things. I'm working through it."

"Are you using me as a crutch, Gabe?"

Beatrice sighed and started affixing butterfly strips on his face. "I take it by your silence, you either don't know or you are."

"I don't think you're an emotional crutch, poppy," Gabe said gently. "You do keep me tethered to this reality. I've accepted what I had to do. As a hit man, I did it for the greed of an organization. But in doing that, a bigger evil was taken down. Someone had to do the dirty job to clean up shit in this world, babe; it just happened to be me. Everyone I've assassinated on that kill roll handed to me was guilty of a crime, I swear."

Beatrice stared at him dubiously.

"Trust me," Gabe whispered. He grabbed her waist and buried his face on her belly. "Just trust me, Beatrice."

She was rigid in her posture; her arms were at her sides. Gabe burrowed his nose further, further down. She inhaled sharply.

Her fingers drove into his hair and tilted his head up forcefully to look up at her. "No distractions, Sullivan. You realize you put me in a difficult position with Travis and with BSI in general."

Gabe scowled. "Babe, you need to stop pulling my hair unless you want me to fuck you afterward, because right now, I have an overwhelming desire to shove up your skirt and eat that pussy."

Her fingers disappeared from his hair as she tried to step back, but he held her firmly.

"Be serious." Her voice was shaky.

"I am being serious," Gabe gritted through his teeth. "I'm as hard as a brick."

Without releasing her, he let her pull away a bit so she could see the undeniable ridge pushing against his jeans.

"Umm . . . Well, you're on your own with that," Beatrice laughed nervously. "Let me go."

Gabe grinned despite the ache in his jaw. Blake had a mean right hook. He watched Beatrice dispose of the used cotton balls and other litter from their little first-aid session. She strutted to the corner of the bathroom to return the medical kit, her ass taunting him in that tight skirt. "You need to stop doing that."

His gaze lifted to hers. "Stop doing what?"

She had a knowing smile on her lips. "Looking at me like you want to eat me up."

Is she flirting with me?

Gabe stood up cautiously; her eyes left his, lowering to his crotch. *Christ! Is she torturing me?*

He cleared his throat. "You need to stop staring at my dick."

Beatrice smirked, turned her back on him, and walked out of the bathroom. "Point made. If you're hungry"—significant pause—"for food, I can fix you something."

Gabe followed her to the kitchen. "What if I'm hungry for something else?"

Beatrice was rummaging through the fridge and didn't answer for a while. After taking out some chopped-up veggies and some chicken cutlets, she said, "Sex is off the table tonight, Sullivan. So if that's what you're after, the door is right there, but I'm not above sharing a chicken stir-fry."

"I'll stay for dinner," Gabe said quickly. Put in place again. *Dial down the teenage hormones will you, Sullivan?*

"Great." Beatrice beamed at him.

That killer smile always did funny things to his chest.

GABE ENDED up staying for a movie as well. A damned chick flick. It was a romantic comedy, so it was at least bearable. Beatrice didn't ask him any more questions about his Russian alter ego. He was relieved, and at the same time, unsettled.

He looked over to where she had fallen asleep at the other end of the couch. Her feet were on his lap. She seemed more relaxed tonight and didn't protest when he started massaging her soles in the middle of the movie. She had changed into flannel pajamas after dinner. If she was trying to look unsexy, she failed. She could wear a flour sack and he'd still think she was the most beautiful woman on the planet.

Gabe leaned over and stole the remote from her slackened grip and turned off the TV. He carefully lowered her feet, stood up, bent over her, and lifted her from the couch.

"What are you doing?" Beatrice murmured sleepily.

"Putting you to bed and then heading home," Gabe whispered. "I don't think Rhino will be too happy with me if I stay much longer."

"Okay."

He lowered her on the mattress and did some maneuvering to get her under the covers. Gabe couldn't help himself and pressed a kiss on her lips. "See you tomorrow, poppy."

Beatrice was already lightly snoring away.

DRESSED IN BLACK, her red hair in a severe bun, Beatrice stood at the back of the gathering for the funeral of Eric Stone. Security was tight, and a larger crowd stood outside the cemetery gates. Though not a national sensation, Titanium Rose had an avid following in Northern Virginia and Washington DC.

Gabe stood beside her. She was surprised when he showed up at her condo this morning dressed in a suit. He was one of those men who could be comfortable in whatever setting was required of him. He would look good in all-commando gear as well as an expensive suit, and judging with her experienced eyes, the one he was wearing today cost at least three grand. It was a sunny day despite the chill; he wore sunglasses, which shielded some of the bruises he had sustained last night.

Her icy walls were thawing. In a weird twist of fate, the revelation last night seemed to have released all doubts that what Gabe had done was crucial to National Security. Taking down an organization intent on selling black market nukes to terrorists who could unleash them on U.S. soil was a strategic accomplishment. Prevention rather than reaction. How could she diminish the success of a brilliant plan? It did not completely dispel her reservations of being with someone like him, like her father, but she couldn't seem to stop him from worming himself back into her life. He was just there, allowing himself to be used. She had not promised him anything; she would see how this played out.

The gathering in front of her started moving. The funeral was over.

"Ready?" Gabe whispered by her ear.

She nodded.

They almost made it to their car when they got ambushed by Kelly Winters.

The reporter eyed Gabe appreciatively. "Beatrice."

"What do you want, Ms. Winters?"

"Hostile." The reporter's lips curved in a derisive smile. "Feeling guilty?"

"Look, it's Eric's funeral. Show some respect."

"There were rumors he overdosed and he had pictures of you scattered in his bedroom."

Beatrice felt her temper rise but strived to remain calm. "I'm sure they're just that. Rumors."

"Are you sure?"

Gabe stepped in front of Beatrice and glared at Kelly. "You're done."

"Who's this? A bodyguard or a new lover?"

"Goodbye, Ms. Winters. I'm not doing this here." Beatrice's tone was somber as she pushed past the reporter. Gabe enveloped her protectively in his arms as he led her to the car and deposited her into the passenger seat.

Heavy gloom descended upon her. She hadn't really mourned Eric's death. Their relationship was so short, so full of drama, and always in the tabloids, it didn't feel real. But death was as real as it got.

Gabe got in beside her. He cursed softly when he saw her face. "Don't let the reporter get to you."

She sighed in resignation. "It just suddenly hit me. He was a real part of my life, however short. Now he's gone. He had so much going for him."

Gabe didn't respond. He just started the car and pulled away.

KELLY WINTERS PUT the finishing touches on her article and sent it to her editor. She had a couple of high-profile stories that had put her firmly on her boss's favorite list. One was the sex scandal involving a Russian diplomat. But it was her coverage of the drama involving Titanium Rose's lead guitarist, Eric Stone's relationship to DC "it" girl Beatrice Porter and his untimely death that had caught public interest. It was a shame the snooty Ms. Porter didn't want to play the grieving ex-girlfriend. She seemed to have moved on pretty quickly.

Kelly wondered what that stuck-up redhead had going for her. Sure she was beautiful, but so were hundreds of other DC socialites, but she always seemed to have the handsomest men at her beck and call. What the hell was up with that? That man she was with today looked like more than just a bodyguard. The protectiveness was more personal than professional, and damn if he didn't look smoking hot in a suit. The bruises on his face only added to his mystery and dangerous attractiveness.

The sound of the cleaning cart rattled by in the hallway. It was almost 10:00 p.m. and the office was mostly deserted. Time to go home. She turned off her laptop. She wasn't taking it home tonight. She deserved a break. Maybe she should go to a bar and meet a guy like Beatrice's man.

Where does she find men like him?

Kelly waved goodbye to the cleaning lady and stepped into the elevator. It was a straight descent to the underground parking garage. The elevator doors opened to the cold concrete and flickering lights of the parking level. Her heels clattered noisily. There was a distant sound of a car's squealing tires turning a corner, and the faint fumes of burnt fuel reached her nose. A man in a trench coat appeared a few steps ahead, walking toward her. He was extremely attractive. A business suit peeked from under his coat, and he was carrying a briefcase. The man's eyes fell upon her, dark and intense. Her reporter's instincts trilled a warning in her head.

"Good evening," Kelly said in greeting.

The man jerked his chin in response as he passed her.

A gut reaction made her turn, but she was suddenly held immobile in a tight embrace. Objects landed on the floor, hers or her attacker's she didn't know. She felt a prick on her neck. She faded steadily into oblivion.

8

Gabe pulled his SUV into the parking lot of a dive bar near the Cloverleaf District. It was late afternoon and the place was quiet, save for a couple of cars and motorcycles in the near deserted gravel parking lot.

Ashe and Duke were waiting for him, lounging languidly against their bikes. He stopped his vehicle beside them and exited. Rounding the front of the car, Gabe put on his sunglasses and walked up to them.

"You have anything for me?"

"Before we give you this information, Crane wants you and Porter to know that this is it. Marker is paid," Ashe said.

"That's not for me to decide."

"Well, maybe it should be Porter meeting us," Ashe shot back. "Our Prez is pissed because he can't get ahold of your boss—"

"Porter is not my boss—"

"Well, why the fuck are we talking to you then?"

"Don't waste my time," Gabe replied coldly. "Either you give me the information or I walk."

Duke, who had been quiet for the most part, stepped into

Gabe's space. The young blond biker was a bit shorter than Gabe, but they were mostly nose to nose.

"Listen, I don't like you," Duke said. "Ashe and I don't trust you, but that lady friend of yours seems to trust you enough and we like her."

Duke nodded to Ashe who held out the manila envelope. "If it was all Fuego, we would have gone deeper, but there seems to be some Russian involvement. We stay clear of them. We need to keep the peace."

Russian. Gabe's blood turned to ice. "Do you have names?"

"It goes all the way up to the Fuego gang leader who everyone knows is Domingo Ventura, but we don't have the name of the Russian dude."

"What kinda fucking intel is that?"

"You have his picture." Ashe nodded at the envelope before getting on his bike. "We're outta here."

Duke swaggered back to his Harley and got on as well. "Later, man."

Gabe returned to his vehicle and just sat there for a while. Finally, he reached into the brown pouch and pulled out a set of photographs. They were grainy, taken from a distance by a low-resolution camera, but the identity of the man in the picture could not be denied. Along with the past returning to haunt him came a myriad of emotions.

The joy was short-lived, ephemeral in its manifestation because what followed was white hot rage. It was Steve Ryker—his brother-in-arms who was supposed to have died in that plane crash. He was the reason Gabe had given up his happiness with Beatrice to carry through the mission that supposedly should have been Ryker's. Why the fuck was he alive, and what the fuck was his role in all this bullshit, and why did the Skulls think he was Russian?

His phone buzzed.

"Sullivan."

"Gabe! It's Doug," Keller's voice came over in such a rush, all his senses went on alert.

"Is Beatrice all right?"

"Those two asshole detectives from the MPD are harassing her again."

"What? Why? I thought Stone's case was closed."

"It is, but Kelly Winters was found murdered this morning and her story depicting Beatrice in a negative light regarding her relationship with Eric Stone hit the tabloids today."

"Damn it!" Gabe muttered.

"I'm in Richmond right now, and I can't get to her for another two hours."

"I got her, man."

"Nate and Travis are not—"

"I got her," Gabe repeated tersely. Beatrice was his responsibility, not fucking Nate Reece or Travis Blake's.

Doug exhaled harshly. "Thanks, man."

Gabe ended the call, started his car, and drove like crazy to get to his woman.

"Beatrice!" Gabe pounded on the door. It had taken him a damned half hour to get to her. He didn't know what he would do if he'd found those damned detectives in there. He was feeling pretty homicidal right now. He was going to demand she give him a duplicate keycard. She could protest all she wanted.

What Gabe didn't expect was Porter opening the door. Beatrice was standing a few feet behind her father.

"Where the fuck have you been?" Gabe snarled at the admiral.

"Good afternoon to you too, Commander," the admiral replied dryly. "I could ask you the same question. Weren't you supposed to be watching over my daughter?"

Beatrice gasped in outrage. Fucking great. Now she was thinking he was with her because her father had dictated it.

"I've been chasing a lead," Gabe snapped and shoved the brown envelope to Porter. "Check that out and explain it to me. Oh, and Crane says his marker is paid up."

He headed straight for Beatrice who had her arms crossed in front of her in annoyance. Daggers were shooting from her eyes.

"Hey, babe" Gabe kissed the top of her head. "What's this I hear about the detectives paying another visit?"

"They don't have a leg to stand on," Porter said absently, a frown had creased his forehead as he returned the contents of the envelope back into it. "Circumstantial evidence is pointing to a Russian diplomat, and they're frustrated because of diplomatic immunity."

"Why a Russian diplomat?" Gabe asked, jaw clenching tensely.

"She did a story on the diplomat and his proclivities for high-class prostitutes. Crime scene photos were leaked on the internet." Beatrice shuddered. "A Russian phrase was carved on her arms. Speculations on social media say it means an *eye for an eye*."

Air deserted his lungs as a series of images hit Gabe.

An assassin from another rival Bratva was tied naked on a filthy bed.

He was taunting Dmitry to do his worst.

Dmitry obliged. Carving the words slowly on the man's arms as he screamed in agony.

After he was done, Dmitry said, "Oko za oko."

Afterward, he sliced the assassin's neck from ear to ear.

Blood soaked the bed before it dripped to the floor.

. . .

". . . EAR TO EAR . . ." Beatrice's voice came back to focus. "Gabe, you okay? You're looking pale."

No. He felt like throwing up. Beatrice was in danger because of him.

Porter gripped his arm firmly, addressing Beatrice, "Sweetheart, can we use your office for a minute?"

"What's going on?" Beatrice glared at both of them. "I'm tired of being kept in the dark, and if your crap is coming back to hit me, I deserve answers, don't you think?"

At that moment, Gabe couldn't speak as he was faced with the possibility that he had to sacrifice the woman he loved again. His heart was screaming *no*. There had to be another way.

Porter dragged him into the study and shut the door.

"Get a grip, Commander," Porter ordered.

Gabe laughed without humor. "Get a grip? Everything's gone FUBAR. Ryker is after me and he's hitting me where he knows it's gonna hurt. Beatrice. He's getting less subtle. I'm not discounting that he took the pictures after he killed the reporter and posted them online."

"Are we certain now that Ryker was Crowe's man inside Fuego?" Porter asked.

"They have to be connected. I worked closely with Crowe when I was an enforcer. He provided me intel on my targets. He knew my methods. He was probably relaying it back to Ryker."

"There's almost no question on that point," Porter replied. "Crowe was inserted into the Zorin Bratva before you were. I made a quick jaunt to Germany these past two days to follow up some leads with some human assets. It's highly possible that Crowe tipped Ryker off about the hit on Zorin's plane. He could have made an offer to Ryker then to join his boss. The reason why Crowe wanted Caitlin was because she almost discovered the identity of the mastermind when she'd been the hacker Sarah Blake. Now that she's almost at a hundred percent of her tradecraft, she's becoming more of a threat."

"If someone is still after Caitlin, we need to bring Travis into the loop."

Porter's lips thinned.

"We are not using her as bait," Gabe said. He was sick and tired of doing things for the greater good at the expense of people he cared about. Gabe scrubbed his face with his hand in frustration. "I'm trying to make sense of who Ryker is after. Me or you?"

"I have a theory," the admiral said. "You've been in Grigori Zorin's inner circle. You've been present in several of his meets with his associates. Whoever his contact was in the CIA fears that you could identify him and is siccing Ryker on you."

"Why not kill me outright?"

"He wants me as well. I'm not always in plain sight. Taking you out is going to put me on alert, so he's messing with us the way he knows will get our attention."

"Beatrice."

"Exactly."

He locked stares with Porter. "Now is the time to tell me to stay away from your daughter."

Porter sighed. "Will you?"

"Fuck no. Even if I stay away from her now, there's no guarantee Ryker won't go after her," Gabe said. "This is where we're different, Admiral. I can't change my past, but I'm changing myself now to be the man she deserves. She deserves a man who will love and cherish her."

"Or get her killed?"

"Fuck you," Gabe snarled softly. "Fuck you." He repeated even louder.

"All I ask, Gabriel, is give her a choice to walk away. She deserves to know what she's signing up for."

Porter handed him a phone. "This is an encrypted line.

I've uncovered some troubling intel and may not be able to meet with you for a while, but I will keep you apprised of what you need to know."

Gabe wondered how much the admiral knew and wasn't telling him.

The admiral straightened his suit and walked to the door. "By the way, the tox screen report for Eric Stone came back from our labs."

"And?" Gabe held his breath.

"It was Hybernabis. He was murdered."

". . . so, babe, that's most of the story that you need to know."

Beatrice's face remained stoic as the details poured out of Gabe. Eric Stone, Kelly Winters, Luisa Delgado, and her friends were possibly murdered because of an op Gabe had been involved in. Someone was seeking revenge on him and her father, and she was in the center of it all. Her dad left him to tell her everything. She had the sinking feeling that she wouldn't be seeing her father very much in the near future. Same old story. Deep inside though, her heart was singing because Gabe hadn't walked out. He stayed and was adamant that he wasn't going anywhere. There was that wee fact this could get her killed.

"So you're saying it's better for me to stay away from you. Not see you at all?"

"In theory, yes." Gabe said. His jaw was taut, and the planes of his face were etched with frustration and a hint of helplessness.

"And if I tell you I don't want to ever see you again because I don't feel safe, you'll respect my wishes?"

His jawline hardened further, but he nodded jerkily.

Beatrice pursed her lips, walked to the wide picture window, and stared at the Washington DC skyline in troubled contemplation. She heard faint movement and watched Gabe's tall form approach from the window's reflection before his heat hit her back.

Two warm hands rested on her shoulders, pulling her into him.

"Take a chance on me, poppy," Gabe whispered. "Please. I promise to protect you, guard you, and shield you from everything that would harm you until there's no breath or life left in me."

She exhaled deeply, slightly shaking her head. His arms came around her, hugging her tighter. "If you need me to crawl and beg you to take me back, I will." Desperation dripped from each word. She was terribly conflicted.

He turned her in his arms, his whiskey eyes were dim in the limited lighting, but their intensity was drilling right into her soul. "The sane part of me tells me to give you a choice," Gabe whispered, "but this crazy part of me that just needs you . . . wants to lock you up and not let you leave me even if you try."

Her heart swelled with emotion. "And which part is winning?"

He squeezed her tight. "The crazy part."

"Hmm . . ." Beatrice smiled. "I'm not telling you to go away. I'm not saying we're a couple again, but I'm willing to try and get to that point. We're taking this slow—"

His mouth came down hard on hers as a hand went to the back of her head to hold it in place as he devoured her lips. His other hand cupped the flesh of her ass and hauled her closer against him. Heat bloomed between her thighs as her body arched against his hardness. Her arousal dampened her panties. She pulsated once, twice.

She dragged her lips away. "Gabe . . ." Her tone was censuring.

He chuckled softly, leaning his forehead on hers. "Right. Slow. Can't blame a guy for trying."

"You're incorrigible."

"I ache for you, babe," he whispered. His lips scorched over hers again, nibbling her bottom lip. A guttural sound of reluctant self-control vibrated at the back of his throat as he finally pulled away.

"Will you come home with me?"

"I don't think that's a good idea. Security in the building is good. I'll be fine."

"I hate leaving you alone. I'll sleep on your couch if I have to, but I have Rhino," Gabe said. "I don't think your building regulations allow pets, you think?"

"I've seen a poodle," Beatrice deadpanned.

The handle on the entryway door rattled. Gabe tensed and hugged her protectively, pivoting his body so it faced the door.

Doug walked in and paused, his eyes squinting at the intimate embrace he was witnessing.

"I need to get myself a key," Gabe muttered. "And we need to do something about people walking in on us."

STEVE RYKER STARED at his buzzing burner phone in irritation. His boss was a pain in the ass. So his last act was a bit dramatic. So what? He was doing his job, and he was just having some fun.

"Ryker."

"You are taking too many risks." A cold chilling voice came over the phone.

"Just sending a message, boss."

"To whom? Sullivan? The plan was to get rid of him. He is not the biggest issue; Porter is. The admiral is a man who's a master of misdirection. He will always look beyond the obvious."

Ryker felt his temper flaring. "I have it under control."

There was silence for a while. "There's too much at stake here, Ryker. You've already taken more exposure than I'm comfortable with when it's not even related to our prime objective."

"I got the results you want, haven't I?" Ryker bit off.

There was a heavy sigh on the other end of the line. "Yes. It's good to know that shipment did not reduce its viability and its dosage matched our expected results. Our buyers will be pleased. I'll be in touch with more instructions."

The call ended.

He threw his phone on the table and cursed his boss.

Ryker did not board the doomed plane that crashed into the Atlantic three years ago. He received an anonymous tip about the hit. He had lain low for a few days not knowing who to trust, but still intended to report back to Admiral Porter. Only, he found out he'd been quickly replaced by Sullivan. Ultimately, the admiral got his way and his favorite Navy SEAL got the assignment. Ryker felt bitter and betrayed. He would always play second best to the great Gabriel Sullivan. He later found out who saved his ass from getting on that flight. Philip Crowe had a lucrative proposition for him, so Ryker gave up his integrity to live the life of a mercenary.

So yeah, he didn't need this dressing down. He did his job. He got his boss the required five test cases. Ryker pulled out the file on Luisa Delgado and the other four to whom he'd given the ST-Vyl virus. Inert in powder form, it was safe and easy to hide with the cocaine shipments. It needed to be activated by a separate compound before it could deliver its deadly potency—malaise and mild fever during the first forty-eight hours. After seventy-two hours, hemorrhagic fever begins. It was further genetically modified with a self-kill DNA so after 120 hours it became inert to prevent mutation. Controlled epidemic. A perfect bioweapon.

THE POUNDING of the hammer echoed sharply in the orange glow of the afternoon. When Gabe purchased the house, it needed a few repairs. Although mostly cosmetic, like a fresh coat of paint, the flooring of the back patio had become warped and needed to be replaced. He glanced furtively to where Beatrice and Doug were having a quiet conversation further up in the stamp of backyard that came with the house. It was a relatively warm day for November, but still chilly enough to have a mug of hot chocolate. Rhino was lying on his belly at Beatrice's feet. His dog looked as smitten as Gabe was.

Gabe stood back to observe his handiwork. One more floorboard to go. His father had been a construction worker and always had projects around the house. Gabe helped him when he wasn't in school. It had always been the two of them ever since he could remember. His mother died when he was five. His dad never remarried. Sullivan men loved only once and forever, so it seemed. His eyes drifted to Beatrice. It had been a week since he had laid it all out for her, pretending to give her a choice to walk away when in fact he didn't think he could ever let her go. He was thankful the outcome didn't include him kidnapping her and holding her hostage until she agreed to stay with him. It had also been a torturously long week of cold showers and inappropriate hard-ons. He respected her wish to go slow, although he didn't think he could last another day. He had tasted her again, though not under ideal circumstances. The memory of him eating her pussy and sucking her tits while his dick stretched and slid in and out of her, had played a starring role in his dreams. Gabe stared down the front of his jeans. Yes. That would do it.

Down boy.

It took him a few more minutes to finish the repair work. When he straightened up, he saw Beatrice on the phone with a frown on her face. Doug's face was also unhappy. What was going on? It was a Saturday; surely dignitaries and politicians could give her a break.

Her voice floated up to him.

"No, Brian, I don't believe that person has been vetted by either BSI or by me. Can you delay them until I get there?"

Brian. Gabe racked his brain. Brian Haines was a guy on Senator Mendoza's security detail.

"Zach should know how this should be cleared with Ed, Nate, or Travis." Beatrice walked toward Gabe. Her face was etched with frustration. "I can't make that call. Look, is Zach Jamison there? Can I talk to him?"

She was now standing close to him. Gabe wanted to hug her, but he was a bit sweaty. She appeared to be on hold; their eyes met. She shook her head and rolled her eyes.

"Zach? . . . What's this I hear about this excursion to the Cloverleaf Junkyard? . . . A lead about what? . . . I don't . . . Wait . . . Damn it."

Beatrice put her phone away and went straight into the house. She was rifling through her purse.

"What's going on?" Gabe asked. Doug came in behind him.

"I'm not sure, but I don't like it," Beatrice muttered. She eyed him contemplatively. "Are you up for a trip to the Cloverleaf District? We can't waste any time, because the senator is already en route."

"I'll go anywhere you want, but is it your job to get involved?" Gabe asked. "I understand once you've handed over security, you're done."

"I can still get involved, especially if I've overlooked important details."

"They didn't put this person down as a contact, Bee," Doug answered. "Their protection is as good as their honesty on that questionnaire."

Gabe pulled off his sweatshirt together with his undershirt. Beatrice's eyes widened at the sight of his naked chest. He would normally tease her, but now was not the time. He quickly proceeded to the laundry room to pull a clean shirt on.

"Doug, I want you to continue trying to contact Nate or Travis. I know Ed is on a job somewhere in Europe, so it might be harder to get a hold of him," Beatrice said. "Travis may be out of town with Caitlin. I'm not sure."

"I'll handle it," Doug assured her.

Beatrice was already out the door. Gabe cursed and went after her. In a few long strides, he caught up with her and held her back.

"What?" she snapped.

"Easy, killer," Gabe said calmly. "The senator may be running roughshod over his security, but you are listening to yours. I have my reservations about heading blindly into the Cloverleaf Junkyard, but it'll be remiss for you not to give a damn. So we're giving a damn, but you stick close to me. No going off half-cocked. Got it?"

"Got it."

"Tight as a tick, babe."

"All right, jeez, let's go!"

Gabe nodded briefly, steering her to his vehicle as he bleeped the locks.

Minutes later, they were on their way.

9

THE GATE to the junkyard was wide open. The chain and lock holding it closed hung undamaged on one side, which indicated that both parties had contacted the junkyard owner. It was a relief not to deal with breaking and entering charges, although she had dealt with these scenarios on more than one occasion. The place was a well-known neutral ground for warring gangs from the Cloverleaf District. Still, there had been instances when the meets deteriorated into violence.

Beatrice was able to contact Brian Haines again to get confirmation for where the meeting was taking place in the junkyard.

"What you got?" Gabe asked when she got off the phone.

"They're on the north side of the junkyard. The man they're meeting is a relative of Senator Mendoza and was a longtime informant whom they haven't heard from in a year. At least that's the explanation Zach had told Brian."

"How long has Zach been in the employ of the Senator?"

"Two months."

"So he's not exactly an expert on the Senator's associations."

"Yes. And I see where you're going with this."

"Do you? What happened to the senator's former Chief of Staff?"

"He died of a heart attack almost three months ago."

Gabe uttered a noncommittal response. Beatrice's attention was drawn to their surroundings. Piles of crushed metal and, well, junk were stacked as high up as twenty feet. She had to applaud the location of the junkyard because the Cloverleaf District is a dumping ground of stolen vehicles and most of the buildings were close to being condemned.

"There's Zach," Gabe said. The Chief of Staff was standing by the senator's vehicle. Brian and one other BSI security personnel were standing facing outward and watchful. There was another car parked close by. It had rental tags. As Gabe's SUV rolled by, Beatrice took a picture of the license plate.

Gabe was circling the area, probably looking for a less exposed parking space. He pulled in between two junk piles.

"Wait for me," Gabe instructed. He exited the vehicle and looked around. Then he came to her side and opened the door. "Come on."

He was shadowing her the entire way.

"Zach, what the hell is going on?"

The Chief of Staff looked duly chastised. "I'm sorry, Beatrice. The senator was ready to drive himself if we didn't go with him. There was no stopping him."

"Who's the guy?"

"His uncle."

"A relative from Colombia?"

"No. He's an American citizen. His son—the senator's cousin—is involved with the right wing paramilitaries who protect the cocaine jungles, and there are rumors of a breakdown of peace talks with the government."

"Why meet him here? Why not at his house?"

"His wife and children. He doesn't want this issue to touch them."

"Well, it's too late," Beatrice snapped. What was it with these men? They try to separate their duty from their family. There would always be blowback from people unhappy with their choices. "He had involved his family once he'd decided to take on this crusade against the drug traffickers. It will only be a matter of time before they get to his wife and children."

"Beatrice," Gabe said her name quietly, but it was rife with caution. She was projecting.

The door to the senator's SUV opened and a man Beatrice didn't recognize alighted. The senator followed, grimacing when he saw her.

She was about to introduce herself to the senator's uncle when a single gunshot cracked through the air.

Everything seemed to happen at once.

The senator's uncle fell to the ground.

More shots were fired and Zach Jamison crumpled as well. Brian went for the senator and shoved him back to the SUV. The other security guy jumped into the driver's seat.

"Go! Go! Go!" Gabe shouted at Brian. "We got Jamison. Get the senator out of here." Tires spinning, the senator's SUV shot forward toward the exit of the junkyard.

Gabe heaved Zach over his shoulders. "Beatrice, get moving!"

She ran as fast as she could, ignoring a burn in her side even as bullets exploded around them. When they reached the safety of their vehicle, Gabe tossed Jamison in the backseat.

"What about the senator's—"

"Dead. He was shot through the head," Gabe muttered as he turned to her and practically dumped her into the passenger seat.

Soon, they were burning rubber out of there. Their SUV flew through the gates at top speed, the back of their vehicle fishtailing when Gabe made a sharp turn onto the road. Beatrice looked back and saw a car and several motorcycles tear after them.

"They're coming after us!"

"I know." Gabe's eyes shifted from the road to the rearview mirror. They sped through a deserted stretch of road with abandoned buildings on both sides. A harsh indrawn breath beside her drew her attention from the back of the vehicle to Gabe, and that was when she noticed the spreading map of red on his jeans.

"You've been shot!"

"Flesh wound."

"Bullshit, flesh wound. That's a lot of blood, Gabe!"

"Babe, calm down," Gabe ordered. His voice was steady, but the way his jaw clenched tight afterward gave away the gravity of his injury. "The senator's car is up ahead. If the bikes get any closer, I'm going to run interference. Prepare to brace."

The words barely left his mouth when there was a loud pop.

They shot out their tire!

Gabe cursed as he struggled to maintain control of the vehicle. The buildings appeared to jar crazily on all sides as their car careened from one corner to the other. Just as the SUV was about to tilt over, it righted itself, and finally jumped the curb. The back of the vehicle slammed into a building before skidding to a halt. Gabe shoved a gun at her. "I want you to get out of here, turn right, and call 911. I'll provide cover fire."

"I'm not leaving you." Beatrice opened the passenger door and was dismayed to find out it opened enough to only allow her lithe form through, not Gabe's big body.

Gabe quickly exited his side amidst a rain of lead. She watched in horror as another bullet whipped his body around. He collapsed chest first on the hood. Unfettered fear gripped her heart. Their eyes met across the hood.

She loved him.

She was not losing him today.

"Gabe!"

"Damn it, Beatrice. Get out of here," he growled as he returned fire and tried to get between the car and the building, but he got hit again and fell.

She concentrated on firing rounds in the direction of the enemy's assault as she made her way to him, assisting him to take refuge behind the car.

"Beatrice, get away from here," he repeated, his breathing getting more serrated by the second.

"Shut up," Beatrice snapped, flinching as a couple of shell casings ricocheted and hit her face. She smiled grimly when a voice howled and cursed. At least she got someone.

Gabe pulled himself up and rejoined the firefight. Out of the corner of her eye, she noticed the back of his head was soaked with blood; he was becoming alarmingly pale as the blood seeped out of him.

They needed to get out of here because they were outgunned and outnumbered.

Gabe seemed to be aiming with cold precision as he felled several of their assailants, but they were not prepared for this type of assault.

It didn't take long for them to run out of ammunition as Beatrice used up her last magazine.

Gabe said he had a few shots left.

He dragged her down to sit beside him. He didn't look good. Blood was mixed with sweat on his face. His lips were white, but his gold-flecked eyes were blazing. He handed her his gun before gripping her face with his bloody hands. "Please, Beatrice, I need you to go."

"I am not leaving you."

The gunfire ceased.

Words rushed out of Gabe's lips as footsteps approached. "Goddammit, Beatrice! I don't want you here."

"Sully! You dead yet?" a voice called out. There was a cackling of laughter and heckling.

"Oh, no you don't, Gabriel," Beatrice whispered harshly. "You are not pulling your fucked up reasoning on me again. You begged me to take you back just a week ago. Well now, I'm taking you back. You better not fucking die on me. Got me?"

Gabe's lips twitched. "Why didn't you say so earlier?" His lighthearted words were dampened by a wince of pain. "This sucks."

"You're riddled with bullet holes and all you can say is 'this sucks'?" She was trying to keep her voice steady, but it cracked. He was fading, bleeding out right in front of her. Beatrice found herself praying that if only they'd make it out of here alive, she would forget all the hurt of the past three years and only move forward.

"Gabe?"

"Love you, poppy," Gabe whispered. ". . . damned much . . ."

"Don't die . . ."

"Trying . . . not to . . . but you . . . go . . ."

"Never."

"Now doesn't this look tragic?" A man Beatrice had never seen before appeared a few feet from them. Her grip tightened on the gun. She lowered her hand fractionally.

"You're not looking too good, Sully." A wariness passed through the man's face. "And not surprised to see me. Now why is that?"

"Fuck you, Ryker." There was renewed vigor in Gabe's voice.

Ryker? This was Ryker? The man who killed Eric and Kelly Winters just to send a message to Gabe. Another man, this one a Latino, appeared behind Ryker.

"No, buddy, I think you're the one who's about to get fucked," Ryker said.

"Why are you doing this?"

"Why else? Money," Ryker sneered. "And I'm so tired of

being second best to you. Well, guess what? I'm smarter. Better." He laughed maniacally. "You know why? Because you handed some bitch your balls and it made you stupid." Ryker's eyes landed on her. A chilling fist gripped her heart. "But before I let you bleed out, you're going to watch me shoot her."

"No!" Gabe snarled. Where he got the energy, Beatrice had no idea, but he managed to get on his knees, and then using the wheelbase, he boosted himself up in an upright position, shielding her fully. "You will *not* touch her."

"Tsk . . . tsk . . . You're as good as dead, Sully. Look at you."

Beatrice readied the gun; Gabe was giving her the opportunity to shoot and she was taking it.

Before she was able to surprise Ryker, shots cracked through the air. Not losing focus though, she leaned to the right. Both Ryker and the Latino guy were already on their way down, but because Beatrice liked insurance, she shot Ryker anyway, forcing his body to jerk backward. Gabe sank beside her. He was done and all strength had left him.

More shots were exchanged.

"Gabe, hold on, please," Beatrice begged. His eyes were closed and he was about to fall sideways to the ground. She steadied him against the tires of the SUV and took a tentative peek through the vehicle's windows.

The Iron Skulls!

But how? She didn't even hear their bikes.

Beatrice leaned toward Gabe and planted a kiss on his cold lips.

"Babe," he rasped.

"Hang on, Gabe. The Skulls are here."

There was a wailing of sirens in the distance.

"Ms. Porter!"

"Ashe?"

The Iron Skulls VP walked toward her, the blond biker

Duke and an older man about the age of her dad followed close behind.

"Gabe's badly hurt." A sob escaped her. She fought for calm, but her knees were like Jell-O. "How did you guys—"

"We had some intel," the older man said. "I'm Nicholas Crane. Sorry we're meeting under these circumstances, Ms. Porter. You okay?"

She could only nod.

"Good. We can't hang around; police and ambulance are on their way."

"But—"

Crane let out a loud whistle to round up his men. "Let's go!"

The sirens grew closer.

Crane nodded to her. "Until next time, Ms. Porter."

The bikers disappeared.

After a few more minutes, the ambulance and police arrived.

BEATRICE WATCHED Gabe through the ICU window.

She closed her eyes momentarily as the memory of seeing him loaded on the gurney, pale as death and barely breathing, assailed her mind. He almost died. A few minutes more, it would have been too late.

She had been afraid to tell him she loved him because saying so felt like saying goodbye. She refused. They had put him under a medically induced coma for four days so his body could recover. They were bringing him out of it today.

Right now, watching all the apparatus in the room breathing for him, monitoring his heartbeat and blood pressure, he still looked formidable. There was a static energy simmering inside him. He was alive. She struggled to wrap her head around his injuries. His heart had stopped once. He lost almost forty percent of his blood. He suffered a collapsed lung and three gunshot wounds to the body. A fourth bullet took out a piece of his skull.

His skull.

The doctor said if he wasn't in excellent shape, his body would have succumbed to all the trauma.

Doug came up beside her and squeezed her arm. He was the only other person who had been a constant in the hospital. Not a peep from her father. Beatrice was offended for Gabe, but she guessed she shouldn't be surprised.

A few minutes later, Gabe's doctor walked up to them.

"Ready, Ms. Porter?"

Two weeks later

"Gabe, if you don't stop behaving like an asshole, a piece of your skull missing or not, I'm going to whack this purse over your head."

Beatrice issued the threat with much conviction. Gabe paused and clenched his jaw. It had been two fucking weeks for fuck's sake, almost three if he considered the time he was under. He'd been going insane with boredom in the hospital. They had fit a quarter-size metal plate in his head. Beatrice had started calling him Terminator.

"Wanna get the fuck out of here." The way he issued this demand was actually the tamest of his recent rants. "I'd rather stay at home than be here."

When Gabe woke up from his coma, he was relieved to see Beatrice's face. Even in the darkest recesses of his medically induced sleep, she had been ever present. He woke up thinking of her. His second thought was of Rhino. He found out Beatrice had moved into his house, so she could take care of his dog. His woman. In his house. Could she really blame him for wanting to be there with them?

"You still require medical supervision and you shouldn't be moving too much."

"You can take care of me," Gabe grumbled.

"I have to work."

He looked away from her, staring out the window. "I'm not there to protect you." A frustrated anger exploded from him. "I'm stuck here. In this hospital. A damn invalid! Some kind of bodyguard I turned out to be." He slapped his thigh to release some pent-up rage. Part of the rage stemmed from the fact that Beatrice had refused to leave him when things got desperate, and she could have been killed. He understood her reasons, because he would have done the same if their situations were reversed, but he was the man, damn it. It was his job to protect her, not the other way around.

"Calm down."

"Fuck calm down. Get me out of here," he demanded anew. "Get me the nurse or whoever the fuck is in charge so I can sign the release forms."

"You be reasonable, Sullivan." Beatrice now had both hands on her hips. His annoyance escalated if it were even possible. She totally looked fuckable. His dick was tenting his pajamas, and he couldn't do a damned thing.

"I am. Before I become truly unreasonable, have me discharged."

Her jaw, which was set stubbornly since the beginning of his rant, slackened. Her lips trembled, and suddenly, to Gabe's horror, she burst out crying.

"Babe, what the—"

"You almost died!" she yelled. Tears spilled from her eyes, her fists were now balled at her sides. "I watched you bleed all over the pavement. There was a puddle of your blood, Gabe. A puddle! Can you even imagine how I felt when I realized I loved you and I wanted you back and all I could do was watch you die? Can you?"

His frustration and anger evaporated. "Babe, come here," he whispered softly.

"Seven hours in the waiting room. You had a hole in your head. You died on the OR table. I thought I would go crazy because they wouldn't let me see you. I'm not your next of kin, and Dad wasn't returning my calls so I couldn't have him do whatever magic he does to fix your records. And you had no family. You had no one."

"But you did get in to see me, babe," he said gently.

"Thank goodness for Senator Mendoza."

Gabe scowled at the mention of the senator. "I hope you ripped him a new one."

"He lost his uncle, Gabe," Beatrice quietly reminded him.

"It's still no excuse for putting a lot of people in danger," Gabe said darkly. "There are protocols for a reason. Was it even worth the information he got from his uncle? Wait. How did you miss the uncle on your background check? Even if he didn't list him down, he would have popped up."

"They use the term uncle loosely. He's the"—Beatrice paused, as though working something in her head—"husband of his mother's second cousin. His cousin—the uncle's son, and I'm using the term cousin also loosely here—is the head of the leading paramilitary force in the country."

"The purpose of the trip was a directive from POTUS though. That's already a conflict of interest right there. Even with the degree of blood separation, family ties in South America are very close."

"True, but Senator Mendoza already knows how to work the bureaucracy of the Colombian government."

Gabe leaned against the pillows, suddenly tired. Maybe he did need to stay longer in the hospital. He held out his hand. She curled her fingers with his as he tugged her closer.

"I didn't mean to upset you," he whispered. "I know I would lose my mind if something like this happened to you."

Beatrice gave a small smile, and with her other hand, she stroked the side of his jaw. "Just another week, okay? Please? I don't want anything to happen to you, Gabe."

"I love you, Beatrice."

"I love you, too."

THREE WEEKS later

THERE WAS some truth that an idle mind was the devil's playground. He had been home for two weeks after almost spending a month in the hospital, and he was extremely restless. His brain was working through several theories, none of them making sense. He wanted to do his own investigation on Steve Ryker. But since the police were involved, all evidence had been sequestered and inaccessible. BSI was able to get some information because the attack affected their client. Domingo Ventura, who was the leader of the Fuego gang's northeastern chapter, maintained that Steve Ryker, who Ventura knew as Vladimir Volkov, was a Russian mercenary hired by an enemy of the senator. Ryker/Volkov bribed some gang members who were sympathetic to the groups fighting the Colombian government and who didn't want the armed conflict to end.

Somehow that didn't add up, because the Skulls already confirmed that Ventura was aware of Ryker/Volkov's previous plans.

Did Ventura double-cross Ryker/Volkov and tip off the Skulls?

Was it about money? A cut in the drugs?

Why did they kill Senator Mendoza's uncle? They could have easily taken out the senator instead.

Unless the senator was dirty.

"Fuck," Gabe muttered, rubbing his hand over his face. Rhino whined, got down from his dog bed, and shuffled over to Gabe. Laying his head on his lap, Rhino looked up at him with concerned dark eyes.

"I'm okay, boy." He scratched Rhino's head affectionately. "Just a little frustrated and feeling helpless." *And useless.*

Rhino's ears perked and turned his head toward the door. Gabe really wondered about his dog's deafness because it appeared he sensed his surroundings very well, or was it just a sixth sense?

Gabe strained his ears and heard the faint click of heels. Beatrice was home.

Because of his injuries, their relationship was developing at a crawl. She insisted on sleeping in the guest bedroom, saying she was such an active sleeper, she might hit him accidentally. He was so happy she'd finally taken him back—even though it took him almost dying to do so—he let her have her way. However, it was getting ridiculous and he was feeling strong enough to manhandle—correction—handle her. Gabe smirked at the direction of his inner monologue.

Keys jingled at the door before it opened. Rhino gave a happy woof and eagerly circled Beatrice as she made her way into the house. Gabe frowned. He had noticed this since he got home. Apparently, the four weeks he had spent in the hospital had been detrimental to his dog's obedience. Beatrice had spoiled him.

He had to take back control of his house, damn it. "Rhino, bad dog."

"Oh, Gabe, he's fine," Beatrice said, cooing down to his dog and scratching his ear. "Such a handsome dog. Yes, you are."

Oh, hell no, Gabe thought darkly. "Babe, a word please."

Beatrice straightened up. "I picked up Chinese food. I hope you don't mind."

"Chinese is fine."

Gabe watched her lower the bags on the kitchen counter while he patiently waited for her to give him her attention.

"What do you want to talk about?" Her eyes searched his face.

"First things first." He pulled her into his arms and gave her a deep thorough kiss. He lifted his head. "Hi."

"Hello to you too, Terminator."

Gabe mock scowled at her. "You'll pay for that later."

Beatrice's tinkling laughter made his cock jerk. Hmm . . . why not sooner?

"Well?"

"Well, what?"

She smiled at him knowingly. "You wanted a word with me?"

Oh, yeah. Shit.

"You need to stop babying Rhino. He's a military dog."

"I'm not babying him. He's a sweet dog."

Gabe groaned. "Babe, he's a war hero. You're turning him into a pussy."

"Don't be ridiculous, Gabe." Her lips were twitching.

"Babe, I'm serious here. When anyone comes in, he needs to sit patiently until you give him attention."

"He's not in the military anymore, Gabe."

"He's a huge dog, Beatrice. I don't want him knocking people down because he gets too excited."

"All right, you have a point there."

"Also, I know you've seen nothing but his playful and gentle side, but make no mistake, he can get aggressive and deadly. It's important you establish control over him."

"How aggressive?"

"He'll rip someone apart if they hurt you."

Beatrice's eyes widened.

"His senses are not all there. He's partially blind in his left eye and he's deaf in his left ear. He may not react positively if he's startled."

Gabe lowered his voice. "To calm him down against strangers you say *friendlies*."

"Okay," Beatrice smiled as she looked at Rhino who was lying down on the kitchen floor with his head between his paws. She beamed at him. "Are we like—talking about being responsible parents to Rhino?"

Gabe's breathing hitched. Beatrice's eyes were teasing, and maybe he was reading too much into her words.

"Yeah," he whispered, his head lowered again to capture her lips. His tongue penetrated her mouth, feeling extremely possessive.

He suddenly had Beatrice on her back on the kitchen island, her skirts bunched around her hips—and fuck him—the sight of her lacy garters clipped sexily to the top of her stocking shit sent all his blood rushing to his dick.

"Gabe, your wounds—"

"Shut it, poppy."

He ran his hands up and down her legs before lifting them up and spreading her before him.

"Look at that pussy," Gabe whispered reverently. Her pink nether lips were peeking out from the minuscule crotch of her tiny panties and they were glistening. She was as turned on as he was and he was aching to lick her clean.

"Gabe, stop—"

"Hell no," he rasped.

"Not in front of Rhino."

Damn it to hell. Cockblocked by a dog.

Gabe straightened and yanked Beatrice to a sitting position. He plucked her from the kitchen island, wincing a bit when some of his injuries bitched at him, and ignoring her protests, he carried her to the guest bedroom.

"GABE! You're going to hurt yourself," Beatrice screeched as Gabe carried her across the bedroom. He dropped her on the mattress making her bounce.

"I've endured enough of your coddling, woman," Gabe muttered. He got on top of her, shoving her legs apart to accommodate his hips. "That shit stops now." His eyes blazed with so much heat, so much want, she thought she'd combust under their intensity. The golden flecks in his whiskey eyes glittered as they basked under the glow of the lamp.

"You're insane—umph!"

His mouth crashed down on hers and shut her up. His tongue demanded passage between her lips. She yielded. He groaned deep in his throat as his pelvis rubbed against her own heat. She could feel her wetness against her panties, a throbbing need begging for release.

Gabe slipped his hand under her sweater and squeezed a breast. He pushed up the fabric, using both hands now to push her breasts out of her bra.

"Love your tits, love them," he murmured against her skin before his warm mouth took over. As he suckled one breast, a hand slipped between her legs, his fingers insinuating past the crotch as he fondled the slick, swollen folds of her pussy.

"Ah, fuck, babe." He released her nipple with a pop as he captured her lips once more, thrusting his tongue in her mouth as he worked a finger inside her. A guttural sound came from his throat as he slipped a second finger inside her, stretching her further as his thumb massaged her clit. His fingers curved up and she exploded.

Beatrice pulled her lips away and screamed. Her hands gripped his hair pushing his head lower. "Gabe! Oh, God. I need more . . . please . . ."

He dropped small kisses down her chest, kissing each breast once more before trailing a path down her torso. He pushed her thighs apart, for a moment, the cold air clashed with the heat emanating from her core. Gabe released her garter clips and then her panties disappeared. A warm breath and a wet stroke lifted her in an arch as his mouth began its torturous assault on her pussy. First gentle, then voracious, he sucked, licked, and thrust his tongue into her core, meeting her wetness with a feral hunger.

She felt a renewed gush of moisture leave her, felt him growl closer into her pussy, and when he fastened his lips on her clit and sucked, a pulsing sensation burst from her center.

She cried out, her legs quaking, toes curling. An elemental desire to make him lose control flushed through her blood.

He was still lapping her up when she carefully positioned her feet on his shoulders and pushed him away.

"Not done eating you, babe," Gabe growled, his eyes pinned her down with a possessive gleam. Seeing his mouth wet with her juices renewed the throb between her legs, but she was determined to suck that gorgeous cock. She had not done it in three years. And she wanted to blow his mind.

"Don't you want my lips around your cock?" she asked suggestively.

Gabe visibly shuddered. He closed his eyes. "You don't have to, poppy."

Men are such hypocrites. Beatrice pushed Gabe down on his back. She pulled down his sweats and exhaled sharply. All of Gabe was hard all right—the man, his muscles, and his thick, long, suckable erection. Even the way it was veined was beautiful, angry and pulsating hungrily on her palm. He hissed sharply when her fingers closed reverently around it.

"Oh, my God," Beatrice just stared and licked her lips. "How I've missed this."

"Babe, you gonna do something about my dick or are you just gonna stare at it?" Gabe said in a strangled voice. "Dying here. Just wrap those fuckable lips around it and suck."

Beatrice laughed briefly before taking the head of his cock

between her lips. She swirled her tongue around the sensitive tip. Cupping his balls, she bobbed, stroking her tongue down his length and sucking on the way up. His fingers dug into her hair as he cursed.

"That's it, babe, take me deeper." He pumped his hips into her face in rhythm.

She continued her assault. Going faster, harder, relaxing her throat to take him in—almost gagging. He was too big and she couldn't take him all. She was out of practice and she teared up, but she relished the power of driving him crazy.

"Take me deeper." There was desperation in his tone now as he punched his hips up. Beatrice felt his cock bunch and harden at the point of release. She took him the deepest she could manage and hollowed her cheeks for maximum suction.

"Holy sweet fuck!" Gabe groaned as his cum geysered straight to the back of her throat. She swallowed as much as she could, licking him up and savoring every last drop of him. She swiped her tongue around his girth until he was spotless.

They were both breathing hard when she was done. She looked up at him. His hooded eyes looked down at her. His hand reached out and wiped a tear from her cheek.

"You okay?" he whispered.

Beatrice kissed him right at the sexy hollow of his pelvis; his still erect cock jerked in response. "Never better."

"Sorry I didn't warn you."

"I know when you're about to come, Gabe."

He smirked. "I guess we went straight to dessert."

"Yes, we did. Now I'm hungry for real food." Beatrice pushed away from him, but he caught her hand.

"Babe." His eyes searched hers as if gauging her mood. "Will you sleep with me tonight?"

Beatrice paused. She had made excuses about sleeping in the same bed because it was too intimate, too fast. She realized she didn't have the same reservations she had two weeks ago when he had come home from the hospital.

She met his steady gaze. "I would love that."

FRANK WILKES JOGGED LEISURELY along the length of the National Mall. There was a thin crowd of tourists who braved the nippy mid-January morning. He stopped by a bench and checked his shoelaces. A man in a trench coat approached the bench and sat a respectable distance away and flicked open a newspaper.

"Any news?" Wilkes asked the man.

"Not a peep from Benjamin Porter in almost two months."

"He hasn't made contact with his daughter?"

"Not from what I can glean."

"This troubles me greatly. Someone's been poking around in our Colombian operation, asking questions. We've already gotten rid of the senator's uncle, and I've increased encryption around our project. I was hoping with Ryker's death, they would lower their guard," Wilkes replied, straightening up and jogging in place. "How's our friend Sullivan?"

The man turned the pages on the paper. "He's recovered enough to be guarding Ms. Porter again."

Wilkes sighed. "I never intended to use her as a pawn. That was all on Ryker. However, I'm not above giving the admiral some incentive to come out of hiding. Will Sullivan be a problem when we execute Plan B?"

"I've thrown in enough issues to redirect everyone's attention to Senator Mendoza. With Ryker dead and with not one attempt on either Ms. Porter or Sullivan in the last six weeks, I can say it won't be too long before we'll have a clear shot at her."

"Good. Do what you have to do, Zach." Wilkes drew his hoodie closer and took off on a brisk run.

10

THERE WAS much chatter and ribbing in the brainstorming session at the BSI conference room. It was packed with security personnel; most of BSI's team leads were present as well as their field agents. Beatrice just finished her presentation of job forecasts for the current fiscal year. She was fabulous. Gabe could get a hard-on just listening to her talk about threat matrixes, security protocols, and ambush preparedness. There was a lot of hooting when she told the story of how she busted the balls of a rival security consultant who tried to steal her client. He had a disgruntled feeling that half the men in the room were having the same lascivious thoughts as he was and that made him want to break something.

Beatrice curtsied dramatically after her presentation. As she made her way to the back of the room—back to him—she was waylaid by more than one man too many. Handshakes were fine, but it was the bear hugs that hazed Gabe's vision in red. There was one particular son of a bitch who was copping a feel; even he could tell by Beatrice's tight smile that she didn't like it. She firmly removed the man's hand from her ass and patted the guy's cheek.

Fuck it. Scene or not, he was dragging her out of there. As

he moved forward, he caught Reece's eyes on him, expression unreadable. Gabe ignored him and noticed Beatrice was about to pass Reece when the asshole pulled her on his lap. Beatrice laughed, while Nate chuckled.

A frisson of jealousy burned through his veins because, unlike the other hugs, Beatrice seemed perfectly comfortable on Nate's lap, as if it was something natural that always happened between them. It felt like an eternity before he reached the pair, probably because Gabe had been imagining several ways to tear the other man apart.

His displeasure must have been evident because Beatrice's laughter died when her eyes fell upon him.

"Gabe?"

"Let's go." His demand brooked no argument. He grabbed her hand and yanked her out of Nate's lap.

There was a beginning of a smirk on the other man's face.

Gabe leaned in so he could rasp in his ear. "Keep your hands off her if you don't want to lose any fingers."

"Gabe," Beatrice berated in a harsh whisper. "What the hell is wrong with you?"

Nate's mouth curved into a grin, but his eyes were hostile.

The jerk did it deliberately to get a rise out of him. Asshole.

The room had gone quiet, all eyes on the three of them.

Beatrice jerked her hand out of his grasp and walked over to Travis who was regarding the scene with amusement. She said a few words to the BSI boss and left the room without a backward glance at Gabe.

Everyone was now staring at him. Gabe had taken a lot from her. His pride had taken a beating. He'd been cautious with her because he destroyed her three years ago. He had a lot to atone for, but this was humiliating. He was put in his place. He was a bodyguard, not her man.

A bodyguard would follow her without question. Fists clenched at his sides, head slightly bowed, he stalked after her.

The door to her condominium slammed open and Beatrice walked straight to the kitchen to get a glass of wine. She was pissed, seething actually, at Gabe's unreasonable jealousy. The trip to her condo was planned since she had to pick up some more clothes, but she had a strong desire to remain behind and let Gabe go home and stew by himself.

The man in question prowled right behind her, anger evident in every line of his body.

"You had no cause to confront Nate!" Beatrice had been repeating the statement like a mantra since the encounter in the BSI conference room.

"You never answered my question," Gabe said coldly. "Do you always let his hands get all over you?"

"It's Nate," Beatrice screeched in frustration. "Nate is affectionate. He is never inappropriate."

"He pulled you on his lap; that's as inappropriate as it gets," Gabe shot back. "I've let the hugs pass a couple of times, but I have my limits. I merely told him if he didn't want to lose his fingers, he should keep his hands off you."

"That was embarrassing."

"No, I'm merely establishing that I'm not the type of man to stand by while another man gets your ass on his lap. Reece understood. He gave me the stink-eye, but did you hear him say anything?"

Beatrice's eyes narrowed. "Wait. Back up. You've let it pass a couple of times? So now because I've taken you back, you think you can start acting like a Neanderthal as if you own me? What's this? Lull me into false complacency? Get your hooks into me and then start acting like a jerk not only to me but to my friends?"

His face hardened perceptively. "I wasn't being a jerk at all. You need to be able to tell the difference when your man is being a jerk or when he's giving a damn. Because, babe, if I'm not reacting when other men have their paws on you, you should be worried."

He was right, but Beatrice still had her jaw set stubbornly, her arms crossed over her chest. Gabe stepped into her space, his arms circling around her and pressing fully into her. His mouth lowered to her ear. "You've given me an in, babe. I'm not getting out. So you can scream and protest as much as you want. Tongue-fucking you and you sucking me off ain't enough anymore. I've given you plenty of time to get used to being back with me."

"What are you saying?"

Gabe backed her against the center island and spun her around, bending her over the edge. Beatrice felt her heart pound against her breastbone in . . . anticipation? There was a twitch between her legs and her panties were already damp. Gabe's crotch hit her ass—he was already hard.

"Gabe," she hissed weakly in protest.

"Shut up!" He growled in her ear as he bent over her. His hands shoved her skirt up. She got wetter. "That attitude is sexy, and it makes me hard as hell. But it's only because I can't wait to fuck it out of you." His hands fisted her panties and ripped them off.

Beatrice tried to lever up. "Gabe, damn it, that's an expensive—" He pushed her down and started rubbing his erection against her.

"I'll buy you more," he groaned. He worked his fingers inside her and started stroking in and out. Beatrice writhed underneath him, her climax building as his fingers hammered inside her. She was on the brink when she vaguely felt his hand between them working his fly.

She felt the blunt head of his cock at her slick entrance. Without another warning, Gabe slammed his cock deep inside her. She moaned as he filled and stretched her to her limit.

"Fuck, you feel so good," he whispered raggedly, still holding her down with his upper body while flexing his hips and thrusting his cock inside her like a battering ram. He relentlessly pounded her into the kitchen island. She was reaching a new height with this joining, not having felt this connection the past two times they'd had sex. This time it was with the security of commitment, and this warmed her over until he pulled out.

His weight left her and she was flipped around, her legs hit his shoulders and his mouth was on her, feasting on her pussy. The wildness of how he devoured her had her exploding in unending pulsating sensations. She must have screamed or cried; she didn't know anymore.

Just when she thought she was cresting on her pleasure, he lifted her and before she knew it, her back crashed against the wall and he was deep inside her once again. Hammering her hard, his cock was driving deep into her womb; she felt some pain mixed with pleasure.

"Am I hurting you?" Gabe grunted, not letting up on the pistoning of his hips.

Does it hurt?

"Beatrice?" The intensity in his eyes seared into hers.

She moaned low; she wanted everything, the pleasure, the pain. All of it. "Harder, Gabe. Make me yours."

Her words snapped whatever control he had. She heard a growl, almost inhuman in its utterance, as he canted his hips, shifted her in his arms and pounded deeper. They were banging hard against the wall; she'd probably have bruises on her back tomorrow, but it felt too delicious to care about that right now.

"Oh, God, harder!" she cried when it hit her. The incandescent release shook her entire body, curling her toes as she arched away from him. Her pussy closed down on him and clenched his cock in a silken fist.

"Fuuuuuuck!" Gabe roared, turning rigid with his climax, his fingers gripping her tighter. His face hit the curve of her throat; rivulets of sweat hit her as a warmth cloaked her body.

They sank to the floor together with her cradled on his lap. She realized, save for her missing underwear, they were still fully clothed.

"That . . . was good," Beatrice murmured. Gabe had been nuzzling her neck, nipping her skin playfully.

He lifted his head and stared down at her. "Good? If you'd screamed any louder, you would need new windows. Fucking incredible was what that was."

Beatrice giggled. God, she had been a giggling ninny lately. She buried her face in his chest as she inhaled the pure masculine scent of him.

"I didn't use a condom," Gabe said.

"I'm protected and I'm clean."

"That's good."

She narrowed her eyes at him. "Not sure what you mean."

"It means we're skipping condoms from now on," Gabe said. "That's what I mean."

"You're getting bossy, mister." Beatrice poked a finger at his chest.

"Time to lay down the law, babe."

"Excuse me?" Beatrice retorted.

Gabe eyed her intently. "I feel a discussion coming. I'd like to get off this floor because my ass is killing me."

Beatrice slid off him, and with her skirt hitched up, crawling on all fours to get up, her bare ass was like waving a red flag at a bull.

She was attacked from behind, her hips yanked back, Gabe behind her already working his stiff cock into her. He bent over her and whispered, "Discussions can wait, my dick can't."

He fucked her hard on the floor.

Gabe sat back against the headboard, his eyes lazily following Beatrice around while she packed some clothes in her suitcase. He'd finally fucked her in every sense of the word. They had been circling around the sex thing for weeks now—had been doing oral the past two weeks—both of them wary to take it further to the next step because the two times they had fucked ended up disastrously. For his part, he was afraid that if she rejected him after the third time, they would be done. He patiently renewed their friendship, their need for each other—and yes, she was right, he wanted to get his hooks into her because hers had always been deeply embedded in him. So deeply interlaced in the fiber of who he was there was no way for him to simply yank her out of his system because she was knit tight in every cell of him.

Still, it wasn't enough. He was a possessive son of a bitch, and he wanted more. The fates must be laughing down on him because he had to go and fall in love with possibly the most stubborn and independent woman on the planet.

"Move in with me," he stated simply.

"What?"

"Move in with me, Beatrice. You know that's where we're heading." Gabe shrugged. "So, just move in with me."

"Gabe, you know how excited I was when I scored this condo?" Beatrice unloaded her dirty clothes from the suitcase to the laundry bag. "Prime location in Washington DC."

"I bet the annual fees are a killer," Gabe muttered.

"Beats renting office space," Beatrice said. "Now that you're feeling better, maybe I should—"

"Stop right there," Gabe snapped. He got up from his relaxed perch on the bed and walked toward her. "You're doing it again. Backpedaling. What the fuck do I need to do, huh, Beatrice? Why are you afraid to get close to me?"

She opened her mouth as if to protest, but shook her head. "I don't know. I like how you make me feel and it scares me." Her luminous green eyes locked on his with all honesty.

"I'm trying, Gabe. Believe me, I am. Because deep down, I know you're not going to hurt me again. But I need you to have a life outside of me."

"What do you mean?" Gabe glared at her.

"Threat's over, right? Ryker is dead. It's been quiet for over six weeks." Beatrice sighed. "We need to go through normal. You know what I mean? I don't want you to be my bodyguard. I was never the target to begin with, you were."

"I still don't know what you're asking."

"I'm asking you to find something else to do besides babysit me."

"You've done nothing but babysit me for a month in the hospital," Gabe argued. "Why can't I do the same for you?"

"That's different and you know it," Beatrice retorted.

"Babe, are you worried I'm going to run out of money, be the drifter boyfriend? Because I assure you, I have plenty saved up. I'm not letting you support me."

"Don't be ridiculous. That thought never crossed my mind because you're not that kind of man."

He sure wasn't.

"I do have a plan once I'm a hundred percent sure you're out of danger."

Beatrice's eyes lit up. "Oh, what? Are you going to ask Travis for a job?"

"Fuck, no," Gabe muttered. "Protecting that body of yours is one thing, but that's not the type of work I like to do."

"Not—"

"Neither am I doing undercover work ever again—long term ones at least. I'll probably contract out to security companies that work with the government, engaging in short-duration strike operations."

Beatrice didn't look happy. "Not sure I like the sound of that."

Gabe rolled his eyes. "You wanted me to do something else."

"There are only a few security companies I trust, BSI being one of them," Beatrice said. "I don't want you doing anything risky without someone I trust to have your back."

"What do you want me to do, Beatrice?" Gabe asked in exasperation. "You don't want me to be your bodyguard. You don't want me to work for security companies other than BSI. Give me something here."

"How about private investigation?"

Gabe's brow shot up. "That could work. But there'll be some level of undercover work and confidentiality I can't share with you."

"That's fine," Beatrice smiled smugly. "I'll get you in contact with a friend of mine."

Gabe didn't trust that smile. He'd seen it one too many times whenever she was scheming with Doug. "What does your friend do?"

"He's a divorce lawyer."

Hell, no.

"I am not about to sit in a car with an overpriced camera," Gabe pushed through gritted teeth, "just so I can spy on unfaithful spouses."

"I'm telling you, Gabe, that market is red hot in DC." Beatrice walked up to him and pressed her body against his. "Think about all the perverted politicians you're going to take down."

"You're joking, right?" She better be. Otherwise, she didn't know him at all.

She grinned. "It was worth a shot."

She tried to pull away from him, but he tightened his arms around her. "You need to trust I'll find something that you're going to be comfortable with. I'm not saying it'll have no level of danger. I'm not saying my whereabouts might be secret. All I'm saying is, I'll always come back to you."

"You can't promise that, Gabe," she whispered.

"Yeah, I can. I did this last time. Took me three fucking

years, but I held on to the promise of you, Beatrice. The difference is, I'm not putting you through that unknown again."

"I'm wondering, what if I had been married or with someone else?"

His grip tightened. Beatrice yelped, so he eased up. The thought of her with someone else was triggering a dark part in him. "I'd kill him."

Beatrice laughed nervously. "No, really, what would you have done?"

His eyes must have changed because she frowned at him. "Gabe?"

No. It's Dmitry.

He pulled her close and whispered the warning in her ear. "I will kill to have you."

Gabe released her before he frightened her more. He backed away from the room, holding her eyes. "I'll wait for you in the living room."

WHAT THE HELL JUST HAPPENED?

Goose bumps ran down her back. That was not Gabriel Sullivan. That was not the Gabe she knew. That voice was menacing. Her hands were suddenly clammy, and they were shaking when she folded some clothes into her suitcase.

I will kill to have you.

Why didn't that sound like an empty threat? It certainly didn't sound like mere alpha-male, chest-thumping posturing.

It was a warning issued with conviction.

Beatrice spied her wine by the nightstand and took a heavy sip. In fact, she drained it. Yet, she didn't want to flee or retreat from him. Behind his dark gimlet eyes was a storm pulling her into its center. There was a yearning for her to be his anchor. His sanctuary?

She finished packing and rolled the suitcase to the living room. Gabe was sitting on the couch, bent forward, elbows on knees, hands linked.

He looked up, and Beatrice flinched. His face was hard, harsh even.

"Don't," he rasped, standing up. "I will never hurt you."

"I know you won't," Beatrice replied levelly.

"You look frightened."

"Frightened, no. Seeing this side of you, though, is unnerving."

Gabe gave a short bark of mirthless laughter. "I don't have a split personality, Beatrice."

"I know you don't."

"What exactly do you see?"

"Ruthlessness."

His expression shuttered. "Ruthlessness has always been a part of me. You know that."

"I don't know; it's just . . . weird, okay?" Her knees went weak so she sat down.

Finally, his face softened and he crouched in front of her. He captured her knees between his, splaying his hands on her thighs. "You have nothing to fear from me."

Beatrice huffed. "It's not that. You're just intense."

His jaw tightened. He gripped her chin and the ruthless gleam was back in his eyes. "Yes. I'm intense when it comes to you. I'm ruthless when it comes to you. That is never going to change. Deal with it."

Beatrice jerked her chin away. "Not helping, Gabe," she hissed.

"Babe, I am who I am. In all the time we've been together, have I ever given you a reason to fear me?"

"No." Even now she was not afraid of him, but she was afraid of what his jealousy, coupled with this cold ruthlessness, could mean to people around her. "Just . . . just control your jealousy, okay? Threatening to kill a hypothetical husband or lover is freaky enough."

"I'll rein it in." His chilly smile was not reassuring and neither were the words that followed. "Just make sure your male colleagues know their place. In deference to your professional reputation, I'll try not to act like a psycho boyfriend."

"That'll be appreciated."

"Just remember—I have my limits."

Shit.

"Honey, I'm home."

A smile played on Beatrice lips. It had been three days since Gabe finally let her go about her business without shadowing her. Not that he'd been an intrusive bodyguard at all. Despite his imposing presence, he had a way of disappearing and reappearing as needed. It freaked her out sometimes, these Houdini acts, but she knew even if she couldn't see him, he had his eyes on her constantly.

Rhino greeted her at the door, and like she and Gabe had discussed, she'd been more firm with the dog, but no less affectionate. She'd admit to bending the rules a bit, and Rhino, being the clever dog, played along. It was like she and Rhino had a little secret all their own.

Rhino sat obediently this time and waited for Beatrice to give him attention.

"Hey, boy," she bent down and rubbed his ears. "Where's your master?" She straightened and called out. "Gabe?"

That was when she saw the note.

Meeting an old buddy for coffee.

Picking up groceries on the way home.

Left you a voice message.

G.

"DAMN IT," Beatrice muttered. She was drained from the last meeting today and forgot to take her phone off silent and check her messages. She did have several missed calls from different numbers and an equal amount of voice mails. She'd check them tonight or tomorrow morning. If they were urgent and business-related, Doug would get a call as well, and so far, none of the calls were from her assistant.

Which means . . .

She could take a leisurely walk around the neighborhood with Rhino. She quickly changed into more comfortable clothes and sneakers and was out the door with an eager German Shepherd at heel. Trotting right beside her as she broke into a slight jog, Rhino snuffled repeatedly in canine contentment.

Beatrice welcomed the shock of frigid air in her lungs replacing the stale stuffy one rendered from dry-heated office spaces. She loved taking walks in this historic neighborhood with its brick walkways and quaint Victorian row houses. If there was one place that would make her give up her DC condo, it would be a house in Old Town Alexandria.

A nagging sensation suddenly prickled her skin. She noticed a beat-up car slowing to crawl right beside her. There were two occupants and the way they were watching her trilled the alarms in her head. They were approaching an intersection and her uneasiness escalated. Paranoid or not, she wasn't tempting fates.

"Come on, Rhino, let's head back," she muttered to him. She turned around and was startled to see a man approaching with menacing eyes intent on her. A white panel van was also slowing down.

She looked back at the first car. It had parked at the intersection and the passenger stepped out clearly waiting for her to make a move. She was trapped.

Before she could react, the man in front of her yanked down his ski mask. Rhino immediately went ape-shit and tugged in front of her, growling fiercely. Ski-mask man pulled out a gun and aimed for Rhino.

"No!" Beatrice screamed as Rhino lunged straight for the man's gun hand, wrenching the leash from her hold. She heard the muted pop of the silencer, but the shot went wide as Rhino brought the man down.

Everything happened simultaneously. She was going for Rhino and making a run for it when the side doors of the van flew open and masked men jumped out. Beatrice didn't waste time counting how many, her intent was getting herself and Rhino out of there.

Spectators were starting to gather and shout for help.

An arm banded around her waist and she was hauled off the ground, a sweet-smelling substance filled her nose. She kicked out, and heard a grunt, but she was fast losing control of her limbs and her vision was fading into black.

There was yelling, from the crowd or from her assailants, Beatrice didn't know. She heard another muffled sound and Rhino yelping in agony. More angry shouting.

Noooo . . .

11

GABE CURSED the car that pulled into a parking spot closer to his house. Thankfully, there was no vehicle behind him, so he backed up to another space a couple of cars down. Exiting his Chevy Silverado, he collected the grocery bags, bumped the door close, and bleeped the locks. Balancing the bags, he took a leisurely pace to his home.

When he turned on his street, he grew alarmed to see a crowd gathering right in front of his house and a smear of red on the pavement.

"What the fuck is going on?" Gabe demanded, shouldering past the throng. What he saw brought him to his knees. He dropped the bags.

Rhino was bloodied, panting hard, and whining softly.

"Buddy?" Gabe whispered, checking quickly for the source of the bleeding.

"He crawled home," a person in the crowd said. "Some of us tried to help him, but he was growling and snapping at us."

Gabe found the wound near the neck.

One of the spectators shoved a roll of gauze in front of his face. "Here. I ran home and grabbed this." Gabe recognized his neighbor next door.

Recovering from the shock of seeing his dog bleeding out on his front stoop, the implication hit him like a ton of bricks.

Beatrice!

While working first aid on Rhino, Gabe asked. "Did anyone see a redhead?"

Everyone started speaking simultaneously. Frustrated, Gabe decided to finish treating Rhino before interrogating any witnesses. When he lifted him, Rhino tried to fight the movement and cried in distress.

"Easy, boy," Gabe fought the heart-rending emotion of seeing his dog injured. He lifted a chin to the nearest person. "Did you see what went down?"

"Yes, I—"

"Come with me," Gabe ordered. He wended his way through the assembly, which parted easily before him. "Tell me everything. How many? What car."

As the details of what happened were revealed, Gabe tried to quell the rising panic in his chest. Beatrice was rendered unconscious and dumped into a white van. There were three men wearing ski-masks—one would be sporting a dog bite on his right arm. Gabe thanked the man for the information and loaded Rhino in the vehicle. Police cruisers turned into the neighborhood, but Gabe had no time to talk to them.

Pulling up emergency veterinary hospitals from his phone, he was relieved that there was one a couple of blocks over. Afterward he called Travis.

"Blake."

"Travis, it's Gabe."

"What do you want?"

"Cut the hostility, Lieutenant," Gabe snapped. "Beatrice was taken. They shot my dog, and I'm on my way to the emergency vet."

There was a muffled curse before Travis said, "What can I do?"

"I need you to scope out my neighborhood. The cops just

got here. Get them to back off. Find out more from witnesses if you can." Gabe dictated his address as well as the intersection where Beatrice was nabbed. "See if you can gain access to traffic cams."

"Porter should have it."

"He's been off the grid for almost two months. But I'm calling him next."

"Gotcha. Anything else?"

"Hurry, Blake."

"Will do."

Gabe punched the admiral's number. It went straight to voicemail. *That son of a bitch.* "Porter, you better be dead or dying. I couldn't raise you for weeks. Your daughter almost died, and you couldn't even fucking show up. Well, now they've taken her, you hear me? They've. Taken. Her. Got your attention yet, Admiral? Just"—Gabe didn't know what else to say—"thought you should know."

He put the phone away and looked over to Rhino, who was whining softly. "Hang in there, buddy. We're almost there." His dog did not survive an IED blast only to be cut down by a sorry-ass schmuck's bullet.

He was innervated with rage so powerful he had to grip the steering wheel tightly to keep from punching the dashboard. His vision blurred, and the sound of cars got louder. He willed his heart rate and breathing to even out.

His woman. Taken.

His dog. Shot.

The past six months were a struggle to define his place in normal society. But maybe he shouldn't fight who he really was, because that person from the past was the person needed to fight this unknown enemy.

The people who took Beatrice knew him, but they had forgotten what he could become.

A stone cold killer.

IT WAS A WAITING GAME.

Waiting for the emergency vet to tell him if Rhino would live or die.

Waiting for Travis to call him back with a clue to find Beatrice.

Waiting.

Gabe hated feeling helpless. He hated how things were out of his hands and out of his control.

He had been on the phone with Travis, desperate to join the search for Beatrice, but the need to know that Rhino was okay was his brain's way of managing his emotions in order to get centered. Travis further set him straight. "Gabe you need to let us handle this. You are in no shape to do the investigation objectively. I'm not saying Nate and I are any better given our friendship with Bee, but you don't have your head on straight right now. Do you remember back with the SEALs, before we headed out on a mission, our minds needed to be clear? We needed to be square?"

"Yes," Gabe bit off.

"Same rule applies here. You're emotionally compromised. You need to get a grip on your shit, or you're going to hinder rather than help find Beatrice. You have to back off. We got this."

HIS ATTENTION RETURNED to the present when a female veterinarian dressed in blue scrubs opened the door to the reception area.

"Mr. Sullivan?" the vet addressed him. He had met her earlier when he brought Rhino in and his dog was admitted for immediate surgery.

"How is he?" His voice was gruff.

"He's stable. You did good administering the first aid."

The vet's voice and face were grim, belying the good news. "How did Rhino get shot?"

"I didn't shoot him, if that's what you're implying," Gabe responded. "That matter is under investigation. I don't have any details."

"Fair enough. I do need to report incidents of animal abuse."

"I don't give a fuck what you need to report," Gabe snapped. "All I give a fuck about is my dog."

Exhaling deeply, the vet said, "There was an exit wound above the scapula. To be sure, we did an x-ray and there were no signs of the bullet. There were some bone fragments we had to clean up."

"Will he make a full recovery?"

"I'm optimistic, but it will be slow because of his age and there might be occasional pain for the rest of his life."

Gabe nodded.

"We would like to keep him overnight for observation." The vet scanned through Rhino's chart. "He's partially deaf and blind?"

"He was a military dog. Got caught in an IED blast."

The vet's face softened. "You have a tough boy, Mr. Sullivan."

A lump lodged in Gabe's throat. "Can I see him?"

"Sure. He's heavily sedated though, but we've moved him into recovery."

The vet nodded for him to follow her through the door.

A long stretch of hallway with smaller rooms on either side led to a sprawling facility with glass walls. Monitoring equipment was grouped around several surgical tables. Toward one corner were two additional glass-paned operating theaters, while another corner were sections separated by curtains.

A veterinary technician was laying Rhino on a table.

"We need to monitor his blood pressure and other vitals throughout the night," the vet said.

A section of his fur was shaved above his shoulder, revealing the stitches holding together battered flesh. Gabe let the vet-tech finish getting Rhino settled in before he stepped close to the table.

"Take your time." The vet drew the curtains closed.

His fingers gently threaded through Rhino's fur. Gabe couldn't believe in such a short time this creature had come to mean so much to him. His dog courageously protected the woman he loved. Gabe didn't know how he deserved such loyalty and selfless love that Rhino had shown him. During the early days of his transition back to a normal life, Gabe would sit on the floor against the wall with his head on his linked arms resting on his knees as images of what he had seen and done haunted him. Rhino would poke his muzzle through his arms to rest his cold nose on his cheek, forcing Gabe to pet him. His dog wouldn't let him wallow in his darkness. Rhino knew what he needed. Amazing what a simple connection could do, bring a human back from fucked-up man-made misery to experience the basic reason for being—love without exception, given without personal gain, selfless and innocent. Gabe scratched behind Rhino's ears. "You did good, soldier." He absolutely did, in more ways than one.

GABE DROVE BACK to his neighborhood thirty minutes later. Travis called to inform him they had retrieved the bullet that had struck Rhino. Travis also acquired street surveillance footage of the abduction.

Pulling his truck right in front of his house, he watched Nate and Travis exit a black Escalade a couple of cars up. Gabe cut off the engine and got out of his vehicle. His eyes took in the trail of blood still visible on the pavement.

The two men jogged up to him.

"Hey," Nate said. For the first time since Gabe had met the man there was no challenge or animosity in his eyes. Instead, there was sympathy and concern. "Sorry your dog got hurt, but I'm glad he's fine."

Gabe gave a slight nod. "Did the cops give you guys a hard time?"

"I know their chief of police and had them back off. They can't sweep this under the rug forever, so if none of the alphabet agencies take over, they may come back to question you. BSI can take over the case if we can establish what happened to Beatrice impacts the security of our client."

"Thanks for all you've done, man."

Travis clapped one hand on his shoulder. "Listen, Gabe, I know we haven't seen eye to eye since you came back, but Bee missing, trumps all the bullshit between us. We want her back as much as you do."

"Thanks, man," Gabe mumbled. He motioned them to follow him into the house as he strode up the walkway to the front stoop.

Unlocking the door, his eyes fell on Beatrice's purse and other things, which reminded him that just a few hours ago, she had been here . . . safe.

His fists clenched at his sides as it took all he had to control his emotions. As if sensing his struggle, Nate said, "We'll get her back."

"I need to change out of these clothes," Gabe muttered. His shirt and jeans were stained with Rhino's blood. "You can set the laptop over there." He wrote them his Wi-Fi password.

He took a quick shower and threw on a Henley and a fresh pair of jeans.

Nate and Travis were already studying the surveillance footage when he returned downstairs.

"Wait," Nate said. "Back up a little. See that?"

Gabe walked over to the two men. "You guys have something?"

"Fuck," Travis muttered. "You're right."

"We first zeroed in on the white van," Nate said. "Unmarked. Fake plates—we already ran them. Unless a 75-year-old man kidnapped Bee, the plate is a dead end. However, before the van appeared, there was a blue Honda Civic that was shadowing her. Our girl noticed and started to turn back."

"Caught the plates on the Civic when it turned into that intersection," Travis said. "Running tags on it right now."

"A guy stepped out, but he was facing away from the cams," Gabe muttered. Beatrice didn't stand a chance. She was cut off from all corners. "Damn it."

"She did everything right," Nate said sadly. "They were just prepared for everything. Rhino could have surprised them though."

"I doubt it," Gabe said. "They've been watching her." Just the thought of it made him sick. "What did I miss? Who could be after her?"

Porter's enemies, and there were many of them. To the public and to the world, the admiral was a respected officer in the U.S. Navy. His connection to the CIA was simply a rumor. However, if what the admiral said was true and there was a bad seed inside the agency orchestrating the events of the past three to four years, no one was safe.

"We're trying to figure out if it's any of our client's enemies," Travis said. "This has not happened before, at least not to Beatrice since she's simply a top-level contact." Travis's eyes narrowed at Gabe. "If there's anything we need to know, Gabe, now is the time to tell us. You say the admiral is off the grid? We're all you've got."

"I don't know everything myself," Gabe said carefully. "Before the admiral disappeared this last time, he said he had uncovered some troubling intel and may be gone for a while.

Eric Stone was murdered; he was killed with an assassin's concoction." The look on the other two men's faces hardened, so Gabe pressed on. "Five people were killed in the Cloverleaf District; three of them masqueraded as fans of Titanium Rose and attacked Beatrice. Finally, the reporter—"

"Kelly Winters? That was blamed on a Russian diplomat."

"All were Steve Ryker's hits."

"The man who was after Senator Mendoza?" Travis frowned. "This doesn't make sense."

"The target was Senator Mendoza's uncle," Gabe said. "I still don't know why he killed the uncle but left the senator unharmed. I was the secondary target, Travis."

"This explains a lot," Nate said. "We've always wondered why they didn't go after the senator after they had disabled your vehicle."

"So what does Ryker have to do with all the other deaths?"

"He killed them the way Dmitry Yerzov made his assassinations," Gabe replied and told them how he was supposed to be dead.

"Wait, how did he find out your methods enough to do a copycat killing?" Nate asked.

"We suspected he was in cahoots with Crowe."

Just the mention of the double-crossing Crowe brought a storm cloud over Travis's face. "Is Caitlin in danger?"

Gabe wasn't about to sugar coat the situation, because after what had happened, he knew exactly where Travis was coming from. "I don't know, Travis. I have a feeling Ryker's actions were personally motivated, but Porter always believed he had a sponsor for his actions. His exact relationship with Crowe remains a mystery unless we can dig into his background."

"We tried," Nate said. "Short of raising alarms in the CIA databases, we couldn't delve deeper."

"There is a whole other layer on the internet where we can find information," Gabe said. Crowe had functioned as his intel guy. "However, I'm not set up nor savvy enough to navigate those layers without getting caught by the feds."

"You're talking about the Black Plane?" Nate asked. "I'm set up for it and can manage enough, but I think Caitlin is better."

The Black Plane was websites that were not easily categorized by URL-filtering databases because of their ad-hoc infrastructure. Simply put, they were hard to trace and frequently used for clandestine and covert communication and illegal activities. They were also a source of leaked classified information—that was if one knew where to look.

"I hate to get her involved," Travis said. "She freelances for the NSA, and after what went down with the whistleblower, things are too hot right now." He sighed. "However, I know she would do anything to get Beatrice back. And where the hell is Porter?"

Fuck if I know, Gabe thought.

SHE WAS SITTING ON A CHAIR; her hands and feet were tied against it. Her senses were groggy from the chloroform, but Beatrice suspected they had injected her with something else as well. She dazedly took stock of her surroundings—three walls and a mirror, which she suspected was a two-way one. The lighting was from a single fluorescent lamp above.

She was thirsty.

"Good morning, Ms. Porter."

Morning? How long had she been out?

She tried to focus on the mirror. "What do you want from me?" she croaked.

"Your father's whereabouts. We suspect you don't know, do you?"

"You suspect correctly. But why take me?" Beatrice knew, but she wanted them to spell it out.

"He's been causing us problems, Ms. Porter. We want him to back off. Taking you is our message to him."

Beatrice laughed derisively. "You don't know my father. He doesn't care what happens to me. All he cares about is his job."

There was a long stretch of silence.

She tried to place the voice but couldn't. She figured they had used a voice enhancer anyway.

"Poor girl. Seeing how you've been operating so high-profile in Washington DC and no attempt has been made on you so far, you may be right in your assessment."

Beatrice snorted. "Right is an understatement."

"And Sullivan, he seems to care about you?"

Gabe was probably losing his mind right now. *Oh, no, Rhino.* "He probably cares more that you shot his dog, you assholes. We're fuck buddies. I'm sure he can find my replacement easily enough."

Another stretch of silence. A different voice came on. "Ms. Porter, I'm surprised you let a man like Sullivan into your bed."

"He's . . . well-endowed." Despite her situation, Beatrice smirked.

The voice chuckled. "You're just like all the other women he killed."

She reacted. Froze. She struggled to regulate the quickening of her pulse and breathing. "I don't know what you're talking about."

"You mean you don't know he killed people for the mob?"

"No," Beatrice lied. She wasn't sure if these people were just fishing for information. "All I know is he did what he had to do."

"Vague. Was that his answer to you? Did he give you specifics of what he had to do as Dmitry Yerzov?"

Beatrice didn't respond.

"Did you know he was called the *Angel of Death*?"

No she didn't, but she was sure she was about to find out.

"No answer?" This time the laughter was smug. "He didn't tell you, did he?"

Beatrice braced and held her breath.

"He killed children, Ms. Porter. First born sons."

She realized too late she was shaking her head. "No," she whispered.

"He probably told you everyone he killed was guilty," the voice continued. "That's what enforcers of the mob say, Ms. Porter. That's how they justify the kill. Anyone who's in the mafia is a made man, guilty by virtue of association. It doesn't matter whether you're sixty years old or six, you're fair target."

She couldn't control the single sob that escaped her. Her lips were trembling, so she bit down to steady it. No! Gabe swore. Even if most of her senses were numb, the rending of her heart delivered a stabbing pain. How could she accept that the man she loved killed children? How would that be acceptable?

He was protecting a cover.

It didn't make it right.

Don't jump to conclusions.

What if he couldn't deny it?

Ask Gabe. Trust him.

At that moment, Beatrice felt fear. Not fear for an imminent death, but fear that she would die with these conflicted emotions about the man she loved.

As her turmoil continued, she almost didn't notice the voice was speaking to her once more.

". . . so you had no idea, poor Beatrice."

The inflection on her name made her ears prick up. It sounded familiar, but she couldn't place it.

The first man came back on. "This presents such a wonderful opportunity. You do realize that Gabriel Sullivan acted with full orders from your father. That the killing of those children was sanctioned by the admiral."

"You're lying about Gabe and my father," Beatrice lifted her head and stared at the mirror defiantly.

"Ask them."

"How can I when you've abducted me?" she retorted.

Diabolical laughter echoed around her. She was feeling dizzy and the room spun.

"We'll return you to your father, but we'll have a little fun with you first."

"Wh . . . What?"

"Do you know how Dmitry Yerzov sent his messages to Zorin's enemies?"

This time her fear had morphed into something else. Terror.

After the last threat, someone in a ski mask came in and gave her water, but not food. She couldn't eat anyway for her stomach was tied up in knots. They let her use the restroom, but marched her right back to the chair and secured her once more. This time they blindfolded her.

They kept her guessing a few hours more. Maybe it was another whole day. She had lost concept of time.

Footsteps came up to the door. It opened. Her ears picked up maybe three men shuffling into the room.

Something was dragged into the center of the room, probably the table she spotted in the corner earlier. Her chair was suddenly shoved forward and the edge of the table hit her rib cage. She didn't react or say anything.

Her hands were untied and her arms were pulled forward across the table, and held down firmly.

No!

Panic seized her for she knew what was about to happen. Images of Kelly Winters's brutalized body flashed through her mind.

She attempted to fight, yank her hands away, but they were slammed painfully down on the table when she tried.

"The more you fight, the more it's going to hurt," a voice said by her ear.

"You sadistic bastards . . ." she whispered hoarsely.

"Just sending a message."

The pain hit her and she screamed. Unrelenting agony tore through her flesh. Her arms burned with each slice. After a while, all the pain faded, but someone was still screaming.

"Gabe, help me." Beatrice reached out to him in the darkness.

She was suspended in the air, wearing some kind of white garment.

He ran toward her, but never got closer.

Blood started from her hairline, streaming down her face.

Soon, it drenched her body and soaked her clothes.

"Gabe!" she screamed as she was swallowed into the darkness.

"Beatrice!" Gabe shouted, jackknifing into a sitting position. A nightmare, thank fuck. He buried his face in his hands. They were shaking.

Rhino whimpered beside him.

"I'm okay, boy," Gabe whispered, leaning down and petting his head. He had brought Rhino home today, settling him in a dog bed pulled close to the couch where he lay.

But Gabe wasn't okay. Beatrice had been missing for over 24 hours and there were no demands from anyone and every lead they'd taken was a dead end. Was she even still alive?

Stay alive, Beatrice. Please.

Don't give up.

I'll find you.

Gabe swung his feet to the floor and picked up the laptop from the coffee table. Leaning against the couch, he checked his emails again, but there was nothing from Nate or Travis. Gabe was also able to get in touch with the Iron Skulls, but they had nothing for him either.

There was a rap on the door. Despite being injured, Rhino growled. It was 1:00 a.m. Gabe grabbed his 9mm from the table and walked stealthily to the door. He peeked behind the blinds and saw a familiar shape.

Relief or rage, he didn't know what he felt as he disabled the alarms and opened the door to his early morning visitor.

Benjamin Porter.

12

THEY LOCKED GAZES at the door.

Gabe didn't know whether to punch the admiral or to hug him in relief. The older man looked weary, like he had been traveling for weeks. He had never seen the admiral this disheveled.

"May I come in, Sullivan?"

Because Gabe didn't know what to say, he simply stepped aside to let the admiral enter the house. Porter removed his coat and hung it on the coat stand near the foyer table.

The admiral faced him. "Beatrice?"

"Nothing."

Porter's shoulders slumped. He walked further into the house and noticed Rhino. "What happened?"

"Whoever took Beatrice, shot him," Gabe pushed through his teeth. Rage was consuming him. Porter looking so calm when his daughter was missing didn't sit well with him. She could be fucking dead, for Christ's sake. And Beatrice thought he was like her father? This was proof to himself that he was nothing like Porter, because Gabe was barely hanging on to his shit right now. "He protected her."

"Where were you, Gabe?" Porter asked.

"You son of a bitch," Gabe snarled viciously. He itched to slug Porter across the face. "I should be asking you, Ben. Where the fuck were you?"

"We'll come to that soon," Porter replied. "I didn't mean the way it sounded." The admiral rubbed his fingers across his forehead. "Best you tell me what happened." It took less than five minutes to get through all the info Gabe had. It sickened him that he had so little to go on.

"I'm very close to finding out the mastermind of operation Red Bridge," Porter said.

"Red Bridge?"

"Red Bridge is a series of interconnected ops starting with the destruction of Project Infinity, the downfall of the Zorin Bratva, and the possible manipulation of the Russian conflict in Ukraine."

"Are we still talking about weapons? Arms dealing?"

"Yes. There were two major players—Komarov and Zorin. You infiltrated Zorin, and Project Infinity agents went undercover with Komarov. My counterpart handling the Komarov side got assassinated. I suspected his boss was the culprit. This was a few weeks before John Cooper and Sarah Blake died in the car accident. Red Bridge had become operational. CIA was cut off from Komarov, so whoever was the mastermind of Red Bridge received most of its profits from weapons sales to South America. He was also receiving a cut from Zorin, which is why I think you may have met him and is his motivation to get rid of you, because of the possibility that you could ID him."

The admiral paused, waiting for some acknowledgment from Gabe. "Go on."

"Zorin made an enemy with our Red Bridge suspect when he decided to go into the black market nuke business without Red Bridge."

Things began to click into place. This was around the time John Cooper, who was then known as Jase Locke, met with

Gabe at the behest of the admiral. "Had you always known that Travis's wife was alive?"

"No. I only had my suspicions."

"You never told me how you got in contact with Jase Locke," Gabe asked.

"He contacted me through a common operative. He never mentioned Caitlin, only that he may have the location of the missing nuclear material."

This started a series of meetings between Gabe and Locke. The last time was when Locke handed him a letter for Caitlin. Probably the same meeting where Caitlin had seen him.

"So what's this got to do with Ukraine?" The region had been in turmoil since the revolution that ousted their president. The interim Ukrainian government was at odds with Russia ever since Russia annexed the Crimean peninsula, but there was fear in the International community that this was just the beginning of a more nefarious goal.

"You know the rumors that Russia is supplying arms to the rebels?" Porter asked.

"That's not even a rumor, is it?" Gabe snorted. "Rumor is Russia is about to invade Ukraine."

Porter nodded. "There's reason to believe they're going to use unconventional weapons to suppress the Ukrainian army."

"You're not talking about chemical weapons, are you?" Gabe asked. It had been done recently by the Syrian government. "They'll be shunned, even by their allies."

"No. I'm talking about—"

Rhino started growling softly.

The admiral stiffened in front of him, their eyes meeting in unspoken comprehension.

Someone was at the door.

Gabe drew his 9mm once more, but before he reached the window, he heard a door slam and a car pull away. He peeked outside and saw nothing. Usually the light from the street lamps would illuminate a silhouette at his door. His eyes drifted further and his throat caught. There was a big lump sprawled across his front walkway.

A body?

No. No. No.

He threw open the door, ignoring the admiral's shout of caution.

"Fuck me. Fuck me," Gabe muttered hoarsely as he ran toward the unknown mass and sank to his knees. A body was wrapped in a blanket, nothing exposed except strands of long hair. It seemed like forever before he could bring himself to peel away the blanket. What would it reveal? Gabe had never been more terrified in his entire life.

"Babe . . ." his voice broke.

"Don't!" An arm banded around his chest and pulled him back.

"What the fuck, Ben?" he growled with half a mind to knock the admiral on his ass.

"Not chemical weapons, Gabe," the admiral whispered harshly in his ear. "Bioweapons. A virus. Check if the body has a fever."

His blood chilled. Gabe wrenched free of the admiral and immediately crawled to the mass on the walkway. This time he didn't hesitate to pull back the blanket. The lighting cast a ghostly glow over Beatrice's features; her lips were pale. Her skin was cold, but that wasn't the reassurance he sought. His hands circled her throat, fingers searching for a pulse. When he found a strong beat, Gabe fell back on his ass, an overwhelming relief momentarily robbing him of strength. He shifted to his knees and uncloaked her body further. He felt for injuries that might discourage lifting her. Finding none, and ignoring the wetness he'd felt along her arms, he carried her back into the house.

. . .

"Remove the laptop from the couch," Gabe ordered the admiral. There was blood all over the blanket. Laying Beatrice carefully across the furniture, the blanket fell open. She was wearing sweats and blood soaked the sleeves of her hoodie.

With grim resolve, Gabe unzipped her top and gently eased her arms out from it. Even if he expected it, he inhaled sharply at the ugly letters carved into her forearms. *Oko za oko.*

The admiral cursed behind him.

"How, Ben?" Gabe asked tonelessly. "Ryker is dead."

No answer.

Gabe rose from his crouch, turned on Porter, and without a second thought, he punched the admiral right across the jaw. Not giving the older man a chance to recover, Gabe slammed him against the wall.

Bringing his face close, he said, "That's for calling your daughter *a body* to check for fever. Jesus, Ben, you think I'd care to go look for a bio-suit and let Beatrice freeze to death outside? You can quarantine us both because no way in hell am I getting separated from her."

"You done?" The admiral's eyes were unflinching.

"You're unbelievable." Gabe released him and went back to the unconscious Beatrice. "I need to take her to the hospital, have her checked out."

"No hospital. She could be infected. We cannot risk it."

"So you'd risk your daughter instead?"

"You think this is easy for me, Commander?" Porter took out his phone.

"No. I think for once in your life, you should think like a father and not like a damned robot," Gabe snapped in disgust as he crouched down again. He stroked Beatrice's cheek gently, willing his anger at Porter to subside because losing his shit right now was not going to help his woman. He considered the admiral's reluctance to take Beatrice to the hospital and mulled his options. Gabe wouldn't be satisfied until she was thoroughly looked over by a physician. His gaze drifted over her body, grimacing at the cuts, yet wondering if something far worse had happened. Did they . . . he couldn't form the words.

"I've contacted Dr. Ryan. She'll be bringing in a special medical van equipped with a biological containment chamber. I don't think any of us are infected. The virus doesn't appear to be airborne but more the type to be transferred via bodily fluids." Porter looked at him. "Did you get blood on you?"

Yes. He did.

"You better fill me in on what's going on with this fucking virus," Gabe muttered.

"Believe me, I will."

BEATRICE WAS TAKEN to a facility in the same building that housed the NEST. All equipment was mobile, brought in by a small commercial truck. The admiral and Gabe were told to wait in a separate room while Dr. Fern Ryan examined Beatrice. For precautionary measures, both of them were sequestered and subjected to a high-pressured hose down and given scrubs to wear afterward. Rhino was taken in by one of Dr. Ryan's assistants while Gabe's house was being decontaminated. It seemed overkill to Gabe at first, until he found out what type of virus they were dealing with.

From what Porter had told him so far, the ST-Vyl virus originated from an indigenous bat in Colombia. It was a largely dormant virus, but a geneticist who worked for the CIA, the same scientist who created the Berserker serum, was able to alter the virus's DNA to make it as lethal as the widely feared Ebola virus. Porter had spent weeks in the Colombian jungles tracking down the lab that was manufacturing the pathogen.

"So you haven't located the lab?" Gabe asked.

"Not the current one," Porter said. "But we've found two previous locations."

"What makes you so sure?"

"We found mass graves. They burned the bodies, but we were still able to type the virus."

"Jesus Christ! They tested on humans?"

Porter nodded. "Colombia was the perfect location. It had the virus host, jungles where they could hide the labs, and test subjects that could be used and passed off as victims of the armed conflict or drug trafficking vendettas."

"Shouldn't Senator Mendoza be made aware of this?"

The admiral exhaled deeply. "This op is classified. I'm already breaking protocol by telling you."

"Do we know how Red Bridge is going to get it to the Russians?"

"I don't think a deal has been made yet," Porter said. "But the virus has reached the U.S."

"How?"

Before Porter could answer, Dr. Ryan stepped into the room.

"How is she?" Gabe asked anxiously.

"We immediately tested for the ST-Vyl strain, it came back negative," the doctor said. "She's dehydrated. Her tox screen hasn't come back yet, but I suspect they've given her drugs to keep her unconscious. X-rays and CT scan show no internal injuries. The rape kit came back negative. Beatrice mentioned as much. They cut her," Dr. Ryan's lips thinned in anger, "but did nothing else."

"She's awake?" Porter asked.

Gabe needed to see her, to look into her eyes to see for certain that she was okay. He didn't spend enough time with her before she was taken to this facility. The 24 hours he spent thinking he would never see her again made him overly paranoid of losing sight of her. Beatrice might just lose her mind with his hovering, but at this moment, Gabe didn't give a fuck.

She could be pissed at him and hate him, but as long as she was alive and breathing he could live with it.

It was some kind of safe house, or so Beatrice was told. Rhino was asleep in the backseat of Gabe's Silverado. She was feeling oddly apathetic. Dr. Ryan said her body and psyche had suffered too much and the shock shut down her mind. Her system hadn't fully expelled the drug cocktail they had given her, which would explain her whacked out sense of self.

Gabe sat tensely beside her. He attempted to hold her hand earlier, but she pulled away. When he tried to touch her face, she flinched. He probably thought it was because of her torture. It wasn't. It was what she found out. Maybe that was why she was keeping her emotions on lockdown. She was actually hanging on by a fragile thread.

"This is it," Gabe muttered as they finally reached the house at the end of the long unpaved driveway. "Your father should follow us here in a few hours."

"And you're sure we'll see my dad, again?" Beatrice had told them what her captors wanted—to flush out Benjamin Porter. Gabe and her father didn't seem surprised with her revelation.

"Beatrice, I know you're angry at the admiral," Gabe said. "You're also probably blaming me."

She didn't respond, just walked into the house when he opened the door. She could feel his gaze burning against her back, but she didn't turn to face him.

"I'll go get Rhino," Gabe sighed with her continued silence. His footsteps faded back to the truck.

Beatrice took off her coat and grimaced at the bandages on her arms. She knew what lay underneath were puckered zigzagged lines laying in stark contrast against her fair skin. They would heal and she could have them surgically erased, but would the horror of having her flesh mutilated ever leave her mind? She had screamed until her mind left her body. She blinked her eyes. Not a single tear. She couldn't even cry.

She heard Gabe curse behind her and saw him lower Rhino on the couch. Beatrice froze as he embraced her from behind. She tried to pull away again, but he held on.

"Don't," Gabe whispered hoarsely. "Don't pull away from me, babe. It's killing me. I get you can't stand to be touched right now. But please tell me it's not because you hate me and blame me for this."

"I don't blame you for my abduction, Gabe. I knew what I signed up for when I agreed to take you back."

"Then why—"

She turned in his arms to face him. "Did you fuck women only to kill them afterward, Gabe?"

He flinched, but held her gaze. "Once."

"Was she collateral damage?"

"No. She was a human trafficker. I didn't even c—"

"I don't need specifics. I don't think you would want to hear about all my fucks after you left me, do you?"

An unnamed emotion flashed across his face, a mixture of anger, pain, and remorse. He was trying to hold on to his temper, and she almost regretted her callous words. But she knew she was delaying the inevitable because even if she was afraid of asking the next question, his answer would decide if she was willing to move forward with their relationship or end it.

"Angel of Death." His body turned rigid before his hands fell away. "Is it true how you earned that name?"

A stoic mask fell on his face.

"You heard that from the people who took you?"

Beatrice nodded.

"How much do you trust me, Beatrice?" Gabe asked softly. There was something sinister behind that question. She refused to be cowed.

"You expect me to trust you? Stop hiding information that would ruin that trust." She raised her chin defiantly.

His eyes darkened. "You know I can't give you specifics."

"Did you kill children, Gabe?" Might as well ask him point blank.

"I did what was necessary to perpetuate my reputation."

"I'm sick of your vague answers. I'm not even sure why I let you get away with them for so long. Maybe I'm in denial!" She threw up her hands in exasperation. "I'm tired of this roller coaster, Gabe. How can I let myself love you freely when ugly truths about your past keep cropping up unexpectedly?"

A hand gripped her left shoulder, while the other tilted her chin up. "Believe me, Beatrice, I wish I could tell you everything, but to do so would put lives in jeopardy. You have to trust me."

Beatrice stared into Gabe's eyes. There was a pleading in them she had not seen before, almost begging her not to force him to tell her. And in his eyes, she finally saw the truth he couldn't say in words. A singular clarity replaced her earlier uncertainty: the man she loved wasn't capable of killing children.

She melted into him. Her hands clutched his hips. She wanted to embrace him and never let go, but her injuries prevented that impulse.

"Thank you," Beatrice whispered softly. "Tell me this is the worst of it, that our enemies can't use anything else against us."

She felt Gabe shudder against her. "That's all of it, babe."

"You won't feel a thing. I'll be quick."

Dmitry administered the Hybernabis, a precise dose to sedate the boy and keep his vital signs undetectable. If there was anything Dmitry was thankful for, it was that Zorin didn't believe in torturing children. They still had to die, but this sleeping death was preferable.

Zorin's physician walked in. He examined the boy and then nodded. "He's gone."

Dmitry had done this a handful of times. Each time wasn't easier than the last. There was something gut-churning about putting fear in innocents who were in no way to blame for the sins of their parents. But that was the way of the Russian mafia.

He carried the unconscious boy out of the cellar door and deposited him inside a van. Closing the vehicle's back doors, Dmitry got into the driver's seat and drove out of Berlin into a forest where he could bury the body.

This time he had to be more careful because the boy was the son of a high-ranking lieutenant of Zorin's who had betrayed the Bratva to a rival mob. Dmitry parked the vehicle behind a black van. A CIA operative was waiting for him.

Without another word, the man opened the back of his vehicle and shined a light on a corpse.

"This is the best I can do."

The corpse bore some resemblance to the unconscious boy, but one familiar with the victim could spot the difference straight away. But it didn't matter.

"The elements should take care of the difference soon enough," Dmitry said.

"You can't save them all, man."

"I have to," Dmitry said shortly. He went to the back of his van to retrieve the boy. The boy would find a new life in the United States. A life away from the violence he was born into. There were families who would be eager to take him in, people who had escaped the Russian mob with the help of the CIA.

Dmitry just had to do his part.

GABE GINGERLY STRETCHED his right arm over the back of the couch to restore blood circulation to that limb. Beatrice had fallen asleep against him and he loathed moving and waking her up. He'd been watching her sleep; disturbing as that sounded, he couldn't help it. Her eyes had been vacant when she woke up from her drugged unconsciousness, and her ensuing disdain for his touch had driven him out of his mind. He thought he should give her space, but he was afraid she would build those walls again. Finally coming clean—well, as much as he could—about the myth surrounding his "Angel of Death" persona was a cathartic relief. A spark of life returned to her eyes before she laid her head on his chest and pressed her body into his. At that moment, Gabe felt the ultimate gift of her trust, and he wasn't going to let her down ever again. He could never tell her straight about what happened to all those children he supposedly had killed, because even the slightest fracture in its secrecy could jeopardize the integrity of the relocation program.

He couldn't risk the safety of those kids for his personal happiness. This reinforced what he knew all along: there was no one else for him but Beatrice. She understood where he was coming from, not demanding detail but just the assurance that she could trust him not to have done anything irredeemable. Redemption was subjective, but he was fast gaining an understanding of what she could accept.

The sensors in the driveway triggered the CCTV cameras. An Escalade was approaching. Travis and maybe Nate. They didn't waste any time hauling ass to the safe house after Gabe let them know Beatrice was safe. He didn't have the opportunity to tell them that the admiral would also be arriving shortly.

The situation was about to get awkward.

13

Awkward was an understatement; tense was more appropriate.

Travis was clenching his jaw so hard when Porter walked into the house, Gabe thought he'd break it. It was the first time the two men had come face to face after Crowe had shot Caitlin, nearly killing her. Gabe also had to reel in his jealousy when the BSI men fussed over Beatrice, especially Nate. The shithead almost had his woman on his lap again. It was probably through extreme throat clearing—all right, growling—from Gabe that Nate must have figured it was certainly not okay.

Caitlin stood back chatting with the admiral. Travis was casting suspicious glares their way.

So, yeah, tense.

Clearly, Beatrice was having none of it.

"Okay, now that you two stubborn mules are in the same room, maybe it's time to kiss and make up?"

Scowl from Travis; Porter had a blank expression.

"Seriously, guys? I've been carved up like a pumpkin and you two won't finally put all the bullshit behind you?"

Gabe tried to smother a grin; he was thrilled to see Beatrice so feisty.

"That bullshit nearly got my wife killed," Travis snarled.

"You think Crowe wouldn't have gone after her some other way?" Porter challenged.

"You brought that piece of shit into our lives, Admiral."

"Only a matter of time, Lieutenant, just like all other things."

"What's that supposed to mean?" Nate asked, frowning.

Porter glanced briefly at Gabe before briefing those present on Red Bridge and the ST-Vyl virus.

"Are you telling us the same person responsible for shutting down Project Infinity is planning to sell bioweapons to the Russians?"

"This is the perfect smart virus. It's modified to have a suicide gene so it'll become dormant after five days. A controlled epidemic."

"That's extremely dangerous," Caitlin said. "If it is indeed a smart virus, what if it learns to defeat its suicide gene and decides to mutate?"

"I don't have the technical data on the ST-Vyl virus," Porter said. "I do know communications with buyers are being done on the Black Plane."

"That'll be hard to trace," Caitlin said.

"Not for you," Porter said.

"No," Travis growled, standing up and facing the admiral. "No fucking way."

"You said the virus has reached the United States?" Gabe interjected.

"What?" Beatrice exclaimed.

The admiral eyed Travis intently. "I've been on the trail of several individuals I felt were involved with Red Bridge from the beginning. One of them is the medical examiner (ME) who faked the DNA results on Sarah and Cooper's death."

"And?" Travis prodded anxiously.

"He has resurfaced in DC." This time Porter looked at Gabe. "When you told me about how those five people were killed in the Cloverleaf District, I didn't give it much thought at that time. However, when Ryker came into the picture, I decided to investigate further. The same ME did all five autopsies, but covered up the real findings on the official report."

Gabe was having a bad feeling about this. Everyone was waiting with bated breath.

"The wounds were given post-mortem. They didn't die from a bullet or the garrote, they died from hemorrhagic fever. Their internals looked like an IED blew up inside them," Porter said. "Needless to say, the ME is in custody."

"Holy fuck," Nate whispered.

"That was how we were able to get a tissue sample to trace the genome of the virus."

"How are they transporting it?" Travis asked.

"Cocaine shipments, that's our suspicion," Porter said. "We also think it's in powder form."

"Wouldn't that be too unstable?"

"We know Ryker performed experiments. The problem is, we couldn't find the location or the data."

"You keep on saying *we*, Porter," Travis said. "Who exactly is *we*? Do you even trust anyone right now in the CIA?"

"I am working with a covert group."

"Does this covert group have a name?" Gabe inquired. This was the first he had heard of this.

"Their name is not important. They won't want to work with anyone else at this point. But we do need someone who can hack through Red Bridge communication."

"That someone won't be Cat," Travis reiterated ominously.

"I can speak perfectly for myself, Travis," his wife retorted.

"Think on it," Porter said. "I'm sure we can manage eventually, but Caitlin can do it faster. We don't have the luxury of time. Intel is pointing to a transaction within the next three weeks."

"If this has something to do with cocaine shipments, shouldn't we be keeping an eye on Fuego?" Gabe asked.

"We already are," Porter said. "Especially since Beatrice disappeared. The entire gang has gone to ground."

"How about the Skulls? Do they have any intel at this point?" Travis asked.

"Crane is keeping his club out of this since the Russians are involved. We're not getting help there."

"Is there anything we can do besides involving Cat?" Travis asked.

Porter sighed. "There is something. Your team is handling Senator Mendoza's security?"

"You don't think the senator is involved in any of this, do you?" Beatrice asked.

"No, but they killed his uncle for a reason," Porter said. "The assassination was blamed on the armed conflict in Colombia, but I'm not discounting he may have been a convenient patsy to mislead us about Gabe being the real target. It would be beneficial to have ears in his office, just to keep a pulse on the political landscape in Colombia."

"I'm up for it," Nate announced.

Porter nodded in approval. The admiral turned to Gabe. "How about you, Commander?"

"I'll leave the security of the senator to BSI." His gaze fell on his woman. She had an unguarded look on her face, looking so lost. Despite her earlier feistiness, she was in no way over what happened to her. "I want to comb through what we have of Beatrice's abduction. We could be missing a clue here." Beatrice looked at him apprehensively. She wasn't ready to relive the nightmare, but they needed to debrief her while everything was fresh in her mind. Still, he couldn't help adding, "When you're ready, okay, babe?"

She sighed in resignation and nodded.

Gabe looked on as Beatrice's assistant kept her company in the living room. If Doug Keller wasn't gay, Gabe would definitely have a problem with him. Right now, Doug had his arms around Beatrice; she was leaning against him with her head on his chest. They were murmuring, so Gabe had no idea what they were talking about. He was getting impatient with people showing up, although it was understandable given how many people cared for Beatrice. Travis, Caitlin, and Nate left an hour ago. It was ironic that the person who should be the most concerned was nowhere to be found. Gabe was getting dinner ready, something as simple as popping a frozen casserole in the oven.

"You want another beer, Doug?" Gabe called out.

Doug raised his bottle. "I'm good, thanks."

Gabe went looking for Porter. He sure hoped the admiral didn't leave without saying goodbye. Beatrice was used to her father's indifference, but Gabe's blood had been on a simmer since they got her back. Save for the shock of seeing his daughter's arms brutalized, the admiral had remained mostly detached.

The safe house belonged to Porter. Whether it was CIA-owned or not, Gabe had no idea. Before they left his house in Alexandria, Porter told him to pack a bag for himself and Beatrice, plus whatever he needed for Rhino, enough for at least a few days. Gabe agreed. Until they knew exactly what was going on, Beatrice's condo and his house were not safe. This place was also equipped with state-of-the-art computers and a communications room. This was not just a safe house but a satellite op center.

He found the admiral on the back patio, smoking a cigar in the chilly January evening.

"Dinner should be ready in an hour."

The admiral said nothing for a long time. He took a few

puffs of his cigar and said, "I never planned to marry Lorraine."

Beatrice's mother. Gabe stilled, not sure where the admiral was going with this.

"She got pregnant," Porter said. "At that time, it seemed like the honorable thing to do." The admiral snuffed out the cigar under his boot. "I didn't want a family to tie me down, but, Gabe, when I first held my daughter, I fell in love with her." The admiral laughed derisively. "Hard to believe, huh, Commander?"

"What happened then?"

"I loved Beatrice, but she was a reminder that I was trapped in a marriage I never wanted, and that love slowly grew into resentment. When I realized what was happening, it sickened me. Why blame an innocent girl for my mistake? Seeing you with her now, how hard you're fighting for her, reminded me of my failures. I failed to fight for the woman I loved, failed to cherish my daughter, and failed to make my marriage work."

"Ah . . . Beatrice doesn't know of this other woman, does she?"

The admiral's eyes flashed a warning. "No and she never will. This is between you and me."

"Of course. Where is the woman now?"

A pained look crossed the admiral's face. "She died about six years ago. Cancer. She didn't want to be the wife of a career military man. She wanted me to quit after a few years. She married someone else, never had kids."

"Do you still resent Beatrice?"

"Oh, that resentment didn't last long. It quickly ended soon after her fifth birthday, which I had missed." Porter's lips tipped in a rare smile. "I missed almost all her birthdays. When I came home a few weeks after she had turned five, she made it known exactly how unhappy she was with me. Feisty even at that age."

Gabe found himself grinning, imagining Beatrice as a little girl, facing up against a stern admiral.

The admiral sighed. "Had me wrapped around her fingers by that time. A year later, I got recruited into covert and clandestine operations. I saw a lot of shit, Gabe, did so much shit. How could I go home and hug my little girl after I'd killed someone else's father?" Porter leaned forward and rested his elbows on his knees, turning his head to look at him. "At that time we didn't have the training nor the available help to work through the aftermath of a mission. It was a stigma then to show weakness; we were expected to tough it out and deal."

Gabe couldn't agree more. There were many veterans who came home messed up, homeless, and hooked on drugs.

"I remembered clearly the first time I pulled away from Beatrice. I shot and killed the leader of a drug cartel. We had intel that he was at home. He was guarded well, but we were able to breach his defenses. He refused to surrender, and the firefight that ensued was bloody. I shot him in the head and he dropped right beside a bed. I nudged him over and that was when I heard it. Crying. His daughter was under the fucking bed, saw her father shot down." The admiral rubbed his face. "She was Beatrice's age. I couldn't go home and face my own daughter afterward. Then I thought of all the other reasons why I couldn't let myself get close to her. Our covers were solid, but the longer you're in this life, the probability of blowback becomes higher. That was when the rift started, and I just let it happen."

"I think," Gabe said carefully, "you spent your life being scared of loving someone again. Those are excuses, Admiral. You could have quit."

"I let myself get drawn deeper into the CIA," Porter admitted. "An op would take months sometimes. Before I knew it, Beatrice was all grown up, and Lorraine was divorcing me."

For a fleeting moment, Gabe felt sorry for the admiral and

his shitty personal life, but Porter had chosen his path. He wondered if the admiral would have given up the clandestine life if he had the woman he loved by his side.

As if reading his thoughts, Porter said, "I think about it sometimes, if I chose *her*, but then I wouldn't have Beatrice. Even if I was the worst father, I couldn't deny that she is the best part of me."

Gabe didn't even want to think about a world where Beatrice didn't exist.

"Don't fuck up with my daughter, Gabriel," Porter said. "I've done enough of that in her lifetime. I don't think I can change my relationship with her. You saw how I was after her abduction. I don't know how to be a father."

"You can try," Gabe said.

"Thirty-two years too late."

"Ben, it's not too late. We nearly lost her. Don't you think this should be a wake-up call? Doesn't this defeat your excuse of trying to protect her by showing your enemies you don't care?" Gabe nudged the admiral. "Maybe you should see the shrink at the NEST."

Porter stared at him dubiously. "Don't push it."

"Okay, then, let's help you become father of the year. You can help me get dinner ready."

"Does it hurt, honeybee?"

Doug shifted her in his arms to peer down at her. Next to Gabe, Doug probably had the hardest time dealing with what had happened to her. Unlike Gabe though, her assistant didn't have the training most military guys had to shut it down. He cried when he saw her arms in bandages. Afterward, he hugged her and had not let her go since he arrived, which was over two hours ago. As for her, she still didn't know how to feel: anger at the people who did this to her, relief that she was alive, or an underlying anxiety of what still lay ahead. They let her go. Why? Beatrice could only surmise that they wanted her to be a constant reminder to her father and Gabe that they failed to protect her. This was why Beatrice tried to act normal around everyone, because showing how terrified she was with her recent ordeal was letting the bad guys win. But pretending was exhausting.

"It does; I just don't care," Beatrice replied.

Doug chuckled. "Pain meds will do that to you." He brushed her hair away from her face affectionately. "So how are you and Gabe? The man looked ready to slam the door on my face when I arrived."

"We haven't spent much time together since I returned. Prior to Travis, Cat, and Nate showing up, I was asleep." Beatrice warmed over. "Such a great feeling being held in his arms. I feel safe."

"Hey now, my feelings are hurt."

"Don't be silly, Doug. Tell me you wouldn't feel the same if a man like Gabe was holding you."

Doug cackled with laughter. "You have a point, sweetie."

The back door slammed. Gabe and her father appeared in the hallway.

"What were you two up to?" Beatrice asked suspiciously.

"Nothing," Porter said.

"Hanging out," Gabe answered.

The two men didn't look exactly guilty, but Beatrice was pretty sure something was up.

SOMETHING WAS DEFINITELY UP. Gabe and her father were busy getting dinner ready. Seriously, how hard was it to reheat a frozen casserole? You really didn't need a former Navy SEAL and an admiral in the U.S. Navy for it.

She and Doug were already sitting at the dining table. Her

assistant leaned in to her. "I think this is the first time I've seen your father toss a salad."

"I've got some great wine here, Doug," her father said, bringing over a bottle. He looked at Beatrice. "Sorry, baby, you can't have any with the meds you're on."

"Thank you, Admiral." Her blond assistant looked perplexed as her father lined up some glasses and poured the wine. Not that Beatrice could blame him. Her father had barely said two sentences to her assistant in the three years Doug had worked for her.

"And here's the chicken mushroom risotto casserole," Gabe announced with much flare. The delicious aroma perked up her appetite at least. After he set down the still-bubbling dish, Gabe muttered something about getting the bread.

Beatrice was controlling a grin. Emotion innervated her body once more as her heart swelled at the sight of her father obviously making an effort to be less rigid. He called her "baby." He hadn't called her that endearment in years. Gabe returned with the bread on a cutting board. It happened quickly, the flash of the silver edge, the pounding in her ears, and the fear that gripped her body. Her chair toppled over as she scrambled to her feet. She couldn't breathe.

The knife Gabe was holding clattered to the table. He was suddenly in front of her and her nose filled with his familiar scent. Her arms were stiff at her sides, but his banded around her securely.

"It's okay. It's okay," Gabe crooned in her ear. "I got you, babe. You're safe."

"I'm sorry," Beatrice whispered. "I don't know what came over me."

Gabe held her slightly away as he stared at her. "It's been less than 24 hours, Beatrice. Cut yourself some slack."

"I don't want them to win."

"They won't," her father said, coming up beside them. "In

fact, they've lost." Her father's eyes searched hers with an emotion she hadn't seen in a long time. Tenderness. "They don't know how strong you are, baby."

Her dad looked at Gabe. Something unspoken passed between the two men as Gabe's arms loosened around her. Her father tentatively reached out for her. Some unnamed feeling held her heart in a vise and squeezed as a burning sensation burst behind her eyes. She was once again his little girl.

"Daddy!" Beatrice launched herself into her father's arms, which came around her tightly. His voice was calming, soothing, still commanding but gentler. She knew that would never change, but something subtle shifted in their relationship, something opened up, and that something, Beatrice knew, would be for the better.

Through the film of her tears, she caught sight of Gabe. His own eyes were suspiciously glazed, expression unguarded, leaving no doubt of his intense feelings for her.

Their enemies had failed, because between Gabe and her father's strength, and with the support of such caring friends, there was no way Beatrice would let this fear control her.

Dinner was delayed for a while. She was sure no one minded.

Beatrice stretched on the couch, stroking Rhino's head absently. Gabe's dog seemed to know she was hurt and did his best to act like her guard even if he was probably worse off than she was. Her father and Doug had left a few minutes ago, and Gabe was checking the perimeter.

It was a day of healing. Not only for her physical wounds but emotional as well. Beatrice wasn't expecting a total 180 from her father, but seeing his usually stoic face crack with regret and tenderness did a number on her heartstrings. She wasn't even thinking it would last, but being a father when it mattered was enough. Another thing she was pleased about was the grudging reconciliation between Travis and her dad. Even when they weren't seeing eye to eye with what should be done, arguing was better than complete silence. Yes, this was a surprisingly good day.

The alarm beeped as the door opened. Gabe walked in and entered the code to arm the security system.

"This place is fucking wired," Gabe said, lowering the flashlight on the table. "We're surrounded by woods, but there are trip wires surrounding the property. I followed the schematic and made sure they're working." He was holding a blueprint of some sort.

"The room adjacent to the one before the backdoor seems like a command center of some sort," Beatrice said. She accidentally walked into it earlier.

"Yes, it also functions as a panic room. There's an interior sliding door," Gabe looked at the plan again. "Walls are six inches thick all around, including the ceiling. There are weapons inside, but we also have an armory right about . . ." He nudged the area rug in the kitchen to reveal a trap door. Wasting no time at all, Gabe hefted the door and let it fall back in a decisive crash. He disappeared down a flight of steps.

Curious now, Beatrice rose from the couch and walked toward where Gabe disappeared. She could hear him whooping in excitement. Hmph, men and their guns.

"Gabe?" she called out tentatively from the top of the stairs.

His head appeared at the bottom of the steps. "Hell yeah, babe. You gotta take a load of this."

Shaking her head at Gabe's childlike elation, she followed him to the cellar. Beatrice had to admit, even she was in awe. Different types of guns, assault rifles, and carbines were pegged on the wall. Gabe was already checking out what looked like the latest model of the M4-carbine—a firearm heavily used by the U.S. Military. Ammunition cans were stacked by another wall.

"Is that . . ."

"RPG," Gabe muttered, lowering the carbine and picking up the rocket-propelled grenade weapon. "Jesus, there's enough firepower here to start a war."

"Uh-huh," she agreed, her eyes landing on another shelf with plastic explosives.

"Come on." Gabe cupped her elbow and led her to the steps. "I'll take stock tomorrow of what we have, although the inventory is in the file your father left me." He kissed the top of her head. "Right now, I need to change your bandages and Rhino's."

"Poor man," Beatrice teased, "reduced to playing nurse to me and dear Rhino."

Beatrice was on the first step when Gabe gently turned her around to face him. They were almost eye to eye, his gaze scorchingly possessive. "You're mine, Beatrice. I'll always take care of you."

Gabe carefully wrapped fresh bandages around Beatrice's arms. He kept his face blank, even though the fury he had kept at bay since she'd been taken threatened to consume him. Beatrice wasn't the only one pretending. He knew she was trying to put on a brave front, so the people who cared for her wouldn't feel righteous anger and the need for revenge.

"It doesn't look as bad," Beatrice whispered.

"Yes, I think the swelling hasn't gotten worse." Lie. It had gotten more swollen. The skin around the stitches bulged red. "You took your antibiotics?"

She nodded.

"Okay, poppy." He kissed her forehead.

She frowned at him when he tucked her in but didn't slip into bed beside her. Instead, he headed to the door.

"Where are you going?"

"I need to check on something." Gabe needed to get out of the room. Seeing the ugly cuts marring her once flawless skin made him want to howl for retribution. He couldn't sleep beside her peacefully. Too much vengeful energy was bottled up.

He quickly disabled the alarm and headed out the back door. Taking deep inhalations cooled the rage pulsing in his veins, but they weren't enough.

An anguished growl escaped from the back of his throat. Hauling his right arm back, he smashed his fist into the concrete wall in front of him. He repeated the movement with his left fist and then a couple more with both hands.

Some of the toxic energy left his body and dissipated into the pain that radiated from his knuckles. He wasn't stupid enough to injure his hands permanently, but there would be swelling. Where was a damned punching bag when he needed one? Gabe prowled the length of the back patio, willing himself to take back control before he actually maimed his hands.

Inhale.

Exhale.

Repeat.

A whine sounded behind the door.

Rhino. Shit. His dog was always perceptive of his emotional upheavals.

"Hey, buddy," Gabe mumbled when he went back inside. He must not have shut the door to their bedroom firmly, and the poor boy followed him downstairs despite the pain in his shoulders. Gabe crouched in front of his dog; Rhino's dark eyes were soulful and comforting. "Fuck, boy, I'm so messed up."

Rhino pressed his cold nose against his jaw.

"I can't help but think I brought this upon her," Gabe whispered. "But I can't walk away from her. Never again."

Rhino whined softly; his pink tongue shot out and licked Gabe's scruffy cheek. "Ugh, okay, no need to kiss it better." He fondly rubbed the fur on his head. "Come on, you're supposed to be guarding her, not following my sorry ass around."

After engaging the alarm, Gabe headed up the stairs, Rhino trudging beside him. He hated seeing his dog move with difficulty, but he tensed up whenever Gabe attempted to carry him. They made it back to the bedroom soon enough. The light from the hallway illuminated as far as the edge of the bed. He saw Beatrice shift slightly.

"Gabe, Rhino followed you downstairs."

"He's with me."

"Okay."

He turned off the hallway lights and headed for the bathroom. There were slight cuts on his fists, but not bad. The purpling skin promised bruising and swelling tomorrow. He should ice it, but he didn't want to be away from Beatrice any longer.

He crawled into bed beside her. She was on her side, facing away from him. He tagged her around the waist and pulled her into his arms. He took a deep breath, taking in the clean floral scent of her hair. The warm softness of her body melted away the remaining tension in his body.

Gabe savored the feeling of having her back in his arms. He didn't, for a minute, want to miss any moment of this in slumber. Even as he struggled to remain awake, his consciousness eventually slipped away until finally, he eased into a dreamless sleep.

14

FRANK WILKES STARED at the manifest of the incoming cargo ship from Colombia via Jamaica that would be docking in Virginia Beach next week. The situation was getting complicated. Benjamin Porter was too close on his tail and Wilkes had no idea who the admiral was working with, only that an incursion group had found the old laboratories in Colombia and was aware of the virus. Wilkes thought of keeping his daughter hostage in exchange for the man Porter had in custody—the medical examiner who did the autopsy cover-ups for Wilkes. But since the ME had no idea who he was working for anyway, he was in no way a problem. Besides, Wilkes had been too late to bargain for his man back because the fool had revealed the existence of the ST-Vyl virus.

Zach Jamison assured him it was better to keep Beatrice Porter alive since Zach had easy access to her anyway. The admiral's daughter was too precious to kill immediately, and it was better to keep them off-kilter with what other nefarious plans they had planned for her.

His phone buzzed.

"Wilkes."

"It's Zach. I have the updated rotation on customs inspection. We're clear with our upcoming shipment next week. Our man inside Customs and Border protection is on duty."

"Excellent."

The line went dead. Short, quick communication had become the norm. The benefit of having Zach Jamison working with a senator on the Homeland Security Senate committee was easy access to border security strategies. All Wilkes and his crew had to do was work around those strategies. There was also the added bonus of keeping tabs on the political maneuverings in Colombia, which was beneficial for Wilkes who was navigating the treacherous slopes with his business partners—drug traffickers and dirty businessmen. However, sharing this intel with Fuego sweetened the deal he had with the Latino group. The derailment of the peace talks between the Colombian government and the other players in the armed conflict ensured an uninterrupted influx of cocaine into the country. So in a way, Wilkes and Fuego shared the same agenda.

For now.

Beatrice thanked her lucky stars that coffee was allowed while she was on painkillers and antibiotics. Gabe had enough to deal with besides adding a caffeine-deprived banshee, which she tended to turn into when she didn't get her fix in the mornings. The aroma wasn't the Colombian Excelso coffee beans she was used to. She took a sip, hoping it would taste decent. Her tongue balked at the flavor and she ran to the sink, spewing out the coffee.

"What? What?" Gabe's alarmed voice came from the doorway. He had let Rhino outside to take care of early morning business.

"What kind of coffee was that?" Beatrice screeched.

Gabe scowled at her and pointed to a supermarket brand

on the countertop. "That's all they had at the convenience store. I can go pick up the ones you like later."

"Don't bother," she snapped. "Doug can pick them up for me." She grabbed her phone to call her assistant, but Gabe's hand closed over hers as he gently, but firmly, pulled her close.

"Stop being a brat about it. It's just one morning—"

"You don't understand!" It irked Beatrice that some people didn't grasp the concept of good coffee.

"I'm beginning to understand," Gabe replied levelly. "I understand now that you're picky about your coffee. I guess I didn't realize that before because you're always stocked up with that shit wherever we are."

"I can't drink this." She dumped the offending beverage in the sink and went to the refrigerator, praying there was soda. Sighting a chilled caffeinated cola, she immediately started feeling better.

"Soda in the morning?" Gabe frowned at her.

"Would you rather I be a bitch all morning?"

"Beatrice—"

"I'm high-maintenance, Gabe," she cut in. Now was a good time to show him what he was signing up for. "Best you know now. I have creature comforts. I want things a certain way; I want my coffee a certain way—"

"Stop," Gabe said softly, leaning in and brushing his lips against hers. "You're doing it again, trying to scare me off."

"I'm not. I'm just a bitch when un-caffeinated."

"Maybe you should drink less of that shit. Not a good idea to be addicted. What if there's a shortage?"

"Of coffee?" Beatrice thought in horror. "You're talking about an apocalyptic end."

"Don't be so dramatic."

She narrowed her eyes when she noticed his lips twitching. "You really think it's funny, don't you, Sullivan? You really want me this mouthy first thing in the morning?"

"Believe me, you can be mouthy with me all you want," Gabe drawled, "especially around my dick."

She rolled her eyes, but had to admit she walked straight into that one. "Can I call Doug now? You don't have a coffee grinder, do you?"

Gabe scrubbed his face in amusement and frustration. "Jesus Christ, Beatrice, you are high maintenance."

"Told ya." She grinned slyly at him and called Doug. Her assistant once more proved why he was invaluable. He had already picked up two pounds of her favorite coffee beans and packed up her coffee machine including the grinder from her condo.

"You know, you probably need to write down the name of the coffee beans and your roaster," Gabe said when she got off the phone.

"Why?"

He affectionately tapped the tip of her nose. "Because, poppy, when I said I'd take care of you, I meant every word. And if caring for you includes keeping you supplied with your favorite brew, so be it."

Her heart fluttered.

AN HOUR LATER, Beatrice managed to make herself useful and made some French toast and bacon for breakfast. Gabe heartily ate what she prepared. Her man could eat. She guessed it took a lot to maintain all those stacked muscles under that tee. She didn't think he deliberately wore tight shirts, but more like he simply filled them out. Beatrice was tall and not many men managed to make her feel dainty and secure. Gabe managed to do so effortlessly.

"Okay, that's the second sigh in five minutes." Gabe eyed her warily. "What's wrong?"

She blinked. "Is it a crime to sigh?"

"Beatrice—"

"Okay, okay," Beatrice laughed lightly. She noticed his eyes grew heated. She smiled smugly. It didn't take much to get her man riled with lust. "If you must know, I was thinking about your muscles."

"What?" he croaked.

"Not many guys make me feel safe. You do it with no effort at all." This time her tone turned serious. "I play hardball with all these macho-security guys all the time; there's very little room to feel feminine. But with you, Gabe, you make me feel all woman and beautiful."

Gabe was the picture of male satisfaction. She could have imagined it, but it appeared he'd puffed up his chest. He linked their fingers together and kissed the back of her hand. "Pleased you feel that way."

Beatrice's smile disappeared when she noticed the bruise on his hand. "What happened here?" Her thumb stroked the light scratches on his knuckles.

He looked away. "Nothing."

He tried to pull his hand from hers but she held on.

"Gabe, tell me the truth. Did you punch something?"

"I couldn't get it out, babe," he said quietly.

"Please don't hurt yourself anymore." Her heart was breaking. This wonderful man was trying so hard not to lose his shit in front of her. "I know you feel anger, and frustration. You may even blame yourself, but it's on them, not you."

"I'm going to kill them," Gabe swore vehemently.

"Easy, sport," Beatrice said gently. "They'll pay one way or another."

Before Gabe could reply, her phone buzzed.

Why was Caitlin calling her?

"Cat?"

"I'll be at your safe house in five minutes."

"What?"

"Travis is a few minutes behind me, and just a warning, he's pissed."

Shit.

Travis was a minute behind Caitlin, or maybe even less. Just when Caitlin was pulling up in her Audi, her husband's Escalade was bearing down the driveway.

"Did she say what's going on?" Gabe asked.

"I have no idea," Beatrice admitted, but she was very curious. Caitlin kept Travis on his toes every single time. It was fun to watch them clash. Travis definitely met his match in his wife. If there was someone who could stand up to his arrogant ass, it was Caitlin.

Caitlin slammed out of her car and stalked up to the front of the house. Travis exited his vehicle, and was glaring at his wife's back.

"Okay, it seems there's trouble in the Blake household," Beatrice quipped.

"Tell them," Travis snapped. "Tell them what you did, Cat."

"Uh-oh, what did you do?" Beatrice asked.

Caitlin huffed angrily, craning her neck toward her husband but not looking at him. "I'm just trying to be helpful. Shall we take this inside?"

They retreated into the house. Beatrice was a bit worried because she had not seen Travis this angry in a long time.

"Okay, what's this all about?"

Caitlin actually looked excited. Ignoring the dark scowl on her husband's face, she said, "You know I hang out in hacker chatrooms on the Black Plane?"

Not that she did, but Beatrice shrugged, prodding her to continue.

"There's been chatter for some weeks now about this bioweapon about to be auctioned off. I thought it was just someone stirring up rumors until the admiral mentioned it last night."

"What? There's an auction site for bioweapons now?" Gabe scoffed.

"Not on the Black Plane. You can be anonymous there but for something like coordinating a terrorist strike or communicating in top secret, you need to delve into a more complex setup we call an IP-MESH." Dramatic pause.

"Okay . . . spit it out, Cat." Beatrice noted briefly that Travis was pacing impatiently behind his wife, as if wanting to throttle her but controlling himself so she could explain herself.

"One of my hacker buddies is very active in the IP-MESH. You see, to get into these clandestine cell networks you need to know someone via Internet Relay Chat. I already do, so all I had to do was set up my own peer-to-peer public key encryption network where only me and that person shares the key. But I also have a private key that would validate—"

"English, Cat," Beatrice interrupted dryly.

Caitlin scowled, exhaling in irritation. "These networks are highly encrypted and are by invitation only. My hacker buddy managed to get me on some of them, and I think I've zeroed in on the Red Bridge auction for the ST-Vyl virus."

This got Beatrice and Gabe's attention.

"The moderator is Redrook843. There's a short description of the virus. Its mode of delivery is in a liquid vial that breaks open and vaporizes; they call it a liquid evaporate. It also has a compilation of some test results and pictures." Caitlin shuddered.

"But didn't the admiral say they suspected it was in powder form?" Gabe asked.

"Redrook said this final composition of the virus is for the sample sale. For bulk orders, its mode of delivery is different."

"It sounds like a basement sale for designer clothes," Beatrice muttered, turning her attention to Travis. "I don't get why you're so pissed. I'm sure Cat's smart enough to cover her sleuthing. Dad can take it over from here."

"That's not everything." Travis glared at his wife.

"Um, I kinda sorta put in a bid," Caitlin said, not looking at her husband.

"What?" Gabe exclaimed. "Are you fucking insane? What do you think is gonna happen if you don't honor your bid when it goes through?"

"My point exactly," Travis muttered, still glaring at his wife.

"Okay, guys, let's calm down." Beatrice thought what Caitlin did wasn't a bad idea at all. Besides, the whole point of the Black Plane was anonymity. "How much did you bid, Cat?"

"Five hundred."

"Grand?"

"No. Five hundred bitcoins," Caitlin said. "That's almost two hundred thousand dollars depending on current exchange rates."

Bitcoin was an internet currency that was fast gaining popularity, especially on the Black Plane where anonymous transactions were preferred.

"When will you know you're in?"

"A week. Well, there's about fifteen buyers interested, five samples being sold. So my chances are pretty high. There are three vials in each sample. Redrook will be sending a private message to those selected. I was hoping if my bid gets selected, the admiral can take it from there and send someone to the meet."

"I don't like the sound of this," Gabe said. "That was way too easy. What if it's a set up?"

"The opportunity was there; the bids were about to close," Caitlin said. "But I did consider that possibility."

"Did you also consider that you're FUCKING PREGNANT!" Travis roared, obviously unable to hold in his anger any longer. "That you don't need this stress, not to mention you could have put yourself in danger again. Jesus Christ, Cat! Is it too much to ask for some fucking peace and quiet for a year, if not for the rest of our lives?"

Beatrice could completely see where Travis was coming from. Losing his wife and thinking she was dead for three years had changed him, and he was only now piecing himself back together. Travis was terrified of losing Caitlin again.

"I know, but Redrook must be stopped. He's taken away so much from so many people already, Travis. You think he won't come after me eventually? I'm a loose end with Project Infinity."

"She has a point," Gabe said.

Resignation was evident in the slump of Travis's shoulders. Caitlin stepped into his space and he clutched her tightly to him, burying his face in the curve of her neck.

"I don't want to lose you, Cat," Travis whispered hoarsely. "I can't lose you again."

Caitlin murmured back words of comfort.

Beatrice tugged Gabe away to give the couple a moment.

EVERYONE WAS CRAMMED into the control room of the safe house. The admiral arrived within the hour of Gabe calling him about Caitlin's breakthrough. Travis and Porter greeted each other cordially. Gabe thought that was an improvement. There was no use harboring grudges at the moment because with what Caitlin had done, there was no room for second guessing, only action.

"What are Redrook's precautions for himself?" Porter asked. "Is it going to be a drop-off or a face-to-face meet? I don't think he'd risk exposure."

Caitlin suddenly looked unsure of herself. "Technically,

I'm already vetted by the person who invited me into the network."

"Except you don't really know the person who invited you. You know him online," Travis said.

"He's been my chat buddy since I got my skills back, Travis," Caitlin said. "We've worked on hacks together actually."

Travis scowled at her. "What kind of hacks?"

"Um, we instigated a denial-of-service attack against an Al Qaeda website," Caitlin mumbled.

Porter chuckled. Gabe didn't think it was funny, because he could feel Travis's frustration.

"What else?" Travis's voice was soft.

"You know, other similar stuff." Caitlin threw up her hands nervously. "So you see, I trust him and his causes."

"Let me play devil's advocate here, sunshine. Why would he be on IP-MESH networks that auction off mass-destruction weapons if he was fighting terrorism?"

"Because he was trying to prevent it?"

"Exactly," Travis said, "and why would he want you onboard?"

"So I can help him?"

Travis shook his head. "Babe, you're too trusting. Yes. He wants you to do the dirty work. Let you take the fall, maybe? Well, over my dead body."

"I don't think Saber Boy wants to see me hurt."

"Saber Boy?" Gabe's lips twitched.

"Saberboy528. What can I say? He's a Star Wars fanatic. Anybody who's got a Luke Skywalker fixation is set on fighting the dark side, don't you think?"

"I see you've been catching up on the movie list I gave you," Beatrice grinned. "I have to agree with Cat. But I'd still take precautions, okay, sweetie? Once you get confirmation of how Redrook wants to do the transaction, you're done." She turned to the admiral. "That's as far as Cat goes. Right, Dad?"

Porter nodded. "Of course. We've got agents ready to take over, but we still don't know what Redrook looks like." He turned to Gabe. "We may need you to do surveillance. During meets like this, the main player is usually in the background. You are the only one who can potentially identify him."

Beatrice looked ready to argue; instead, her gaze locked with his. They both knew everyone had a role to play if Redrook and Red Bridge were to be taken down once and for all.

For a safe house, there seemed to be a constant rotating door of people coming and going. Porter left a few minutes earlier, Travis and Caitlin stuck around for a late breakfast, and now, Doug called to say he was coming over. Gabe had reservations about too many people knowing their location, especially with the risk of being followed. But Beatrice assured him that Doug, being an assistant to a security consultant, was adept in all manners of evading and shaking a tail.

Would he ever spend one whole fucking day alone with Beatrice?

Apparently, Beatrice had been helping Caitlin with some interior design ideas for the Blake residence as he watched the two women look up shit on the laptop. Gabe realized he wanted Beatrice to put her personal touches in his home, too. *Their home.* He bought that house for them, but if she didn't like it, he'd go wherever she wanted. Hopefully, she would give up the condo, because no way would he and Rhino be comfortable there. The two seemed to have formed an unbreakable bond after their shared ordeal, so Gabe was sure Beatrice would consider Rhino's comfort if they were to move.

Christ. *You haven't even asked her, you moron.*

There was no question in his mind that Beatrice was it for him. He just needed to convince her there was no other man for her as well.

"Things going well between you and Bee?"

Gabe turned his attention to Travis. Both of them appeared content watching their women share an animated conversation.

"I hope so. It's hard to gain traction in our relationship with all this crazy stuff that's been going on."

Travis nodded in understanding. "I hear you, man. When I got Caitlin back, I couldn't wait to get started with our life together, but aside from her amnesia, shit just kept on happening."

"She never got any of her memory back at all?"

"Nope."

"She got her skills back though."

"The brain is a complex organ." Travis shrugged. "Her aptitude for computers was always there, I guess."

"You've got one smart woman."

Travis grunted. "Too smart for her own good if you ask me."

Gabe chuckled.

Both women glanced their way.

"What are you two talking about?" Caitlin asked.

"How much of a pain in the ass you are," Travis said, deadpan.

Caitlin grinned cheekily; Beatrice snickered.

Gabe sighed. His woman was so fucking beautiful.

"Jesus, I thought I had it bad. You're just as pussy-whipped," Travis murmured.

"Guilty."

Travis smirked.

"Shut up," Gabe muttered.

The driveway sensors alerted them of an approaching vehicle.

"That's probably Doug." Beatrice hopped out of the chair and glanced at the CCTV screen. "Yep, sure is."

Gabe intercepted Beatrice before she could get to the door. "Babe, when I'm around, I answer the door. Got me?"

Her brows furrowed.

"A familiar car doesn't always translate to friendlies," Gabe added. "I'm not being paranoid, Beatrice, just cautious."

"I know that, Gabe." She pursed her lips. "I wasn't simply going to throw open the door."

"Glad we have that clear." He wasn't taking any chances with her. He knew she worked in the security business, so she understood, but sometimes when one was the person being protected, it was hard to gauge the danger surrounding you.

They watched Doug exit the car before opening the door. Beatrice's assistant was carrying a big box.

Beatrice was like a kid at Christmas when she picked up the coffee beans from the container even before Doug lowered it. She grabbed the coffee grinder and started pulverizing the beans. Gabe took over for Doug and lifted out Beatrice's fancy coffee machine. Soon enough, the aroma of freshly brewing coffee permeated the house. A twinge in his chest wished he was the one who put that look of excitement on Beatrice's face. He was looking forward to that day.

"So, honeybee, Mr. Zach Jamison wants to talk to you," Doug called out from across the room.

"Yes, I've been avoiding work messages," Beatrice responded. "Figured you could handle them."

"What did he want?" Travis asked, standing up. "If this is about Nate being included in the senator's security, he should talk to Nate."

"That's what I told him. He said Nate wouldn't give him a straight answer about the security change. If there was a known threat against the senator to include a very senior security person on the detail, the office of the senator should know."

"And he thinks I have the answers for him?" Beatrice asked.

Doug shrugged. "No idea. What's your schedule like tomorrow?"

"I'm taking her to a sketch artist friend of mine," Gabe said. "I'm still investigating her abduction. No way am I waiting for them to make their next move. This catch and release scenario bugs the fuck out of me."

Too late, he realized he had spooked Beatrice again. Her face had turned pale.

"I'll protect you," Gabe said.

"We will, too, Bee," Travis added. "BSI's got your back as well as Gabe's."

Gabe nodded as Travis clapped his back in reassurance.

Brotherhood.

"My abduction stays under wraps," Beatrice said. "I don't want any of our clients losing confidence. Thank goodness it's still winter and I can wear long sleeves."

Gabe scowled at her. "Can't you take a break from work until we get a handle on what's going on?"

"He's right, Bee," Travis said.

Beatrice and Doug exchanged glances. Her assistant shrugged. "I've already cleared your appointments tomorrow and rescheduled them for later this week. But Tuesday's are still on."

"Keep them the way they are," Beatrice said. She looked at Gabe. "I can't let the bad guys win. Hiding out here is letting them win. Besides, it'll drive me crazy waiting for their next move." She linked her hand with his. "You got me, don't you?"

"I'll assign Sam Harper to you as well," Travis said.

"I like Sam." Beatrice's face lit up.

"Who the hell is Sam?" Gabe growled.

"He used to be my bodyguard," Caitlin said. "I gave him a dislocated shoulder and a very bad headache."

Gabe wasn't sure if Caitlin was joking and looked questioningly at Travis.

Travis rolled his eyes. "Poor Sam. You're not going to conk him over the head with a vase, are you, Bee?"

Caitlin glared at her husband.

"Of course not. I'm not some ninja chick like Cat," Beatrice said.

"All right, stop teasing the pregnant woman," Caitlin grumbled.

Everyone started laughing as Travis hugged his wife affectionately. Gabe glanced around him, and seeing how Beatrice's friends cared so much about her, he started feeling guilty about his earlier resentment. He guessed he would get used to them, although he still couldn't wait to have her all to himself.

15

"Need a break, babe?"

Beatrice shook her head, but her face was pale, and she had trouble keeping the quaver out of her voice. Gabe had been debriefing her from her ordeal. It had been more than 48 hours since he got her back. He couldn't delay the debriefing any longer.

He knew he was being too easy on her, refusing to push her. His experience in the military had prepared him for every type of questioning. But having a personal stake in her, he probably wasn't the best person to do this, and should've let one of Travis's guys do it. However, Gabe's instinct to protect won out.

"What did they say after they came back into the room?" He braced himself for what was to come. He just prayed he could keep it together.

"You know," Beatrice whispered and held out her arms, "this happened."

"They didn't say anything?"

She pressed her lips in a thin line and concentrated on a spot on the table. "Just that if I fought, it would hurt more. And they were just sending a message."

Gabe's fingers curled into fists before him. *Don't lose your shit, Sullivan.* He breathed deeply. "How close was the voice?"

"He was right by my ear."

"Did you recognize the voice this time?"

"It was raspy, deliberately low. So, no."

"Think, Beatrice. Earlier, you said the altered voice seemed to have an inflection you recognized."

She closed her eyes for a second as if trying to recall the events. When her green eyes met his once more, the agony in them clawed at his insides.

"No," she whispered.

"Okay," Gabe relented. "Can you tell me how many people were in the room?"

"I think there were three of them. I was still blindfolded." She looked at him pleadingly. "That's all I remember, Gabe. Are we done?"

"Did you lose consciousness or were you sedated?"

"I don't know!" Beatrice snapped. "Pain, Gabe, that's all I remember. And screaming. I don't know . . . I don't know . . ." she mumbled over and over. She had tried to wrap her arms around her earlier but winced and realized her forearms were fucked up. Right now, the fingers of her left hand were digging into her right palm.

Christ, he hated himself right now. Gabe immediately turned off the recorder, got out of his chair, and knelt in front of her. He folded her hands in his and said gently, "Hey, we're done, okay?"

"I'm sorry if I can't provide anything useful," she sniffed. "It's just that they kept me drugged up most of the time."

"We got a sketch of one of the guys who abducted you, that's something," Gabe said. Not to mention Rhino had mangled his arm.

"What are we doing next?"

"I doubt the guy Rhino injured has sought medical attention in area hospitals, but it's worth checking out. I'll call around." Gabe looked at her. "Do you mind hanging around DC for a while or do you want me to take you back to the safe house?"

"You can drop me off at BSI if you've got stuff to do. I'll be safe there."

Gabe rose from his crouch and sat on the table. "Who's usually at BSI at this time?"

"Close to lunch? Probably, Emily. Sometimes Travis is around," Beatrice said.

"I don't want to leave you without a bodyguard. Didn't Travis mention this guy Sam Harper?"

"Travis called me this morning. Sam can start tomorrow. Let me call Em and see who's at the office."

Gabe nodded. He hadn't worked security in a team in a while. Being an assassin, he worked alone, only using intel he acquired from Crowe. Remembering his former partner reminded him that Ryker's link to Crowe had yet to be investigated. Judging from the debrief, Beatrice's abductors had intimate knowledge of Dmitry Yerzov's kill roll and methods, but it seemed they didn't know about the fallacy regarding his Angel of Death reputation. Even as Dmitry, Gabe had maintained a strictly professional relationship with Belov/Crowe. Gabe called someone else when it had to do with switching his young victims with corpses. Porter preferred this decentralized system of clandestine work.

"Em said Ed will be at the office," Beatrice said after she ended her call.

"Ed Shephard, right?"

"Yes. Em's husband."

"Fine," Gabe muttered. He still didn't like being away from her, but he couldn't do his own investigation if he didn't get himself out there.

After leaving Beatrice at the BSI office, Gabe met a mutual acquaintance he had with Ryker. The man was a fixer—a specialist in the fabrication of assumed identities. Alphabet agencies, including the CIA, used the fixer for clandestine operations that were politically sensitive and strictly off the record.

The fixer was reluctant at first to reveal his dealings with Ryker, but since Ryker was dead and apparently owed the guy ten-grand for some falsified documents, it didn't take long to get some actionable intel—a drop-off place for said documents.

Money talked.

Gabe paid him five grand for the lead, which was more than the man was ever going to get back.

So now, he was back in the Cloverleaf District. Steve Ryker was known as Vladimir Volkov around these parts. That was why the Iron Skulls said he was Russian.

He pulled his Silverado in front of a rundown dry cleaners in a relatively isolated area. These types of businesses were so clichéd as fronts for organized crime, but realistically, still common.

The bell chimed when he pushed open the door. A young Latino man came to the counter, eyes widening as he caught sight of Gabe.

The man was going to run.

The Latino guy turned and sprinted into a back room. Cursing under his breath, Gabe drew his 9mm, jumped over the counter, and ran after him. When he reached the entrance to the room, he leaned past the frame and quickly pulled back when he saw a gun. A shot fired past him. Gabe immediately crouched, thanking his instincts as another bullet punched a hole where his head would have been. He didn't think Beatrice would appreciate him missing another piece of his skull. He leaned past the door jamb again and squeezed the trigger. He heard a grunt followed by a thud on the floor. Gabe didn't waste any time getting to the Latino man who was writhing on the floor and clutching his leg. He straddled the man and pointed the muzzle of his gun to his head.

"Volkov. You know where he lived?"

"He's dead, man."

"I know that, dickhead," Gabe snarled. "I said lived. Where did he stay?"

The guy's mouth clamped shut. Gabe's fingers tightened around the man's neck as he jabbed the tip of his 9mm into the Latino guy's wound.

The man yelled in agony. "Upstairs!"

"You better not be lying." Gabe hauled the guy up and pushed him toward the stairs. On their way to the floor above, he asked. "Why did you run? Do you know me?"

No answer.

Gabe's blood boiled through his veins. "Were you involved in the kidnapping of the redhead?"

This time the man turned his head to look at Gabe. "No. Not me. I wasn't involved."

"But you know who was involved?"

"No."

"What's your name?"

"Johnny."

Bullshit that was his name, but that would do for now.

They reached the top of the stairs where there were two rooms.

He yanked Johnny close to him and muttered, "Which room?"

"The one on the right."

"Who else lives here?"

"No one. Fuego is not here anymore. I'm not Fuego."

Gabe heard rumors that the gang was laying low ever since the hit on the senator's uncle. He nudged the guy forward and instructed him to open the door on the left. It revealed a large bathroom, except it wasn't. It was covered in tiles with a raised structure in the middle that was twice the size of a regular bath tub. Gabe didn't have any doubt what this place was used for—bloody executions.

"Did Volkov use this room?"

"Yes. This whole space was his." Johnny was groaning in pain.

Jesus Christ. *Was Ryker a sadist?*

"Why did you run from me?" Gabe asked as he pushed the man into the other room. There was a bed and other furniture. The dresser had its drawers open and clothes strewn all over. The desk drawers were empty, the contents scattered on the floor as well. Someone had been looking for something.

"I recognized your picture."

"Volkov had pictures of me?"

Johnny nodded and pointed to a bare wall. "He had a few pinned on the wall, but mostly they were of a redhead."

Gabe's gut roiled in distaste at the thought of Ryker stalking Beatrice. "If you're not Fuego, what were you doing with Ryker?"

"Ryker? I do not know—"

Gabe shook his head. "Volkov."

"I ran errands for him. He didn't like to be outside much, especially during the daytime."

He noticed that Johnny was starting to look pale. Might as well patch him up before he keeled over. Gabe instructed him to sit on the chair and took out a roll of duct tape. The innocuous household item had many uses, like securing a captive and temporarily fixing a bleeding injury. He checked the gunshot wound and realized the bullet went through.

"You'll live," Gabe said curtly after wrapping several layers of tape over the bleeder. He checked the man for the Fuego tattoo and found none, so he must have been telling the truth. "Who ransacked this room?"

"The Fuego big boss—Ventura and another guy."

Gabe knew how Ventura looked from the pictures the Iron Skulls provided. "Describe Ventura's companion."

"Listen, *hermanò*, I told you too much already." With the bleeding stemmed, Johnny was thinking coherently again and not running his mouth. "I'm sure they're having this place watched."

"I thought you said they've disappeared." Gabe got to his feet and started pulling out the drawer of the dresser, dragging the furniture forward to also check the back.

"I just know. Look, I'm lucky they didn't kill me—"

"Why would they? I'm sure you store shit for them, don't you?"

Johnny didn't say anything.

Taking out a switchblade, Gabe moved to the desk and started poking at the corners for hidden compartments.

"Description of the man?" He repeated as he eased under the desk. "Don't make me repeat that question for a third time." He tapped his knife at the edge of the desk, his warning not lost on the Latino guy.

"He . . . He was dressed well. In a suit."

"What?" Gabe emerged from under the table, sat up, and stared hard at Johnny.

"He had dark hair, and skin. Not too tall."

"Was he Latino? How old, you think?"

"Hard to tell. He didn't have an accent. He's around mid-thirties."

For a minute he thought it was Senator Mendoza. "Was he heavy-set? Thin? Any scars?"

"He was wearing a coat, but he's definitely not fat. I don't know of any marks on his face." The man sighed. "I don't look at them, you know. They come in and do their shit. The less I know, the better."

Gabe got to his knees and·peered underneath the space between the claw foot dresser and the floor. Having trained in clandestine ops with Ryker, he knew how the man operated.

He tapped under the base of the dresser and noticed the thin plywood bulging on the right corner.

Bingo.

He inserted his knife at the corner and dislodged the piece, revealing the edges of a stash of papers. Gingerly pulling them out, Gabe's brows shot to his hairline as he read the contents of the documents.

Getting back to his feet, Gabe slashed the duct tape bindings and released Johnny. "You're coming with me."

GABE KEPT his eyes peeled as he waited for Johnny to lock up the doors of the dry cleaners. There were a few people milling around who immediately looked away when they saw the pair of them. Cloverleaf was known for violent crimes, so Gabe guessed that a form of self-preservation for those who lived here was to ignore the happenings and keep their mouths shut.

When they got into his pickup, Gabe took out his phone and made several calls. First was to Dr. Ryan, the second was to the sketch artist who had worked with Beatrice earlier. He told them to head to BSI. Lastly, he called Beatrice.

"I'm on my way back," Gabe said when she answered.

"Did you find anything?"

"Interesting stuff. I'm also bringing in someone who may know what Redrook looks like."

Silence for a beat and then, "Do you trust him?"

"Not sure yet, babe. It's all we've got right now."

"If he pans out, that'll be some breakthrough."

"Yeah. I've got some documents your dad needs to look over. Can't talk about it on the phone."

Beatrice dropped off for a bit while she spoke to someone. It also sounded like she was outdoors.

"Beatrice?"

"Yes, sorry. I'm about to head out to a meeting with Zach."

"What?" Gabe snapped. "I told you to stay in the fucking office."

"Don't worry, Ed's coming with me."

"I don't give a damn if you have an entire security entourage," Gabe snarled, starting the truck and steering out of the space. "I told you to stay put."

"Things have just gone to crap, Gabe. Zach and Nate had a confrontation earlier today. The senator got involved, and he's thinking of canceling the BSI contract. Travis is over there smoothing things out right now. The senator told Zach to go cool off. I'm taking care of Zach," Beatrice said.

"Jesus Christ, not one day and Reece got into trouble?"

Beatrice laughed briefly, though not really with humor. "Don't let his easy personality fool you. When Nate's got a hair up his ass, he could push your buttons."

Gabe couldn't agree more, remembering the many times the man irked him and made him jealous.

"Where are you meeting Zach Jamison?"

"Coffee shop at the corner of O St. and 35th." Beatrice told him the name.

"Okay, text me Ed's number."

"Will do. I gotta go."

Gabe ended the call and looked over at Johnny. The man was quietly staring out the window, his face lined with pain.

"We'll have someone look at your leg," Gabe said.

"For what? I'm dead anyway."

"You have any family around here?"

"No. In Florida."

"You might want to visit them, lay low for a while."

Johnny sighed. "I have a business, you know."

"Yeah, right. You probably make more using your business as a front," Gabe said. "It's only a matter of time before they tie up loose ends and circle back to you."

Johnny remained quiet for the rest of the trip.

BEATRICE ENTERED the coffee shop in Georgetown and spotted Zach Jamison immediately. She hadn't met him outside the senator's office since she visited his hospital room after the junkyard ambush.

He stood when he saw her, his face looked grave, unhappy. He tried to smile, but it didn't reach his eyes. His gaze drifted behind her. Seeing Ed, his mouth tightened.

Ed escorted her up to the table.

"Zach." Beatrice held out her hand in greeting. Zach already knew Ed because he was the team lead on Senator Mendoza's security detail. After the two men exchanged handshakes, Ed excused himself to scope out the area and vanished into the background.

"Everything all right, Beatrice? Where's Sullivan?" Zach asked after a server came by and took her order.

"He had somewhere else he needed to be."

"I hope I didn't needlessly drag you out if you're in danger," Zach said anxiously. "What's going on?"

"I'm fine. Just precautions. It happens sometimes with this job."

"Is it because of our contract?'

"No." Beatrice was uncomfortable with the questions. "Speaking of the contract, what happened between you and Nate?"

"He's getting too intrusive to the point of offending some of our supporters," Zach huffed indignantly.

"He's been there a day," Beatrice reminded him. Actually, less than a day.

"Well, he's already gone and interrogated one of the senator's visitors from the Colombian government who oversees exports."

"Was the man on an advance dossier given to the security team?"

Zach pressed his lips together.

"Zach?"

"With the trip coming up, we've had an influx of dignitaries from South America. Our staff is overworked," the Chief of Staff defended. "So no, he wasn't. But Reece overreacted." Zach's eyes bore into hers. "Is there a threat you're keeping from us, Beatrice? We've already beefed up security after the junkyard incident. Why was Reece suddenly inserted into the senator's detail without an accompanying re-assessment? You even have Shephard guarding you. I understood when it was Sullivan, but now . . ."

He let his words trail off and flipped his right hand in an irritated gesture. She also could have imagined a slight sneer curving Zach's lips.

She wished she was more prepared for this meeting and had formulated a standard answer. Good thing a server brought their coffee and pastry orders, which gave her a few seconds to compose her reply.

"No different threat than was assessed after the junkyard ambush," Beatrice said. "It's just that the Senator's trip to South America is approaching; I did warn you that we would ramp up security leading up to the trip and the addition of personnel is fluid up to ten. Also, I've been hearing dissent with regards to the Immigration and Border Security bill, which goes to vote after the senator's trip. That's still two months out, but you can be sure those in opposition will take action before then. BSI can never be too careful."

Beatrice didn't like the way Zach's eyes scrutinized her, as if stripping her defenses to get to the core of her lie. Her answer was weak at most, too generic, but was valid.

Zach's phone buzzed. He checked it, his face tightening. When his eyes returned to hers, they were so chilly; she felt a shiver snake up her spine.

"Is everything all right?" Beatrice asked. "Was that the senator's office? I know Travis went over there to talk to the senator."

"I know he did," Zach said. "I told Senator Mendoza we couldn't have a man like Reece on our security team and we'd have to shop for a different company if BSI insists on including him. This is why I wanted to talk to you. I like you, Beatrice." The way he said her name sparked a deadly sense of déjà vu.

. . . so you had no idea, poor Beatrice.

She ignored the ringing in her ears and took a sip of coffee, trying to concentrate on Zach's words.

"You're astute, smart, and capable," he continued. "Surely you can recommend a different security firm."

"You were the ones set on BSI. I was recommending a different company."

"My point exactly," Zach purred. "You knew our needs more than we did. We should have listened to you. Reece is too inexperienced to handle the complex day-to-day activities of our office."

Beatrice bristled at the obvious dig at Nate. At that moment, she despised Zach Jamison. Nate may not have an impressive resume like Travis, but that was only because he had worked clandestine missions for the CIA, missions he couldn't list as accomplishments. She valued her clients, but she loved her BSI boys more and would protect them like a lioness defending her cubs, even if she lost business.

"Nathan Reece is an invaluable member of BSI," Beatrice said carefully. "From what you've told me of what had transpired, I can only conclude he was doing his job. Your assessment of Nate's skills is different from mine. BSI's track record speaks for itself. Foreign and local dignitaries all have glowing reviews of their services. If our basic beliefs about what is crucial security for the senator are different, I'm not your person. Trust goes both ways, Zach. If the security team can't trust the person they're protecting to do what they're told, then a working relationship is not possible."

The Chief of Staff's expression turned more remote; gone was the charm that Beatrice was used to.

Her phone buzzed with a text message. It was from Gabe.

Her stomach bottomed out.

16

GABE PERUSED the document in front of him while he waited for the artist to finish the facial composite of the man Johnny saw with Ventura. It was a long shot because the last time Johnny saw them was around a week after Ryker's demise. Dr. Ryan stepped out of the room, her eyes zeroing in on Gabe. She was not pleased.

"I gave you my number just in case Beatrice had issues, not to call me for your own problems," the doctor said sternly.

"This guy may lead us to who abducted Beatrice," Gabe replied.

"That's what you told me on the phone and the only reason I came. Don't make it a habit, Mr. Sullivan."

"Can't promise that, Doc," Gabe grinned.

"Save that charming smile for Ms. Porter. It's not working on me," the doctor said dryly, but amusement twinkled in her eyes. "Here's a prescription for antibiotics and pain meds."

Just then, Travis and Nate walked into the office.

"Doc? What are you doing here?" Travis asked.

"Sullivan here had someone for me to patch up," Dr. Ryan replied. "I gotta go. See you around, Travis. Give my regards to Cat."

After the doctor left, Travis turned to Gabe. "What's going on?"

"Everything squared away with the senator?" Gabe asked.

"Yes," Nate replied. He and Travis wore identical frowns as they regarded Johnny in the conference room.

"Are they keeping you on?"

"Nate's out," Travis said, "but I told the senator I'm a hundred percent behind what Nate did." Travis paused. "Why am I telling you this? It's none of your business."

Gabe shrugged. "Beatrice is in a meeting with Zach Jamison right this moment. I was curious."

"Are you telling us what's going on?" Travis looked pointedly at Johnny. "Who the hell is that?"

"Sorry, I didn't tell you Travis, Nate," Em came up behind them. "Both of you were busy with Senator Mendoza, I didn't want to interrupt."

"Juan Rodriguez, otherwise known as Johnny," Gabe said. "I had some intel about Ryker's hideout in the Cloverleaf District." The other two men stilled. "I found where he did his executions, which were really medical tests."

"Damn," Travis muttered. "Let's go to my office."

"Can't. Need to keep an eye on Johnny."

Travis looked at Em, who understood and returned to the reception area out of ear shot.

"Speak," Travis prompted.

"These documents hold the technical information on the virus." Gabe held up the stack of papers recovered from Ryker's room.

"How is it different from what we already have? Porter said they've typed the genome."

"Yes. But here"—Gabe held up the paper—"it states it's inert when in powder form. It's transformed into a liquid evaporate by a careful ratio of the indicated compounds. Ryker experimented on five test subjects. It's all there." Gabe handed the paper to Travis, with Nate looking grimly over his friend's shoulder. "Everything from time of exposure to time of death."

"Fuck me," Nate whispered. "This is sounding too damn real."

"Damn straight," Gabe muttered. "I already left a message for Porter."

Travis nodded. "Whatever covert group Porter is working with needs this data." Though Gabe agreed, he wanted in on that mission, so he could personally gut whoever tortured Beatrice. His anger was under control, but it would spike to a killing degree whenever he let his thoughts drift to the cuts on Beatrice's arms.

"I'm done," the sketch artist said, walking up to them. "Johnny agrees it's not an exact likeness, but it's the best he could remember."

Gabe looked at the sketch and balked. He could feel the blood leave his face as a fear like he'd never felt before ratcheted up inside him. Travis cursed while Nate said, "Fuck! Tell me that's not Zach Jamison."

ZACH JAMISON IS DIRTY. He was working with Ryker.

Beatrice read the message twice to make sure she hadn't misunderstood.

"What's wrong, Beatrice?" Zach whispered.

Her gaze lifted reluctantly to stare into dark soulless depths. The gears in her brain tried to make sense of who was clearly before her.

The person who tortured her.

The more you fight, the more it's going to hurt.

"You," Beatrice whispered.

Zach's smile was nothing like his regular megawatt smile. This time, it was laced with malice. "So, the cat's out of the bag. Pity." His eyes shifted to a point over her shoulder. Ed

Shephard had probably been alerted. Beatrice was frozen; she didn't dare take her eyes off Zach.

A scuffle erupted behind her. There was screaming and seats scraping as the crowd panicked. She still didn't dare look away.

"See, I'm not stupid to come here by myself." Zach's lips curved derisively.

"I'm not going anywhere with you." Beatrice finally found her voice. Her phone kept buzzing. She couldn't take her eyes off Zach. She just didn't trust him. She couldn't be taken again. It would destroy her. The thought of never feeling safe, not knowing who to trust, would destroy her.

"You won't have to," Zach sneered. "You'll be dead."

He lunged forward, a hand shooting out, but Beatrice, even in her terror, was ready for him. She shoved her chair backward and managed to block a knife swipe aimed for her neck. She stood up and saw Ed engaged in a hand-to-hand with Zach's goon. She faced off with Zach, who had indecision written all over his face as he stared beyond her again.

"I'll see you around, pretty girl." He backed away from her and disappeared into the back exit. It would be foolish to follow him. Beatrice stood unmoving.

Ed suddenly appeared by her side. "Jesus, you're bleeding."

She was cut? Before she could reach up to touch the right side of her face, Ed had her chin tilted at an angle.

"It's a shallow cut," Ed observed. "But fuck me, Sullivan's going to go ape-shit."

She had no doubt. Remembering her phone, she saw additional text messages from Gabe.

Talk to me.

Damn it. Tell me you're okay.

And then.

Babe, please be okay.

Beatrice called him.

"Beatrice? Christ, babe, are you okay?" Gabe growled into the phone.

"I'm fine. Oh, God. Oh, God, Gabe, I can't believe it's Zach." She half-sobbed into the phone, collapsing into a chair as the adrenalin withdrew from her body. It was as if a ghost had walked over her grave, and she felt chilled all over. Her life had once again flashed in front of her. It was only through her endless sparring exercises and continued training that saved her from having her carotid artery slashed.

"Ed's with you?" Ed was on the phone, probably with Travis or Nate. Zach's goon also disappeared.

"Yes, he is," Beatrice said. Protection of your principal was always a priority, not chasing after an assailant. It was a primary rule of executive protection.

"I'm on my way," Gabe said, his voice now guttural. "God, Beatrice, I love you."

"I love you, Gabe." She felt cold, so cold. "I need you," she added on a whisper.

"I'll be there soon."

"CAN'T you go any damn faster?"

"I'm going as fast as I can, man," Travis muttered as he wove his Escalade around DC traffic. "It's rush hour and they're in Georgetown."

A skin peel with muriatic acid was probably less torturous than what Gabe was experiencing right now. He had calmed down a bit after he'd talk to Beatrice, but the sucker punch of discovering that Zach Jamison had been deceiving them all this time caused him to almost lose his shit at BSI.

He was ready to charge out the door when Travis and Nate pounced on him to calm him down. He nearly punched Travis, but the other man assured him there was no one more capable than Ed Shephard and he'd been alerted. It did little to assuage Gabe's panic, especially when Beatrice didn't reply to his text message warning. But he agreed to let Travis drive while he'd been imagining several ways to deliver a slow painful death to Jamison. Finally, he had someone to direct his rage. A focus.

Parking in Georgetown was terrible. Gabe was doubly thankful now that Travis was driving. It wasn't difficult to find the coffee shop; there was already a police cruiser double-parked in front of it.

"I'll need to drop you off here and find parking," Travis said as he approached the intersection a block before the establishment.

"Thanks, man." Gabe exited the Escalade and broke into a sprint. There were some curious onlookers at the entrance. He shouldered past them and yanked the door open. He spotted Beatrice talking to a uniform.

Their eyes met across the room, her luminous green ones flooding with relief, probably mirroring his own. His relief quickly turned to outrage when he noticed the cut right under her right jaw.

Beatrice abandoned the police officer and walked briskly toward him. He opened his arms and quickly engulfed her in a crushing embrace. If given a choice, she would never leave his arms.

"Babe, you scared the shit out of me," Gabe murmured into her hair.

"I'm sorry. You're right again," she mumbled, pulling away to look up at him. "I shouldn't have left the office."

Gabe exhaled deeply. "Yeah. But it's done. Next time listen to your security, okay?"

"I know. I keep on preaching it, but I had Ed with me, so I felt safe enough."

"You didn't know Jamison was dirty." He hugged her tightly to him again before he asked as calmly as he could muster, "What happened to your neck?"

Beatrice stiffened in his arms.

"Babe?"

"He tried to cut me."

Gabe closed his eyes at the thought; the close call was killing him.

"Ouch, Gabe. Ease up. You're squeezing the air out of me."

"How . . . you blocked it?"

"Yes."

"That's my girl."

"Um, excuse me, Ms. Porter, but I need more information from you." A police officer was standing beside them, assessing Gabe warily.

Gabe forced himself to let Beatrice go. He kissed the crown of her head and nodded to the uniform to proceed. He hovered nearby though, spotting Travis talking to Ed. He wanted to join that huddle, but leaving Beatrice's side was not an option right now. He didn't know who to trust in this coffee shop and the crowd outside didn't exactly give him the warm fuzzies as he scanned the spectators for suspicious elements.

His awareness was heightened; all his senses were engaged as he called upon all his training to protect the woman he loved. Right now, the only way someone was going to hurt a hair on her head was through his cold, lifeless body.

ZACH JAMISON GOT into a white-colored van a few blocks away from the coffee shop. He needed to go to ground and fast. That had been too fucking close. He turned to the driver of the van, Domingo Ventura, the leader of the Fuego gang.

"How the fuck did Sullivan find out about Volkov?" Zach demanded.

Ventura had no idea the Russian they had been dealing with was actually former U.S. Special Forces Steve Ryker.

"I have no idea. But one of my *hermanos* saw him drag Johnny from the dry cleaners. We should have whacked that *pendejo* when we had the chance."

Now that BSI had outed him, it would only be a matter of time before they establish his connection to Philip Crowe. Too bad he had not finished off Beatrice Porter. He relished wreaking psychological agony more than physical damage. Maybe he could still play with her. She was right when she called him a sadistic bastard.

Frank Wilkes would be one unhappy boss, but Zach still had information he needed. Unless someone figured out what information he'd been siphoning from their office, Zach was still indispensable.

It was Benjamin Porter he wanted dead. Zach had nothing against Sullivan. That had been all Ryker. However, Sullivan being in the way of his revenge against Porter made him Zach's enemy as well.

So be it.

It was obvious now that "safe house" was a misnomer, and the place was intended to be a command center for Porter's agenda. Right now, the house was like a fucking party. Okay, maybe Gabe was exaggerating. With Caitlin around, food was a necessity, especially since she was almost four months pregnant. She had hacked into the Metropolitan Police Department database because they were officially the ones investigating the assault on Beatrice in Georgetown. They had lifted a partial fingerprint of Zach Jamison from the coffee cup.

Caitlin was using those prints to do a search of her own against a larger, more classified database with a couple of modified input parameters to widen the search to individuals other than Zach Jamison in case the name was an alias.

Travis's wife had been shoveling food in her mouth as they waited, much to Porter's annoyance. Clearly, the admiral was old school and didn't want anyone eating in the command center.

Gabe stuck his head out of the command room to briefly check on Beatrice. She just received a call from Senator Mendoza who received a visit from the MPD detectives. Judging from Beatrice's face, she was trying to make the senator feel better for unleashing Zach Jamison on her. Neither the MPD nor the senator knew of her torture at the hands of the motherfucker. The truth would open a whole line of questioning that could compromise what the admiral was working on. Until Porter and his covert team could shut down Redrook, they had to keep their intel under wraps. All the senator and the MPD knew was Zach Jamison had snapped and attacked Beatrice. Tough sell to the senator since Zach had apparently worked for a former friend of his and came highly recommended.

Gabe stood beside Porter. "Hundred bucks says that the senator's former Chief of Staff was murdered and didn't die from a heart attack."

"Short of exhuming the body, we couldn't prove it," the admiral said. "But I'm going with your hunch. You did say Hybernabis could mimic a heart attack in those with pre-existing conditions."

"Correct."

Caitlin gave a whoop that made the admiral and Gabe switch their attentions to her.

"Found anything?" Porter asked.

"I've kept an open-match algorithm against Philip Crowe's records, including both living and deceased people," Caitlin said. "The fingerprints bear a 91% match against Zacharia Alvarez. Deceased. Car accident." She shook her head and added derisively. "Sounds like a common cause of faked deaths. Anyway, Alvarez and Crowe were in the same college together until the second year when Alvarez supposedly died. They were both computer science majors. Crowe dropped out to join the Army soon after his death."

"Let me guess, Alvarez is Colombian?" Gabe asked.

"Irish-Colombian. That's why it's hard to tag his ethnicity."

"So Zacharia Alvarez becomes Zach Jamison."

"You think Crowe and Alvarez were acquainted with each other? Going to the same college and sharing the same major would assure they'd at least moved in the same circles."

"Hacking into school records now," Caitlin announced. It took maybe fifteen minutes for her to find what she was looking for, oblivious that he and Porter were looking over her shoulders. She zoned them out. By this time, Travis had quietly entered the room. "Yep, they belong to the same fraternity and . . ." She covered her mouth with her hand. "Um . . . Yeah, they know each other." Caitlin's eyes angled toward the three men in the room. "Does someone get the vibe that they're more than just friends?"

All three men shifted uncomfortably. There were several pictures of Crowe and Alvarez in rather compromising positions. The images were faded, probably over fifteen years ago.

"Aren't those pics too racy for fraternity websites?" Gabe asked. "You'd have thought with Zach's new identity, they'd have erased every trace of him."

"I'm not on a fraternity website," Caitlin said. "That had been sanitized. I went to one of their former frat brother's micro-blogging site. That's where you'll find interesting pictures. Get Doug in here, let's get his opinion."

Gabe was trying not to chuckle as Travis left the room to get Doug. Beatrice returned with her assistant.

"Oh, my," Beatrice said. "That explains a lot, doesn't it, Doug?"

"Oh, yeah," her assistant replied, eyes wide on the screen.

Doug looked at everyone in the room. "There's something between those two all right."

"If he and Crowe continued to be lovers, that would explain his hatred against you, Admiral," Caitlin said.

There was silence in the room as everyone absorbed the motive. It made perfect sense, Gabe realized. Although a lover's revenge seemed to be simply the tip of the iceberg because everything had been set into motion long before Porter had shot and killed Philip Crowe. This meant Zach Jamison had been recruited to be a sleeper agent, meant to infiltrate the political system and keep the CIA apprised of its schemes, totally clandestine and not sanctioned by the U.S. government.

"You think Zach is bi?" Beatrice asked suddenly.

"Now why the fuck would you think that?" Gabe asked.

"Well, he's been trying to ask me on a date," Beatrice explained. "But he reserved his goo-goo eyes for Doug and Nate."

"Nate?" Travis asked in amusement.

"By the way, where is Nate?" Caitlin asked.

"The senator called him to his office, probably to apologize," Doug replied.

"This late?" Beatrice asked.

Doug shrugged. With the loss of his Chief of Staff, burning the midnight oil at the senate office wouldn't be surprising.

"Okay, let's get back on point here," Porter interrupted. "Caitlin, we can focus on Zach Jamison. See how he moved through the ranks to become Chief of Staff for a United States senator."

"That's easy," Caitlin said. "Pretty much public record. He switched his major to Political Science and graduated with honors from Miami University. Everything before that time was definitely fabricated. He worked as an aide for a state senator before he worked as the Director of External Affairs and then the Chief of Staff of the Florida governor."

"Wasn't there some scandal surrounding the governor?"

"Yes, for federal corruption charges. Senator Mendoza was good friends with the governor and stood by his side despite the accusations. So the senator had known Jamison a while before hiring him."

"Man, that blows," Travis said.

"Are we sure the senator is innocent?" Gabe asked.

"Now that's the sixty-four thousand dollar question," Caitlin piped in.

"Criminy," Beatrice muttered, "if he's dirty, I quit. I really like the man."

"I've known Mendoza for years, followed his career. He's legit," Porter said. "Of course, as we all know, nothing is as it seems."

"Jeez, thanks, Dad," Beatrice groused.

The admiral chuckled and planted a kiss on Beatrice's forehead. "I gotta go, baby. I need to keep another team apprised."

"So when are we going to meet this A-team of yours?" Gabe asked darkly.

"Jealous, Commander?" Porter asked; his eyes held some wiliness Gabe didn't trust.

"No. But I sure want to get my hands on Zach and this Redrook guy," Gabe shot back. "Don't want to miss all the fun."

"I'm sure that can be arranged," the admiral answered enigmatically.

"STAY THE FUCK AWAY FROM HER!"

Beatrice's eyes snapped open, her heart in her throat, pounding wildly. Gabe thrashed beside her.

"Beatrice, God, no!"

He was dreaming or having a nightmare.

"Gabe," she whispered. Beatrice made the mistake of touching him and found her wrist gripped painfully as she was flipped over him and then under him. A hand squeezed her neck.

"Gabe!" she choked out, her concern morphing to fear as he straddled her, his dead weight pinning her legs to the mattress.

"Beatrice?" The hand on her throat slackened and moved to cup her face. "Oh, fuck." His other hand skimmed her body as if checking for injuries. "Did I hurt you, babe? Fuck. Fuck. Fuck."

"I'm okay. Just, um . . . surprised."

He rested his forehead on hers. "I'm so sorry. I . . . I . . . frightened you. Maybe I should sleep on the floor." He pulled back and linked his hands with hers, drawing them together and kissing the back of her fingers. "I'm really, really sorry."

"Gabe, it's not your fault. I shouldn't have woken you that way when you were already agitated in your sleep." She heard him curse softly and looked to the side. "It was about me, wasn't it? I heard you call out my name."

He nodded jerkily. His weight left hers, shifting to sit on the side of the bed. He hunched over, elbows on his knees, head bowed.

"I can't decompress," Gabe admitted. "My nerves are wound so tight right now. I just"—he exhaled harshly—"just keep replaying everything in my head, searching if there was a way I could have kept you away from those motherfuckers. Did I miss any signs?"

"Stop. It was beyond your control, Gabe." Beatrice knee-crawled across the bed, and sat on her heels. "You need to move on from this, so I can, too. Please?"

He tilted his head in her direction, not quite looking at her. "I'm sorry," he repeated. "I need some air." He quickly rose and ordered Rhino to *stay* when the dog moved to follow him. He left the room, his body rigid with tension. Beatrice knew he was going to visit the wall outside again.

She got off the bed and grabbed a robe to wrap around her body. She found him pacing the darkness of the back patio. He must have turned off the motion sensor lights. Beatrice watched his silhouette through the window for a while. Every now and then he would pause in front of the wall as if contemplating what to do, and then he'd resume his prowl across the patio over and over. Minutes passed. Finally, she couldn't take it anymore. He was in agony over her, and her heart ached to comfort him.

She opened the door. He continued pacing; he knew she had been watching him.

"Go away, Beatrice."

"Gabe—"

"Stay the fuck away from me." His voice was so harsh, she flinched.

"No!" Beatrice shivered in the cold, wrapping her arms around herself. "You can't let everything that happens to me get to you this way."

"Not your fucking problem. I'm trying to deal with it," Gabe growled. "But you have to stay the FUCK away."

"Why?"

"Beatrice, I'm begging you." A guttural sound grated at the back of his throat. "Get back upstairs. I'll be with you in a few minutes."

"When? After you've hurt yourself again?" Her teeth chattered; a tremor rippled through her. Why Gabe thought this frigid February air was mind-clearing didn't compute. However, she would rather turn into an icicle before she'd allow him to stew and kick himself for what Zach and this Redrook guy did to her.

He cursed softly and dragged her into him, rubbing her arms briskly to get her warm. "It's freezing out here, babe."

"So come inside. We can talk, stay up. You can make me hot cocoa."

His mouth skimmed the side of her cheeks; his breathing turned ragged. Hands that were meant to warm her from the chill emanated a different kind of heat. Their contact was still elemental, but the caresses turned sensual, teasing, arousing. A groan escaped him. "I need to be inside you."

A frisson of unspoken need sparked between them, kindling the beginnings of desire. Her core swelled and pulsed.

His mouth played along the edges of her lips. "Tell me if it's okay."

"You want to fuck me?" Beatrice asked breathlessly, gasping when the back of his fingers brushed between her legs.

"Yes." He pressed her against the wall; a finger worked through her panties and stroked her slit.

"Out here?"

"Yes," he snarled softly.

"Cameras."

"I'll take care of it, and it's too dark," he muttered. "Last chance, Beatrice. Tell me to stop. Either get out of here, or be prepared to get fucked. Hard."

A finger plunged inside her, causing her to inhale sharply. He wasn't kissing her. His face was millimeters from hers and the warm air fanning her cheeks reminded her of a predator sniffing his prey. It was . . . exhilarating. The kindling fire of lust was quickly turning into an out of control inferno.

She grabbed the back of his head to close the distance between their lips. He growled low, their mouths smashing into each other. Their kisses were hot, frantic and desperate. His fingers left her pussy to work between them, pushing his pajama bottoms down to free his cock, then returned to get at her panties.

"Hold on to me," Gabe muttered. "Watch your arms."

That took her out of her sensual haze for a second, her chest filling with the knowledge that even when they were driven by primitive instincts, he was still careful with her. But she wanted to be fucked with abandon, needed it.

He kissed her again, his hands gripping her ass to boost her. She responded by wrapping her legs around his hips, wedging him between her thighs. She could feel the blunt head of his cock slipping through her folds and prodding her slick entrance. He powered his hips forward, thrust fiercely into her, and grunted as he impaled her with his hard, thick length.

Beatrice felt her body shudder with each upthrust, his cock stretching her inner walls with each delicious slide, her clit rubbing against his hardness. Her skin was on fire, and she felt more alive than she'd been in days.

"Please, Gabe, I need it . . ." Her body hummed along the edges of fulfillment and she was greedy enough to demand it. "Harder . . . Oh, please."

"You got it, babe," Gabe growled by her ear. "Fuckin' you until you scream." Shifting his arms under her thighs, he plowed into her without mercy. Even as the rough wall abraded her back, she didn't care. Her nerve endings were electric, the current seizing her body until it coalesced into pulsing sensations in her core.

"Gabe!" she screamed as light exploded behind her eyes. She grabbed his hair; he grunted in response and relentlessly pounded into her like a runaway piston. She was raw, full of Gabe, and alive. That was all that mattered.

"Ah, fuck . . . fuck . . ." he groaned, convulsing against her. His arms shook as the spasms hit him. Warmth filled her core, his cum spilling inside her. He uttered a feral sound as she clenched her pussy on his cock.

"Take it all. Take it all, babe . . . ah fuck!" A palm slapped the wall beside her head, and his chest collapsed against hers as his release tore through him. His heartbeat hammered against hers, their harsh breaths mingled. Slowly, the after-shocks ebbed between them. His mouth brushed across her face, his nose ghosting over her cheeks tenderly. He slowly lowered her to her feet and chuckled when she stumbled. Her legs were limp like noodles.

"I needed that," Beatrice whispered.

"Me too, babe," Gabe kissed her lips lightly. "Me too."

17

CHOCOLATE SHAVINGS SWIRLED in a saucepan filled with heated milk. Gabe whisked along the edges of the pot, allowing the chocolate to melt and turn the bubbling liquid into a dark, thick mixture redolent with the addictive aroma of cocoa. A smile played on the edges of his mouth as he remembered the first time he prepared his version of hot cocoa for Beatrice.

They were on their fourth date. It was late February and there was snow on the ground, but they went out for a walk after dinner anyway. Gabe had his arm around her, hugging her close as he savored the feel of her arms around his torso. They traversed the National Mall at a leisurely pace, their breath vaporizing into visible swirls on a chilly winter evening.

"How is it, you've had that big steak dinner and your abs are still hard and flat?" She felt him up playfully. "Well, hard ridges of muscle."

Gabe chuckled. "Just made that way, babe."

"It's not fair. I have to work hard to stay in shape." Beatrice pouted so prettily Gabe wanted to capture those luscious lips with his mouth and explore their depths. Self-control was a challenge around her.

She stopped walking and extricated herself from his embrace. She unbuttoned her coat and revealed the black, tight-fitting dress that Gabe had been imagining the different ways of stripping off her all evening.

"This is hours of Pilates and running, and I'll never have the zero body fat you have."

He circled her back into a hug. "I don't have zero body fat, but I love your curves; although, I have yet to see them bare."

She pulled back slightly from him. "My, my, Mr. Sullivan, that sounds like a blatant proposition."

"Come back to my place," Gabe said abruptly.

Indecision spread across her face. "I have an early meeting tomorrow."

Gabe sighed. He wasn't sure if Beatrice was simply stringing him along. It had taken him a couple of attempts before she even agreed to go out with him. She told him outright she didn't date military men, more so when she found out he was a former Navy SEAL. It was ironic that his emergency meeting with the admiral regarding an upcoming op made him rethink what he wanted in life. Because that was when he saw her, and a craving he had never felt before electrified him. He thought, maybe after a date or two, he'd find there was nothing beneath that beautiful facade. He'd never been more sucker-punched in his entire life. She had such sass, intelligence, and a beguiling personality under all that gorgeousness. She captivated him in such a way that he never wanted to break free. But he had no right to claim her at that time. Not yet.

"Can I see you Friday night?" He wasn't going to let her brush him off so easily. It was Wednesday right now.

An evasive expression shadowed her face. "Um, I already have plans."

Gabe's jaw clenched. "A date?"

Her eyes flashed emerald fire, her chin tipping up defiantly. "Yes."

"With whom?" Fuck him. Why couldn't he keep his mouth shut?

"I don't think it's any of your business, Gabe." She attempted to pull away from him, but he tightened his grip.

"I'm sorry," No, he wasn't. He was going to seduce her tonight and pleasure her until she forgot every single asshole she was dating. "I'll make you hot chocolate so good, you'll forget your name. Then I'll take you right home. It doesn't need to be a late night." After I've fucked you so hard, you will never want another man inside you.

"Make hot chocolate?"

"The works—milk and chopped Belgian dark chocolate—meticulously simmered for a perfect emulsion of pure heaven," Gabe coaxed.

"Tempting, but we just finished dinner."

"It's freezing. Our bodies are burning more calories to stay warm. We've walked a mile, and if you want to feel less guilty, we can go another mile. By the time we get to my place you'll be asking for it."

"Hmm . . . That sounds like a double-entendre."

Gabe could taste triumph. "I won't deny I want to feel the heels of your boots digging into my back."

Beatrice laughed nervously. "You're very sure of yourself, aren't you?"

"I can read body language, babe," Gabe whispered, drawing her close. "Your mind is fucked up with all your own rules, but I bet you're wet for me right now."

Her breath hitched. Gabe went in for the kill. "I can't wait to fuck you."

It worked. He had her up against the door with his cock driving inside her within seconds of crossing the threshold of his apartment. He did keep his promise to make her the hot decadent drink and then took her home afterward. The following day, he made his intentions known to Porter that he was bowing out of the op. It would be another two months before he was released from his obligations, but it was worth it. And then he fucked up.

"That chocolate is going to burn, Gabe." Slender arms came around him lightly. The hand not holding the whisk came up to her bandage-covered forearm.

"Is Rhino okay?" Gabe asked.

"Yes. He's snoring on his dog bed. I think he knew he wasn't getting any of this delicious concoction."

Gabe added a bit of brown sugar and then a pinch of salt to the hot beverage before turning off the stove. He poured the dark, thick liquid into two mugs and handed one to her.

"What were you thinking about?"

He grinned crookedly. "The first time I made this for you." They sat on the barstools around the kitchen island.

A blush stole up Beatrice cheeks. Damned cute.

"I remember that night."

"You still insisted on going home," he chided. "I wanted to fuck you all possible ways that night."

"Judging by our lack of control when we got to your apartment, I'm thankful that one of us was still thinking of the consequences," Beatrice retorted. "I don't think I would have been able to walk the next day if you had your way."

Gabe snorted. "Damn right. You were a very difficult woman to pin down."

"I couldn't trust you," Beatrice said. "You would disappear for weeks, and then suddenly you would hound me every single hour of the day. All along you were still working for Dad."

"Not after I'd asked you to become mine," Gabe said. "You had no idea how much I wanted to tear apart every man you've dated, especially that fucking lawyer."

"You expected me to pine for you?"

"In a selfish way, yes." Gabe's hand tightened around the mug. "You certainly had no shortage of men taking my place."

"I never slept with them, Gabe," Beatrice said quietly. "It never got that far. Contrary to what you think, I dated, but I don't sleep with two men at the same time."

Gabe nodded. When they first got together, he had been wary of asking her if she was sleeping with anyone else, thinking it would drive him to extreme jealousy and destroy their relationship even before it began. It didn't take long before he destroyed it himself, and it had been the biggest regret of his life. "It killed me to leave you."

"Gabe, we're past that. It's done."

"Is it?"

"Why are you bringing this up again?"

Gabe finished the hot cocoa before he turned on his barstool to face her. "I killed the person inside me when I thought I could never have you. It was the only way I could function and do my job. Now, having you back, it scares me that I actually have this second chance with you. I can't lose you, Beatrice. If you leave me, I'm nothing. If you get taken away from me, I'll have nothing left. Nothing and no one will ever be enough to make life worth living."

"Gabe, I don't define you—"

"You do. More than you know. The man I am now is the man I've created to be what you need. Do you understand what I'm telling you, Beatrice? Everything I've done for the past three years destroyed the man you knew, except the part that loved you."

Beatrice lips trembled, her eyes glazed. "Gabe—"

"I hung on to the memory of you," he whispered. "It was buried deep down, but that was the only part of me I couldn't let go. The promise of you saved me, Beatrice. That's all that's left of me now. My love for you. I'm not telling you this so you'll pity me or think I'm emotionally blackmailing you to stay with me. I need you to understand why I'm consumed with keeping you safe. Because keeping you safe is keeping my sanity safe; it's keeping my heart safe. It's a selfish reason in a way. You need to know I'm not the same." Gabe clenched his jaw. "You're not getting a whole person."

"Oh, Gabe, you're so wrong." Beatrice reached out and cupped his jaw. He caught her hand and turned his head to kiss it. "I can never define you, because no person, entity, or words can define you. You defy limits. I loved the man you were before, but I'm crazy in love with the man you are now. Telling me you've been able to come back from all the ugliness because you've kept your love for me burning inside you? You have no idea how romantic that sounds."

Gabe snorted. "I'm the least romantic person."

"Uh, I'm pretty sure everything that came out of your mouth in the last two minutes was romantic."

"In a needy kind of way, maybe," he grumbled.

"Hey, even superheroes can be needy once in a while. You're arrogant and domineering 99% of the time."

"Sass," Gabe's eyes crinkled at the corners. "You're sassing me right now, right?"

"You're denying that you're bossy?"

"You don't listen to me anyway, so I can't be that bossy."

"We're such a pair," Beatrice said. "We'll never be a boring couple."

Suddenly, he had a vision of him and Beatrice, older and with graying hair, walking along the neighborhood of Old Town Alexandria holding hands.

"What?" Beatrice's question interrupted his thoughts.

"Nothing." Gabe grinned at her. "Nothing at all."

He liked that vision of them very much.

THE CRATES WERE UNLOADED from the tractor trailer. Inside were boxes of canned ground coffee from Colombia, except three of the boxes contained cocaine. Three of those cans were the ST-Vyl virus in powder form.

Frank Wilkes nodded to a skinny, bald man wearing spectacles.

Dr. Devlin, or Dr. D as he was known, was the brilliant scientist who created the Berserker serum and now the ST-Vyl virus. Soon, the D in Dr. D would be known as Death for there was no question of how lethal this new virus could be.

The Russians would be pleased and could settle their war in Ukraine once and for all. The internal wars within Syria and Iraq with ISIS should be the focus of the CIA, but the mess in Ukraine was taking away much needed resources.

ISIS (Islamic State of Iraq and Syria) was a new jihadist terror group known for its extremely brutal methods.

Dr. D lifted the marked cans from the box and transferred them to a biological containment chamber that resembled an incubator. Using gloves attached to the chamber, he lifted the plastic cover and punched a hole through the cylindrical container to retrieve a sample. As he was conducting the efficacy tests on the virus powder, Zach Jamison strode into the warehouse. He was followed by Domingo Ventura and his men.

When Zach reached Wilkes, he said, "All done. We've amended the record of this shipment on the manifest, eliminating the three boxes." He inclined his head toward the Fuego leader. "Ventura will escort the cargo back to the destination warehouse. Everything is settled there, too."

Ventura would get his drugs and everyone would be happy.

Dr. D turned to the three of them and gave Wilkes the thumbs up.

Wilkes looked at the Fuego boss. "You understand we can't do business for a while. With Jamison out of the senator's office, there is not much we can provide you now."

"I understand. This shipment should last us a while," Ventura replied. "It's been a pleasure, Mr. Wilkes."

Ventura ordered his men to re-seal the open boxes, returning them to the crate. After loading them back into the semi, the truck pulled away from the warehouse. A roar of motorcycles joined the rumble of the transport outside as the shipment of drugs and coffee left the vicinity.

"How soon can you manufacture the virus?" Wilkes asked Dr. D.

"It should take me a day to set up my new laboratory and another two days to produce the samples."

"You're still going ahead with the auction?" Zach asked.

"I told you, Zach, the auction needs to happen," Wilkes

said. "In exchange for getting rid of Porter for you, you've agreed to oversee the transfer of the virus vials to the bidders."

"Why do you need the auction sales? I thought the Russians are buying the whole lot of them."

"It's a million dollars and they can spread the news on the Black Plane about the availability of this bioweapon. Once Dr. D can synthesize ST-Vyl, we will have infinite opportunities."

Zach didn't say anything.

"Are you backing out, Zach? Don't you want to avenge Crowe?"

"Of course I do," Zach snapped.

Wilkes raised a brow at his outburst. The other man lowered his gaze. "I'm sorry, sir. What about Sullivan and Porter's daughter?"

"Sullivan could still be a problem, but if I could get rid of the admiral, I'd have no use for his daughter any longer. I'm not a mindless murderer, Zach."

"Well, you have the location of their safe house," Zach said. "It was easy enough to put a tracker on Doug Keller's car. So when are we going to do this drop?"

"I'm sending out a private message to the five I've chosen. The drop is going to happen in Culpeper, VA. I shall communicate with you on IP-MESH."

Zach inclined his head, turned, and walked out of the warehouse.

"He doesn't know of the ISIS threat?" Dr. D asked when they heard a car leave.

"It increases the risk of the drop. I don't want to spook him. He's an analyst, not a soldier," Wilkes said. "I may be many things, Dr. D, but I'm still a patriot. The whole purpose of this drop is to capture the ISIS operative looking for a bioweapon. We've already identified who he is on the IP-MESH. The other four will be picked at random. There's a strong possibility that ISIS intends to release the virus on U.S.

soil as retaliation for our involvement in their war in the Middle East."

"Isn't it too risky? What if he gets away?"

"That's why you're manufacturing a killed virus."

Dr. D looked miffed. "This was not our agreement."

"It is now," Wilkes told the scientist. Dr. D was a difficult asset to manage. He was a brilliant scientist and knew it. He desired to see the result of his work even when it translated to death. Wilkes had pegged him as a megalomaniac. He was dangerous.

"No one is getting out of that drop," Wilkes continued. "I've got my own paramilitary unit ready to apprehend every single one of them. All, except the ISIS agent, are considered collateral damage. If they resist, they will be killed."

"Very well," Dr. D sighed. "When will your Russian associates need their stash?"

"How many vials does a single can produce?"

"Hundreds."

"Excellent." With weapons sales to Colombia drying up, the shift to bioweapon sales to the Russians could prove lucrative as his last hurrah before he went into retirement. Wilkes had no intention of selling it on the Black Plane, not knowing if it could find its way back into the United States. He was lying to Zach. He had recruited Jamison to be a sleeper agent to be inserted as necessary to keep tabs on the agenda of targeted politicians. Their association had been beneficial. Zach recruited his lover, Philip Crowe, who had become Wilke's best double-agent. When Porter killed Crowe, Zach had slowly come unhinged and had been filled with a singular mind for revenge. Wilkes, being the opportunist, harnessed Zach's thirst for vengeance to further his schemes, but now that Zach's cover was blown, he had become a liability.

The auction meet could be the perfect excuse for an *accident* involving Zach Jamison.

It was too bad he had to get rid of Benjamin Porter.

Wilkes's man had a bead on the admiral in the last couple of days. Porter had been seen in Washington DC, as if taunting Wilkes to nab him. He could put a sniper on him, but he felt the man deserved a face-to-face meeting. Wilkes respected the admiral in a *worthy adversary* kind of way. Porter wasn't a sanctimonious prick like the others in the agency. The admiral was willing to get his hands sullied to get the job done, but unlike Wilkes, he'd never done it for personal profit or cut a large swath of collateral damage.

Wilkes only cared about the homeland. Screw the rest of the world.

Beatrice curled up on the sofa and studied the report Doug had brought in this morning. She hadn't left the house in ten days. Gabe rarely left her side. He only did so when he had to take care of Rhino, otherwise he was always in her face. Thankfully, they had not killed each other yet, because she was getting stir-crazy with this isolation. She was very much a city girl. Washington DC was her playground. Living in the middle of nowhere, surrounded by woods, was not her idea of a sabbatical. Beatrice sure hoped her dad tracked down Zach Jamison soon or this Redrook guy. He called Gabe once a day to keep them updated, but so far there was no solid lead.

Gabe seemed to have no problem adjusting to this change of pace. He said he'd done time as a sniper. In training to be one, you were required to stay motionless, under cover, staying alert, and attune to every change to your surroundings for hours. It freaked Beatrice out sometimes when she'd be working behind Gabe, and he would make comments as if he had eyes in the back of his head. He said it was the minuscule sounds she made, the rustle of fabric that alerted him to what she was doing.

Her sanity was also helped by the presence of Sam

Harper, a relatively new recruit of BSI. He was one of the few employees of the company who was not from the military. His background was mixed-martial arts and security for high-end clubs. Sam was coming off a security detail for a French dignitary—a deal brokered by Beatrice for BSI.

"How did you like Europe, Sam?" Beatrice asked.

"Fine," he said shortly. Then a lop-sided smile softened his serious face. "Hated wearing suits."

She laughed. "Most of the guys do. Limits their movement. Although," she angled her eyes at Gabe, "didn't you wear suits all the time when you were the *other* guy?"

Gabe chuckled. "Yes, but it was a bitch to keep my weight down."

"Muscles, you mean?" Beatrice looked appreciatively over her man's delicious body.

"Yes, muscles," Gabe muttered. "Muscle weight is heavy. It slows you down, and wearing a suit doesn't help. I've been experimenting in some training methods. The thing is, my body needs a lot of calories and I'll be damned before I starve myself."

"How much cardio do you do?" Sam asked

"I normally run six miles every day and then lift weights," Gabe said. "I need a sparring partner for mixed-martial arts."

"We use the gym on the first floor of the building where BSI is located," Sam said.

"I have privileges there because I'm affiliated with BSI and can get you in," Beatrice said. "Well, once this whole mess is over," she added in a grumble.

Sam's phone buzzed. He looked up at Beatrice and Gabe. "Travis says he and Caitlin are coming over. They've got something."

Beatrice sat up straighter. This could be it.

. . .

Twenty minutes later, Caitlin breezed through the door with Travis. She already had her laptop open.

Without much greeting, she said, "Redrook sent me a message. Tomorrow night is the meet."

"What? That doesn't give much time for preparation. What if his buyers are not in the country?" Beatrice asked.

Caitlin shrugged. "I know. It's take it or leave it. It's as if this meet is not the major event but a precursor to something."

"Where's the drop?" Gabe asked.

"Coordinates are pointing to an area in Culpeper," Travis said.

"Let's go into the control room and pull up satellite images," Gabe said. The group marched down the hallway into the communication and control room as he took out his phone to call Porter.

The admiral answered on the second ring.

"Porter."

"Admiral, Caitlin made contact. Meet is tomorrow night."

There was a long stretch of silence. "I've a strong suspicion that the meet is a distraction."

"What?"

"I have reliable sources that say Redrook has already made a deal with the Russians."

"What is this meet for then?"

"Not sure, but I don't think Redrook is going to show up. He's our priority."

"Shouldn't stopping this virus from getting into the hands of the bidders be our priority?"

"Look, Commander, I'm in the middle of something—"

"Goddammit, Ben. Stop keeping us in the dark," Gabe growled. "What the fuck is going on?"

"Trust me," Porter responded. "Plausible deniability, Gabe. What I'm doing is unsanctioned and entirely clandestine. I don't want to bring you down with me if shit hits the fan. Give me the time and coordinates."

Seething, Gabe punched in the information in his phone and sent it.

"Okay, got it," Porter said. "Have you guys figured out where it is?"

"Culpeper."

"Okay, we'll do this. I'll pick you up two hours before the meeting. I suggest you recon the area via satellite if you can."

"Already on it."

"Good. I'll see you tomorrow night."

18

It was 8:10 p.m. the following night. No sign of Porter. Gabe tried to call him earlier today. It just rang and rang. He had tried again a few minutes before the hour. No answer.

"Fuck. What do we do now?" Gabe asked Travis, who had returned to the safe house with Caitlin. The plan was Caitlin would work the communication systems and process whatever surveillance photos Gabe was going to transmit from the meet. Satellite imagery and timings were not sufficient to observe remotely. "If I don't leave now, I run the risk of encountering the people involved in the rendezvous."

"You're not going by yourself," Beatrice said. "You don't even have the contact information of the covert group; they might make a mistake and shoot you."

"If Porter hasn't shown up, they might not be there and may be assisting him somewhere else."

"I'll go with him," Travis announced.

"What?" Caitlin exclaimed. "I think the best idea is to forget this." She turned to Beatrice. "I'm sorry, Bee, but your dad is a big pain in the ass. He tells us to do something and we do it and then he turns around and changes his plans without telling us."

"What if something happened to him?" It was obvious it took an effort for Beatrice to vocalize her fears. Her face was pinched with worry. That thought had occurred to Gabe, but he hadn't wanted to add to the anxiety of the group. Caitlin suddenly looked remorseful, and Travis looked stony-faced. Sam was standing quietly against the wall.

"You know the admiral better than that, Bee," Travis said. "He's too smart to let something happen to him."

"If they have him, the more we need to get to the meet," Gabe stated resolutely. "He told us to do recon on the area. We did so thoroughly yesterday, Travis." The meet was at an old barn on a farm. Because it was winter, cover was scarce. There were no leaves on trees and only skeletal bushes dotted the area. At least, there was no snow on the ground because there was no white camouflage gear available.

Gabe was already suited up. Black cargo pants, military boots, black tee and jacket. The rest of his equipment and ammunition was in a backpack. He had a carbine to tote, a pistol in a thigh holster, and another in the back. He looked at Travis. "We've got an armory downstairs. Go gear up."

"Just recon, okay?" Caitlin linked her hands with Travis. "Don't get too close and don't engage."

"Just recon, babe," Travis agreed. "Sam, can you call Nate and have him come over. Two men should be covering the safe house while we're away." Sam nodded and left to make the call.

"That goes for you, too," Beatrice looked pointedly at Gabe. "Even if you recognize Redrook, let my dad deal with it. Right now, you guys are vigilantes and acting outside government sanction."

Standing down with a target in sight, knowing he played a role in torturing Beatrice, was going to be difficult, but he would give Beatrice the reassurance she needed.

"You got it, poppy," Gabe said, drawing her close and kissing her forehead.

"I GOT THE BARN IN SIGHT," Gabe murmured through comms. The farm was set amid rolling hills and he had hunkered down along the crest of one, training his binoculars at the structure in question.

He and Travis parked their SUV a mile from the location and hoofed it the rest of the way. The short hike was beneficial in keeping them sharp. Oxygenated blood kept them warm and aided their focus. They had agreed to split their area of coverage. Travis covered the back of the barn, while Gabe was in charge of the front. There were guards stationed at the beginning of the long driveway leading to the barn, probably to check the buyers before they were allowed through. Caitlin was issued a QR-code for identification. Gabe and Travis knew what areas to avoid.

"Two guards," Gabe added. "They don't look like Fuego. I'd say they're ex-military."

"Mercenaries?"

Gabe adjusted his optics closer. "Yeah." His reply was noncommittal. "But not too sure."

"Copy that, buddy."

Buddy. Gabe allowed the word to sink in. It might have been a slip on Travis's part, but the man's willingness to be his wingman in this op reminded him of their brotherhood in the SEALs.

"I see a car approaching the back of the barn." Travis's voice crackled through comms. After a few minutes, he said, "Fuck, it's Zach Jamison."

"Alone?"

"He has some underling carrying a couple of briefcases."

The ST-Vyl virus.

"I don't think Redrook is in that vehicle," Travis added.

Unless Zach was Redrook, which was highly unlikely given his background. He checked the time. It was 9:45 p.m., the meet was set at 10:00 p.m. Usually in transactions like this, timing was very precise. Too early was not good and increased the risk of getting caught. A minute past meet time was a no-no as well because it increased the tension in the waiting party.

The buyers should be arriving in the next fifteen minutes.

There was a muffled curse from Travis, followed by a grunt.

"Travis?" Caitlin's panicked voice crackled over their communication system. "Gabe, what's going on?"

"Fuck," Gabe muttered as he levered himself up from his prone position. A twig snapped behind him, and he heard a muttered expletive. The sounds were on top of him, so without looking back, Gabe fell to his side and swept his leg in an arc. His fishing expedition caught someone's leg and sent the person crashing to his back. Gabe pushed to his knees and grabbed the pistol from his thigh holster, but a swift kick from his assailant, who was still on the ground, knocked the gun from his hand.

Stunned at the lightning reflexes of his opponent, Gabe withdrew his knife and pounced . . . and found himself flying in the air, somersaulting actually, and landing on his back.

What.

The.

Fuck?

Thankfully, he had the knife flush to his forearm and didn't end up stabbing himself. Realizing the unknown figure was highly trained and not the random goon, Gabe scrambled to his feet to assess the man warily. By now, his assailant had risen to his feet. From the light of the full moon streaming through the bare branches, he discerned he was around his own height of six-four and probably around two-twenty pounds. The man was suited up in all black with a skull cap on his head and dark paint camouflaging his face.

They squared off.

"Who the fuck are you?" Gabe growled.

"Funny. I should be asking you that question," came the gravelly response.

"Look, man, we could be on the same side."

"I know who's on my team," Gabe could hear the sneer in Face Paint's voice, "and you're not. Come on, motherfucker, show me what you've got."

Face Paint held out his arms in a challenging gesture. This was nuts, Gabe thought, but he'd be damned before he threw the first punch. They circled each other. Finally, his opponent got tired of waiting and spun, his leg went flying. Anticipating every move, Gabe caught the foot and twisted it. The man's body pivoted with the leg and his other foot headed straight for Gabe's head. He managed to duck, but he had to let Face Paint go.

Staggering backward, Gabe made a mental note to engage Sam in sparring exercises because he was barely keeping up with this guy.

They went at it, the man's elbow jarring Gabe's jaw, but he managed to sink a fist into Face Paint's solar plexus in retaliation. More jabs and punches were exchanged, and although they seemed evenly matched, Gabe was breathing heavily while the other man was barely panting. He needed to end this now because the meet was starting in a few minutes and this son of a bitch was going to outlast him. With a suppressed roar, Gabe blocked the oncoming blow, and with a leap in the air for added momentum, came crashing down with his elbow into the side of the man's head.

"Fuck!" the other man grunted and fell to one knee. Seeing his opportunity in finishing this off, Gabe followed up with a kick, and for the second time this night, found himself flat on his back.

He was really, really, getting pissed at this guy.

Face Paint straddled him; Gabe tipped him over. They

rolled and punched. Over and over. Gabe was starting to get dizzy, and he was praying so was the other guy.

"I don't know; they seem to be having fun," a female voice spoke beside them.

"Damn it, Maia, we don't have much time!"

Travis.

Gabe and Face Paint stopped fighting.

"Travis, what the fuck is going on?" Gabe growled, angry that at the end of the fight, the other guy was on top of him.

"Figured out who Porter's covert group is," Travis said conversationally. "Gabe, meet Viktor Baran of AGS." His friend motioned to Face Paint.

"This, here, is Maia." The woman with Travis was also similarly dressed as Viktor.

Viktor pushed away from him, got to his feet, and held out his hand. "Good fight, Sullivan."

Gabe had heard of Artemis Guardian Services (AGS) and their inimitable leader. This fucker knew who he was, and they wasted time fighting senselessly. Gabe ignored the proffered hand and stood to his full-height to go eye-to-eye with Viktor. "I don't know what the hell your game is, Baran, but we're wasting precious time."

"Agreed," Viktor answered curtly. "Maia, what's the bead on the buyers?"

"They're arriving at the moment." Maia pushed down on an ear piece, listening to updates. "Our team has the barn surrounded and is waiting for word to go in."

Gabe resumed his position on the hill, surveying the activity in the barn.

Just then, a crackling of leaves and footsteps got everyone on alert. A big guy, even taller than Gabe and almost twice as wide, emerged from the trees. He had a skinny guy following in front of the business-end of his assault rifle. Big Guy was obviously one of Viktor's men because he was dressed similarly. Skinny was dressed in dark military fatigues.

"Who's this?" Maia asked, referring to Skinny.

"Found him skulking on the third quadrant. He was with another guy," Big Guy reported. "His buddy got away. They were doing recon." He ripped off the velcro holding the cover on the arm of Skinny's uniform revealing the insignia. "Green Beret."

"What the fuck?" Viktor muttered. "Why is Army Special Forces operating within the homeland?"

Skinny remained stonily silent.

"Listen, we're under CIA directive to handle this situation," Viktor said. "Our order trumps yours."

"We're under CIA directive as well," Skinny finally spoke up. There was a hint of confusion on his face.

"Redrook," Maia whispered. "He's running their show."

Gabe was slowly losing patience listening to the hushed conversation behind him. His mission was surveillance, damn it. He promised Beatrice he wasn't going to get involved in this CIA bullshit, but he was biting on his tongue not to comment on the clusterfuck.

"Maia, warn our guys to expect another team. Keep their eyes peeled for an ambush," Viktor turned to Skinny. "You better tell your men to stand down. Your boss is dirty and is conspiring with Russians to kill innocents with the virus."

"You're wrong," Skinny said. "Our boss is entrapping an ISIS operative who plans to launch a terrorist attack on U.S. soil with a virus."

Wait. What? Gabe turned his attention to the gathering behind him. This was getting more FUBAR by the minute.

"Tim was right. He mentioned something about an ISIS plot to attack the U.S. after what happened in Iraq," Maia said.

"Who's Tim?" Gabe asked.

"AGS data analyst," Travis answered. Obviously, his friend knew these people very well.

Viktor put his comms back on. "All in position? . . . Damn it. Okay we gotta move in. We're heading down. It's a go."

The second the AGS boss gave the command, gunfire erupted in the barn area. Viktor gave Big Guy instructions to secure Skinny.

"You coming, Sullivan, Blake?" Viktor asked. He gave the signal for Maia to go ahead.

Gabe locked gazes with Travis.

"We're not sponsored by any government agency in this op," Travis said.

"You think we are? CIA directive or not, we're totally clandestine on this one," Viktor said. "We fuck up, we're on our own."

This time it was Viktor who leaned his face close to Gabe's. "You like playing by the rules, Sullivan?"

"You like playing games, Baran?" Gabe fired back. "We could have killed each other earlier, you know."

A chilly smile curved Viktor's lips. "If I wanted you dead, Sullivan, you wouldn't have seen me coming."

With that parting shot, Viktor Baran disappeared into the shadows.

PANIC GRIPPED the control room at the safe house as everyone listened to the scuffle breaking out through comms.

Soon after Travis failed to respond, they heard a fight break out from Gabe's feed and judging from the distant sound coming from communication devices, both had been knocked off.

Caitlin and Beatrice gripped each other's hands while Nate tried to get the guys back online.

"Travis, do you copy?" Nate's voice was calm, but his expression was worried. "Gabe, do you copy?"

Finally, there was a distant, *What the fuck, Maia?*

"Travis, come in, buddy!" Nate spoke loudly.

"This is Blake." There was a loud irritated huff. "I'm okay."

Caitlin sighed in relief.

"What's going on?" Nate asked.

"Can't talk now. Need to get to Gabe and Viktor Baran before they kill each other," Travis said. His voice jarred, indicating he was jogging.

"What?" Beatrice exclaimed, grabbing the mic from Nate. Viktor was one of the most lethal operatives in the history of security companies. "Tell me you're joking, Travis."

Travis didn't respond for a while until he said, "They're alive."

Beatrice sank in the swivel chair in relief.

HER RELIEF DID NOT last long because Gabe and Travis were planning to join up with the AGS team in the raid, which was already underway. There was no time for discussions; split-second decisions were the order of the night.

"I'm not so sure about that, Travis," Caitlin said. "You promised you were just doing recon."

"I know, sunshine, but with Viktor at the helm, we should be fine. Gabe wants to get his hands on Zach Jamison," Travis said. "Besides, I don't think you want BSI to be labeled as a bunch of pussies, do you?"

Nate and Sam chuckled. Beatrice was leaning toward the plan. She had huge respect for Viktor and his team.

"Speak for yourself, Travis," Gabe mocked, then addressing the control room, he said, "I think we'll be fine going in. You okay with that, Beatrice?"

"It's Viktor. There's no one else I trust more," Beatrice said. "You're in good hands, Gabe."

There was a stretch of silence and Beatrice thought they

had lost communication again. Finally, Gabe's voice crackled over comms.

"Hmm, not sure I like your total confidence in this guy."

"Knock it off, Gabe," Travis muttered. "We're going in. Out."

They watched the two blips of Gabe and Travis travel down the hill on their tracking map.

"So you know Viktor?" Caitlin asked Beatrice.

"Most of his team, actually," Beatrice said. "You might even know Maia. I frequently bump into her in high-society functions. How she keeps doing undercover ops, I have no clue."

Just then, the alarm on the driveway beeped loudly.

"Are we expecting anyone?" Nate frowned into the monitor as they watched the dark outline of a car come up the driveway. "Are you expecting Doug, Beatrice?"

"No. And it's 10:00 p.m." Beatrice said urgently.

Nate got moving and punched the button that would flood the front of the house with lights. In seconds, he and Sam were armed to the teeth with pistols and assault rifles as they strode down the hallway to the front door.

Beatrice watched in horror as the figure staggered out of the car, obviously hurt.

"It's Dad," she whispered.

19

GABE'S FIST smashed into Zach Jamison's face.

Fucking exhilarating.

He and Travis caught up with Viktor just as they entered the perimeter of the yard fronting the barn. By the time they got there, it had been mostly a clean-up job.

The four buyers who showed up were quickly subdued. Much to their own detriment, they were only allowed two security guys for this meet. One of them was a French defense company, another one was a security firm based in Africa. The third guy was connected to a German pharmaceutical corporation, but it was the fourth buyer who Viktor had his Guardians haul off to the main house beside the barn to await interrogation. The man was the ISIS agent rumored to be looking for a bioweapon to unleash on U.S. soil.

Maia had secured Jamison to a chair while Viktor, Gabe, and Travis looked on. Afterward, Viktor looked at Gabe. "Consider this a bonus. He's all yours."

"Not sure I know what you mean, Baran," Gabe said warily. Everyone seemed to trust Viktor, not sure he did quite yet.

"I mean, I know what he did to your woman. If you

decide to cut him into pieces," Viktor shrugged, "we'll clean it up for you."

Zach's eyes widened in disbelief.

"You can't be serious?" Gabe asked, almost choking at the offer.

"I am. However, I don't think that's what you should do at this point."

"Oh, yeah? Enlighten me."

"Priority is establishing Redrook's identity, not revenge."

"I know that."

"Although, I'm not too concerned because I've made contact with the leader of the special ops team that was supposed to ambush this meet. We'll find out soon enough who's pulling their strings."

"And you trust this guy?"

"As much as I should," Viktor said. "Understand this, Sullivan. Unless you're on my team, I don't fully trust you."

"It's mutual at this point, Baran, so luckily, I'm not on your team."

Viktor cracked a slight smile. His expression was one of innate stoicism. Add the face paint to the whole facade, and it was damned near impossible to read the man. Now in the light of the barn, Gabe could see ice blue eyes that had seen too much death. He should know—Gabe had seen the same reflected in his own eyes.

Viktor moved closer and lowered his voice. "I know what you've been through, Sullivan. You're still trying to claw your way back from who you once were. Killing Jamison at this point is not the road back. But make no mistake, I understand you. Just remember, you have to live with the consequences of your actions."

So now, Gabe was staring at Zach with much unparalleled rage and he was torn with what he had to do. If Viktor hadn't made his little speech, would he even think twice about slitting the man's throat?

"How do I know this Frank Wilkes isn't some name you pulled out of your ass, huh, Zach?" Gabe scoffed.

"You think I like being made a punching bag?" Zach asked, spitting blood on the floor.

"What's the matter, Zach? You can dish it, but you can't take it, you sadistic son of a bitch!" Gabe growled as he unsheathed his knife from his boot.

He waved the weapon in front of Zach's nose, who was at the moment, just staring at Gabe, daring him to do his worst. In his peripheral vision, he saw Travis make a move forward.

Gabe held back a hand. "Stay out of this, Travis."

"Gabe, think about it, man, would Beatrice want you to do this?"

"Are you suggesting I call and ask her?" Gabe asked derisively.

"Don't be ridiculous—"

"She screamed, you know," Zach sneered.

"You will shut up if you know what's good for you!" Travis snapped at Zach. "Gabe, killing Zach is not what Beatrice wants."

"She'll never be safe," Zach said and laughed chillingly. "While her father is alive, she'll always be fair game."

"Oh, you'll be wasting away somewhere," Gabe replied. His voice was calm, but the desire for retribution scalded his veins.

"You think that will stop me? How do you know she's safe even now?"

Both men froze.

"Ah . . . your little safe house. You never considered we'd track Douglas Keller."

"Impossible. There are sensors—"

"Technology changes every day, trackers become more advanced, more difficult to trace. When was the last time those sensors were updated?" Zach asked mockingly. "Everyone who knew the location of the safe house was careful and experienced in security, but it's not difficult to determine the weakest link."

"Travis, call the safe house," Gabe said before turning back to Zach. "Why are you telling us this now?"

"Why did I give up Frank Wilkes's name easily? It appears the bastard double-crossed me. Even if he killed Porter for me, what good would savoring that knowledge be if I was locked away behind bars? Even for Crowe, that wouldn't be worth it. If I get charged with treason, it'll be the death penalty. I have nothing to lose now."

"No one's answering," Travis said. "I've tried everyone's cell phone numbers. Something could be jamming the signal."

"They're probably all dead," Zach continued to taunt them.

"Here," Gabe tossed Travis his secure phone. "There's a direct line to the landline in the control room."

"I should've let them rape her," Zach continued. "Ventura had the hots for Beatrice."

"Shut up, Jamison," Gabe growled as unwitting images of the Colombian gang leader's hands all over Beatrice flashed through his mind.

"He loves her spirit; he would enjoy breaking her—"

Gabe didn't reply. It took all his self-control just to keep his hands by his sides.

"Push her to her knees, shove his cock in her mouth, spread her open and— urrk . . ."

Gabe detachedly observed the blood spurting from the C-curve he had carved across Zach's throat. Ear to ear. He felt like he was a heat-forged sword plunged into water, hardened and tempered to become the deadly weapon he was meant to be. Rage had dissipated into a chilly regard of the bloody scene before him.

"Ah, fuck," Travis muttered behind him.

"Funny that my regret at the moment is giving Zach what he wanted," Gabe said tonelessly. "Did you get through?"

"The admiral arrived at the safe house. He's injured."

"What?"

"We need to head back. Now," Travis said, turning and marching to the gate of the barn.

"Tell me what's going on?" Gabe sheathed his knife into his boot.

"Zach Jamison was right; Harold Baxter knows the location of the safe house."

"Harold Baxter—"

"—is Redrook, and my bet is Frank Wilkes is an alias he's used to run Red Bridge since its inception. Porter has the evidence." They exited the barn, and Gabe followed Travis's lead into the main house, presumably to look for Viktor. "He needs to send the information to AGS for safekeeping. But to do that, he has to have Viktor's analyst open a secure socket so Caitlin can transmit the intel."

Viktor was walking out with another guy who was dressed in fatigues. This must be the Special Op guy Viktor was talking about. Both men looked grim and unhappy, but at least they didn't look like they were about to kill each other.

"Our man is Harold Baxter," Viktor said to Gabe and Travis. He made the introductions with the newcomer.

"We got confirmation from Porter as well," Gabe said.

"So he's okay? He went off the grid this morning," Viktor said.

"He's injured," Travis announced grimly.

"What?"

"He's got intel he needs to transmit to Tim," Travis said. "He's holed up in the safe house right now, but that location is blown. We need to get over there, ASAP. No telling if Baxter is going after them."

Gabe and Travis were about to return to their vehicle when Viktor stopped them. "Hold on. If Baxter's after them, you'll need backup. And you need to get there quickly."

"You're not saying—" Gabe started.

"We have a chopper on standby," Viktor said. "I can round up a team and fly you guys out there and provide cover fire. If there's no landing site, you guys still know how to fast rope, right?"

"Hell, yeah," Gabe snorted as Travis nodded his affirmation.

Viktor nodded in approval. Gabe didn't change opinions very quickly or often, but he was actually beginning to admire this motherfucker.

TIM BURNS, the AGS data analyst, was on video conference with Caitlin while the two worked on establishing a secure connection between the safe house and the AGS data center. Beatrice was crouched down in front of her father, wrapping a bandage across his torso. A bullet had torn through the side of her father's abdomen with no apparent internal damage.

"I can't believe you let yourself get captured." She was so pissed at her dad right now that was probably the first full sentence she had spoken to him since he stumbled through the door.

"I knew I was being watched. I knew Baxter had suspicions it was a trap. But I also knew he couldn't resist the bait."

"You are just as insane as Baxter." She pulled on the bandage with more strength than she intended. The admiral winced, and she felt guilty, but not enough so she'd back down from giving him hell. He let himself be taken by Harold Baxter, also known as Frank Wilkes and a host of other aliases. In the CIA though, the man was known as Baxter. Beatrice had a sneaking suspicion that the two men actually admired the other's cunning. Judging from what her father told her, he and Baxter had a civilized conversation in the man's hideout until Baxter ordered one of his men to kill him. Somehow, the admiral gained the upper hand and managed to transfer some files, but soon after, Baxter's security team swarmed in. Her father managed to get away but had been shot. "What's on the jump drive?"

"Everything that incriminates him with weapons sales to Colombia and allowing drugs into the United States so the rebels could pay for them," the admiral said. "I'm hoping there's enough information there regarding ST-Vyl virus that would tie in to what Gabe had retrieved from Ryker's room. We can nail him on the charge of conspiring with a faction in the Russian government to commit a terrorist act."

"You think the Russian president is involved?"

Her father shook his head. "Not likely. He is up for re-election and can't afford to take risks. I'm putting my money on one of his generals with the support of some companies poised to gain from the end of the Ukrainian conflict."

"How has the world become so fucked up?" Beatrice muttered. "War everywhere. Terrorism on the rise."

"Is there anything on Project Infinity or the specter agents?" Caitlin asked. The expression on her face broke Beatrice's heart.

Her father's face softened in regret. "I'm afraid not, Caitlin. I've dug into it before, believe me. Those files have been destroyed. There's also strong evidence that the foster homes used by Baxter to recruit the kids for the program have been razed to the ground."

"Oh, my God." Caitlin's eyes widened, mirroring the shock Beatrice was feeling.

"What kind of soulless bastard is this guy?" Beatrice asked incredulously.

"One you don't want in charge of National Security," her dad said. "Baxter was next in line for Deputy Director of the CIA. This was over fifteen years ago. He fucked up a high-profile op and was demoted to missions that have low political risks, which is how he became involved in South America. At that time, the war and attention of the public was shifting to the Middle East. He took advantage and made money."

Footsteps thudded outside the control room. Seconds later, Nate burst in. "Three black SUVs are speeding down the driveway. I want you girls to lock yourselves in here. You up for a fight, Admiral?"

"Of course."

"I'll alert Viktor and the others," Tim announced from the video feed.

Beatrice was feeling something else. "I can help." When both men were about to protest, she added, "If any of you say I should stay behind, think again. I'm good with a gun." She looked at Nate. "You can have the RPG."

"I—" Caitlin started.

"You need to stay here, Cat," Beatrice said, nodding to Nate who signaled he had to head back outside. Porter followed Nate. "You're the one who can operate"—she looked around at all the monitors and keyboards—"whatever these are. And it looks like you're still transferring the files."

"Be careful," Caitlin said.

"I will," Beatrice replied.

Nate started yelling that the SUVs had pulled up in front of the house.

"You have the schematics of the underground tunnel leading outside, right? Just in case they trap you in here."

"Bee," Caitlin whispered and couldn't say anymore. They hugged each other tightly. Afterward, Beatrice exited the room and dragged the sliding door shut.

"Seal it!" Beatrice shouted.

Hydraulics whirred as the locks bolted into place.

Seconds later, the frenetic din of assault rifles blasted through the night.

"BEE, go upstairs and cover the back! Take Rhino with you," Nate shouted, taking a moment behind the reinforced wall by the door to instruct her. Sam was at the other end, firing at will. She didn't see her dad, but the trap door leading to the armory was open.

The German Shepherd was circling in excitement in the middle of the living room.

She nodded and grabbed her two Sigs and a can of pre-loaded magazines that were under the kitchen cabinet. Grabbing a short-wave radio from Nate, she confirmed the frequency and scrambled up the stairs.

"Come on, boy!" She looked back to make sure Rhino was following her. The walls and windows were bullet-resistant, but wouldn't hold off a continued assault for long.

Beatrice had Rhino lie down on the side of the bed away from the windows. She fitted the suppressor on her Sigs. The lights in the room were off. She slowly slid the window open a smidge. For a while there was no movement in the backyard. Her eyes roamed far and close to the side of the house. The lighting in the back was also behind bullet-resistant glass.

She ignored the raging war that seemed to be taking place in the forefront of the safe house. At least with the fierce exchange, it was a good sign that her father, Nate, and Sam were putting up a good fight. The bad news? So were the hostiles.

Her eyes caught a stir by the wall, a minuscule peep of a leg that quickly disappeared. She focused on that spot, though in a way, she was omnipresent-aware. It was hard to describe the feeling where all she could hear was her breathing and all her senses were alive. Three figures broke away from the cover of the wall. Beatrice didn't fire yet, waiting to see what they would do.

One of them was carrying a large weapon that looked like—

Oh, my God! It's a RPG.

Before the hostile could shoulder the weapon, Beatrice aimed and squeezed off two shots. The remaining two scuttled in opposite directions, firing haphazardly at the house. She ducked behind the walls momentarily, gauging where the bullets were hitting. The suppressor disguised her muzzle flashes and the sound of her gun, so they didn't know from where she was shooting. The line of the lights that ran along the middle of the house also made it difficult for the attackers to aim and fire into the house.

Satisfied that they were shooting far from her location, she peered over the window edge again. Her blood turned to ice. There was a body on the ground, but the RPG was missing.

It was a split second before she caught the movement right behind the tree line. She fired the same time she heard the *whoosh* of the rocket. An instantaneous explosion rocked the floor below her.

Cat!

The control room was reinforced, but Cat better be ready to make a quick exodus.

She heard shouting on the first floor and from her radio. Nate was yelling out orders to put out a fire. Beatrice was able to pick off another shooter, but her eyes were searching for the man with the RPG. Rhino was whining in agitation.

"Shh . . . quiet, boy," Beatrice said. She spied a gunman lurking, trying to sneak into the back patio. She managed to disable him, sending him crashing to the ground. She was about to fire another shot when a bullet ricocheted off the edge where she was shooting from. Amid the crazy ruckus of gunfire and more explosions, Beatrice thought she heard the blunt rhythm of a chopper.

Another bullet struck near her. Same spot. Shit, they were using a special scope and must have clocked her.

Which meant . . .

Oh, shit.

She saw it, the rocket heading straight for her.

She scrambled to her feet and ran across the room toward the bed.

"Rhino!" she screamed.

A thunderous roar and a fireball shot past her, sending her flying on top of the bed. The blast wave further rolled her off the mattress. Pain exploded on the back of her head before darkness claimed her.

IT WAS A WAR ZONE.

The muzzle flashes of carbines and assault rifles lit up the front yard like a firework show. Smoke was rising from the safe house and the stucco walls were heavily pockmarked.

Their Black Hawk's machine gun did quick work on the attackers, not giving them an opportunity to use the RPG on them.

"Get us down there," Travis growled.

"Hold on, Blake," Viktor said. "You don't want to drop dead before you hit the ground, do you?"

Gabe clenched his jaw as he gripped his carbine tight, but Viktor was right. He also understood how Travis felt because an overwhelming desire to make sure Beatrice was all right prickled the expanse of his skin.

The chopper swooped to the back of the house and raked the ground there as well, tearing a path and taking down two more of Baxter's men. The assailants appeared to be a different faction from the guards at the meet and they were not the U.S. Special Ops team either. How many schemes did Harold Baxter/Frank Wilkes have?

"Looks good here," Viktor spoke to the pilot. "Lower the bird."

Gabe jumped off, got on one knee, and had his carbine shouldered, sweeping the area. Maia followed in seconds, repeating the same motion and clearing the other side.

Travis exited the chopper but walked toward the house with his weapon trained in front of him.

A hand landed on Gabe's shoulder as Viktor shouted into his ear. "Go! We got you guys covered."

Gabe nodded, rose from his crouch, and trailed Travis into the house.

His heart sank when he walked into the debris of destruction. The back door was partly blasted in, the windows shattered, and plaster littered the floor. Gabe walked through the door just as the control room door slid open and Caitlin launched herself into Travis's arms.

Porter was leaning heavily against the stairs, a fire extinguisher in his hand. He didn't look good and was bleeding steadily. Gabe's eyes scanned the room. "Beatrice?"

"Nate went to check on her," Porter gasped out. "Explosion. Upstairs."

Gabe saw the hole and smoke coming out of their bedroom when they first landed. The gears in his mind clicked as he processed Porter's words. Beatrice was in the bedroom when the warhead exploded? Fuck no!

He leapt on the landing and was about to bound up the steps when he heard his name.

"Gabe?"

He looked up. Green eyes framed by a face covered in soot stared at him. Beatrice was standing at the top of the stairs with Nate's arms around her. This time, Gabe didn't feel any jealousy at all, just a buckling relief that she was alive and standing.

"Fuck, babe," Gabe said raggedly. He took the steps two at the time and pulled her from Nate's arms, clenching her so tightly, he was probably squeezing her too much. It was as if he couldn't get close enough to her.

He shifted away slightly and kissed her desperately, deeply.

"I love you so fucking much," Gabe muttered.

"Oh, Gabe," Beatrice whispered. "I thought I would never see you again."

"Don't ever think that. Don't ever," he growled fiercely. "I will always come for you."

He kissed her again.

"BAXTER'S DEAD."

Viktor was speaking to the admiral who was being patched up by Maia.

Caitlin and Rhino were the only ones who escaped unscathed from the siege on the safe house. Nate, Sam, and Porter received non-life threatening gunshot wounds with the admiral possibly sustaining a couple of broken ribs from the explosion. Beatrice had a concussion and a few minor lacerations. Since she was unconscious when Nate found her, Gabe would be insisting she receive the full battery of tests. Dr. Ryan had been notified and was on her way with a medical van.

"We have confirmation?" Porter asked. The body of Harold Baxter was found alongside the other dead hostiles who attacked the safe house.

"I sent an image to Tim for facial recognition. It's a 99% match," Viktor said. He looked at Gabe. "You also confirm that you've seen him with Zorin?"

Gabe nodded. He definitely had seen Harold Baxter meet with his former crime boss at least twice before.

"Too bad he couldn't be held accountable for his crimes," the admiral said. His eyes drifted to Beatrice. "However, I, for one, will sleep better at night with Baxter gone."

Porter's gaze continued moving and landed on him. Gabe inclined his head in silent agreement. It was a selfish thought because they could have found out the depth of Baxter's deception if he were alive. But in this, Gabe was sure that he and Porter were of the same mind—fuck the whole world, they had paid their dues in blood for far too long.

There had been a revolving door of Guardians in the safe house, which was technically not safe anymore given the blasted doors and windows. The big guy who Gabe had met in the woods earlier walked in and approached Viktor.

"Our Quick Reaction team was able to apprehend Dr. Devlin and sequester the ST-Vyl virus. Should we inform the CDC?"

Viktor contemplated the question before deferring to Porter. "Admiral?"

"Fucking tired of making decisions," Porter said wearily.

"We'll actually have to involve the FBI and Homeland Security on this one since it's on U.S. soil," Viktor said. "I'm sure the CIA will have to work intel on the Russian buyer. Tim is mining the data right now."

"This would mean a POTUS brief," Porter muttered. "I don't have time for this shit."

Gabe pushed back from the wall and walked over to where Beatrice was talking to Travis. She looked at him questioningly when he sat down beside her and pulled her into his arms.

Travis cleared his throat and grinned knowingly. He stood up, squeezed Gabe on his shoulder, and muttered that he was going to look for Caitlin.

"You okay? Dizzy?" Gabe asked.

"My head hurts."

"You've got an egg-size lump on the back of your head."

"After all the craziness of the past few months, it's nothing."

"Zach Jamison is dead. I killed him," Gabe stated flatly. "He was tied to a chair and I slit his throat."

Beatrice closed her eyes, and for a brief moment, Gabe was afraid of what he would see in them.

When she opened them, they were hard. "What prompted you to kill him right then?"

"He threatened you. I couldn't turn him over to anyone else knowing he'd send someone after you again."

Beatrice didn't say a word, just nodded.

"I can't change who I am, babe. I'll always be ruthless when it comes to you," Gabe added. "I would kill for you, no hesitation. Anyone who threatens your life is dead."

"I wasn't saying anything, because the first thing I felt was relief." She released a weary breath. "I'm also feeling guilty because right after they cut me, I wanted to tell you to hunt down whoever did this to me and kill them all. It frightened me, the violence and anger consuming me, though eventually they faded. It doesn't mean I'm not glad he's dead. If that makes me an evil person, so be it." Her eyes searched his. "If that makes us two of a kind, so be it. There are no rainbows and unicorns in our world, Gabe, especially yours. You've seen too much of its evil that in order to fight evil you had to become like it. I fully accept that part of you."

"I know how lucky I am; I don't deserve you." He held her gaze. "You're brave, smart, incredibly beautiful—"

"Don't forget, I give good head," Beatrice said in a hushed whisper.

Gabe choked on his chuckle, caught unaware by his woman's sass even after she nearly got blown up. She never ceased to amaze him.

"That you do." He tipped her chin up to look at him. "You know I'm never letting you go, right?"

"If that's your version of a proposal, Gabriel, that sucks."

He could see her sudden nervousness through her sass. He knew they would have to compromise between her aversion to being tied down and his consuming desire to make her irrevocably his. He needed to show her that he had a life outside of her, but she needed to accept that she was the center of his world. "It's not. When I finally ask to you to be my wife—take note, that's when and not if—you will know."

"Is that so?" Beatrice's brow arched, but her lips were tipped in a genuine smile.

This was promising, so he added, "Yup. You might as well start picking paint colors and furniture for the house." He remembered how Beatrice was so animated discussing home decorating shit with Caitlin. He wanted that enthusiasm channeled for them.

"Wait . . . Uh, what house?"

"Mine. I'm not living in your fucking condo. I doubt Rhino would like it, and I'm not doing this 'your place or mine' bullshit."

"I need time—"

"You're moving in right after you get checked out by Dr. Ryan. We're packing your shit. It's moving next to mine, and you're sleeping in my fucking bed. I'm not sleeping under a damned canopied one."

"Whoa there, buster." Beatrice looked more dazed than earlier and Gabe felt guilty. "No ragging on my beautiful bed. But I agree, you'd look silly under all those frills." Her green eyes were luminous. "So, you're asking me to move in with you? Officially?"

"Yes. We got sidetracked with that discussion because of your silly concerns about my job choices," Gabe said. "I agree, I wouldn't be your most effective bodyguard long-term, but I've been offered a job as an instructor at the Farm before. I'm sure they'd have no problem accepting my application."

The Farm was the CIA's training facility.

Beatrice looked at her hands. When she lifted her eyes, her brows furrowed as she stared past him. "Uh, we probably shouldn't be having this conversation in a room full of nosy people."

Gabe paused, realizing that for a few seconds there the chatter around them had died. He turned his head to the side.

Sure enough, everyone from Porter, Viktor, Maia, Nate, Travis and a host of other people were listening in on their conversation. When had badass security guys become such gossips?

"Seriously, baby, put the man out of his misery," the admiral said dryly.

"You got all the images, Tim?" Caitlin transmitted all the photos from the scene outside. She didn't particularly care to see pictures of mangled, dead bodies, but someone had to get it done.

"Yup. The team who guarded the meet at Culpeper was mostly South African mercenaries. These are checking out to be Russian," Tim replied. "Different security companies."

"Well, I guess that's it for tonight—or morning," Caitlin yawned. It was close to 2:00 a.m.

"You did very well tonight, Caitlin," the data analyst said. "I had the satellite images up on your location; it was quite a fire fight, but you remained cool as ice."

"I trusted the people around me," she replied. "And I knew Travis was on his way."

"I'm sorry you didn't find what you were looking for," Tim said softly.

"I've accepted it for a while," Caitlin replied truthfully. "Catching a break with Redrook and knowing he held the key to my past did raise my hopes, but I can't regret not remembering my past, because I welcome my life with Travis so much more. I feel it deep in my gut, you know, that I've never been this happy and fulfilled before." She put a hand on her baby bump.

Tim simply smiled at her and Caitlin got self-conscious.

"Oh, Lord, I don't even know why I'm telling you this. I'm so sorry. I just met you," Caitlin stuttered in mortification.

"Are you sure?"

Caitlin stared at Tim, confused. "What do you mean?"

"I'll see you around, Star Pixie." Tim smiled wider, winked, and cut the feed.

Caitlin was left staring at the screen, her mouth open in an O. Star Pixie was her alias on the Black Plane.

"Saber Boy?" she whispered.

EPILOGUE

Two weeks later

Gabe glanced impatiently at his watch, the third time he had done so in the past half hour. She was probably stuck in DC traffic again. The past two weeks had been a difficult time for him, letting her go about her day without him. It felt similar to coming back from a series of missions where one had become hyper-vigilant. He was slowly decompressing and his senses were coming to terms that Beatrice was going to be okay without his hovering.

He resisted the urge to track her on his phone. That would make him no better than a stalker; although, he didn't give a fuck if he became *her* stalker. Gabe needed to get his act together. He had invested his money wisely. The house was paid for, and even if he could keep Beatrice living in the style she was used to, he needed to keep his mind and body occupied. Otherwise, he would go insane with boredom. Gabe stared at his emails on his laptop. He escorted Beatrice to a high-profile gala the night before and met with several politicians and officials from alphabet agencies and security companies all eager to engage his services. This morning, he switched on his laptop to a barrage of emails including one from the Director of CIA black ops who Gabe had worked with on several SEAL missions. The director had approached him years ago, right before he left the Navy SEALs, about training new recruits. Gabe was tempted to call him back. But was being an instructor what he really wanted to do?

Rhino walked toward the door and snuffled at the corner. As if on cue, the doorknob turned and Beatrice walked in. After petting Rhino on the head, his woman headed straight for him.

"Hmm . . . missed you," Beatrice breathed into his lips. He kissed her, engulfing her in his arms, lifting her slightly, one hand digging into the meat of her ass, while pressing her tightly against him.

"Hey," he whispered after he had kissed her thoroughly. "Why so late, babe?"

"Nate," Beatrice groused. "He had reversed roles with Travis in the slave driver department. But don't worry, I've informed him I have a man now waiting for me at home. I'm not as cutthroat as I used to be."

Gabe chuckled. "Not sure I like playing the 'man waiting at home' bit."

"Oh, knock it off. You know your sabbatical isn't lasting long. I can tell you're getting bored out of your mind despite the house projects. I received calls from a couple of security firms today, asking if you're looking for a job. You made quite an impression last night. I told them if you're interested, you'd call."

"You can be my agent," Gabe teased, helping her remove her coat and hanging it in the closet.

Beatrice rolled her eyes. "I'm a consultant, not a head hunter."

"I'm considering the CIA post as an instructor," Gabe said, walking into the kitchen to check on the roast. "I may have to be onsite for several days, but I'm sure I can work out a schedule that would work for both of us."

Beatrice's brows furrowed. "Are you sure that's what you want to do, Gabe? I know you're limiting your options because of me, but this past month"—she exhaled a shaky breath—"I've come to trust that you're going to do what's right for us. I want you to be happy and fulfilled in your job, Gabe."

Her words meant a lot to him, and in a way, he was choosing the CIA instructor position because it was the least likely to keep him away for weeks and make her worry about him. But he wasn't thrilled about the prospect.

"Why don't you change out of those clothes before I end up attacking you. I've set the roast to keep warm while you freshen up," Gabe said, deflecting her question, but there was some truth that he was tempted to have her as an appetizer, knowing she wore those sexy garters underneath that skirt. "We can talk about it after dinner. Deal?"

"Good idea," Beatrice laughed. "We can't have a repeat of this morning."

Gabe grinned salaciously. "That was a delicious way to wake up." Beatrice had gotten up early this morning for an 8:00 a.m. meeting. Gabe woke up to her bent over the desk in their bedroom, typing an email on the laptop. She had been wearing garters, stockings, and a bra. What did she expect when she presented him with her delectable ass? Hazed by sleep and a surge of lust, he snuck in behind her on his knees and buried his face into her pussy. He nudged her panties aside, and ate her, licking her into a quick orgasm.

"I had to change my panties," Beatrice chided as she made her way up the steps. "You almost made me late."

"We have rules about bringing work into the bedroom," Gabe said. "I just meted out some punishment."

"You know that's a poor form of punishment, right?"

"Go change, babe, before I spank that ass."

"Still not a punishment, Gabe," Beatrice called out playfully as her voice faded up the stairway.

He shook his head, grinning. She made him incredibly hard with that smart mouth on her and he looked forward to more.

Rhino suddenly got up and growled at the door. His dog tilted his head to look at him warily. Gabe stiffened, going on alert. He listened for Beatrice's movements upstairs and heard the shower turn on.

"Rhino, guard," Gabe ordered. His dog snuffled in agreement and stood by the stairway. Gabe grabbed his gun, checked the magazine, and slotted a round in the chamber.

He approached the door and took a peek through the window. There was a man leaning nonchalantly at the top of the stoop. It wasn't Porter, but the guy's silhouette looked oddly familiar. It didn't take long for Gabe to figure who it was.

He turned on the front lights and opened the door.

Viktor Baran.

"Why are you here?" Gabe asked tersely, but his mind was racing with the possibility that something else had come up and the danger was not over.

"That's a hostile way to acknowledge a friend," Viktor replied with amusement.

"I would hardly call you a friend, Baran."

Viktor's smile didn't reach his eyes. "I'm a busy man, Sullivan. Do you want to step outside, so I can tell you why I'm here? Beatrice is upstairs and—"

"Don't," Gabe snarled, flicking the lights off and plunging them into darkness save for the light from the street lamp. "I fucking swear, if you were spying on my woman—"

"Calm down," Viktor chuckled. "I don't want my own

woman to hand me my balls, so you can be sure I have no perverted designs on Beatrice."

Gabe was baffled for a moment that there was a woman on the planet who could hand Viktor Baran his balls. And having the AGS boss admit to such a thing was disconcerting.

"Finding it hard to believe, Sullivan?" Viktor wagged his left hand, and sure enough there was a gold band.

Well, I'll be damned.

"So why are you here?" Gabe asked.

"I'm in need of a tactical analyst."

"You're offering me a job?" Gabe asked incredulously.

Viktor shrugged. "I've seen what you can do."

"Wait a minute, was that fight some kind of test?"

"You could say that."

"Fucking unbelievable," Gabe growled. "Why would I want to work with someone as insane as you?"

"Because whether you deny it or not, Sullivan, you see yourself in me."

Eyes that had seen too much death.

"You'll have to find someone else."

"Do you honestly think you'll be happy as a CIA field instructor?"

"What?—"

"I have eyes and ears everywhere," Viktor said. "I have access to classified databases. You want to protect your woman and keep her safe? Information has the power to protect her. I can give that to you."

"I'm still not your guy. I'm not going on covert missions abroad or going undercover, and leaving Beatrice for weeks on end. I'm not doing that shit again."

Viktor huffed irritably. "Didn't you hear what I said? I need a tactical analyst. You remain at the data center, analyze the intel with Tim, and you plan TAC team strategy. You don't have to go on the field unless it's in DC or anywhere close by and they're usually short duration strike operations.

With increased terrorist threats, I need help running ops from the data center."

"Why? I heard you practically live and breathe AGS."

"Why? Because I'm fucking married. I love my wife, Gabe, and priorities change. She comes first, and if it means I have to give up some control of running AGS to spend more time with her, I'm willing to do it."

Gabe was shocked speechless. Whatever Viktor's reasons were, he had not expected anything this . . . sappy.

"I need someone I can trust," Viktor added.

"Then why not pick someone internally?"

"We need new blood, new perspective," Viktor said. "Why do you think AGS is at the top of its game?"

"You still don't know me well."

"Oh, I know who you are. You were a Commander with SEAL Team Six, Sullivan—one of the most decorated and most lethal. You were feared as Dmitry Yerzov."

"I'm not the same man—"

"I sure hope not," Viktor fired back. "People who go undercover usually have no ties that bind them, and yes, having no family makes them effective to a certain degree. But you fight terrorists who want to destroy our freedom, you need to have someone at home worth fighting for. You'd kill for Beatrice; you'd kill to protect the life you have with her."

Their eyes locked. He *had* killed for Beatrice.

"I'll always choose her above everything else," Gabe warned. "If she gets put into danger and I have to choose, I will choose her every single time."

Viktor tightened his jaw. "We have safeguards in place so you wouldn't be put in such a position."

"It's happened before?"

"It had. You become a Guardian, Gabe, you will have access to the best security for Beatrice—information and personnel."

"Gabe!" Beatrice's worried voice called from inside. "Rhino, let me pass, boy!"

"I need to discuss this with her," Gabe said as he made a move to head back into the house. He thought for a moment to invite Viktor in, but fuck if he knew what Beatrice was wearing.

"Give it some thought. If you have any concerns, give me a call. Beatrice has my number." Viktor gave him a chin lift, turned, and walked away.

Eight months later

"Gabe's here," Emily's voice sounded over the intercom in Nate's office.

"You did that on purpose," Nate accused.

Beatrice smiled sweetly. "You've been keeping me past eight p.m. for the last few weeks. My man's not pleased. You're lucky Viktor's been keeping him busy as well, but Gabe's starting to grumble about my late nights."

"So, he likes his job?"

"He bitches about Viktor sometimes," Beatrice laughed. "But I think they thrive on pushing each other's buttons."

Gabe had accepted the position as tactical analyst for AGS, and Beatrice couldn't be happier. It was the best of both worlds. He got to plan and run point on missions from the data center as well as participate in quick-reaction strike operations as needed. Sure there was a level of danger, but her exposure as a security consultant more than prepared her for it. Besides, she trusted Viktor to have Gabe's back.

Beatrice packed up her laptop and eyed Nate. "You know, you probably need to share some responsibility with Ed and promote someone else to team lead. Or just hire more people."

Travis had cut back on his work schedule with the arrival of Abigail Blake. Little Abby was so adorable and at almost three months, definitely had her parents, especially Travis, wrapped around her tiny fingers.

Senator Mendoza's South American trip was a success with no glitches in security whatsoever. BSI received glowing commendations for the outstanding security work provided, and now their company and Beatrice's were besieged with inquiries and new clients. Also, the escalating threats from ISIS had prominent politicians, dignitaries, and businessmen on edge and beefing up security.

Nate scrubbed his face wearily. "Yeah, you're right." He shut his laptop and stood up. "Might as well call it a night. Where're you guys going? Wanna grab a drink?"

"Um," Beatrice hedged, "I think we're heading straight to dinner." Gabe hadn't been happy about her spending too much time alone with Nate, and now, walking out with her friend into the reception area, probably wasn't a good idea. Speaking of not so good ideas, she was thinking that having Gabe pick her up at BSI was a bad one as well.

"He still doesn't like me around you, does he?"

"Well, you do nothing but wave the red flag at the bull," Beatrice answered.

"He's just too easy to rile up." Nate smirked.

Beatrice shook her head and grinned, irritated and heartened at his jealousy-inspiring antics. Even if Nate wouldn't admit it, she knew it was his way of torturing Gabe for what he had done to her four years ago. It was Nate's way of letting Gabe know that if he fucked up again, Beatrice would be fine without him.

"We've been together for almost a year, Nate," Beatrice said. "He's all in."

Nate's expression softened. "I know, Bee, and I know the man's crazy for you. Old habits just die hard."

"I know," Beatrice said, "but I see his point. If I saw a woman sitting on his lap, and if that same woman was spending too much time holed up in an office with him, I'd be jealous, too."

Nate gripped his chest dramatically. "Oh, God, he's brain-washed you!"

"Don't be a dickhead," Beatrice retorted. "I'm still the same me. You just need to find a new girlfriend to spend time with instead of sticking your nose in my love life."

"No one wants me," he deadpanned.

Beatrice rolled her eyes. "Because you can't commit. You know how many of your girlfriends were jealous of me because you did more for me than for them?"

Nate shrugged. "Can't help it. The more they demand things from me, the more I push back."

"Because you knowingly go for gold-diggers," Beatrice grumbled. "You go for the surgically-enhanced bimbos when you obviously can't stand them outside the bedroom."

"It works for me," Nate muttered under his breath and his steely gaze told her he was done with the conversation.

He opened the door to the reception area, gesturing for Beatrice to walk ahead. Gabe was leaning against the sprawling curved reception counter, chatting with Emily. He usually wore tees and cargo pants to work, but he had gone home this time to change and walk Rhino before they headed out for dinner.

Now standing before her in dark slacks and a slate-blue dress shirt, she was struck with how equally hot he looked dressed-up or casual or nude. Warmth suffused her cheeks as an image of him all naked, all stacked muscles . . . all hard, flashed through her mind.

"Hey." He walked up and brushed his lips on hers lightly.

His gaze went past her shoulder and narrowed at the man behind her. "Reece."

"Sullivan."

"You leaving, Nate?" Emily asked. "I'm about to head out."

"Yup, might as well since Bee, here, is slacking."

"I'm not. You're just OCD about contracts."

"And that's a bad thing?" Nate shot back.

Gabe cleared his throat. "We're going to be late for our dinner reservation, Beatrice. We need to get going."

A hand settled on the small of her back, firmly guiding her to the door.

She had a feeling she was going to get the caveman treatment from Gabe later. Her man controlled his jealousy in public in deference to her reputation, but the signs were there. A narrowing of the eyes, a hardening of his jaw, and the most obvious of signs, a seemingly calm tone. It was when he got her in private that he let her have it, reminding her to whom she belonged. She wasn't complaining; she just didn't want him feeling needlessly jealous.

A delicious ache between her legs caused her steps to falter.

It was going to be a long dinner.

DINNER WAS an enjoyable affair as usual. Between discussions of their work and home improvements, the renovation of Beatrice's home office took up most of the conversation. Gabe was tired of Doug walking in on them in the mornings, especially when Beatrice was feeling frisky and her man had to take a cold shower because of an unfulfilled hard-on. He was redesigning their home so there would be a separate entrance to her office, which was in the back of the house anyway. It would have been simple enough, except Old Town Alexandria was a historic neighborhood and every exterior change had to go through the City Council and the Board for Architectural Review. Tonight was a celebration of the approved plans.

However, Beatrice noticed that Gabe was a bit off, distracted even. He had grown quiet around dessert time, and on the drive home, he barely spoke a word. Their vehicle was an AGS-issued black Ford Explorer. Gabe never replaced his wrecked SUV from that mess with Ryker, and since he was working on the house anyway, he used the Silverado pickup.

"You're okay to walk a few blocks or do you want me to drop you off at the front of the house?" They had circled twice for closer parking, but since it was late, the ideal spots were taken.

"I've walked blocks in heels before, Gabe," Beatrice quipped.

"Next project will be off-street parking; at least for one of the cars," Gabe declared.

Zipping into an empty space, Gabe muttered for her to stay put as he quickly exited and rounded the vehicle to her side.

"Pulling out all the stops tonight, Sullivan?" Beatrice teased.

"I want it to be perfect," Gabe replied simply.

Suddenly, her heart thumped wildly under her breastbone. *Oh, God.* Was it what she was thinking?

Gabe smiled at her almost boyishly, which was a feat, because boyish Gabe was an oxymoron.

Silence fell between them as he took her hand in his and started walking toward the house. The annoying click-clack of her shoes echoed on the pavement. Gabe, as usual, maintained a stealthy gait.

When they reached the wrought-iron fence of their home, he unlocked the gate and guided her through, keeping a firm grip on her elbow as though he was afraid she would escape.

He didn't waste any time with his objective. It was evident in the look he cast her when he came for her in the car.

He dropped to one knee.

"Gabe. What?—Here?" Beatrice breathed, partly in panic and partly in elation. He was holding on to her hand.

His brows scrunched in a frown. "Proposing? Yes."

"Uh—"

His eyes drilled into hers even when he was the one in a vulnerable position. There was a stubborn set to his jaw. "You are going to hear me out before you start panicking." His grip tightened on her hand.

"Okay," she whispered. She was going to tell him to go ahead and ask her, but hey, if he intended to go all bossy about it, she wasn't going to stop him.

Gabe pushed out a deep breath. "The start of our relationship had not been ideal. In truth, I was afraid I could never get you back. But I think we have what it takes to make this work. This"—he waved to the house—"I've always meant for you to have this whether you took me back or not. Even with everything that separated us—the distance, the years, and the hurt, you've always been mine, Beatrice. I may have let you go then, but in my heart, I never did. All my life, I've never felt an emotion this intense. I. Fucking. Love. You. You are my oxygen; you are the heart of me, poppy." His voice thickened. "God knows you've suffered too much because of me." His fingers shifted from her hand and trailed up her forearms, his thumb caressing the smooth expanse of skin where her scars used to be. Cosmetic surgery, at its finest, took care of all the physical evidence of torture. "And yet, you've accepted me as your man. You've taken me at my darkest and brought me to this dream. I'm almost afraid if I don't bind you to me now, I will lose you. I can't lose you. So put me out of my misery. Be mine in every way. Marry me, Beatrice." He reached into his pocket and took out the most gorgeous diamond ring Beatrice had ever seen. Three carats at least, her discerning eye told her.

She must have stared at the ring for too long, and made Gabe nervous. He visibly swallowed. "I took the liberty of choosing the ring, but if you don't like it—"

"Yes."

"You don't like it?" His face fell.

"No, you silly man. Yes, I'll marry you." Her laugh was choked because her heart was almost beating into her throat and she might also be crying. She didn't care. She had the most perfect proposal given by the most perfect man. She loved him so much; it frightened her sometimes, but knowing without a doubt how deeply Gabe loved her, made such fears inconsequential. "Don't you dare return the ring. It's mine."

A roguish smile broke through Gabe's face as he slipped the ring on her finger. He stood up and immediately swept her into his arms, crashing his lips on hers and devouring her like a man starved for too long.

"I love you so much, Gabe," Beatrice managed to say when he stopped kissing her, which was a while. "Words cannot describe how happy you make me." She brushed her lips lightly on his and felt him shudder, closing his eyes as though strongly affected by the slight contact. "You never gave up on me."

Gabe's face turned solemn. "And I never will. You're it for me, poppy."

Beatrice snuggled closer and buried her nose in his neck, inhaling his musk, feeling secure in his tight embrace.

"God," he whispered. "Who knew proposing could be so nerve-wracking."

"You didn't seem all that nervous."

"I was. And it's only because it's you." His hands slipped to her ass and squeezed. "Dismantling an IED would have been less stressful." He smiled wryly. "You're the most unpredictable, infuriating, and independent woman I've ever known."

"And you want to sentence yourself to a lifetime with me?" Beatrice teased.

"You bet," Gabe muttered. "I wouldn't have it any other way. You're my unpredictable, infuriating, and independent woman. Make no mistake. All mine."

"Hmm . . . that goes the same for you, my cocky, bossy, and infuriating man."

"Speaking of cock . . ."

Beatrice snorted and leaned away, but Gabe molded their bodies together, making her aware of, well, his cock, which was presently springing to life.

His warm breath fanned her ear as he whispered, "Don't think I've forgotten that you need some hard fucking to be reminded just how mine you are."

"But—"

His mouth hit hers, stilling her protests, not kissing her, but murmuring further, "You're walking inside, stripping your clothes off, and laying on our bed, legs spread and ready for my mouth."

Oh, yes, Beatrice thought lustily. "Gabe—"

"Inside," Gabe rasped. "Now."

THINGS DIDN'T HAPPEN EXACTLY as planned, especially when you have an eighty pound dog waiting for his evening walk. Beatrice smothered a giggle as Gabe groaned when Rhino met them expectantly at the door.

"I'll wait for you upstairs," Beatrice said as she mounted the stairs, looking over her shoulder and shooting him an exaggerated come-hither look. Gabe's heated eyes followed her up the steps with a promise of retribution.

She took a quick shower and donned a robe. Then she

remembered Gabe's instructions of being naked and ready, so she discarded the covering and crawled into bed. The warmth of the shower lulled her into total relaxation, and she must have fallen asleep. She awakened to a sound. The room was dark, except for the outline of Gabe in front of the bathroom, a towel hanging low on his hips. Light from the outside window illuminated the ripple of muscle across his torso. He dropped the towel and prowled to the bed.

"Gabe?"

"You fell asleep?" There was amusement in his voice.

"You took too long."

The bed dipped as the blanket was drawn away, revealing her nakedness. Gabe sucked in a deep breath as he took in the expanse of bare skin.

"So beautiful," he murmured. His mouth sought her lips, his tongue dueling with hers, teasing, arousing. He did this for a while, just kissing her, the back of his fingers caressing her side. Finally, he moved on top of her, coaxing her legs open to cradle his hips. His hardness pressed against her core. But he didn't rock against her. He kept his lower body steady even as she sought to rub herself against him.

"Easy," he broke off. "I want this to last." He slowly trailed his lips down her throat, leaving open-mouthed kisses along her collarbone until he reached her breasts. He gently sucked one taut peak into his hot mouth.

"Gabe . . . oh . . . ah," Beatrice mewled helplessly. He swirled his tongue and flicked one nipple, and then he went to the other breast and did the same. He lightly bit on the turgid tip and Beatrice arched her back in response. "Oh, Gabe, I need . . . I need . . ."

This man had broken down her walls and made her need. She *needed* all of him—his body, heart, and soul.

"What do you need?" he mumbled against her skin as he went lower.

"All of you."

"I'm all yours, babe." He kissed her belly button, and then the sensitive area of her hip bone all the time muttering, "Mine." Her skin was tingling with anticipation. Every pore was alive to his touch, and when he pushed her legs further apart, moisture pooled between her thighs. Beatrice tilted her head down and watched Gabe's head move up and down one leg and then the other.

"Gabe, please . . ."

And then he was there. The roughness of his tongue lashed up and down the seam of her sex. Parting the dewy folds to invade the core of her, he fucked her with his tongue. Tunneling inside her pussy and then sucking her clit between his lips before fluttering his tongue maddeningly on the swollen evidence of her arousal. He slid two fingers in, curling them up and touched her sweet spot. She went off like a firecracker, spiraling into ecstatic heights, climbing and climbing until . . .

"Ahhhh! Oh, stop!" She just couldn't breathe as her climax crested. She just kept coming, over and over. Her body trembled; her pussy throbbed. He ate her out, lapping every drop of her wetness, groaning into her and licking, sucking even harder. She had never come so hard in her life.

He bolted up her body and crashed his mouth against hers to swallow her cries. His kisses turned brutal as he ground his erection against her clit, prolonging her pleasure. He lifted her legs under his arms, spreading her wider. His hips rocked against her, the head of his cock nudging ever so slowly inside her, driving her insane with want. He broke the kiss, stared down at her, and growled, "Fucking love you."

He slammed in, and she gasped as his girth stretched the sensitive walls to the limit.

"You okay?" he whispered. He always asked this because she had trouble taking in his unusual thickness sometimes.

"Give me a sec," she whispered. Oh, God, how he filled her and stimulated every corner of her sex. She nodded for him to go ahead and anticipated to be taken over the edge once more.

Gabe was drunk on Beatrice. Sinking inside her always felt amazing; nothing ever compared to the feeling of her squeezing him tight like a silken vise. He started moving, raising himself slightly to watch where his cock disappeared into her pussy. The slide in and out excited him. His burning gaze returned hungrily to her face. Her hooded eyes were intent on him. He liked that; having her watch him fuck her, possess her.

He quickened the pace, thrusting in and out, hearing her moan and whisper his name. His name on her lips spurred a possessive satisfaction that he was the reason for her sexual frenzy.

"Gabe . . ."

He was close, but he held back, wanting to make her crave him the way he craved her.

"Come on, Beatrice . . . give me one more, babe." He nearly came when her nails raked his back. He grunted with a decisive thrust, the force pushing her up. He adjusted his grip on her, locking her down as he bucked harder.

"Yes . . . oh, yes . . . hard . . . like that."

Fuck, yes. He drilled into her, crashing their pelvises together. Her eyes widened then squeezed shut as a scream ripped through her. He went crazy, rotating his hips and fucking her harder. He canted the angle of his thrust, taking her savagely, rutting into her. His spine tingled; the muscles of his neck bulged. He pumped once, twice. Finally, he tumbled over the precipice, slamming home and emptying inside her.

His climax rippled through him in sensual aftershocks. Gabe sagged on top of her, but quickly fell on his back, so he could gather her in his arms.

Beatrice touched her nose to his neck; her lips brushed against his jaw in feathery touches.

"Love you," she mumbled. Her head rested on his chest, her breathing evening out as she fell asleep.

Gabe's arms tightened around her, shifting slightly so he could press a kiss on her damp skin. He savored these moments when he had her in his arms, watching over her.

The moonlight illuminating the room reminded him how Beatrice had pulled him from the darkness. Overcome by emotion, he could only exhale and whisper the words he felt in his heart. She couldn't hear him right now, but he would spend the rest of his life showing her just how deeply he loved her, and just how much he treasured this second chance with her.

She was his light.

His prize.

His redemption.

The End

Nate's book is next with A Love For Always.

Curious about Viktor's team?
Find them here: Guardians
Turn the page after the bonus scene to find out how to connect with me!

BONUS SCENE

If you want to read about what went down between the admiral and Frank Wilkes/Harold Baxter, turn the page. Treat this like those surprise scenes at a movie's end credits.

*Harold Baxter/Frank Wilkes

Harold Baxter stared at his nemesis. Admiral Benjamin Porter had been a pain in his ass for the past four years, but Baxter had managed to stay one-step ahead of him. Barely. It had been too easy snatching him in front of his house. Baxter had no doubt Porter deliberately let himself be captured. The man must have a death wish because no way was Baxter letting him get out of here alive.

"I trust you're comfortable?" Baxter asked. The admiral was tied to a chair.

Porter shrugged. "Can't say I admire your hospitality."

Baxter chuckled, but quickly turned serious. "You finally surfaced and made yourself an easy target. Why? You know I'll only kill you."

"Should I call you Baxter or Wilkes?"

"Baxter is fine."

"My daughter. Most of my enemies were wise enough to leave her alone, Baxter, but you've made your biggest mistake going after her."

"I let her go."

"You don't have children, do you?"

"You know I don't. They're a weakness," Baxter said. "You're proof right here. Tell me, Porter, how can you protect her when you'll be dead?"

The admiral didn't answer, but Baxter quickly corrected himself. "Ahh … I see it now. You think Gabriel Sullivan is all she needs to keep her safe?"

Still no answer. But the chilly expression in Porter's eyes momentarily had Baxter doubting the prudence of bringing the admiral to his hideout.

"You cut her," Porter finally said. "She's innocent of this war between us. Avoiding collateral damage was never one of your strongest suits. The moment you'd taken her, you made it personal. And yes, you should be very afraid, Baxter. You keep on forgetting who Gabriel Sullivan once was."

"You'd have someone so ruthless be with your daughter? One could question your parenting skills," Baxter scoffed, but cold sweat beaded his forehead. He'd seen Dmitry Yerzov kill a man with chilly precision when Baxter had met with Zorin on one occasion. His assassin dragged one of his enemies in front of them. Zorin simply nodded and Dmitry sliced the man's throat. No hesitation. Stone-cold eyes. Hard to believe this was the same man who seemed desperately in love with the admiral's daughter.

"She was born to survive a ruthless world," Porter said proudly. "My daughter is tough enough to handle one Gabriel Sullivan. I can't imagine either of them settling for less."

"You've always been a grand manipulator, Porter," Baxter said. "But a matchmaker?"

"Are we done with the niceties?" the admiral cut in abruptly. "What the fuck do you think you're doing selling bioweapons on the Black Plane? Selling firearms is one thing, but you've gone too far this time, Baxter.

"The virus I'm selling to the bidders is inert."

"What?"

"Contrary to what you think of me, Porter, my only purpose is to help with this fight against ISIS."

"I have no time for your riddles. Spit it out, Baxter."

"There's an ISIS operative looking for a bioweapon. We've confirmed he's a high-ranking member of the Islamic State. He'll be a fountain of information if interrogated correctly. Several people died an ugly death to give us his identity and the method of how to track him on the Black Plane," Baxter said. "As much as I want to protect the homeland, our citizens live in a bubble. They think because the crisis is a world away, it's not going to touch them. They always realize this too late. Look what happened with 9/11. Even now our people's image of terrorists is that they live in caves or in mud huts. This new wave of jihadists is well-funded, and their computer networks are sophisticated. We have to concentrate our resources on ISIS, not getting involved in Russia's war with Ukraine."

"So your answer is to help the Russians suppress the Ukrainian government by providing them a virus?"

"A means to an end, Admiral."

"You're sick, twisted," Porter growled with so much vehemence, Baxter nearly flinched.

What did he expect? That he could sway the admiral to his agenda?

"Our little talk is over," Baxter said coldly. "I thought we were the same, you and me. Obviously, I was wrong."

"I may be many things, Baxter, but a mass murderer I am not," Porter shot back. "One more question—"

"I am not accountable to you—"

"The Project Infinity files—"

"Have long been destroyed," Baxter said with much satisfaction when a look of dismay flashed across Porter's face. "You sentimental fool. You still want to help Travis Blake when the man all but shunned you when you were the one who facilitated the return of his wife."

"I nearly got her killed as well."

"Sarah Blake. She was a good agent and hacker," Baxter said wistfully. "They all had to die, you know."

"Are you still going after her?"

"I haven't made up my mind."

"Leave them alone, Baxter. Travis and his wife have suffered enough."

"I hate loose ends. That includes you."

As if on cue, a rap on the door heralded the entrance of one of his mercenaries.

"Kill him," Baxter stated shortly. "Make it quick."

"Not doing the job yourself?" the admiral asked.

"I abhor blood spatters," Baxter replied cynically.

It was then that the situation deteriorated quickly. Porter

surprised his goon as he shot up, chair and all, and rammed the back of his head against the man's face. Then he sprung and flipped his whole body with the chair, feet coming up to push back into Baxter's desk for momentum.

The edge of the table struck Baxter's ribs, robbing him momentarily of breath. He heard a crash, a splintering of wood, and a grunt. He had already reached for his gun when Porter came into view, a sharp stake that was once a chair leg in his grip.

Baxter fired and caught Porter on the side, but the admiral just kept on coming. Before he could squeeze off another shot, a blunt force struck his head, followed by an excruciating pain jolting up from his fingers to his arm. The son of a bitch drove the stake through his hand! Baxter howled in agony.

Porter grabbed his gun and aimed it at him. "Don't move or I'll shoot you."

"You've become careless, Baxter," the admiral added. "Wooden chair, my legs untied, underestimating an old man like me?"

The admiral went to Baxter's laptop and took it out of hibernation. He produced a jump drive. How his men missed it when they patted the admiral down, Baxter didn't know. Apparently, this batch of mercenaries were imbeciles.

Goddammit his hand was killing him and his head was throbbing. Baxter cursed all that was holy that his room was soundproof and his men in the outer rooms couldn't hear the scuffle inside. So much for paranoia being his eventual downfall. If only he could reach the alarm under the desk. But both hands were on top of the table and the edge was pushed so far into him with his chair already against the wall, he couldn't wedge his hand easily to reach it. The admiral premeditated his moves with calculating precision.

"There's nothing on that laptop," Baxter gritted through his teeth.

"I know. You've stored it in a cloud somewhere on the Black Plane."

How the fuck did he know that?

"All I need is your private key, which I know you've stored somewhere . . ." Porter's voice trailed off. "Got it." The admiral was in profile to Baxter, so he knew the man was keeping an eye on his movements. The gun was pointed unerringly at him while his other hand flew on the keyboard. "My, my, Baxter, you've been a busy man."

"You'll pay for this," Baxter snarled.

"Am I missing something here?" Porter's eyes met his briefly. "Am I not the one with the gun?"

As the minutes ticked by and a ghost of a smile appeared on Porter's face, Baxter knew he had to act now, and kill the man, because getting charged with terrorism was not his end game.

Fuck it.

Baxter shoved the table forcefully and dove under it, praying the wire of the alarm had not been severed. He pushed it. He heard Porter curse and his footsteps retreated to the side door exit—another allowance to his paranoia that was backfiring. Shouting and footsteps rushed down the hallway, and finally, the door crashed open, but Porter was gone.

His crew found him hiding under a table. The humiliation.

"Get him! He went out the side door," Baxter roared, brushing off his men's help and rising to his feet. He yanked the stake from his hand. Blood gushed, but he was too furious to care and wrapped his hand in a shirt his goon handed him.

Gunfire exploded outside, but subsided quickly. His man came back with his broken laptop, looking grim. The admiral must have used it as a shield. Without his mercenary telling him, he knew Porter got away. There was only one place the admiral could go that was a mere ten minutes away.

The safe house.

CONNECT WITH THE AUTHOR

Find me at:

Facebook: Victoria Paige Books
Website: victoriapaigebooks.com
Email: victoriapaigebooks@gmail.com
FB Reader Group: Victoria Paige Reader Group

* Sign up for my newsletter and receive **Beneath the Fire** for free.

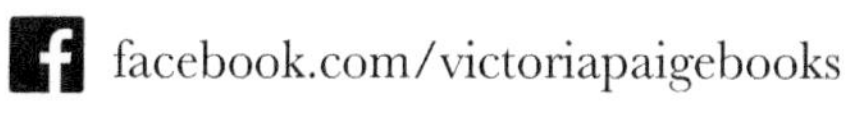

facebook.com/victoriapaigebooks
twitter.com/vpaigebooks
instagram.com/victoriapaigebooks

ALSO BY VICTORIA PAIGE

Guardians

Fire and Ice

Beneath the Fire (novella)

Silver Fire

Smoke and Shadows

Susan Stoker Special Forces World

Guarding Cindy (novella)

Reclaiming Izabel (novella)

Always

It's Always Been You

Always Been Mine

A Love For Always

Misty Grove

Fighting Chance

Saving Grace

Unexpected Vows

Standalone

Deadly Obsession

Captive Lies

The Princess and the Mercenary

* All series books can be read as standalones

Printed in Great Britain
by Amazon

23165468R00175

The man who shattered her heart is back and he wants a second chance.

Beatrice Porter swore she would never fall in love with a man like her father. For years she watched her mother self-destruct in bitterness, married to someone who only lived for his job. Gabriel Sullivan was such a man—a Navy SEAL, a man who put duty and country above all else. Yet falling in love with him was inevitable. She thought their relationship could work until he'd left her one night with a broken heart and her pride in tatters.

Having committed atrocities for the greater good, Gabe has nothing left but darkness inside him. The only flicker of light is the memory of Beatrice--the woman he left behind, the woman whose love he threw away. Winning her back won't be easy, but when Beatrice finds herself at the center of an assassin's deadly game, Gabe has a decision to make: stay in the shadows or step into the light and fight for the woman he loves.

Winning her back won't be easy, but convincing her that he's all in is the only redemption worth having.

As danger closes in on Beatrice, he is even more desperate to keep her safe. But a shocking revelation threatens their second chance. Unless Gabe finds the specter behind this twisted conspiracy in time and put an end to this nightmare, once and for all.